Praise for Ella M. Kaye

"Kaye's characters not only come alive, but will jump out and yell at you, pour their hearts out to you, and you will laugh and cry right along with them. The fun, witty banter and the expressive sorrow will keep you on the edge of your seat."
Liz, Reader Review

"I was so intrigued by the characters. I loved the intensity between Eli and Delaney. I felt part of the book. I couldn't put it down."
Kristie, Reader Review

"I could really appreciate what Delaney was going through while still being a strong, independent person and not a weak victim. Great read ...that I highly recommend."
Kathi, Reader Review

"Shadowed Lights is a MUST read. It draws you into the characters' world like you are actually there and can feel/touch & smell the things that they are actually doing. A masterfully written book. Another of Ella M. Kaye's book needs to be on your reading list if it isn't already there."
Annette, Reader Review

"Warning! This is not a book for skimmers. You'll want to read and savor every word of this sensual romance."
Muddy Rose Reviews

Barnegat Lighthouse, Long Beach Island, New Jersey

Elucidate Publishing
PO Box 1262
Hermitage PA 16148

United States of America

Shadowed Lights

Ella M. Kaye

~ *One* ~

Eli's boots sank into the damp sand as he stared out at the abandoned flooded house swept into Barnegat Bay. He should have gone out with the crew, his crew. Instead, he studied the structure from the shore. A beautiful home, former home, with an enclosed porch. One he could imagine living in, if it was farther from the water. At least far enough it would never get swept up and taken into gaping, consuming, drowning level water.

He had been told often that you could also drown in only a tablespoon of water, but the thought was so ridiculous, he brushed it off easily. As long as his feet touched something firm and his head was in the air where he could breathe, Eli was fine with water. He could wander the shoreline up to his waist, even up to his shoulders. And he could swim if he knew he could stand up and touch bottom. His parents had tried to get him out farther, but panic always ensued and his father had to pull him back in. It frustrated the hell out of him, made him feel weak and ridiculous.

Dread had knotted his stomach when his Indiana crew decided to come to the east coast to help with cleanup from Hurricane Sandy. Work was slow in his area. The idea of helping with cleanup sounded right. But ... the ocean.

Eli had never in his life been to the ocean and he hadn't wanted to come, although he wanted to help. He wanted to work. He always wanted to work. Even when he was no more than ten years old, his greatest pleasure had been going to work with his father, mixing mortar and learning to apply it neatly and carefully. The praise he got for a job well done stirred his soul. Construction was in his blood. It was his life.

This... A shudder consumed him as he stared out at the vast blue green brown of Barnegat Bay, New Jersey. This was a whole hell of a lot of water. Unpredictable water. Life taking water.

An irony, he knew, even as he thought it. Water was the ultimate survival need. But like anything, too much of a good thing was still ...

deadly dangerous.

A light chill in the wind echoed his chilled soul. Wet air. Indiana had its share of humidity, but it was nothing like this cool wet air that reeked of ... fish, he supposed. Seaweed. Dead things rotting. He'd always enjoyed fish dinners, particularly those deep-fried all-you-can-eat fish dinners presented by his local fire hall as a fundraiser. Now, after seeing the dead and rotting fish carcasses strewn along the beach, Eli wasn't sure he could ever eat another fish.

A shame that would be. He enjoyed helping the fire hall. He always found a few people to take with him who hadn't been and they often went back in following years and gave him a big thumbs up when they saw him there with a new group.

Possibly, once he got away from the shore and back home, he could let the current images go. He was good at letting go. Sometimes.

With a sigh, he headed back to the base. Maybe he could make himself go on out where he should have been.

Something under his foot threw his balance and, unable to let himself see that he stepped on something he didn't want to even look at, he shoved it away with his steel-toed boot. It was hard enough to walk in the damp shifting sand in heavy boots. He didn't need anything adding to...

"Hey, *careful.*"

Eli turned and found a girl with a messy wind-blown pony tail wearing jeans and a sweatshirt, both too big for her, coming at him. Not at him. At whatever he'd kicked away. She squatted to pick the thing up with gloved hands and examined it.

He couldn't help his curiosity. "What is that?"

"A sea star."

"Sea star? Is that like a falling star? Meteorite or something? Is it valuable?"

Brownish-green eyes met his, briefly, and pulled away. "It's a starfish."

"Now, that I know. Why didn't you just say that?"

"I used its real name. It's not actually a fish. And yes, it's valuable." She spoke more to the starfish than to him, barely loud enough he could hear.

"Did I hurt it?"

"It's missing a leg. I don't think you did it." She crept over to where water lapped against her age-lightened gray-black galoshes covered in wet sand and green stringy stuff and crouched to set the thing back in the ocean, then held her pose, watching it. Now and then she pushed a strand of light brown hair that seemed to have escaped the ponytail behind her ear with small fingers. She'd taken off her gloves. Beneath them were pale thin hands, with narrow but long fingers. Delicate. Unpainted nails. No ring on her marriage finger, or on any of them.

Eli moved closer but not close enough to get water in his boots. "If it's valuable, why are you letting it go?"

She glanced up at him as though he'd said two plus two equaled green. "It's only valuable in the ocean, alive. Not if it's dead." Apparently satisfied the thing was happy and alive, she straightened and walked away.

Her attitude annoyed him. A tree hugger, he supposed. More concerned about animals than people. He could understand to a point, but to him, turning against your own kind was ... well, unforgivable. Maybe he was wrong. Maybe he wasn't. He'd done his share of helping critters out of places they shouldn't have been. Using the cage and snare pole he kept in his truck for when he rescued someone's frightened pet out of a burning house, he'd take the critters out to a wooded area and let them go. Neighbors who knew he had the equipment had even called him for help with coons and such, sometimes in the middle of the night, and he never refused. But if it came to a choice between human and animal, he wouldn't think twice.

He supposed he liked people more than other people liked people. And he understood that at times, too. Lots of people just weren't all that likeable.

Curious despite his annoyance, Eli followed. She glanced back as he caught up. Probably scaring her, he figured, since she was alone and not many people were on the storm-littered beach so early in spring. "You said it's missing a leg. Will it live that way or is it going to bleed to death out there?"

"They don't have blood." She kept walking.

"Serious? Okay look at me like I'm a moron again, but this is my first time to the ocean. I don't know jack shit about sea critters other than fish, actual fish that live in freshwater ponds. I have friends who have starfish and sand dollars in their vacation collections, but that's the extent of my knowledge."

She stopped. "That's cruel, unless they found them already dead. It's kills them, you know, to take them out of the water. That sea star can re-grow its leg and be fine, but only if it stays in the ocean. It dies if you take it out, and if you don't pick them up just right, they're easily injured."

"Everyone takes them home if they find them, don't they?"

"Not everyone." She turned back and walked away faster.

He caught up. "I haven't done it. Don't get mad at me." When she didn't answer, he stopped and let her go on her way. *Freaky girl. Not a girl, exactly.* She had to be close to his age and he was pushing forty pretty damn fast. He didn't have that much need to know more about starfish. What did it matter? He didn't plan to take one home.

Cruel? Dead sea life was scattered along the beach. People hadn't done it. Nature did it. A huge storm. It killed people, too. Eli had to wonder if she cared about that at all.

Either way, lunch break was over. Time to get back to work.

Hopping up on the scaffolding, he clipped a safety harness around his thighs and hips and headed up. Eli didn't mind up. Up was fine with him. He had the harness. He had decent arm muscles and strong hands. He had good common sense and quick thinking. And he loved the view from the air, higher than most would go. He often thought the biggest reason men joined construction, high rise construction anyway, was because they could, and would. And they were adrenaline junkies, he supposed. Speaking for himself, it was true enough.

~ *Two* ~

By four o'clock, Eli felt the strain of his muscles that told him it was quitting time. On the other hand, he thought it would make more sense to keep working while the sun gave them plenty of light and get the job done faster. His company would yell. Overtime cost too much. Hell, he'd do it on his own time if they'd allow, just to get things back in order for all those lives thrown into chaos during and after the storm. He couldn't work alone, though, and he knew the rest were waiting for the figurative whistle that allowed them to go roam restaurants and bars and unwind for the night.

Eli enjoyed unwinding as much as anyone. Socializing. Flirting with pretty women with no rings on their marriage fingers, as his dad always called them – *Eli,* he'd say, *you be sure you always look for that ring, or where it looks like a ring has been, and you stay away from that* – as though he had to be told. Why would he want a woman some other man couldn't trust to keep her vow? He'd already had an untrustworthy woman. Thank heavens he hadn't been married to her, but close enough. He sure as hell wouldn't be part of doing it to some other poor sap.

Of course as he got older, his options in that department would get more limited, but it didn't concern him. He'd stopped looking for that. If it was meant to be found, he'd find it, he figured. If it wasn't meant to be, then it wasn't. Eli had his work. He planned to keep working for just as long as his body allowed, and then he'd tone it down and work differently, supervisory maybe. Retiring was nowhere in his plans. What was the point of it?

To travel, his mother said. His folks did a lot of traveling these days, since his father had semi-retired, and when he wouldn't go, she went without him. It was good, Eli supposed. She'd worked hard since she was young and deserved the time to travel. By plane only, if it was farther than a couple of hours. Eli found it funny she would rather fly since the woman hated heights. With a passion. But she hated long drives even more. She also hated that Eli worked so high up, said it made her stomach hurt to even think of it, so he told her not to think of it.

Eli liked traveling just fine, but he didn't much like doing it by plane. He hated that as much as his mother hated heights. The lines. The voices over the intercoms. People shoving through and in between and running their bags over your feet. Getting half undressed just to get through security and putting your hands over your head like you were some kind of criminal. Being squashed against someone taking more than his fair share of space or having some kid kick the back of his seat. No thank you. He could do it if he had to, just like his mother could do heights if she had to, but he preferred driving.

A friend once invited him to do a singles cruise. No way would that happen. Eli didn't want to be looked at like a piece of steak by a bunch of women desperate enough to pay for a cruise just to hunt for a man. He wouldn't even do the whole bar-hopping-to-meet-chicks thing as his friend did most every weekend. He wasn't desperate to find a girl and if he was, he sure wouldn't do it on a boat, over water. He might as well jump right in and let the sharks have him.

Meeting up with some of his crew at Rhode's Den, Eli scanned the place as he pulled in. A little place. Cabin-like. A porch to the side, surrounded by a log rail fence he could barely see behind large un-trimmed bushes full of white blooms, looked bigger than the interior could be. It was out-of-the-way enough he never would have found it without looking for it, and there were few cars in the gravel parking area. Not a great sign, as far as he was concerned, but Ted swore the food was incredible.

Eli had to brush past flowering shrubs, pink over on this side of the building, to walk up three weather-beaten wood steps to the door. The little flowers smelled. Strong. Not bad, kind of spicy for flowers. His mom would know what they were. She was as obsessive about flowering things as he and his father were about constructed things. The door squeaked as he entered and he half considered offering to fix the thing for them, but he wasn't back home, so he thought better of it.

It was bright inside for a bar and grill, but the smell of sizzling beef made his stomach growl. As small as the place was, it was easy enough to find Ted and Carmine at the only table being used out of a row of four that ran along the bar, with just enough room to walk between. Dividers stood along the other side, so Eli figured there were more tables he couldn't see. The light came from the mostly glass wall overlooking the patio. Only one table used out there, too. The bar was nearly packed, however.

Nudging Carmine over so he didn't have to squeeze into the space between his coworker and the divider, Eli ordered a beer and helped himself to the fried pickles on the table while he perused the one-page menu. With spicy chicken wings and another order of pickles requested from the girl doing her best to ignore Ted's flirting, he kicked back to listen to the guys talk of the house-turned-island, of fish swimming through the living room, of what must have been careful decorating now turned green and moldy. When they told Eli he should go with them the next day to see it for himself, he made the excuse that help was needed where he worked earlier, and they could handle it without him.

Last thing he needed was to be even more up close to the results of deadly ocean water.

While he ate, Eli studied the place. Not the work of skilled builders, obviously, since there were sloppy corners on the ends of the bar that showed ridges and peeling yellowed varnish, which meant it wasn't done right in the first place; ceiling tiles starting to bow, which meant bad tiles or a moisture issue; gaps in door frames that showed bad cutting and fitting; and the shelving behind the bar was slanted toward the back, causing all of the alcohol to tilt enough to notice. Still, the pickles were among the best he'd tried and the thick burger just delivered to a girl at the bar smelled like it had been cooked perfectly.

"Well, look who that is. Ain't she the crazy woman who was walking on the beach talking to fish today?"

Eli looked over where Ted nodded: the girl with attitude who rescued the starfish. Her hair was still back in a ponytail, but it was now neat instead of windblown, and she was in a bulky beige sweater instead of the big sweatshirt, still over loose jeans, with clean brown boots rather than galoshes covering her feet. Definitely her, though. Same delicate, graceful features. Same uppity attitude. She sat at the far end of the bar.

"Talking to fish?" Carmine snickered.

"Yeah, looked as though she was. Saw a guy from another team try to talk to her and she looked at him like he was talking Swa-hilly or something. The girl walked right on away from him without even answering the poor guy."

Eli rolled his eyes. "Swahili, not Swa-hilly. You even know what Swahili is?"

"Some sort of language." Ted shrugged and chugged part of his beer. "Who cares? Just a saying."

"You should know why you're using a phrase if you're going to use it. It's an African language that barely anyone knows."

"Yeah, so? It works. I bet more people can understand *Swa Hee Lee* than can understand fish gurgle."

"You're an idiot. She wasn't talking to them."

"Yeah and you know?" He drained his fourth beer. "A girl who talks to fish but not to men's got something wrong with her."

"Depends who the man is and what he might have said. If it was you, I wouldn't blame her." Eli got some snickers but then they joined in with Ted, laughing about her mental issues or being sarcastic about her snobbishness. Eli had to wonder if they'd kicked a sea star, also, and been yelled at for it, which, at this point, he found amusing.

"Think she has gills under that sweater?"

"Or flat flappy feet."

"Yeah, maybe she's a mermaid in disguise and those fish are her friends. Like the nasty ones with big teeth in the movie."

Ted guffawed. "I can see it. Should we ask?"

"Naw, man. She might turn into one and bite our heads off."

"Hey, keep it down." Eli glanced over at her, hoping the noise in the crowded bar would keep the conversation from their booth hidden.

They did lower their voices but didn't stop. Annoyed by the childishness, Eli went to the bar and asked for coffee. As he expected, the bartender didn't particularly want to brew coffee at seven o'clock at night, but Eli was never bothered by that. They offered it. It was their job to do it. It tended to bother them less if he ordered something with his coffee, and since he was feeling less stubborn than he sometimes did, he ordered Irish Coffee instead of plain black.

Turning on the bar stool to watch the activity around him as he waited, Eli looked forward to going home. He enjoyed New Jersey itself fine, and he even had to admit Barnegat Bay was a nice sight, even with all the water. The different work kept his active mind interested. But the people were far different, which was okay, except he was a talker. So far, from what he found, they weren't. At least not to him and his Midwest accent, they weren't. A friend who had traveled east a few times warned him not to be offended. Northeasterners kept to themselves and their little groups. They didn't say hello in the street like small town Indiana did. They meant no offense; it was just their culture.

He supposed there was a good side to that, as well. Now and then his rural town 'everyone knows everything going on' was a bit hard to take, even for him.

The bartender apologized to someone about it taking so long to come get her order because he *had to make coffee*. Eli nearly called him on it until he realized the guy was talking to fish girl, as one of the juveniles at his table called her.

"It's fine, and I'd love coffee, too, since you're making it."

"Yeah? At this time of night? Won't keep you up?"

"It's been a long day, so not likely."

"Need to give yourself a break more often." The man smiled at her. "What do you want in it?"

"Nothing. And thank you. I'm glad someone else ordered it, even if you aren't."

"You know I'd make it for you anytime. Just ask, hon." With another grin, he walked away.

Someone she knew well. Boyfriend? Family? Hard to tell. Judging by his age, could be either. Eli studied her as she pulled something from a brown fabric side bag and set it on the bar. A book. The girl planned to read in a bar? He saw a man nearby try to get her attention, but she ignored him, moved the bookmark farther back in the pages, and settled in.

Eli had to laugh. Not only reading in a bar, but reading a thick hardcover with an actual bookmark and putting the thing farther back in the book instead of laying it on the bar? The girl was priceless. Snobbish maybe, as they'd called her, but ... to be honest with himself, he found her kind of adorable. Most women in the bar were in T-shirts, too many with rolling bulges plastered against the material, or in frilly, feminine things meant to catch a man's eye, but this girl was in a bar alone doing what she could *not* to catch a man's eye, or so it seemed.

He had half a thought to move around and talk to her, or try to talk to her. Not that he got far with it earlier, but there were plenty of people around now. Surely, she wouldn't worry...

What the hell? Eli figured it could be interesting to try.

Thanking the bartender for the Irish Coffee, along with a quick look to tell the guy he didn't appreciate the rude comment, he wandered down to the end of the bar. In case she was still wary, he moved to her other side and stood partly in the barely open space meant for bartenders to get in and out. Let the guy bitch at him. He didn't want the girl to feel cornered. Still, she pulled back, slightly. Her eyes didn't raise from the pages.

He sipped his drink and shook his head about how weak it was. "Glad I'm not the only one who wanted coffee. Makes me almost feel bad when I am."

She pulled back more, shoulders hunching in as she almost looked at him. "What?"

He raised the glass mug. "Coffee. And a bare touch of whiskey. Not sure I should have bothered with that since I can hardly tell it's there." Damn, a stupid thing to say, since she knew the guy. She went back to her book, but Eli wasn't willing to give up that easily. If she didn't want to talk, she should have got a table instead of sitting at the bar. "So I was wondering: what makes that starfish so valuable?" He propped his forearms over the bar top.

This time, she didn't even acknowledge him.

"You didn't hear me because you're involved in some really sexy steamy story that has you rapt at attention, or you forgot our conversation from earlier? Or you don't recognize me. Don't say so if that's the case. Hard on the ego."

With a slight twist of the head, she blushed and turned the book so he could see the cover. *The Historian.* It didn't look romantic. Eli was almost sad it wasn't.

"Haven't heard of it. Not sexy and steamy?"

"No. Historical."

"Yeah, obviously with that title. About what?"

"The search for Dracula."

He laughed. Too loud. She replaced the bookmark, closed the book, grabbed her coffee, and walked away. Damn, another bad move. "Hey, I didn't mean to be insulting." She kept walking like she didn't hear him and the bartender warned him to leave her alone. Eli shrugged and returned to his table while he watched her walk out to the patio. It was chilly to sit outside, and night was falling. And Eli felt bad that he'd insulted her, trying to or not.

His friends jibed him for striking out with even the crazy fish girl, but Eli shrugged them off and followed her to the weathered pine patio surrounded by rough-cut log rails but more by those shrubs that gave off their strong spicy-floral scent. Behind the white ones were the same thing in yellow and then orange. Over top the shrubs lay a nice view of a tree-covered hill ... mountain? He wasn't sure. He didn't think New Jersey had actual mountains.

Walking over close to her, he looked out over the New Jersey vista, a very different view than what he'd been dealing with. The flower scent nearly choked him. "Some strong-smelling shrubs, aren't they? Gotta wonder why you'd put these around somewhere people try to eat." Pulling one of the yellow flowers off, he brought it to his nose and shook his head. Then, taking a chance, he set it beside the girl on the table. "Peace offering. Not much of one, of course, since I just plucked it from someone else's vine, but..."

"Shrub. It's not a vine."

"Yeah, just a saying. A joke. Not a good one." He shrugged. "You know what they are?"

"Rhododendrons. And the place is named after them. Rhode's den."

"Ah, I figured it was someone's name."

"No. It's in honor of the owner's mother. She loved rhododendrons. When he lost her and left him money, he put up this place and surrounded it with the shrubs in honor."

"Nice. And at least it makes sense now." Eli sat across from her at the uncovered picnic table that matched the floor. Again, she'd chosen the one back in the corner, and she gave him a wary look, about ready to bolt, he figured. "Okay, I'll let you alone. Just wanted to say I'm sorry I laughed. Surprised me, is all. You don't look like the vampire fan type."

"It's historical." She returned her eyes on the page.

"Dracula isn't real."

"All myths start from reality."

He supposed that was true, if you went back far enough. "Okay, I'll give you that." When her eyes flashed up at his, he knew he'd screwed up again and figured he better change the conversation. "So, about the starfish? Or sea star, as you will. What makes it so valuable? And I'm not being a smartass. I want to know."

She glanced over toward the door that would take her back inside the tavern, but she didn't get up. "They help balance the ecosystem. They eat things that would overpopulate otherwise. Mussels and such. It does matter."

"Kind of the way if not for hunters, deer would overpopulate and start dying of starvation."

"And disease. Yes. Every living thing has to have something to keep it in check. It's about keeping things in balance. People take too many, or take them while they're still alive, just to show them off as a vacation memento, and..."

"Right. They throw off the balance. Same reason there's a hunting limit per season." He'd expected her to cringe at the hunting reference, but she only gave him a quick nod. "You know more about land game than I do about sea critters."

She didn't answer, but he was too intrigued to give up. "So, if they don't have blood, what do they have? Ink?"

Her expression at least said she realized he was being funny. "Why are you asking?" Still, her eyes didn't quite touch his. Her body was tense, pulled in.

"I like to learn new stuff. I'm overly curious and it often gets me in trouble." He shrugged and took a swallow of the weak Irish coffee as the nosy bartender stepped out to tell him his order was at his table and asked her if everything was okay. Luckily, she said it was. Still, he threw Eli a silent warning before he left.

"Friend of yours?"

She studied him now, gauging whether or not she should have sent the bartender away, Eli guessed. "My sister's ex from years ago. He knows I think she was crazy to dump him."

"You go out with him now?"

"No." Again, the moron look. "That's... No. He was around the house for a long time and still treats me like a little sister. He also owns the place, which is why I come here."

"Ah." Eli swallowed more coffee, tasting more of the whiskey as the mug emptied. Good thing, since this girl was making him a bit nervous by now. Probably because she was so nervous. It was impossible not to feel it. Still, he was curious. "So, the sea star? What do they run on?"

Setting the bookmark back in place, she closed the hefty hardcover and sipped her coffee. He loved that she drank black coffee, like his mother did. He wasn't sure he knew one other woman who didn't put a bunch of stuff in it.

"They take in sea water. It circulates through their systems, and it fills the little tubes on their bottom side that are like feet. They can't move otherwise."

"Water. Interesting. And if they can't move, they can't find food."

"Right. They shouldn't even be picked up unless they're still in water. They get hurt easily."

"You said that."

She blushed. "Sorry. I forgot I did."

"No problem. I'm real sorry I kicked it. Didn't look to see what it was first."

She nodded and moved her gaze out to the hill.

"Since I'm new in town, have advice as to what's worth seeing around here?"

She gaped. For a second. "You realize we just had a storm in October?"

"I do. It's why I'm here."

She slipped the book back in her bag, picked up her coffee, and walked away.

What was the girl's problem? He wasn't being obnoxious. Did he know there was a storm? What a smartass question. Did she think no one outside the area paid attention? It was all over the news. Everyone knew. Lots of places were sending lots of stuff and money in support. Did she not realize it? Eli nearly regretted being annoyed at his crew for making fun of her.

Heading back to his table, he couldn't help watching her set her coffee cup on the bar and leave. She had a nice walk, not cocky, not arrogant, just simple and unaffected, as unaffected as her clothing style. Beige and brown and loose. Everything about the girl screamed, "I don't want to talk to you," and he supposed she planned it that way.

Maybe she didn't like men, at all, either way.

Eli put it out of his head as he enjoyed the spicy wings, damn good wings, he had to admit, with the perfect amount of heat to notice it without overwhelming the flavor, and absorbed himself in the inane conversation of his coworkers.

~ Three ~

Delaney pulled her yellow sweater from the closet, held it in front of her in the dresser mirror, and put it back on the closet shelf. She loved the color, like homemade butter, but it was too bright. She'd bought it on a whim: a silly thing to do, and she'd known at the time it was silly because she'd never let herself wear it, but it was beautiful so she'd allowed herself that quick moment of thinking she might. Maybe someday she would.

Her stomach twinged at the thought. Of course she wouldn't. Unless ... maybe with a navy jacket over it she could.

With a sigh, she grabbed the dark brown sweatshirt that was a staple of her wardrobe. Pulling out of her work clothes, Delaney studied her stomach she'd worked so hard to keep flat and strong, also a bit pointless, she figured, since it never showed. She was one of the few coastal Jersey girls who did not go lay out on the beach nearly uncovered. Or at all. She liked to swim, but not in public, so she almost never did it. Maybe some day...

Ricky Martin interrupted her thoughts as *I Like It* streamed through her iPod dock. Pulling on a coral baby doll tank, well-fit and soft, Delaney allowed herself the three minutes of musical release, dancing to it with plenty of hip movement to go with the sensual Spanish rhythm. It was the one time she felt like herself, like who she really was that no one was allowed to see. Dancing. Giving in to the beat, the feel of the sound, the stirring blood. She loved music in general, but something about Spanish sounds got to her faster than any other.

When it ended, Delaney pulled the baggy brown sweatshirt over the coral tee, gathered her medium length dirt brown hair into a ponytail at her nape, and again perused herself in the mirror. Plain brown. Through and through. Except, really, she wasn't. Not deep inside. It was only her wrapper.

Turning the iPod off, Delaney gritted herself, made her way down the hall, called a *see you later,* which was also pointless since her sister and the kids would be far too involved in whatever they were doing to worry about whether or not she was home, and slipped into her brown boots. They were showing too much wear.

Chagrined to realize she would have to replace them soon, she grabbed her bulky jacket just in case it was colder than she expected, double-checked to see that her license and credit card and a few dollars were still in her little brown pocket book with long thin strap that hung over her head and shoulder and down her side out of the way, gripped her keys tightly, checked to be sure the door was locked, pulled it shut and checked it again, looked both ways down the sidewalk to be sure she wouldn't run into anyone, and hurried to her dark blue 2007 Ford. She locked the doors as soon as hers was closed, started the engine, clicked her seat belt, and looked behind her twice before she pulled out, still looking to be sure some jerk wouldn't fly up on her too fast.

Delaney hoped he wouldn't be there again. She had work to do, and she didn't want some guy from somewhere else hanging around badgering her. And why was he? Because she complained about him kicking the starfish? Only a heinous person would actually kick the thing. People who picked them up as souvenirs didn't understand, or at least she told herself they didn't. Kicking the thing... But he said he didn't see what it was. In that case, she could forgive him. Not that it mattered if she did. Since she'd walked away from him the night before, she expected that even if he was around, he wouldn't bother to speak to her.

She could have been nicer, she supposed. He looked okay. Her sister would ask why she didn't talk to him more. Too few men bothered to talk to her and when one did...

Not that she wanted them to talk to her. She didn't. Maybe she did. Some of them. Those who were polite and looked respectable. Yes, she did, but she didn't. It was too hard. Trina tried to understand, but she couldn't. No one could unless they felt the same, and as far as she knew, she'd never met anyone who did. They were out there. She knew from memes on the internet that others did feel the same, but she'd never met anyone who did.

Delaney felt herself tense when a car came up beside her. Too close. She slowed down to let him move ahead and around. "Just go on." When he stayed too close, she slowed more. Then the one behind her got closer. Annoyed, she turned off one exit sooner than she'd planned. It would take more time that way, but she hated traffic. Some day she would live in a smaller area where she could go wherever she needed without the congestion, the speed, tourists. Including those who came only to amaze themselves at the devastation. Gawkers. She couldn't stand them.

And the temp workers. Delaney would be glad when the place got back on its feet and all of the temp people went back home and got off her beach. Of course then the tourists would return. Maybe she needed to live somewhere without tourists.

But where would she go? And by herself? She couldn't, and her sister loved the bay. Delaney loved Barnegat Bay, also. But what she loved was the water, the animals, the beach, and the lighthouse. The thought of moving away from that sent her nearly into a panic, so she stopped thinking about it. Of course it was more the thought of moving away from her sister, the one person she could talk to without the nervousness she hated, or at least mostly without it. How could she leave that?

She couldn't.

And then there were her nieces and nephews, three girls and two boys. At thirty-two, Delaney was unsure she'd ever have her own. Before she could do that, she'd have to make herself talk to a man long enough to get to know him, to really know him, and she didn't know how she would. Her short term thing when she'd pushed herself to date that jerk who pretended to enjoy her "quirks" was a disaster. She couldn't do that again. She'd stay alone forever first.

And maybe she would. She could be known as the crazy fish lady for all she cared, as those stupid men at the bar had called her when they didn't realize she could hear them. People thought she was strange, anyway, and they were probably right. At least it kept them away from her for the most part. Why not use that to her advantage?

To distract herself, Delaney carefully switched from radio to CD. Richie Sambora's sultry, sexy voice seeped *Stranger In This Town* through the speakers. She knew the feeling. She'd grown up right there in Stafford Township, so she knew she shouldn't feel like a stranger, but she hadn't been anywhere yet where she didn't feel like one.

People were right. She was strange. But the animals she took care of weren't concerned that she was. Not that sea creatures got emotionally attached to her the way cats or dogs would, or could. Someday she would have one of those, when she had space and more time. Either was fine. Or both. At the moment, her place was crowded enough.

Slamming his palm against the half-crumbled wall, Eli stalked away. What difference did it make if he didn't belong to the "right" outfit or have the "right" certificate? He knew what he was doing. Recovery efforts had been going on for five months, since the beginning of November, two of which he and his crew had been part of, and there was still so much to be done. If he could do the work and wasn't asking to be paid for the overtime, why shouldn't they let him? No wonder it was taking so long. Lots of them were willing to do whatever they could and they couldn't get past the damned red tape to do it.

Damn stupid.

It was March. He didn't mind a couple of months away or so, and he was glad to be helping, but he was about ready to be home. He'd traveled plenty, but he'd never been away from his family for two months or more. When this job opportunity came up, Eli figured it was time, and since he was the main foreman, his crew wouldn't go if he didn't. Two week vacations once a summer, plus a few long weekends over holidays with whoever could go with him wasn't quite "getting away" from things, as too many said he should. *Get out and find some girl somewhere else, have an adventure, have a fling, see the world...* Maybe they were right.

A spring fling could be nice, he supposed, way out east where his hometown wouldn't see it or talk about it for years to come, where his mom wouldn't hear it and give him that look. He could. He hadn't dated in some time. Well, there was Debi, but that hardly counted since in the six months they'd dated, she hadn't let him get past anything that had to be taken off, which she wouldn't. Not that he was pushy; he knew how to respect a girl, but he was nearly forty and still single. And she was divorced, so it wasn't like she hadn't been down that block already. There was respecting yourself and then there was taking yourself way too damned seriously. When she made a big show about having to celebrate their six month "anniversary" and still sent him home with just a kiss at the door, Eli called it off. Of course, he'd had to tell her that anniversary meant a *year,* not six months, since the root word *ann* meant *year* and it was just plain silly to celebrate six months of hardly more than holding hands at their ages. She'd called him a pompous ass and said she was glad to be done with him and his *silly* sex drive.

Maybe she was right. Maybe he expected too much.

To calm himself, Eli decided to walk down to the beach front. One of these days, he would gather the nerve to go out on Long Beach Island. For the moment, he'd settle for looking at it across the bay and talking to anyone about the storm who was willing, about how much had already been cleaned up, and how much hadn't. Some loved the chance to talk. Others shut him out. Eli loved to guess which would do which. He was often wrong. Most of the time he was wrong, but it didn't keep him from trying.

He tried twice to talk with someone walking along the beach and they both looked him up and down and walked away. By now, it amused him and Eli thought he might keep count. Was it his dirty jeans and old boots, his hair that was mashed down by his hard hat and sweat, or his accent? Maybe they were just sick of outsiders always being in their faces. He supposed he couldn't blame them. So many were still out of their homes, some living cramped with friends or relatives, others moved away.

The second houses, vacation homes, he didn't worry so much about. But those who lost their main homes, and not only the wood and brick, but their belongings, he felt for deeply. He'd been face to face with a family whose house burned to the ground. They'd lost everything. The pain and loss in their faces, especially the little ones, was etched into his memory forever. It nearly made him stop volunteer firefighting so he wouldn't have to see it again, but he couldn't. If his work saved one home and one family from that kind of loss, it was worth it. No matter how it made his parents worry. They were also proud.

So many back in Indiana commented that ocean dwellers should expect such a thing when they lived right on top of the water, but Eli could see the charm in it as he walked along. It would be hard to resist the opportunity to live on a beach and look out over the peaceful expanse of blue-green-gray with no apparent end. Even when you didn't like the water.

He supposed he didn't dislike it too awful much. It scared the holy hell out of him, but he was still intrigued by it. He doubted it was any worse threat than their tornadoes. But then he had a good sturdy basement to hide from wind. Where did you hide from water *and* wind?

Needing to shift his thoughts, Eli tried to decide what to do with his night. Those in charge didn't understand why not letting him work longer when he was away from home was harder on him than a twelve hour day would be. He had to stay busy.

~ *Four* ~

Pulling off, finally, onto North Main, Delaney thought of how the trees would soon be fully green again and how the bugs would come out full force, making the cleanup harder to take. There was still so much debris left to be cleaned out of the wildlife refuge, even with as much as the group of volunteers had already cleared.

She couldn't bear the thought of birds and other animals getting caught in old cans or bathing in paint-laden water or swallowing garbage that would choke or sicken them. Her brother-in-law said creatures could fend for themselves and Delaney could help other people instead, by helping them get back in their houses, but Delaney figured people should be able to help themselves as she had, as she always did. Animals were more at the mercy of nature, and of the messes people made. People were only at the mercy of themselves and what they chose to deal with or not deal with.

As well as those things they were stuck with, not due to their choosing. Still, they had choices. Animals had only instinct. Something about that appealed to her.

Parking as close as she could to the current work area, Delaney debated whether she would need the jacket over her sweatshirt. The breeze was cool but the evening sun was still warm. She considered tying it around her waist until she needed it, but that would get annoying as she bent down into the moist sand. She left it in the car, figuring it would be easier to just walk back and get it.

"Hey, Miss Starfish."

Delaney turned at the familiar voice and saw the smiling stud with wavy brown hair striding toward her. Again, he wore dirty jeans, a plaid work shirt that was mostly clean, this time in green and yellow instead of blue and red, and heavy black boots, probably steel-toed. His walk was cocky but not overdone. Unintentional, she supposed. It didn't look like he was faking it or trying too hard.

Why was he there? And why was he talking to her again after she'd been such an idiot the night before? Trying to decide whether to hurry away or figure out how to talk to him without sounding like a complete idiot, she felt her heart start to race and her face get warm. *Stop it. He doesn't matter.* Telling herself he didn't matter and he would go back to wherever he came from soon, she forced a deep slow breath to try to calm her heart as her feet stuck to the sand.

His pretty deep blue eyes peered into her boring hazel-ish eyes when he came up close, and Delany felt the heat in her face rise. She looked away. At the sand. Shells. Anything else. When he stopped in front of her, way too close, her head started to spin as it had the night before at the bar while she was forcing herself to look calm and speak somewhat intelligently.

"Are you often out here at night?"

It wasn't night. It was evening. But she couldn't answer him. She could hardly breathe. Somehow, she had to figure out how to answer in between remembering how rude she'd been the night before. Unintentionally. But it made her feel like an idiot. Why was he there?

"Okay, bad question. Sorry, didn't mean to scare you."

"No. You didn't." Her voice came out stronger than she intended since she was trying hard not to let it shake. Sweat formed in her armpits. "I have to..." She looked over to where the others were gathering and hurried away.

Why hadn't she told him what she was doing? Because he would have rolled his eyes like everyone did. She didn't want him to look at her that way. Like it mattered what he thought. It didn't. Why did she care? She didn't. But her stomach twisted when he caught up.

"Have to?" He walked beside her, backward. "You're doing all this saving fish stuff because you have to? Let me guess. Community service? What did you do?"

"What?" Delaney stopped.

"Did you cross their red tape?"

"You think I..." Too flustered to finish her thought, she rushed away. Maybe she should have told him he was right, it was community service. It would sound far more interesting than the truth. She would sound far less stuffy, less... But she couldn't.

Eli debated whether to follow or let her be. She clearly had no interest. Except she'd blushed. In his experience, women only blushed when they were interested and were trying not to look it, but then it had been a very long time since he'd seen it. At least ten years. Women in their late twenties, as he assumed she was, didn't blush over men, did they? Not that he'd seen. They were too experienced in some way, too broken in. They knew what a line was and weren't impressed by them. He liked women his age far more these days than he used to like women his age. Of course, if she was in her late twenties, that wasn't exactly his age.

He needed to leave her be. If he was going to have a fling, it wouldn't be with her. She was too jittery. He needed some girl who wouldn't care too awful much when he went back home.

Eli started to turn away, to go back to the by-the-week hotel to shower and eat and find a way to fill the hours before bed, but he was curious as to why she was out there again if she felt she "had to" be there. Or maybe she meant she had to get away from him. Could be. Either way, instead of leaving, he ambled toward the small group she'd met up with.

"Hey." He spoke to a male this time, young, barely twenty-ish, with scraggly hair tied at the back of his neck and a couple days' worth of sparse beard trying its best to grow in. "Is this some kind of community service?"

"Where're you from?" The guy stared him down.

"Indiana. And you're local?"

"I'm as local as it gets, *Indiana*. Why are you here?"

"Working construction. Cleanup..."

"Nice. Another cockroach."

"What?"

"This don't pay anything. You can move along."

"I'm not..."

"Get lost. We have work to do."

"What are you doing?"

"Nothing that concerns you. We'll take care of ourselves." He strutted away.

As Eli considered catching up to the kid and taking him down a peg, he caught a glimpse of Miss Starfish looking over at him. Then

     Ella M. Kaye

she looked away again.

"Can I help you?" An older woman wrapped in a gray tunic that nearly matched her hair gave him an almost friendly look.

"Actually, ma'am, I'm wondering if I can help you. Is this only for a local group or..."

"Do you know what it is we're doing?"

"Some kind of fish rescue, so I assume."

She laughed. "Fish rescue. That's a good one. What do you know about fish rescue?"

"Well." Eli rubbed his chin that was rough already despite the fact he'd shaved that morning, as always. "I nearly committed the ultimate sin of injuring a sea star that wasn't dead and I learned they filter sea water through their systems so they can walk, or ... crawl, creep ... whatever you call it. That's about it."

"Come again?"

He looked over at the girl who was busy scouring the sand for ... fish in need, he supposed.

"Ah. You're here to impress Delaney."

"Who?"

She laughed again. "Don't even know her name but you're willing to help with wildlife cleanup to impress her?"

"No, I'm a good ways from home and I get bored in the evening. Thought I might find a decent way to fill hours since I'm here to help."

"To help? You're not here to take advantage of the nice paying jobs so many are inundating us over while us locals still can't get insurance to pay for our houses?"

"No, ma'am, I came to help. Most of us did."

She stepped closer. "You know, I believe you actually did. I don't, however, believe *most* of you did. Neither do most of us. So you'll have to excuse the attitude of the youngsters. We're all still stirred up good."

"I imagine you are."

She looked him over a while and then nodded. "So you want to help clean up the reserve."

When he asked for more information, she explained, and for

some odd reason, he found himself agreeing to give them a couple of hours a night, at least most nights. She warned him that Delaney wasn't easy to impress, and chuckled as she walked away.

He wasn't trying to ... well, maybe he was. Why else would he be doing this? To fill hours, he told himself. Instead of hanging with the same guys at night that he worked with during the day. He enjoyed their company well enough, but enough was enough. He liked variety. He liked new conversation.

And maybe he wanted her attention, at least enough she'd talk to him.

Figuring he better work up to it slowly, since no matter what she said, she was wary of him, Eli joined a group of older women, not a lot older, maybe five or ten years. A safer group to start with. He used the charm he knew he had to make himself welcome and he listened to those willing to tell their stories and he shared his own, which wasn't nearly so interesting. As he did, he kept hoping Miss Starfish, Delaney, would join them. In a group, she had to know it would be safe.

She didn't. The girl didn't join any group. She worked alone and was the only one to do so. If it wasn't his own wishful thinking, she did look back at him now and then.

Luckily, he had his own gloves, good leather gloves to protect his hands from the wires, rusted cans, and broken glass he grabbed from within marsh grass and sand. Some of it looked new, not from the storm. Stupid kids, he supposed. He'd seen few teens helping with anything in the couple of months he'd been there. A lot of them hung around doing nothing but laughing, making jokes, including about Miss Starfish. When they pointed at her, obviously making comments to each other, Eli straightened, pulling his shoulders back, and took a couple of steps toward them. They scattered quick.

His gloves were soaked by the time dusk was fading into dark and they called it quits. Eli couldn't resist sidling up to the woman who had been friendliest as they headed toward their vehicles to try for a bit more information. Gloria was a mother of four and new grandmother, she said, who wanted the beach safe and clean for her grandbaby when he was old enough to play there. Just before she turned away to her own car, Eli asked how well she knew Delaney.

"How well? Nah, I don't really. She's a sweet girl. Not very talkative. Hard worker, though. She does this on the side along with her two jobs and her full house. Can't believe no man has snatched her up to make her his wife..." The woman stopped and looked at him harder. "You have plans to try?"

Wife? Eli shook his head. "I've barely spoken to her. No, just curious. I'm horribly curious. The bane of my existence, so Mom says, or at least of hers."

The woman grinned. "A good trait to have. Curious means intelligent, and you'll have to be if you want to catch that little fish. She's self-sustained, not needy like a lot of these foolish little girls who think they *need* a man to be happy and that they're lucky when one talks to them." She rolled her eyes. "I tell them as often as I can to think of it the other way, that it's the man should be lucky to get them, and they should make themselves into a good catch that's hard to catch if they want a truly good man. Silly girls just don't listen. Worked for me, though. I been together with my truly good man for twenty-eight years now and still wouldn't trade him for the world, except on days, which we all have."

"Yes, Mom says the same."

"She and your daddy still together?"

"They are. Forty-five years now."

"That's always nice to hear since it's so rare these days. Sad." She shook her head. "Anyways, you want to turn Delaney's head, you best beware not to be pushy. That'll turn her away from you right faster than anything else in the world from what I've seen. Could be wrong, though. I only know her from a kinda distant family friendship. Can't say for sure if anyone knows that one well, except maybe her sister. I don't think she has friends, not the normal kind. That girl's not an easy one to know. Hardly talks. Can't imagine why."

"Bad experience?"

"Oh, not that I ever known about. Her poppa philandered and her momma knew about it, but they stayed together till she lost them both. Seemed like decent enough parents. She just ain't quite like most folks. Can't tell you why about that, either. Well look how dark it's getting. I got to hustle home and get dinner on the table. The roast should be good and slow cooked by now."

"Enjoy." His mouth watered at the thought of it. "And thank you. Nice to find someone willing to talk."

She laughed and tapped his arm. "Now don't mind about people around here not talking to you much. That's just our way in general. I don't much fit, either, since I wasn't raised here. Maybe that's why I like the girl so much. She don't care that she don't fit anymore than I don't. We'll talk more if you come around to help again."

"I will. Thank you."

"You got somewhere to go?"

"Excuse me?"

"For dinner. Where are you staying?"

Making it sound like he had plans to meet up with friends, Eli reluctantly turned down her dinner invitation. He appreciated it, but a few minutes of talking didn't require her to take him into her home. He wouldn't impose.

And as much as he wanted to do so, Eli didn't try to talk to Delaney on his way to the truck. He did keep an eye out to be sure she got to her vehicle alright, then he went on farther to his own. With a grimace about the soaked leather gloves that wouldn't have a chance of being dry in the morning, he unlocked his door, threw them in the bed since they were too dirty to put inside, and saw her pause as she drove by him. She stopped and got out but stood between her door and the running Ford. He was amused they both drove the same brand of vehicle. His mom often said he was too easily amused.

She called over. "I have extras. Gloves. Those won't be dry by morning if you need them."

He gave her a grin. "I have doubts any gloves of yours would fit my monster hands."

With the appearance of throwing a return comment that she thought better of, she looked away. "No, I have men's gloves. I wouldn't..." She leaned down into her car and her trunk popped open. Giving him a wary glance, to be sure he was staying out of reach, he supposed, she went to the trunk, shuffled around a minute, and came cautiously toward him holding a new, still tagged, pair of heavy gloves.

Eli walked up just far enough to meet her in between the vehicles.

"These should work." She kept her eyes averted from his but glanced at his hands as he accepted.

"They don't belong to someone? I'd hate to make your ... husband? or boyfriend angry..."

"No. They don't. I carry them for cleanup in case we get volunteers. They're a donation. Thank you. For your help today. You shouldn't have wet gloves to work tomorrow after giving your time tonight."

Donation. From a local building supply company, Eli guessed. So she was some kind of organizer. Interesting. "Thank you..."

She started away.

"Will I see you here tomorrow?"

She paused and again considered saying something she didn't actually say, but she did finally look at him. "I'll be here." With that, she hurried away to her car, closed the door, and left him staring.

Another bad move. She'd known it was a come-on with the husband or boyfriend question. She was smart enough to know it for what it was. And he definitely could not have a fling with that one. But it was sure as hell tempting.

Monster hands.

Not hardly. They were work roughened, yes, but Delaney liked that in men. Otherwise they were nicely-sized strong and sturdy hands with long fingers, appropriately big for his height, which she judged right around six feet. They were sensual hands. Like the rest of him. A very sensual man with a great smile and pretty, sweet, dark blue eyes. He talked so easily, so naturally. How could she not be attracted to that?

Not that it mattered if she was. He was there temporarily. By now she knew he wasn't vacationing and gawking. He was there working, one of the many temporary workers she kept wishing would leave, even if they did need them. By summer, he would be home with his family, and maybe sooner than that. They all did. She wouldn't be stupid enough again to get interested in a temporary worker.

With the resolve in mind, Delaney realized she'd thought of him

all the way home and sat in her driveway for some time as she delayed
going in to the crowded house. She loved her sister and her nieces
and nephews. She did. And she could deal with her brother-in-law
well enough by now, but she was ready to not have to live in the same
house with him. They'd been there since told to evacuate. Nearly five
months.

At least she wasn't home often. To be honest, that was why she'd
taken the weekend job, volunteer work, at the food bank. Delaney
worked in the back, away from everyone, restocking shelves. She
often took food in with her to add when she noticed something was
too low. It was quiet and she could wear her iPod and headphones
while she worked. Although often, she did wish she could be in her
living room that used to be mostly open space, with her music on
loud, practicing...

How long had it been since she'd been able to dance more than to
a quick song here and there? Five months. Almost. Now and then her
sister's family was out somewhere all together long enough she could
fit in a bit of practice, but most of the time she didn't know exactly
how long they would be and while she danced she worried incessantly
about them walking in and catching her.

No one saw her dance. She was good at it, and she'd always loved
to dance but she pulled out of lessons far too early because she
couldn't stand to do the mandatory recitals. So she quit. Her sister
fussed at her because she was a good dancer, but it was too hard to do
it in front of all those people.

At home, alone, using videos, she'd learned technique and created
her own style and she could get lost in being someone she wished she
could be but wasn't. Or maybe it was who she was supposed to be if
not for... Anyway, she wasn't. Except when she'd had the house to
herself without fear of someone walking in.

She longed for that. With a deep passion, she longed for it.

Giving up on the thought again until Trina and family weren't
there every day, Delaney gritted her soul and got out of her car to
force herself inside.

~ *Five* ~

Glad to finally get the opportunity after working at the refuge nearly every night the past week, Eli jogged back to his truck, which he now always parked close to where Delaney parked, and grabbed a new pair of work gloves. He saw her notice when she handed them to the boy who'd come to help unprepared. Only fair, Eli supposed, since he'd cornered the small group of boys hanging out doing nothing a couple nights before and suggested they'd feel better about themselves if they did something useful. Shocked one of them actually listened, he took the kid under his own wing and got him started.

Delaney still worked alone, but she spoke to him now and then. He'd learned she was a filing clerk forty hours a week. A quiet, not public, job. She hadn't said as much, but Eli figured that was why she did it. The girl wanted to talk. Eli could see she did. And yet she kept to herself. She only spoke to him when he pushed the issue and he didn't push far, or often. Still, he thought it could be a good sign that she worked close to wherever he planted himself each night.

Since it was Friday and the weekend alone loomed fast, Eli gathered his guts together and ambled over. "Hey, Starfish Girl. How's it going over here? Want help?"

She shrugged and kept working.

"You know I don't mean any offense by that."

"By what?" She gave him a quick glance.

"By what I call you. You can tell me to stop. I keep figuring you will."

"Then why do you say it?"

"To see if you will."

She straightened and gave him her full attention. "I don't like to be tested. So you can stop."

He nearly grinned at the quick little blaze of fire in her eyes. "Okay. I know your name is Delaney and I'm sure you've heard mine, but we haven't officially introduced ourselves. I'm Eli. Elijah Forrester, technically, but only Grandma calls me Elijah on a regular basis, and Mom does when I annoy her, which I tend to do a lot, or when she's worrying about me, which I can't get her not to do for some reason." He pulled his right glove off and offered his hand.

She hesitated but pulled off her own glove. "Delaney Griffin." A soft grip, like she didn't particularly want to touch him.

"Pleasure to meet you, Delaney. So do you have a nickname?"

"No." She pulled her glove back on.

"You don't like nicknames?"

"I haven't been called one I like." Starting back to work, she paused and looked at him. "Why are you helping here?"

He shrugged. "Can't stand to be bored and they won't let me work past four. Contracts and regulations. Ridiculous. Anyway, I have nothing else to do ... and that sounded bad. I don't mean this isn't important and I'm just killing hours. I mean I know it's important and I'm here anyway and I don't want locals to think I'm just raking in the bucks I can get and... Well, I'm here to help, so I'm helping."

"Why?"

"Well, you know, I'm not sure. Just because something told me I should. I think it was the right choice, whatever it was, other than my company suggesting I come since they wanted to send a crew and my guys wanted to come. There was that." He gave her a soft grin when she stared, trying to follow his rambling, he figured. And he figured he might as well jump right in. "What would you say to having lunch with me tomorrow? Someone said Bill's Diner out by the lighthouse was pretty good. Have you been?"

"Mustache Bill's. Yes, and it is good."

"So if I pick you up, you can get us there? Thought after the week's hard work, it might be nice..."

"I can't. Thank you." She picked up a rusty can to toss in the bag.

"Can't? Or not interested?" Eli stepped closer. "Because if you'd rather just meet there, I'm fine with that, too. I'll find it."

Light pink spread across her cheeks and she shook her head.

"Delaney." He took one more step, watching for her to get ready to bolt. "To be fully honest, I'm here doing this because you are. I do want to help; that was true, but I'm here picking up garbage because ... because you are. Because I was hoping to talk with you."

"Why?"

"Is that your favorite word?"

The blush deepened and her jaw tensed.

"Sorry. Okay, I don't really know. Again, something just told me I should. Yes, I often work on gut instinct. It usually does well for me and I think it could again. How about you give it a chance? Just lunch. Not a big deal..."

"I'm working."

"On Saturday? Since when do file clerks work on Saturday?"

She met his eyes, then moved away.

He caught up. "Yes, I asked about you. Sorry again. Actually, no, I'm not sorry." He touched her lower arm. "Dinner, then, if lunch won't work. How about it? If you want to ask a couple of friends to go with us, that's fine, too. I know you're nervous about..."

The spark of fire in her eyes returned. "You don't know anything about me." Pulling away, she went to add her bag to a pile of picked-up trash, said something to Gloria, and hurried to the parking area.

Eli caught up as she started to pull forward and stepped in front of her car. When she stopped, he moved to her door, glad the window was already down. "Okay, I know I don't know anything about you, but I'm interested. Is that so bad?" At her hesitation, he tried again. "I can do breakfast if lunch and dinner don't work."

She glanced at their fellow volunteers. The kid he'd first talked to the day Eli started volunteering yelled over to say she should have run him over.

"Think he's right? Should you have run me over?"

"I can't afford the insurance hike."

He grinned. "Guess I'm glad for that. So?" Still, she hesitated, but she was too close to agreeing, so he had to keep trying. *Now or never, Forrester.* "I don't give up easily. You should be aware of that. But, so I don't make it sound like you'll need a restraining order, if we try this and then you just want me to get the hell away from you, say the word and I will. That's a promise. And I know I'm an annoying ass at times, but I'm also a man of my word. Always."

"You often get restraining orders against you?" She eyed him as though truly wondering.

"Nah, not often." He winked. "Okay, bad joke. I do that when I'm nervous. No legal trouble, for anything. I'm pretty uninteresting, to be honest. Have you impressed yet? Should I pretend I'm a bad boy?"

"You're not nervous." It was a question. Curious.

"Kinda am." He figured he might as well admit it.

"Why?"

Making himself not laugh that she again asked *why*, he leaned closer, his hands propped atop her car. "Because I figure you're about half a step away from getting a restraining order, and I'd rather you didn't. And before you ask *why* I'd rather you didn't, because it'd be hard to talk to you that way, and I uh ... I'd really like to talk to you more. This is kind of unusual for me, Delaney. Nervous isn't something I'm used to, particularly not around women. So maybe give me a break if I'm doing this wrong?"

Her gaze fell ... to his chest. And she pulled her eyes away to the direction of her steering wheel as her cheeks reddened. Eli took it as a good sign she might just be a tad bit interested and decided to keep his mouth shut and give her time to think she might be, before he blew it by talking too much.

"I'm heading to get frozen yogurt after I clean up and eat. In Manahawkin. If you want to go out that way, I'll be there around ... seven-thirty."

"Sounds good, but how about something to eat along with it?"

"Oh, I don't usually..."

"I can grab carryout somewhere. Pizza or something? Know somewhere easy we can take it?"

"There's ... a pizza place next to the yogurt place, if you want that. Same building. They're on Main Street right across from the lake. You can't miss it."

Eli wasn't at all sure whether or not she'd agreed to dinner, also. "Okay. So, are there picnic tables at the lake at all?"

"Yes."

"Perfect. Can you do earlier if we're eating, too?"

Delaney pressed her lips together and stared out the windshield, watching her co-volunteers walk around them with a wave goodnight.

"My treat. Since I'm annoying you and all. You'd be saving me from another microwave dinner at the hotel."

She gave him a soft shrug. "Seven?"

"Perfect. See ya soon." With a grin, he started to walk away and turned back. "What do you like on your pizza? I'll get it started."

"Anything."

"Yeah? Anchovies?"

"If you want."

He laughed. "I don't want. It was a test. So anything? Really?"

"I don't say what I don't mean."

Delaney's nerves explode throughout her body as she showered fast and changed into clean clothes. What should she wear? It didn't matter. It didn't. Telling herself she was not trying to encourage Elijah Forrester from Indiana at all, whatsoever, Delaney pulled into her regular baggy jeans and ... and ... they were going to the lake park, so a sweatshirt over a tank top. Good enough.

Pulling a hair band around her wrist to let her hair finish drying before she put it back, she jogged down the stairs and ran straight into Paddy, or rather, Paddy ran straight into her, dumping his sippy cup, with no lid, all over her jeans. "Paddy! Trina, why is he running through my house with his juice again?" She shook her head as she surveyed the mess. It ran down the banister, splashed at least two steps, and flooded the wood floor. "Paddy, you *know* your cup stays on your *table*."

"He's only three, Laney." Trina picked the child up when he yelled about being yelled at.

"He's old enough to follow simple rules. He is. Look at this."

"I'll clean it. I always clean it up. Don't have a holy conniption."

Shrugging her hands, Delaney let it go, again, and went back up to find clean pants. So few rules. She insisted on so few rules. Why was it so hard? She'd have to go back and clean behind Trina since her sister wouldn't do more than mop it up quick with a towel, which would leave the stickiness and attract dirt. In her own house, Trina hired a cleaning service twice a week. Delaney refused to have strangers come clean her house, invading her space more than it was already. Her sister seemed bound and determined to change her mind to allow it. Wasn't going to happen. The arrangement was temporary. They would move out again. Someday.

Five months already. It was time.

Fighting the guilty streak that always came when she had the thought, Delaney tossed the wet jeans in her hamper, pulled into new ones – she'd have to do laundry when she got home now since it was her last clean pair, other than those that fit too snug – and jogged back down again, watching for running little ones. They weren't supposed to run in the house, either, but that never stopped. Never.

"Where are you off to?" Trina caught her as she opened the door.

"Out. I won't be late."

"Out where?"

"Trin, I still don't have to answer to you, you know. Love you. I'm eating out so don't bother to save any." Escaping before Trina could object, Delaney got in her car and breathed a heavy sigh of relief. Out. She was going out. To meet a man. No way was she telling Trina that yet.

~ Six ~

Waiting for a car to go past, Delaney quick-walked across Main and checked her watch on the sidewalk in front of Fusaro's Pizza. Five after seven. She was late, thanks to having to go back and change jeans.

He'd said he would get the order started, so she expected he was already inside. Maybe she'd change her mind. Would he be at the door or sitting somewhere? Would she have to ask someone for his table? Her heart started to thump at the thought, and she paused with her hand on the door. Go in or leave? Why had she agreed to this? She hadn't, really. She only invited him to join her at one of the few places she could go fairly easily.

The door opened and she jumped back, releasing the handle.

"Hey, Delaney. Sorry. I startled you." He held it, suggesting with his look, his stance, that she should go inside with him.

Her stomach turned. "Sorry I'm late."

"You're fine. It's nearly ready. Hope you like what I ordered."

"Anything's fine." She grimaced about repeating his word and grabbed a deep breath to calm herself.

"Coming in?"

"Um. Yeah." Hell. He was wondering what was wrong with her. Already. She shouldn't have come, shouldn't have agreed. Being a Friday night, the place was busy, loud. She wanted to back out and jog over to the park, by the water. But he touched her back and led her just inside the door where an employee told him she was headed to get his order.

Eli stuck a thumb in his jeans pocket. Nice-fitting jeans. Not loose. Not tight. Topped by a long-sleeved tee, medium green, a good color on him, and also nice-fitting, showing him off just enough. "Nice place. Smells great in here. I'm about starving just from that. Maybe next time we can eat in rather than taking it out."

"Sorry."

His head tilted. "For what?"

"Suggesting take-out instead. And being late. I'm not, usually. I had to go back and change again last second. The three-year-old is always running around the house with his drink, although I keep telling him..."

"Three-year-old? You have a kid? Kids?"

"What?" She realized she hadn't told him about Trina yet, other than a quick mention of her sister. "No. Not mine. My nephew."

"Ah." He relaxed and Delaney realized he'd tensed somewhat thinking she had kids.

"Anyway, that's why I'm late."

"It's fine. It wouldn't be ready any sooner if you'd been here sooner. And take-out's good, too. I'm not that picky."

She tried to decide if that was a slam of some kind, but he started talking about his own nephews, also young from the way it sounded, and he knew how messy they could be. Delaney tried to listen well enough to answer intelligently, but the haze that came with too high a level of nervousness had crept into her brain and she focused on telling herself it was fine, she was fine, it was only a pizza place, a nice one, busy, but still only a pizza place, when the girl came back with the food inside a plastic bag to make it easier to carry and Delaney tried to help pay for it, but Eli already had it ready and paid for and was ushering her out the door.

"So, should we go eat this and come back for the ice cream?" He headed toward the parking area.

With the fresh air and being out in the open, Delaney's head cleared enough to answer. "We can get the yogurt first and then head to the park. But it's yogurt, not ice cream. Is that okay?"

"All good to me, but it'll melt while we eat."

"Not if we eat dessert first." She tensed even more. Was that a stupid suggestion? She should have just okayed what he wanted to do and left it alone.

"I'm game. Where's your car?"

Her breath returned. He was fine with it. Maybe it wasn't too stupid. "Over at the park so I didn't have to move it a few feet."

"Okay, well, how about I put this in the truck and then we grab the yogurt and I'll give you a lift over there? Probably shouldn't leave my truck here."

She agreed because it would have been ridiculous not to agree, but Delaney had not planned to get inside his vehicle. It was only across the street. It would be fine that far.

Luckily, the place wasn't crowded. Too early in the season. Eli hadn't ever been in a serve your own frozen yogurt bar, so she explained you grabbed a dish and put in whatever you wanted and paid by weight.

"Now that's cool. Wow, how do you choose?"

"I have a few favorites and just get whichever one they have. They change them out." Delaney went straight to where she wanted to go and tried to decide how much to get. The bowl was plenty big, too big for her, and if she put too little in it, it would look ridiculous maybe, but she didn't want too much, either.

As she pondered in front of the flavor she always chose when she saw it, Eli wandered back and forth, looking at everything, and stopped to get at least three different flavors of yogurt, adding several toppings while he talked to the girl behind the counter who joked with him about being able to handle it. At the end, he topped the thing with two maraschino cherries. Delaney had added one. She would be tempted to add three or four, but it would look greedy, so she never let herself take more than one.

"You have some nice self-control, there." He grinned with a glance at her bowl.

"Some days. Are you going to be able to eat pizza on top of that?"

"Oh, yeah. And this was definitely a good idea. Glad you invited me."

She tried to pay since he bought the pizza, but he wouldn't have it and she couldn't argue because the girl behind the counter was watching and she just couldn't even though she felt bad about it, being that it was her idea. He opened and held the door for her, and then the passenger door of his truck, and let her hold his yogurt while he drove across the street.

He parked next to her car and they wandered down to one of the picnic tables. To calm herself, Delaney focused on the green of the trees and the grass, the blue-green-brown pond, the ducks cruising around leaving V-trails in the otherwise calm water. Nature soothed her. Always. Grounded her. She'd read once about letting tension fall down from the top of her head, down, to the soles of her feet, and down to be absorbed by the earth, letting it return calm and serenity. Often when she came here, she took her shoes off and focused on letting the stress fall.

Of course she would not do it in front of Eli.

Taking the side of the table that faced the water, she nearly laughed when he opened two boxes of pizza, one full of veggies and one full of meat with olives, and grabbed a piece to eat in between eating his yogurt.

"How do they look?" He handed her a few napkins.

"Good, but that's a lot of pizza." It smelled good, too. After eight hours of filing, with only a quick, light lunch, and nearly three hours of working at the refuge, she was starving.

"Thought I'd take the extra back to share with the guys, unless you want it."

"No, they need it more than I do." And she wouldn't get any of it, anyway. The kids, and Pat, would have it gone by the time she'd want it.

Delaney started with the frozen yogurt, cherry first, then the luscious sweet, cold peppermint with chocolate chips. Since her stomach started to growl and she didn't want him to hear it, she followed his lead and grabbed a piece of pizza, also.

"We were supposed to have dessert first, I know." Eli talked between bites from the other side of the table. "But I'm starving, so..."

"I eat shakes along with my cheeseburgers, too. Instead of waiting." She shrugged.

"Yeah? Nice. So..." He looked around at the park and toward the water. "You come here a lot? Are you close by?"

"Recently I've been coming here, usually Sundays when it's warm enough."

"It's chilly tonight. You're not cold, are you?"

"No. Layers. I'm used to it." She had her heavy jacket over the tee and sweatshirt.

"You're outside a lot."

"When I'm not at work and it's not ridiculously cold." She watched the ducks hedge up along the edge of the pond, eyeing them as they considered whether to come close enough to beg for food.

"Right. Me too."

"Aren't you all the time? With your job?"

"Yeah, well, usually. But that's work. When I'm not at work, I'm … still outside a lot. Other than the roughest parts of winter, and then I go stir crazy inside since we can't do much construction during blizzards and I'll go shovel snow in town or such just to get outside and moving. They say it's healthier, right? The fresh air, even if it's cold?"

"I guess." When you didn't already have germs from one of the bunch of kids you lived with, it would be, she supposed.

"I usually take a couple of weeks during the middle of winter, end of January or so, to go south somewhere I can be outside without frostbite. You do that at all? I know it's gotta get cold here, too. It was cold enough when we got here, and worse it seems with the wet air."

"When did you get here?"

"Mid-January."

Two months already? "So you're about to go home?"

"Nah. We probably have another couple of months, depending on how it goes, how much they let us work. That's been a bit debatable. Hard to say. It'd be nice to stay long enough to let spring finish coming in and see it that way, too. I mean, not to sound like an insensitive ass. I'm not here sight-seeing, but it's my first time to the ocean, so…" He shrugged and took a large bite of the meat-covered pizza.

"What do you think of it? The ocean."

"Well, it has its appeal. I'll give it that. I do love the sound it makes, the water rolling in and out. That's nice."

"I love that, too. I can't imagine, really, being away from it. You don't mind being away from Indiana so long?"

"Can't say I'm not at all homesick, although this early in the year, there's not a lot to do anyway. Some construction will be starting up again. More in a couple of months. It'll be good to be back with the family, though."

Delaney nodded, but she couldn't ask the biggest question on her mind. What family did he have? The way he asked if she had a kid told her he probably didn't, but you never knew.

"As long as I'm there by the beginning of July, it's all good."

She almost didn't want to ask, but to be polite, she figured it was kind of required. "What's in July?"

"Big family thing every Fourth. Those who have moved away come back and bring all the rug rats so everyone can get reacquainted. We do a hell of a big cookout and then go to the lake for fireworks, come back and get the little ones down for bed, with the bigger ones playing games and watching a movie and such inside while they keep an eye the little ones in case one gets up, and then we adults hang out in the yard till all hours."

She tried to tell him it sounded nice, but Delaney wasn't so sure it did, other than a cookout and fireworks.

"You have any family traditions like that?" He caught her eyes for a second.

Until she put them back on her dessert. "No."

"That's kinda sad. I know lots don't anymore. So tell me..." Spooning in a good bit of yogurt with toffee topping, Eli at least waited until he swallowed. Luckily. "For someone who loves being outside, why are you a file clerk?"

Delaney looked past him over to the water.

"I don't mean that bad. Nothing wrong with it. You enjoy the work?"

"It's okay."

"Only okay? Nothing else available?"

She caught his eyes in a question.

"Sorry, I'm being rude, aren't I? I don't mean to be. I guess I just always thought of file clerks as stodgy old ladies who hide inside out of the weather as much as possible and like tidiness and orderliness better than about anything else. Bad assumption on my part. Still, everything has its stereotype, right?" He took a big bite of pizza, his second piece nearly gone.

"It's quiet. I can take my music and listen to it and be left alone..." Delaney stopped and fought the blush she could feel moving up from her neck.

"You like alone." His voice was softer, his head tilted.

"Chaos bothers me." Easy way to put it.

"Yet you have two jobs along with your volunteer work at the refuge?"

"I don't have two jobs."

"Gloria said you did. And you said you're busy tomorrow."

"I um..." Delaney took a slow bite of her yogurt. "I volunteer Saturdays at the food pantry."

"Two volunteer jobs? That's nice, Delaney."

She had to wonder if he was being facetious, like most men were when they found how she spent her off-work time. "It keeps me busy." And away from the chaos of the kids, but she wasn't ready to delve into all of that.

He chuckled. "Yeah, well, I know a lot of people who like to *keep busy*, too, when not at work, but it's not useful to anyone but the owners selling the alcohol, or clothes and such. I guess it's useful to them. So, yeah, I think it's nice you do that instead of going bar hopping or shopping for stuff you don't need or whatever. Of course, there is the reading in a bar thing. Guess you do that. Until some jerk disturbs you."

Her face grew warm with his teasing. "Mostly they don't." And it was the only one she ever went in, but she wouldn't say that since at least he thought she was willing to go into a bar now and then, and so maybe he wouldn't think she was too awful stodgy.

"Yeah, you kind of put off that you don't want them to. Is that on purpose?"

Her heart began to thump. Too much. Too personal. Of course it was on purpose. What else would it be?

"Yes, I'm nosy. Curious. I get razzed for it often, and you can tell me to back off." He stuffed more yogurt in his mouth. "This is pretty incredible. What kind did you get? I wasn't watching."

"Snickerdoodle cookie dough."

"Damn, that sounds good, too. I missed it. Can I taste test? I'm not sick or anything, but just in case..." He wiped his plastic spoon on a clean napkin.

Of course she had to let him. He went past the M&Ms to only get the yogurt. "Mm, that's good, too. My favorite cookie, actually. Mom used to make them a lot, but it's been a while. She gets them to stay soft instead of getting all hard so you have to dip them in coffee to eat them. Not that I mind that, either."

Delaney had to wonder if he always talked so much, or if it was his way of showing his nerves, not that he looked at all nervous. She also wondered if he often asked questions without caring whether or not got they answered, or if he was trying not to make her too uncomfortable. Twice so far, he'd asked something and let it go. Or maybe asking questions was only a way to keep talking and he didn't care too much about the answers.

"So. You sometimes come here on Sundays. What do you do if you don't? Go shopping? Did I get myself in trouble with my comment? I do that a lot, too. Get myself in trouble by saying what I shouldn't, I mean, not by shopping."

Wow, he was hard to keep up with. Her head started to spin and she focused on his main question. "I don't like to shop."

"Really?" He grinned. "A girl who drinks her coffee black, spends a lot of time outside, and doesn't like to shop? Sure you're a girl?"

That flush that had crept out of her cheeks crept back in.

"Okay, that was stupid again. A joke. I can tell you are."

Delaney shifted on the bench, thinking about just walking away. It wasn't bad enough Trina constantly complained about her "boy clothes" and always wearing jeans or baggy capris. She didn't need it from this guy, too. And there was no way she could keep up with him conversationally. How he ate so fast between all the talking, she couldn't imagine.

Eli cringed. Stupid thing to say. He'd meant it as a compliment, actually, because he liked how down-to-earth she seemed. She obviously did not take it that way. Chances were good she'd heard too much of it, the same way Eli had heard too often about his questionable level of intelligence because he preferred working with his hands to sitting in some office. He just figured she did, too, so the office thing didn't fit her. Could he explain that without making it worse? Probably couldn't. Best to leave it alone and move along.

She'd only eaten one piece of pizza while he'd chowed down on three plus finished half his yogurt already, even being the one doing the most talking. By now, he wanted to move around and release some of the tension. She'd been surprised he could be nervous, but hell, when she hardly said two words and he had to almost force her to say that much, why wouldn't he be?

"Gonna help with more of this?" He nodded toward the almost full boxes.

"No, thank you. Should I have warned you I don't eat much at a time?"

"Nah, with your figure, I expected you didn't." Hell. She blushed again. She had to, however, know *that* one, at least, was a compliment. Didn't she? "I'm going to take this on back to the truck, then, so we can walk around with the dessert we were supposed to eat first. If you want."

Her slight nod had to work, he supposed.

With Delaney faced away from the parking area, looking toward the water, Eli gave his brother a quick call once he was out of her ear shot. "Hey, got a minute?"

"What do you know? The kid remembered he had family back here."

"Funny, Bill. Been busy. Quick question. Real quick 'cause I only have a couple minutes. So if I tell a girl I hadn't expected her to eat much based on her figure, she'd take it as a compliment, right?"

Silence came over the phone.

"Hello? Really, gotta make this quick. So?"

"Hell, Eli. Don't go screwing around with some girl you're just going to leave. Those people have enough issues right now, don't you think?"

"I'm not screwing around. Just... hanging out."

"Eli..."

"Give me a break, alright? Just answer." He unlocked his door and finagled the bag onto the floor in the back seat while hanging onto his phone with the other hand.

"Since when do you care that much how a girl will take anything you say?"

"Yeah, I don't. Generally. But this girl..." How did he explain Delaney? "She's not your average-type girl."

"No such thing as an average-type girl. There's part of your trouble."

"Okay, I got it, but you don't. Just tell me that wasn't offensive."

"Not sure. Depends on the context."

"I have no time to go into all of that."

"Then I can't answer you."

"Fine. Thanks, anyway. Gotta go. Tell everyone I said hello and I'm fine and staying out of trouble. I'll call later."

"Are you? Staying out of trouble, I mean."

"Doing my best. But she's waiting, so I'll have to call back."

"Eli. Be careful, alright? I know you got burned bad last time, but don't do anything crazy because of it. And don't turn it around on someone innocent."

"It's not like that, but thanks for the warning. Later." He hung up before he got closer to her. *Don't turn it around.* Why in the hell would he?

She turned toward him when he approached, checking to see that it was him, it looked like.

"So, can we walk? I'm not good at sitting."

"Sure." She slid off the picnic bench, gracefully. The girl was ridiculously graceful.

They took their bowls of what was left of the yogurt and Eli told her to lead the way since she knew the place. She took him down around some trees and back alongside the small lake that looked more like a pond, where a wood barricade held the water back from the grass, to where he could see a walkway that went across a dam. He asked if they could go across it, and she hesitated, but she went that direction, tossing her empty bowl into a garbage can on the way.

Eli did the same, saving the two cherries, hanging on to their stems. "You like these?"

"Does anyone not like them?"

"Always possible." He gave her a grin and offered one. Again, she hesitated before she took it. Her fingers brushed his.

"Your hands are cold."

With a shrug, she pulled the cherry from the stem with her teeth, dropped the stem into the grass, and shoved her hands into the pockets of the big coat that looked like someone else's. Eli couldn't make himself ask since he'd already had his foot in his mouth too often.

Stopping roughly halfway across the narrow bridge, he propped his arms, folded, on the metal railing to look down at the water. It yanked at his guts a bit, the thought of standing over top of all that water, but the railing was sturdy. To calm himself, he studied its engineering.

Until he realized she wasn't by his side and looked around to find her. She was standing in the middle of the walkway looking out the other direction.

"View better over here?" He touched her back.

She jumped.

"Sorry. Delaney, you don't have to be afraid of me."

"No, I ... don't like being up here." Her arms were crossed in front of her.

"Could've said so when I asked."

"You wanted to see it."

"Okay, I saw it. We can go back." Which was fine and dandy with him, anyway. Eli offered his arm, but she didn't take it. He tried hard not to be offended. First, she'd missed or ignored his cold hands comment that could have led to him warming at least one of them with his own, and now a flat-out refusal.

Silence filtered through the chill of the wet breeze and the smell of something cooking from across the street, he supposed. French fries. Obviously. He kind of wanted some even though he'd had enough pizza to be satisfied. They went back the way they'd come since he let her lead. He figured that was a sign she didn't have much interest in extending their outing.

When they got near the picnic table and she still hadn't said a word, he gave in. "I should let you get home since you're cold and it'll be getting dark soon." And he was flustered about trying to figure out what to say or not say. "You have any free time this weekend? Coming back out here Sunday? You said you often do."

"Maybe."

"If you do, you want to be alone, right? You can say so."

She was silent as they ambled back toward their vehicles, but before they stepped onto the parking area, she stopped. "I think I'll make snickerdoodles Sunday. I'll bring some in case you're bored and looking for somewhere to be. About three? I can do later…"

"Perfect. You want to just meet here or should I pick you up?"

"I'll be here. If something comes up, don't worry. I'll have my book and I'll just enjoy the quiet."

"Um, okay. Can I give you my number?" At her shrug, Eli went to his truck and yanked a sheet of paper from the little notebook he kept in his center console, wrote his name and number and went to her car to hand it to her. She didn't offer one in return and he decided not to push. "Thanks, Delaney. It was a nice way to spend the evening."

"Thanks for dinner and dessert. I didn't mean to let you buy, though."

"Least I could do for throwing myself at you when you would've been just as happy without me tagging along."

"I didn't mind."

"No? Honestly?"

"Honestly."

"Good. See you Sunday."

"Okay." She said it like she wasn't sure he'd be there, but he let that go, too, and waited to be sure she got her car running and pulled out before he went the opposite direction.

Delaney felt the tension throughout her body, strong enough to make her muscles ache, as she drove home. Sugarland was in her CD player and it helped some, but her feelings about meeting Eli again were too mixed. He was … chaos, in a way, but also calming in a way, and she couldn't figure out how to sort the two out.

Before she even opened the front door, she heard the television.

Loud. With a sigh, she went in and tried to get past the entrance to the living room unnoticed, but Trina jumped up and asked where she'd been and when Delaney said she'd stopped for yogurt and they realized she didn't bring any back to share, they pouted like she was a huge jerk or something and Trina asked if she'd come watch the movie with them, some action/adventure thing.

"Thank you. No. It's too loud for me."

"I'll have them turn it down."

"Then they'll fuss that they can't hear it. It's fine. I'm tired, anyway. Night, Trina." Escaping fast, Delaney went up to wash her hands and face with warm water, letting it soothe her, and then to her bedroom, closing and locking the door. To drown out the noise below, she turned on her music. David Bowie. Because she was in that mood. Without her shoes, to keep it less noisy, she released tension through Flamenco stomps to the beat of *China Girl*. The stamp and taps weren't nearly as satisfying without her shoes making the toe heels clap against the floor, but the last thing she wanted was to hear comments about *her* noise in her own house.

Shoving the thought away, Delaney focused on her arm movements, the wide graceful circles she'd imitated until she had the feel of it down. As always, it melted away her tension and made her feel stronger, resilient, stable.

And worthy of someone like Eli being interested.

Maybe she was, but how did she let herself show him enough of herself to prove it when just talking to him was so damned hard?

Eli couldn't go back to the hotel where his roommate would likely be playing a loud video game on his laptop, as he did every night if he wasn't out with a local girl or out trying to hit up a local girl. Not that he had room to talk.

Bill's warning flashed through his head. *I know you got burned bad last time, but don't do anything crazy because of it. And don't turn it around on someone innocent.* He wasn't turning it around. He wouldn't do that to any girl, much less this one, the one already so wary. If you didn't want something done to you, you didn't do it to someone else. Simple. At least he always thought it was simple. He knew lots of people didn't see it the same. Too many were too bent of vengeance. A stupid thing to do. It only made everything worse.

Yeah, he'd been burned, but Delaney was old enough, chances were good she had been, too. How many weren't? Like she said about the cherries. Kind of common.

Don't do anything crazy. Maybe a tad bit too late for that one. She'd said she couldn't imagine ever leaving the ocean, not being able to hear the waves lapping, and he wasn't about to move away from home permanently. His family mattered too much. He already missed hanging out at his parents' and seeing who dropped by, or dropping by his brother's place and harassing the youngsters. He missed the sweet tight hugs of the niece who was most fond of him, her little arms wrapped around his neck.

Delaney had no family traditions, she said. He couldn't imagine living that way.

Pulling up along the shore of Barnegat Bay, Eli turned off his truck and looked out over the water, his arms over the steering wheel, his chin on top. It was dark enough now he could only see the blackness of the water, with the sheen and reflection of the dwindling sun spread across its top. Yeah, it was nice, a good vacation spot. He got it. But he couldn't stay. To him, the rich earth and pungent smells of growing crops, the wide expanses of tall corn and places you could see nearly forever by breeching a small hill since most of the land was so flat was every bit as luxurious.

He couldn't move away from that. And yet, since he met her, the homesickness had been largely replaced by thoughts of what might be going on inside her head, of her history, her hang-ups, whatever it was that kept her so quiet. What was up with her? How did he get through to her?

And should he even try? He was going back home. Maybe Bill was right that he should let her be.

With a deep sigh, he got out and headed down to the shore, removing his shoes and socks to let the sand sift between his toes the way she did. He wasn't a big fan of the feeling. It was gritty, ticklish although he wasn't ticklish. It irritated the soft skin between his toes. Dirt felt better on bare feet. Though generally, Eli kept his shoes or boots on when he was outside. He even wore socks in the house unless it was too hot.

What about this did she love? Or was it only comfortable being what she knew? Could be it was about time for the quiet little dove to stretch her wings to see if she might like other kinds of shores as well. Not all shores had sand. Maybe dirt would do. And pasture. Waves of grass and wheat and corn.

Of course he was getting way too far ahead of himself. She hardly even spoke to him. He was being ridiculous to ponder whether she'd move. Still, he had trouble making himself not ponder it. There was definitely something about that girl, something he found kind of impossible to resist.

Seven

Eli paced in the grass between what looked like a jogging path and the thin strip of sand in front of the water, just down from the picnic tables where they sat the other night. Two nights ago. It felt much longer.

A check of his watch said he'd been there nearly forty minutes. He came early since he had nothing better to do and, well, he was anxious to see her. Ten after three. She had his number. If she wasn't coming, she'd call, he expected, not that she said she would. She'd made it sound like he was perfectly free to cancel on her without notice, so maybe she meant she'd feel free to do the same.

And she could, of course. Still, it was only polite to call.

A few ducks followed him around, waiting for food, which he didn't have. But then, he'd heard you weren't supposed to give them bread, so he'd stopped doing it a couple years back. Could be it was false info, an overreaction. Hard to tell. Maybe Miss Starfish would know, since ducks were water creatures and that seemed her specialty.

If she came.

Hell, he'd forgotten to call Bill back like he said he would. Since she wasn't there yet, Eli pulled out his phone. His brother would be home from church and done with Sunday dinner by now, in all likelihood kicked up in his recliner while the kids played out back on the swing set and Shirley sat with a book on the sun porch watching over them.

"You have some great timing, you know."

Eli grinned at his brother's harassment. "Catch you sleeping?"

"Just about. In five seconds or so, I would've been."

"Only old men sleep on Sunday afternoon." He crouched to pull the start of a sticker bush out of the grass.

"Yeah, that's me, an old man. You call now 'cause you knew I'd be enjoying some rare quiet time?"

"Damn right. Best time to talk to you."

"Okay, kid. So you got me to yourself. What's up? How's it going out there?”

"Slow as hell. Driving me crazy."

"Yeah? Come home."

"Can't. Too much to be done yet." He stood again to go over and toss the thing in a nearby garbage can.

"Why's it so slow, then?"

"Red tape. Too many of us trying to work together without decent communication. You know how it is. Anyway, could be we won't be here much longer and I'll be back there annoying you in person soon."

"That would be good."

"Miss me, do you?"

"Possible. But of course, there's no one hearing me admit it."

Eli chuckled and put his attention on the far side of the lake, a beach area, it looked like.

"So, how'd it work out with the girl? What's up with her?"

"Well, hard to say. I'm ... out here wandering around a little park next to a pond they call a lake 'cause she said she'd be here, oh, about fifteen minutes ago. So I'm thinking it's not going so well..."

"Eli?"

He pivoted at the voice and pulled the phone from his ear. "Delaney. Hey."

"Sorry. I... You're busy." She glanced at the phone.

"No. Hold on. Just let me get off."

"You don't have to. I'll give you privacy."

He studied her as she walked away, farther down the lake, carrying a bag over her shoulder and one in her hand. She wasn't wearing baggy jeans as every other time he'd seen her. They were jeans, but they fit her well. A long dark blue shirt hung down over top, down to her thighs, topped by her big jacket. Still, at least they were normal jeans.

Remembering Bill was on the line, he apologized and said she got there and he'd have to call back. Eli hoped she hadn't just heard him say it wasn't working and she was late, but then she wasn't very close, so likely she didn't.

Delaney stood right on the edge of the water, surrounded by

ducks. Eli went up close, but not quite as close as she was. "Is that lettuce?" She was tossing them bits of something pale green.

"Yes. You didn't have to end your call."

"No problem. Just my brother. Why lettuce? I figured an activist like you would yell about feeding wildlife."

She glanced at him, only for a second. "I'm not an activist."

"No? It's not an insult." When she didn't answer, he tried again. "So lettuce is fine? Is the rule about no bread true or just hype?"

"Bread has no nutritional value for them. If they fill up on that and don't eat enough other things, they get malnourished, sometimes deformed if they're young. So a bit of it here and there doesn't hurt, but I don't because others do. Lettuce is nutritional. Corn and peas are fine, too. Or oats."

"Interesting."

"And you only give them what they'll eat right away so it doesn't sit and get moldy. That'll make them sick, too."

"Makes sense." He wandered slightly closer. "And the thing about them getting too dependent..?"

"Not likely. As long as there's a natural food supply available, they'll turn back to that easily enough. Just like bird feeders. It's only a small part of what birds eat, anyway. They still forage. It doesn't bother anything."

"Good to know. Mom always has a bunch of feeders outside her windows so she can watch them fly about."

"I did have, but the neighbors complained."

"About your feeders?"

"About the droppings on their cars, and the noise, they called it." She shrugged. "Not worth the fight, so I took them down. Your mom's neighbors don't complain?"

He chuckled. "They wouldn't dare, if any were close enough. But no, they're in the country too far for her birds to bother anyone else." Noticing her glance at *wouldn't dare*, Eli felt like he should explain. "People don't give Mom flak. It's not in their best interest. Now, didn't keep Bill and Rosemary and me from doing it, but then we know her bark's worse than her bite."

"Siblings?"

"Right. Bill's the oldest, seven years my senior. Rosemary's right in between us."

"You're the baby."

"Yeah." He found himself rolling his eyes. "I hear about it plenty, too. How about you? Your sister's younger, right? Only the one sister?"

"Only the one, but she's two years older."

"Really?"

Delaney threw another questioning look as she tossed out the last bit of lettuce to the squawking ducks.

"Um, you just seem more like you'd be the oldest rather than the baby. Not an insult."

"I didn't take it that way."

"Good. I'm never real sure with you. I mean, people back home know how to take me so I'm a bit out of practice... or..."

"Still nervous?"

"Guess so."

"It's fine. I'm not that easily insulted. Really." She headed away from the ducks, up to the table they used two days before, sat on the bench backward, looking toward the pond, and pulled a brown lunch bag out of her shoulder bag. "I brought you cookies, if you want them."

"Heck, yes, I want them." Unrolling the top, he took a good whiff of the sweet cinnamon buttery aroma. "Mm, that's pretty much like home, from the smell."

"You can try them."

"Didn't want to be rude." He offered her one first.

"No, thank you. I've had enough already, in between fighting off the little ones while trying to make them. I'd forgotten why I stopped baking."

Sitting next to her, he bit into one and couldn't help closing his eyes. Soft, even. Perfect. Definitely like home, but better.

"Okay?"

"Delaney, this..." He finished chewing and nodded at the bag. "This even beats Mom's cookies, but don't ever tell her I said so. Nice cure for homesickness."

His grin made her heart jump, just a little. Okay, more than a little. He was adorable. Kind of like the neighbor's puppy dog years ago that followed her around every time she was outside playing, just waiting for attention and going spastic when he got an ear scratch or tummy rub.

Maybe not an appropriate way to think of a grown man, but it was hard not to. He hadn't even said anything about her being late. Again.

"So, how's your day going?" He talked between bites. "Other than the interference with your baking."

"That was the easiest part of the day so far."

"Yeah? Why?"

"There's now marker, permanent marker, in the crevices of my wood kitchen cabinets because someone left them down where the three-year-old could reach them and no one was watching what he was doing."

"That won't be fun to get off."

"No, I expect not. And as I was leaving, the seven-year-old was trying to hide the fact he'd grabbed his mother's coffee off the table, so he twirled around fast, throwing it all over me. Good thing it only got me and not him."

"Was it hot?"

"Very. Just poured. She always pours it and leaves it sit to cool, and I keep telling her..."

"Did it only get your clothes?"

Delaney pulled up her coat sleeve to show him the wide red mark on her arm that still hurt enough it was hard to ignore. "That's why I'm late. Sorry again."

"Forget it." He took her hand and raised her arm. "That might blister. Put anything on it?"

"Cold water. You're not supposed to use anything else, right?"

"Well, not oil or anything oil-based." He stood. "Come on."

She stared at him and pulled her coat carefully back over her arm. "Where?"

"Getting something for that arm."

"No, it's fine."

He sat again. "Delaney, I know a thing or two about burns. You need to get something on that to try to keep it from blistering. And you might want a different coffee maker while you're at it. Shouldn't come out that hot."

She knew he could be right, but she'd had her fill of being around people for the time being and she was in no mood to get in his truck and just go wherever he thought she should go, or to encourage him at all, so she refused.

"Okay, then. I'll be right back."

Unable to resist, she turned enough to watch him walk away. He had a nice saunter, and even in barely more than fifty degrees, he wore only a T-shirt, denim blue, under his plaid long-sleeve flannel shirt in different shades of blue. The sleeves were rolled slightly rather than buttoned, showing off a decent amount of arm hair without being overdone. His jeans were the light denim color she liked, not the brand-new-looking dark jeans that looked like they were trying to be dressy, and nicely fitting, loose enough to look comfortable but not trying to cover anything.

Eli didn't get in his truck, as she expected. He opened the tailgate, rolled the tarp thing that covered it back out of the way, and jumped up. Easily. The man was in incredible shape. Long and lean, but not too lean. Well-tanned, not surprisingly since he worked outside. His brown hair was a pretty color, darkish but not exactly dark, with highlights that also had to have come from working outside, and a nice, soft wave. The tan and the hair color showed off his dark blue eyes like crazy. Delaney had a hard time not staring into them, they were so pretty. And friendly.

Getting back down with an easy leap, Eli caught her watching and she turned back to the lake, hoping the flush in her cheeks would fade before he returned.

He'd left the bag of cookies, wrapped back up and set on the table. Oil stains showed through the brown paper. She'd wanted to put them in a plastic container, one of those cheap disposables she never threw away, but as always, they'd all disappeared. She considered grabbing one as a distraction, but she'd already told him she'd had enough and it would look odd if she changed her mind. Besides, she brought them for him, so he'd have enough to take back to his hotel room and enjoy for a couple of days.

"Let me see that arm." Eli straddled the table's connected bench and set a first aid kit and jar of something between his legs.

Delaney didn't want to look closely enough at it to see what it was, considering where it was. "It's fine, really."

"I'm trained in first aid enough to know what I'm doing here. Let me see it."

Since she didn't have a good reason to argue, she pulled her arm out of her coat and pushed her shirt sleeve up. Her stomach turned a bit when he picked her arm up to look closer. Gently. He had a soft touch.

"Okay, definitely needs some help." He cleaned his hand with an antiseptic wipe, opened the jar, dipped his fingers in, and pulled out a white oily-looking substance. "Might hurt a bit from touching it, but it should stop within a minute or two."

"Isn't that oil? I thought..."

"Coconut oil. Not actually oil, just called that. Trust me. I use it all the time, especially on the little ones. Nice thing is if they stick the sore finger or whatever in their mouth with this on it, it doesn't hurt anything. Completely edible and non-toxic." He tilted his head when she pulled back as a reflex. "It'll help, Delaney. Okay?"

She gave him a nod, despite her better judgment, and gritted her teeth at the pain that increased with the pressure, even easy pressure.

"It only burns more because I'm touching it." Eli, very gently, smoothed it around the red area. "It'll stop soon. Promise."

Unwilling to look like a wimp in front of him, Delaney did her best to keep from reacting, to the pain and to his touch. Wiping the oil off onto the same wipe, he grabbed gauze from the first aid kit and taped it over the burn.

"Better yet?"

She nodded. The fire was starting to wane, at least from the burn. Her own fire was another story.

"Good. Let me help with your jacket."

Delaney needed to walk to calm her nerves, so after he took his supplies and the cookies to his truck, they wandered around the lake, using the sidewalk rather than the little bridge over the water to get to the other side. By the time they got to the beach area where the sand ran down into the water, Delaney was ready to sit. They'd talked some, mainly about ocean life and tourists and sea critters, as he called them, but they also walked silently part of the way.

It was a much more comfortable silence than Delaney was used to, not fraught with tension because she couldn't figure out what to say or if she wanted to say it, but relaxed and easy.

When she sat in the sand, her knees bent in front of her, he did the same, close enough his arm touched hers when they moved. She had to wonder if she took her right side so he wouldn't brush against the sore arm.

"How's it feeling by now?"

"Much better. Thank you."

"That'll wear off. When it starts burning again, just add more. As often as you want. It won't hurt anything."

"Why are you first aid trained? For your job?"

"Yeah. Not the paid job, though. I have used it there at times. Minor stuff." He picked up a rock from somewhere to his right and threw it into the water, causing ripples that came into shore. "I do some volunteer fireman duty."

Fireman. Rescue construction. Volunteering with her at the refuge. He had a good heart. Delaney tried to say something about it, but it flashed memories in her head she didn't want. Instead, she looked up at the bats fluttering just above the trees. Dusk was settling in. She hadn't realized they'd been out there so long.

It was on the tip of her tongue to tell him it was getting late, she should go, but she couldn't make herself do it.

"Have another recommendation for food? If I don't get something real soon, I'm gonna head back to the truck and devour those cookies all at once."

She grinned. "What are you looking for? Take out or..?"

"Nope." He shifted, turning to face her. "Hoping you'll go with me for a nice sit down. Will you?"

Her stomach twisted. Delaney very much wanted to agree. But

she couldn't. It was too much too fast. "Thank you. No, I'm…"

"I'm barging in too much on your too-rare alone time. Yeah? Or I'm getting on your nerves. I'm hoping it's just the former."

The twist turned into a knot and she got up. "I don't … um…"

He stood beside her. "Okay. I got it. Just because I'm bored when I'm not working, doesn't mean you are. So… Thank you for meeting me out here and for the cookies. I'll walk you back to your car unless you'd rather I didn't." He sounded insulted.

"I'm not tired of your company."

"No? I know I can be…"

"No."

"So then..?"

She started walking, back around the pond, on the sidewalk. He let her be with her thoughts that were flying every direction. Delaney wanted to say yes to dinner. She wanted to stay and hang out with him. But she did not want to encourage him just so he'd leave again in a couple of months or less. And she definitely did not want him to pry into why she didn't talk to him much. That would come. If she let it get too far.

If he offered to get takeout and eat in the park, she would likely give in, but it wasn't what he meant and anything else was … too much.

At her car, she knew she had to give him some kind of explanation. Or something.

"Be sure to keep coconut oil on that arm, Delaney. Do you have any? You can take what I have…"

"No. Thank you. I'll stop and get some. I have to get a few groceries, anyway." Which she did not want to do. Her nerves were already too much on edge.

"If you're sure you will. Virgin oil works best, more expensive but worth it. Keep it out of hot water for a while. Cold water's good."

"I know. Thank you. Really. It did help."

"I'm glad. Well…" He took a couple of steps back with a kind of half turn. "Any time you want to get out and not want to be alone, give me a call. Night, Delaney." Eli gave her a light nod and backed away, to his truck.

She didn't want to leave it like that, though. "Will you be at the refuge tomorrow, or are you getting tired of it?"

He smiled, a beautiful charming smile. "I'll be there." His eyes sparkled.

"Good. I'll see you then."

~ Eight ~

Delaney was almost surprised he was there every night after work, all week long. A couple of nights, he'd looked beat when he showed up and she asked if he didn't want to take the night off, but he always stayed as long as she did. They'd somehow turned into a team, with her focusing on the smaller debris while Eli used those muscles of his to drag bigger stuff up to a central pile, or to pull large fallen branches and trunks out into the water where they would become fish havens. Now and then one of the other women called over to him for help, and one of them made a point of doing so whenever she found any reason, flirting with him as he helped, but mainly, he stayed beside her.

They didn't talk a lot, which was nice. Still, she gave up wearing her headphones because it was easier to hear him the first time when he spoke to her than to ask him to repeat it, and it felt rude to wear them now that she had a work partner.

By 5:30 Friday, Delaney realized she was plenty tired enough herself. Dropping a piece of glass in her trash bag, she stood and stretched her shoulders, set her hands on her hips, and looked out over the Atlantic, through the brush.

"Getting ahead of you." Eli paused pulling a large trunk with a bunch of thin branches poking against his jeans to give her a grin.

She stared over at him. As always, he was in a T-shirt covered by an old plaid work shirt and jeans plus a pair of tall galoshes he'd picked up for hauling stuff out into the water in order to keep his boots dry. Even covered so much, he was a very sensual man. And that grin...

"Something wrong?" His grin faded.

"Yeah."

Eli dropped the dead tree and made his way back to her. "What is it? Your arm hurting? Or..."

"No. I'm tired. I think I'm done for tonight."

"Feel okay?"

She wasn't about to admit why she was more tired than normal. "Yes, just... Long week, and I've had enough of this for now. Feel like frozen yogurt tonight?"

He smiled. "Sounds good."

"Actually, there's ice cream just across the street at the lake."

"I saw it the other day. Is it good?"

"It is. Want to splurge with me?"

He leaned in close, still with that grin. "Absolutely."

It made her stomach turn, but a good turn this time. Elijah Forrester was absolutely starting to get to her.

He was supposed to call his brother, but with Delaney willingly hanging out with him until well past dark, Bill would have to understand.

Since he figured she would balk at going out for dinner, Eli told her he had a stop to make and would meet her there. Looking up a number before he followed her out of the refuge, he ordered Asian takeout in a variety, stopped to pick it up just across the street from the park, and still arrived before she did. He was pretty sure she said she'd park beside the ice cream shop, in front of the beach area.

Finally, she pulled up beside him and started apologizing as soon as she got out. "Who accidentally spills a whole bottle of shampoo, my shampoo she wasn't supposed to be using, by the way, all over a floor without realizing it? Seriously." Delaney shoved a hand over the hair again pulled into a ponytail. "I'm sorry I took so long. It would have just been left there if I hadn't thrown a hissy and made her clean it up. And I'm the bad guy, of course."

"The three-year-old?"

"No, the oldest. At least from the three-year-old, I'd expect that. Am I being too particular?"

"I can't say I'd put up with that very well, either."

She grabbed a deep breath. "Sorry. I'll stop. I just get too wound up with the chaos. I shouldn't have stopped at home, but I wanted to clean up a bit since you were making a stop anyway, and I didn't even do that. Anyway, I'm definitely ready for ice cream. I might get as much as you did last week. I am sorry I left you waiting again. Really, it's not something I do."

"You're fine. Stop apologizing." Without thinking, he reached out to touch her face.

She drew back.

"Um, my turn to apologize. I just..." Damn. He hadn't meant to do it. "I feel bad for what you're dealing with. If this doesn't work for you tonight, say so."

"No, really. I'm... It does. And I seriously need ice cream. With plenty of chocolate."

Eli grinned and motioned for her to lead the way, forcing himself to keep his hands off, no matter how much she looked like she could use some friendly comfort.

Nearly at the little place that was obviously an old Victorian house at its origination, he wanted to ask more, about the kids and the living arrangements, and about why she was so out of sorts the past couple of days, even quitting early...

She jumped when her phone rang, then grimaced at the caller ID. "What, Trina? I just left there. ... No, I won't be home early enough to bring dinner. ... Send Pat for it. ... Yeah, well, I'm tired, too. I work more hours than he does. He can deal with it. ... Fine, your call, not mine. ... No, I'm not stopping for dessert, either. It'll be too late for those kids to eat sugar. ... I don't know. ... Don't wait up. I'm a big girl. I can handle myself. ... Bye, Trina." She rubbed a hand over her face as she stuck the phone back in her pocket. "Sorry."

Eli took her hand and stepped in front of her. "Hey. No need. And it really sounds like you need a break. Let's say we buy the place out and see if we can make ourselves sick tomorrow since it's not a work day."

"It is for me, but I might anyway."

He grinned and held the door. *Don't wait up.* She'd told her sister not to wait up. Eli tried hard not to take it for more than it was.

Delaney ate way too much ice cream. But Eli was prepared. He had an old blanket in the back of his truck to spread over the sand, and even as generally uncomfortable as she was, she enjoyed sitting there with him, watching the reflection of the sunset in the water and birds hopping around its edge as she picked at the Lo Mein to counter the sugar, he said, although there was plenty of sugar in most take-out, also, and she knew her system would be unhappy with her by morning. But that was morning and this was evening and she was enjoying the weather now that the humidity dropped some but it was still warmer than the past few days. She was also enjoying his company. The ducks came to visit but she didn't want to get swamped while sitting on a blanket, so they gave them nothing and the pouting ducks went on their own way.

Done eating, apparently, Eli stretched his legs out and leaned back on his bent arms. "Okay, I've gotta ask. You said you live with your sister, and there are a couple of kids, but how many people, exactly, do you live with?"

"Seven. The kids range from three to thirteen, plus my sister and her husband. Trina was aiming at every three years because she always wanted a houseful. Tiffany is the oldest, followed by Tracie who's ten, and then Paulie, who's seven. But then Tammy came accidentally only a year after Paulie, and they meant to stop there. Then came Paddy, the three-year-old. He's a terror. Cute, but ridiculously out of control."

"Wow. Who chose those names? No offense, but..."

She chuckled. "Yeah, I agree. They decided on T names for the girls to go with Trina and P names for the boys to go with Pat, kind of a compromise, I think. Trina finds it cute. Anyway, the house wasn't meant for so many. It's a small place. There's only the one full bath on the top floor and the half bath on the main floor the oldest girls won't use because it's too small, so they constantly hog the one with the shower and their stuff is all over the counter because the medicine cabinet is overfull. It's just not enough room for five kids. I love them. Really. But it's so crowded."

"You haven't thought about finding your own place? I mean, I get it if it's a financial thing..."

"It is my place." Delaney nearly pulled back from the conversation, but since she'd let him in that far, she figured she might as well finish the story. "They were part of the mandatory evacuation from Barnegat Light. Good thing they sheltered with me during the storm, since their house is gone. I mean gone, with everything in it. They brought some of their most important stuff over before it hit, so they have that, but..."

He sat up again. "That sucks."

"It hit my sister hardest. Things, her possessions, matter so much to her."

"Not to you?"

"No. Not really. But mess does. And clutter. It closes the place in too much. Maybe I'm too particular, like she says."

"Nah, I agree, and honestly, with it being your place, you'd think they'd respect that more. No offense to your sister, but still, I'd kick them out if they treated my place like that."

"I can't. Trina... She's emotional still. Until they can rebuild, I can't ask her to relocate again."

"Right." He shook his head. "I can see why you're out and about so much. I'm sorry. For all of you."

"A lot of people got hit harder. A hundred or so people died. So really, we're lucky. Even Trina is. Just don't tell her that."

"Yeah, I know, Delaney. It's why I'm here. Just wanted to do something. Not sure it's making much difference overall..."

"It is to me." It came out before she could stop it, and she felt her face get warm when he caught her eyes. "And Maggie seems to think you are."

"Who?"

"From the refuge, the one who keeps calling you over to help."

"Whether she needs it or not." He rolled his eyes and leaned back on his arms again. "I keep wondering if I should ask if she realizes she's way too young for me. But with so few younger kids helping, I hate to discourage them."

She chuckled and wished she had the nerve to lay down, also, as tired as she was. It would feel better, but Delaney couldn't make herself do it. Too personal. Too open. "It's nice, though. I do appreciate it. Your help."

He flicked a grin her direction. "I'm only doing it to be close to you, you know."

Her face grew warm again. "Too late to convince me of that, but

I'm flattered, anyway."

With his smile, that devilish charming smile, Delaney felt the warmth spread through her body and distracted herself by organizing their little mess, wrapping the leftovers inside the bag to keep insects away and taking the garbage up to the can, stopping him when he said he would. He watched her, though, a guardian type of watching her, it looked like, the way he scanned the dark area around her until she was back beside him.

Delaney had to keep her eyes from him as he settled in, lying on his back, his arms folded under his head. It was nice to enjoy the dark and the quiet unbothered and she let herself get lost in her own thoughts until he got quiet for too long and she called his name. Asleep. Out there in the open. Something about it was way too adorable and she left him alone. Wondering how long she should let him sleep, Delaney jumped when her phone rang and tried to answer fast before it woke him up.

Didn't work. His eyes opened. "What, Trin?"

"Are you okay? You know it's like nine-thirty. Where are you?"

"I'm fine, thank you."

"Okay, where are you, out late again? You're never home recently and you hate to be out alone, especially at night, so..."

"I'm not alone and I'm fine. Headed home soon. I told you not to wait up."

"Laney..."

"You know I hate that name. Please stop." She watched as Eli sat up and rubbed a hand over his face and checked his watch. "Go on to bed. I'm fine. Good night, Trin."

Eli shook his head. "It's not even late. Is she always so Mother Hen with you?"

"No. She knows something's up I'm not telling her. And she's nosy. She's not worried."

"You haven't told your sister you're hanging with the enemy?" He rolled his shoulders and neck.

"Enemy?"

"Temp workers, you know. I do know how locals feel about us."

"Some do, I guess."

He chuckled. "Sure sounded like you did."

"Oh." Something about him waking up in front of her made his sensuality stand out even more than normal. "No, not quite that. Anyway, I should get back home, I guess."

"Why? You work early?"

"No. Ten o'clock. But you're ready to go."

"What makes you think that?"

"You fell asleep."

"I didn't... Did I?" He rubbed his chin. "Sorry about that."

"No, it's fine. But really, I have things I need to do before tomorrow, so..." Delaney stood and he stood with her, grabbing the blanket and tossing it over his arm.

He walked with her to her car and thanked her for hanging out with him, even if he was kind of, almost, the enemy. With a grin.

"Eli... I shouldn't have given you that attitude. I'm..."

"Nope." He held up a hand. "Don't apologize. You've got your reasons. I get it."

"You don't, really."

"Don't I?" He stepped closer. "Something more than just intruding on your beach, your privacy?"

"Yes."

Dropping the teasing, he gave her a light nod. "Can I ask?"

"I um... No. It doesn't matter. Are you awake enough to drive back okay?"

"Yep. But you know, I'm not just being nosy. I do care." He looked for a moment like he'd move in and Delaney felt her heart race, but then he backed away and asked if they could meet up again after she was off the next day.

She couldn't do it. It was too much. And she did have things to get done. But with him standing so close and looking at her that way, somewhere between respect and ... lust, she assumed, it was hard to say no. She barely made herself say she couldn't.

"Okay. Sunday, then? Just an hour or two? How about breakfast? Then you can be free the rest of your day off if you want to be. Not that you have to agree or anything..."

"I eat breakfast late on Sunday. It's the one day I let myself sleep in."

"Brunch, then. What about that Mustache place out on Long Island? They have breakfast, right?"

"Mustache Bill's. They have wonderful breakfast."

"Game? I can pick you up."

The thought of getting in his truck still bothered her. So did the thought of having breakfast on Long Island on Sunday morning when it would be crowded. Maybe she could do it. He wasn't exactly a stranger anymore. "How about I pick you up since I know where it is?"

Agreeing, Eli gave her the name of his hotel and the room number and touched her fingers. Barely. "I look forward to it, Delaney. Have a good day tomorrow."

Her stomach tightened. Her heart raced. Definite flirting. He was flirting, not just hanging out any longer. The dynamics just changed. Maybe she wouldn't be able to do a crowded restaurant with him. Not after that look.

He again waited until she pulled out and followed as far as the traffic light, then turned off in a different direction. Suddenly, she felt so much more alone than ... than when? Than always. She always did, but she was used to that. Eli was starting to make her not used to it.

Not good. Not at all good.

~ *Nine* ~

Delaney's heart pounded as she pulled in front of the hotel. A bad idea. She was starting to fall for him, and he would leave soon, just drive right on back to Indiana and whatever family and girls or whoever he had there, and that would be that.

She nearly drove away again when she saw him, not only him, but a couple of guys with him. Laughing. Looking over at her. One of them was the idiot who had called her fish girl and said she was talking to the fish. She hadn't been. She'd been talking to herself. Muttering to herself. People did that. There was nothing crazy about it.

She couldn't do this. She was out of her mind. Everyone would know she'd again let herself be duped by a temporary worker and she'd never live it down. But much of her wanted people to see her with Eli, who was far above the last one, the one she'd seen only because ... because he paid attention to her despite her best efforts not to be noticed. He'd noticed her. She was flattered. And curious.

As she was with Eli.

No. Delaney could not do this again.

He walked toward her car and the other two followed, still laughing. Her stomach tensed, and her grip on the steering wheel. When she heard something about his *little Jersey fling* and not telling the girl back home, Delaney started to pull away. Jersey fling? She was no idiot. Somewhat naive, maybe, but not an idiot. She'd hardly slept since leaving him at the lake, thinking about his look, the way he'd nearly kissed her. It was too much. She was no one's fling. Never again.

Startled when he jogged over and stepped out in front of her car, she slammed the brakes, barely missing him. "*What* are you doing?"

"Ignore those guys." His voice came through the open window.

She looked back. They'd stopped laughing, staring instead.

Eli came to her window. "They're jerks, okay, but they didn't mean to be offensive to you, only to me. I'm sorry, Delaney. Are we still on for breakfast? Can I get in?"

Her head shook involuntarily. "This was a bad idea. I can't... No. I'm sorry. I didn't mean to mislead you. Please, don't come back to the refuge. It's my refuge, too, to get away from things, and ... I can't do this." Her heart pounding harder, enough the nausea began to creep in, she let off the brake and moved away, careful not to hit his toes.

He said something, but she couldn't hear him through her pounding heart and spinning head. To distract herself, she turned Sugarland on because Jennifer Nettles' voice always soothed her nerves, fast forwarded to *Stay* and almost took the road back home. Instead, she headed to Long Beach, to walk along the shore, to see what progress had been made with reconstruction, how much Eli and his crew and the other out of state crews were actually accomplishing.

The girl back home. Did he have? Eli didn't wear a wedding ring, but then neither had the last jerk. Trina said men often didn't, because of their jobs. They were too likely to catch them on equipment. And he didn't need a ring to be promised to someone. Why wouldn't he be? Her sister had told her to stay away from the last guy after meeting him. She could tell he was bad news. But then considering who Trina married...

Delaney had looked forward to breakfast out for a change and saw no reason she couldn't go ahead with it since she'd gone out that direction, anyway. She'd never done it before, eaten out by herself, and... How did she think she'd be able to sit at a table alone with people staring and wondering why she was alone and ... and she couldn't. Maybe she could. Of course she could.

Panic tried to work its way through her system and she squashed it back by singing along with Jennifer. When she had to slow down through populated areas where the cars were closer, Delaney rolled up her window to be sure they wouldn't hear her singing along, and when she stopped at a stop light, she stopped singing in case they might see that she was.

Not that it mattered. Except it did. She enjoyed when others did it. It made her smile. There was no reason she shouldn't make others smile when they saw her sing along to her favorite music, but she couldn't. Her heart raced at the thought of it.

At the diner, Delaney parked back away from the main traffic where she could pull between two empty spaces and wondered if she had the nerve to go in. Her heart would pound. She would flush. She knew the drill well. Sometimes she made herself do it anyway, whatever needed to be done. But it was Sunday morning and Bill's would be crowded and they'd look at her funny for being alone on Sunday morning taking up a full table by herself and ... and just sitting there. She supposed she could grab a newspaper on the way in, except it was big and made too much noise. A book didn't make noise unless she dropped it, which she might do with as nervous as she was, but she hadn't brought one. She should just go home. Or she could go to the reserve and work so she wouldn't have gone out for no reason. But working alone would give her too much time to relive how she'd freaked out and left him standing in the parking lot, in front of his coworkers.

Maybe she was an idiot. At least he would stop now and she could go back to what she was used to. Being left alone. Except at home where she wanted to be alone and couldn't.

Shoving a hand through her bangs, Delaney considered shopping instead. It was nearly Easter and she always bought her nieces and nephews small things to set beside their baskets. She didn't like to shop on Sundays, though. It was her one restful day and shopping was far from restful. It was exhausting. Of course, going into the café by herself would be exhausting, as well. She might as well ... go walk along the beach at the lighthouse. That, she could do alone, as she often did. It had been a while.

About to restart the engine, she jumped at a knock on the window. Eli. Her heart pounded as she rolled the window down only a crack. "Why are you here?"

He shrugged. "You got my hopes up about the wonderful breakfast, and I decided to do it anyway."

"Alone?"

"Why not? I eat alone plenty. I'd rather have company, but I don't mind finding someone inside to chat with if I need. Was that your plan? If you wanted to eat alone, you could have said so."

"No. I don't. I was about to leave."

His eyebrows raised. "Okay, look. This doesn't have to be so hard, does it? Those clowns were harassing me, not you. If you heard the thing about a girl back home, it was nothing, just an ex they love to harass me about. I've got no girls back home other than my sister and cousins and nieces. No girlfriend. No wife. Not even an ex-wife. They were just being jerks. So if that's what chased you off..."

"I'm not the fling type." She watched a couple hand-in-hand laughing as they walked to their car. "So if that's what you want..."

"No. Delaney, I know you aren't. Neither am I, alright, whatever they said. I'm just enjoying your company and I'd like to keep doing that."

"You don't understand..." She felt her eyes try to water with her nerves intensifying and looked away.

"Right, I'm sure I don't. And I mean that in all seriousness, okay? Let's have breakfast and talk about it. Then if you want me to leave you alone, I will, as I said."

Gripping her keys hard enough they dug into her palm, she heard him ask if she was getting out and she started to make herself, but she was so flustered she couldn't do it. She couldn't go sit in there around all of those people talking loud and happy and easily and again find it so damned hard to even speak to him, to the waitress, to the greeter. It wasn't about those guys. It wasn't even about him. She could only do public things on certain days when she was in the right enough mindset, and that didn't happen often. It sure wouldn't happen after she was already shaken. He didn't understand and he couldn't. Nothing she said would make him understand. No one did. Not even Trina. Her sister knew what she couldn't do, what she had trouble doing, but she didn't get it. She just put up with it.

He walked away. Delaney wasn't sure whether to be relieved or to just go ... throw herself into the ocean and swim out as far as she could and see if she could get back again. At least that fear couldn't be nearly as bad as the constant everyday unending insatiable fear of just trying to ... live in a world where you were supposed to be friendly and social and ... and normal.

The passenger door opened, nearly making her jump out of her skin, and Eli got in. "So. Maybe we should talk here first."

"Why?" Her face was hot. "About what?"

"What in the hell are you so afraid of?"

Her heart pounded enough it made her head start to ache and her eyes threatened to spill over with frustration. She couldn't explain. He'd never understand.

He took her hand gently, the hand with the keys. "Let go."

Despite knowing better, she let him pry her fingers open and take her car keys. Then she yelled at herself for being so stupid...

Dropping the keys into the cup holder where she could get to them, he ran his thumb over her palm, over a spot that throbbed from the keys digging into her skin. "Delaney, what are you so afraid of?"

Also against her better judgment, she enjoyed his touch, his presence. She had to bite her tongue to prevent exploding from the intense friction between wanting him there and not wanting him there.

"Okay, you know what? How about we go take a walk? Will that make it easier to talk to me?"

"No." It was hardly more than a whisper.

"Okay, so ... what can I do to make this easier?"

"Why do you care?" The heat from her face flooded down through her neck and to her armpits...

"I care." He caressed her hand and the heat continued down her body. "I'm not going to try anything. If that's what's worrying you, I'm not that kind of guy. In fact, I've beat the hell out of a couple of guys when I saw them try to push some girl. Can't stand that monster-asshole mentality, and I won't do it myself. I don't want anyone who doesn't want me. So okay? You can relax."

"I'm not..." She forced her breath to slow down enough to answer. "I didn't think you would."

"No? So ... you're not afraid of me specifically?"

"No. And yes. You're... Why do you keep talking to me?" She was now sweating. Hell. The last thing she needed was to sweat like a running pig and then ... smell, but she shouldn't since she had deodorant on. She at least shouldn't smell, but sweating was...

He shifted to face her more directly. "Like I said, I want to get to know you and I can't say why. I can only say it matters for some reason. Can we just talk? I can leave it at that. Of course you've guessed I think more than that could be good, too, but I can leave it at that." He shifted again, brushing off the intensity in his body and sitting more casual. "So, tell me one thing about yourself I should know. Anything. And I don't mean your job or your living arrangements or whatever. I mean about you."

"Like what?" She glanced at him, at his sturdy shoulders, at the way his shirt fit well, not overly tight but enough to show off the toned muscles, and not plaid this time but a soft brown V-neck...

"Like ... favorite color."

"Green."

"Now that's interesting. Green is a friendly color, says you like balance and harmony. Not surprising, I guess. Mine's red which is a little funny to me since it's supposed to symbolize aggression and I'm about the least aggressive person you'll find."

"Except you beat up strangers."

"Well, only if they need beating, and a man who treats a woman that way needs to know how it feels to be under someone else's control without being able to do shit about it. It's ... justice, I guess. I'm big on justice. The real kind."

She glanced over again. "It also stands for joy and vitality. Red." And passion, but she wouldn't say that.

"Yes, that too." Luckily, he didn't say it. "So what else? What's your favorite TV show?"

"*Bones.* And..."

"And?"

"You'll laugh."

"So what?"

She couldn't help but stare. So what? Did he not even care if someone laughed at him? Just how damned secure was he? She wished she could grab at least a little bit of that...

"You know if I laugh, it's just something in my own head, no reflection on you. Why should you care if I do?"

Delaney had to think about that one. Maybe he was right. Still...

"And what? What's your secret TV love? *Jersey Shore?*"

"No."

He laughed. "Okay, I didn't figure. Do I keep guessing?"

"*Dancing With The Stars*. I like the dancing. I don't care much about the celebrities, but the pros are incredible. People don't know, really, how hard that is."

"Do you dance?"

The heat in her face that had started to subside returned full force and she stammered an answer. "I used to take lessons." She couldn't admit the rest.

"Yeah? Not surprised about that, either. I could see it. You're built for it, and you're really graceful. I've enjoyed that."

The heat flooded her body.

"And I embarrassed you. Sorry. Couldn't help but notice, especially when you walk over the sand in those boots." He glanced at her feet. "I'd figured the boots were only for work, cleanup detail protection."

"They're comfortable." And brown. They didn't stand out, or at least she'd thought they didn't.

"And you're into comfort. More than fashion."

She clenched her fist again and tried to decide whether to tell him she had a closet full of shoes she loved, all colors, all Flamenco-type shoes. That she never wore except at home alone when she danced.

She knew she dressed plain, stodgy. Her sister told her often enough she could help with her wardrobe, and Trina would be good at it, but they'd tried and Delaney couldn't imagine wearing what Trina picked out for her. If she dared, she'd love to wear them, but she didn't dare. She'd feel foolish dressing so nice for ... what reason? For people to notice? She didn't want that. Even today, when she was dressing to meet Eli, she wore jeans and a plain blue sweater. Loose. Not clingy.

"Hey, so am I. I've never understood why girls go to such a fuss about the latest styles. Honestly, guys don't care about what's *in*, or at least most of us don't, so I'm guessing it's other girls they're trying to impress and I don't get it. Why bother?"

Right, exactly her thought. Well, almost exactly, except guys did care since they paid more attention to the girls who showed more, but she didn't want the kind of guy who wanted her because of what she showed, body wise. Her brain mattered far more, as far as she was concerned, but Trina constantly told her she had to attract them first and then let them know she had a brain.

Delaney disagreed, but then Trina was married with five kids. She was also a social butterfly. She couldn't understand, although she did try. And really, Trina could have done better than Pat and probably would have if she hadn't tried to get attention first and put her brain second. It was better to be alone than...

"So what else?" Eli interrupted her thoughts as she watched an elderly couple. The old man was tottering himself, and still, he gave his arm to his wife to help support her tottering. Sweet. She wanted that. Yes, really, she did want that.

"What do you do with your time off? Other than wander around the park."

She looked over at him. "How about you answer that first?"

With a light grin, he shrugged. "Okay. Might take a while. I'm a pretty active guy." He gave her a wink. "For starts, I play on a local old folks softball team, and I call it *old folks* because the high school baseball players call it that. Wait till they get there, the little know-nothings. Most of them couldn't keep up with me if they tried." He shook his head with a laugh. "I enjoy wrestling around with the nieces and nephews, playing touch football and such with them. I help my parents around their place when they need it. I also like to fish, or at least I used to. Not so sure anymore..."

"Why?"

"Why what? Did I like it or don't I now?"

"Now. What changed your mind?"

"The work you do. All of the crap on the beach and what it does to them, and all of the rotting carcasses I've seen. Of course, I throw them back most of the time unless I get a nice one that fries up well, but I guess now I wonder if I'm..."

"I fish. Or I used to. It's been a while."

He looked surprised. "Do you? While you're rescuing them?"

"Circle of life. They're meant to be food. It's an important nutrient. They use each other as food. Nothing wrong with it if it's not overdone. Catfish is my favorite."

"Is it? They're bottom feeders, you know."

"Yes, but they're mild and it is healthy, if the fish are healthy, which means if the water is healthy."

"You do this for people to stay healthier?"

She tilted her head. "Why did you think?"

"Well, animal rights and all. Thought you might be vegetarian until you mentioned cheeseburgers. I had a feeling you didn't like people much."

"Because I get mad at the way they trash the beach? Yes, I get mad that they do. It makes the fish sick and the water unhealthy and then it makes the rest of us more unhealthy even when we're not doing it. Yes, it makes me angry when people do stupid things that hurt others because they either don't care or don't think. If they want to do it to themselves, they think it only matters to them, but it doesn't. It's a horribly selfish view and it does make me angry, because it hurts others who have done nothing to them, and when I'm walking on the beach or on a path somewhere, I'm relaxing, or trying to relax, and seeing all of that garbage makes it hard to relax. It's unfair to be lazy and selfish and let other people have to pay for that." The calm that had started to return went right back out the window. She'd said too much...

"And you like people more than you look like you do."

Delaney gritted her jaw. He didn't get it. He couldn't...

"Or ... you avoid them because you care too much? About what they think?"

Her face warmed again and she straightened the CDs in the door.

"Delaney." He squeezed her hand gently. "I'm sorry. I assumed what I shouldn't have. You..." Suddenly he changed tracks. "You know what? I'm about to starve since I waited on a late breakfast with you. Can we go eat?"

She felt herself nod although she wanted to bolt. To walk on the beach. To stare out at the beautiful flowing endless blue-gray-green of the Atlantic. But Eli got out and came around to open and hold her door and she couldn't resist. Maybe he understood. A little. It might have to be enough.

He talked as they ambled to the door, about Indiana and that he felt the same about the garbage along roadways and that he didn't eat the fish from the local river due to how dirty it was. He didn't seem bothered that she didn't answer. She couldn't answer while she was talking to herself, trying to convince herself she'd be fine in the crowded restaurant. She did catch his eyes enough to let him know she was listening and that seemed good enough. At least for now. Delaney had to wonder how long that would be good enough. Until he went back home, maybe.

When given the choice, he asked for a table for two, by the window, back in a corner. That had to be for her. She didn't believe he'd normally sit so far out of the way. Still, her heart raced and the fuzziness threatened her ability to think. She managed to say thank you when they were seated and focused on the menu, trying hard to shut out the noise around her, the loud and muffled voices, silverware clanging, laughter. People. Everywhere.

By the time she got through ordering, Delaney felt a full-fledged panic attack coming on and excused herself to wash her hands. While she veered around tables and chairs pushed too far out, she kept her focus on the floor. Her body pulled into itself as much as possible, her breathing fast enough it made her dizzy by the time she locked herself into a stall.

Just breathe, Delaney. It's fine. You're fine. They're just people. They don't care about you. They're too busy caring about themselves. It's fine. It's fine, really. Think of something else. The lighthouse, the ocean, the waves shuffling in and out. Birds overhead. Sand between your toes. After breakfast, you can go to the beach. Just tell him you need the rest of the day to yourself. It's fine. Just breathe.

Finally calming herself enough with the mental view of the ocean, Delaney unlocked the door, washed her hands slowly, with plenty of warm water. Her head cleared somewhat, and she took a deep breath, walked back through the noisy people, her gaze on the floor so she didn't see them, and back to their table. To Eli. Who grinned at her like everything was fine. It was. She kept telling herself it was.

Through breakfast, he asked simple questions about Barnegat Bay and Long Beach and if she came out this way often or if she preferred to stay more inland. She managed to answer, somewhat, and he shifted the conversation to himself, with stories about his two older siblings, about his cousins, of which he had a bunch, and his parents he apparently admired, his grandparents he also admired. They lived in a small farm town and had to drive thirty-plus miles to "find civilization" which sounded wonderful to her. But away from the water. That one, she wasn't sure about.

He talked about the day and weekend trips he often took, with friends or by himself. She found herself jealous, not only of the big family he was totally comfortable with, but of the ability, the nerve, to just take off and go, to land wherever he happened to be for the night, to jump on some road and drive and look around with no plans.

She couldn't imagine. She had to plan everything. Then she had to reconsider the plans about twenty times before she acted on them and then she was still unsure and nervous about whether she'd checked into things enough, whether she would put herself in a situation she didn't expect, which she hated. She admitted some of that to him, to a small extent.

He leaned forward, his forearms against the table, and held her eyes. "You know, I think you could learn to enjoy it."

"No, I..."

"If you went with someone you trusted?"

She sipped her coffee. "I don't know. I guess I haven't found anyone I'd trust that much."

"What about your sister? You said she's spontaneous. You wouldn't do it with her?"

"Probably not. She's... She tries to push me to talk to..."

"To strangers. And you'd rather not."

"No, I'd rather... I'd rather be more like her and able to talk to strangers, but it's not just a choice."

"You're talking to me." His dark blue eyes sparkled.

"More or less." And her heart was starting to race again.

He grinned and raised his cup as in a toast. Setting it down again, he became more serious. "Did something happen to make you not able to talk to strangers?"

She hated that question. With a passion. It was as bad or worse than when others mentioned how *shy* she was. "No. I'm just not comfortable with it." That was putting it mildly, but it was the best she could do.

"That's a shame, actually. Because I think you probably have a lot to say that would be interesting to hear."

"What makes you think so?"

"I can see it." He shrugged and leaned back in his chair. "So, how about showing me around Long Island since I've made myself come out here, finally, after more than two months of thinking about it. Do you have time?"

~ *Ten* ~

He hadn't really expected Delaney to agree to run around Long Island with him since they'd had such a shaky start to the day, but since she did, Eli asked if there was somewhere she could leave her car or he could leave his truck so they could ride together. She suggested the lighthouse parking area and said it would be a nice place to start sight-seeing. He didn't much care where she took him. He was enthralled by her, maybe because she wasn't at all trying to impress him. If anything, she was trying not to impress him. Mainly, he wanted to know her story, to see inside her thoughts. Being "uncomfortable" was a cover-up answer. It was far more than that.

Old Barney, as locals called the Barnegat Lighthouse, looked to be nearly two-hundred feet tall, a circular column tapered in smoothly, the bottom half painted white, the top half dark red. It was topped by a silo-shaped thing made of glass with some kind of support decking jutted all the way around underneath. The thing wasn't on since it was daylight, but Eli had seen its light flash off and on, or what looked off and on as it spun its slow circle, on nights he wandered Barnegat and the surrounding area in the right places. The base of the thing jutted out into the water from the shore and people walked out around it.

When he realized Delaney was taking him that way, his stomach churned. Concrete. The base was concrete. Solid. Not enough wind to churn up waves. It was fine, he told himself. Only an earthquake was going to break up that big-ass slab of concrete, and he hadn't heard of earthquakes in the area. Only hurricanes. But the sky was nearly cloudless. The sun was hot and direct, breaking up the chill from the past few weeks. Nothing to worry about.

Focusing on the girl at his side who calmed more the closer she got to the water, Eli bit back his ridiculous fear and forced himself to look calm. Even when she went right up to the edge, her hands on the skimpy metal railing just in front of where the water lapped up onto the rocks below. Not far below. The Atlantic was right there, nearly on top of her feet.

Cursing in his head, he forced himself up beside her and refused to grip the railing the way she'd been gripping her keys.

"Beautiful, isn't it?" Wisps of brown hair alongside her head shivered in the barely-there breeze. Again, most of it was back in a ponytail and he had to wonder if she ever let it down. "Eli?" She turned her head with a gentle tilt to look at him.

"Yeah. Beautiful."

Her expression questioned him, but she turned back to the water.

He used the opportunity to study her profile, which he much preferred to staring out at all of that water. A gentle face. Her nose was on the longish side, but not too long, not too thick. Her eyebrows looked unplucked, which he appreciated since they were nice as they were. She had long, thick eyelashes darker than her hair and her lips were somewhat rounded, high on top so they looked like they would make that *sealed with a kiss* logo about perfectly if she wore lipstick. He didn't notice any. He thought she might have a touch of blush on her cheeks and maybe a bit of barely-there eye color, but other than that, the girl was ... natural. Earthy. Unencumbered by stuff that weighed most people down.

There was something, though...

She turned to catch his eyes. "What?"

"Um, just ... enjoying the view."

"The view is that direction." She tilted her head.

"Well, now, guess that depends which view you care more about." With a grin, Eli risked sliding his hand over to hers.

Her cheeks flushed again, but at least she didn't pull away. "Feel like heading out along the walkway?"

"Where does it go?"

"It runs along the edge of the ocean, and it has great views of sea life and birds of all kinds. You don't mind birds, right? I know some don't like it when they swoop too close."

"I'm fine with birds, even if I did watch the movie." The edge of the ocean, however, was a whole different story.

Her grin said she understood the reference. A Hitchcock fan? She liked *Bones*, which meant she liked mystery and suspense, maybe trying to figure things out. And humor. He knew the show; his cousin always watched it and sometimes he got pulled in.

Tempted to keep hold of her hand, Eli thought better of it and instead walked close with an occasional rub of his arm against hers. Against her shirt, actually. She was in a loose tank top in shades of dark blue and green with a thin shirt over top, plain blue, unbuttoned, the sleeves rolled almost to her elbows. And jeans, the better fitting ones again, but still with the long shirt over top to cover her backside.

She stopped now and then to look over the railing, her arms propped on top. A low walkway, very close to the water. Eli had to focus on the rocks, the construction of the railing, the bird varieties she pointed out, or her hands clasped softly. Still his heart beat faster than normal when the waves splashed a bit higher, reminding him where he was, the scent of seaweed and fish adding to the image of depth and darkness.

When he pressed, she talked a bit about her family, how she'd lost her parents at the same time and her sister was all she had, that there were a couple of cousins she no longer had contact with. He thought it sounded like she regretted that she didn't.

"Your parents ... a sudden loss? Together?"

"Yes. An accident. Years ago." She started walking again. "My house was our family home. Trina got married and moved out. I was still there at the time and wanted to stay rather than sell. But that's why they think they can just stay as long as they want, since it was her home, too. It's not, though. It's mine. She got money instead, to equal the house value, and some of the furniture, the stuff she wanted since I didn't care that much. We split the rest. I pay the real estate taxes on the house along with the upkeep, so it's mine. Things always mattered to her more than they do to me. The house, the familiarity of it, the privacy, is what matters to me, and now..." She shrugged.

"So why do you stay?"

"Why wouldn't I? It's home."

"Any place you're comfortable is home."

She picked up a stick from the middle of the path and tossed it aside. "And if you're not? Anywhere? Does that mean you don't have a home, really?"

"Maybe." Not comfortable anywhere?

"Because I was, in my house, when it was still just mine. Now it's a constant battle between wanting it to stay nice and needing quiet and not wanting to insult my sister."

He started to ask about not being comfortable anywhere, but she walked away and he caught up and changed the subject. Birds. Fish. Ocean. She pointed out birds that were on the endangered list but were kept safe on the refuge. The ocean wind tossed her ponytail and the edges of her shirt. She didn't seem to notice.

She was at one with nature, but uncomfortable in her own skin. That's what he kept noticing that he couldn't figure out. Why? She was beautiful, not knock-out turn-heads beautiful, but classy beautiful, elegant. She had a kindness in her face that added to her beauty. She moved nice, graceful, refined, with dignity. He liked that.

Eli never understood why some of his friends admired certain girls for their "beauty" when he could see the nastiness of their attitudes, the "look at me, I'm worth looking at" stances, the selfish, show off nature. He didn't care how perfect their features were, how blonde or fake-colored their hair was, how skinny, how enhanced their breasts were, natural or not, or how much they showed of their bodies. Not that he didn't enjoy looking. He was a regular guy. Of course he enjoyed looking. But he wouldn't want one of them, not for more than ... well, maybe not even for that, these days. He wanted heart-stopping can't-get-enough sex with a girl who was more than looks, a girl fully into him, not just sex, but him in particular.

Probably this girl who wasn't even comfortable with herself wouldn't be that into sex whatsoever. The way she avoided being touched, cringed at his touch, even, told him it was unlikely. Still, she was interesting. He enjoyed the conversation. And he enjoyed trying to figure her out. Of course, once he had, maybe he wouldn't be so interested. The quest was much of the fun. The adventure.

In the spirit of adventure, he had to push a bit. "So what if I gave you a bit of advice?"

Her raised eyebrows when she glanced back at him made him grin. "Okay, I know, I don't know much about you yet so I have no right to give you advice, but I do have some travel experience and I think travel would be good for you. Maybe you think you're not comfortable anywhere because you don't fit here and you think you should. Maybe you shouldn't. Maybe there's somewhere else you should be. Have you considered that?"

"Alone?"

"Sure. I do it. It can be..."

She started walking again.

Eli had heard plenty of people say they didn't go anywhere alone, not even to eat. She apparently did that, since she'd gone to the restaurant without him. Except she was sitting in her car. Maybe she didn't do that, either. It would be good for her. He should encourage it. Not that she'd listen. But it could be a good step. The girl needed to travel. "Take a friend. Share a room and the gas bill and it's not so bad. Or take three friends and share a room. Makes it even cheaper."

"You share one room with three other men?"

"Sure. No big deal as long as I don't get a bunk mate who snores or tosses and turns all night. I've weeded them out pretty well. Sad to choose travel mates that way, I guess, but a good night's sleep is important when you're out and about all day. I can get along with most anyone during the day. It's at night that matters."

She blushed and walked farther down the walkway.

He had to chuckle to himself. Yeah, probably a fantasy with her would be better than the real thing. She embarrassed too easily. But it was cute, not something he was used to.

At the end of the path, she stopped and again propped her arms, crossed, over the railing. Crossed arms were a definite "keep your distance" sign, but Eli often ignored signs just for the fun of it. He sidled right up next to her, his arm against hers, and peered at her profile.

Delaney turned her head just enough to barely meet his eyes and lowered her gaze but didn't move away. She was actually beautiful. A breeze swept the ends of her captured hair that had some red to it under the bright sun. And her eyes ... they were like the ocean itself, a mix of green and brown with a touch of blue at times. Everything about her meshed with nature. She did nothing to try to stand out.

Somehow, she still did.

"Would you consider traveling with me? Different rooms, of

course. I'd love to get you out of here and see what you're like elsewhere, away from here where you've always been."

"Why?"

"A lot of people are different outside their small well-known boundaries. And I like to travel. I have a whole list of places I want to go. Just thought you might enjoy it."

"I have to work."

"Well, yeah, so do I. But you have vacation time, right?"

She started back toward the lighthouse.

Eli found himself unsure what to say as he ambled along beside her. He'd pushed too fast. Not that it mattered. She'd never go. Her feet were too bound to the sand, the shifting sand.

He couldn't imagine how those who lived on sand ever felt really grounded. This wasn't like the hard constant earth of the Midwest. Indiana's borders wouldn't shift by themselves. The coast did, and would, always. It was the nature of water to change things. Of course he knew earthquakes were always possible and they could shift borders a bit, and there had been tremors in the past few years, maybe always there had been. Still, since his childhood, the only thing that changed were buildings going up, houses decaying, man-made efforts that would always change with times. The earth was still the earth. The brown dirt sprang up with life every spring and died back every winter. The hills, what there were of them in Indiana, stayed the same.

Did those on the coast naturally feel less grounded, less ... comfortable? Maybe it wasn't just her. Maybe it was cultural. He'd have to pay more attention to other locals instead of spending so much time on Delaney.

Maybe. And maybe he didn't care quite that much.

Travel with him. He was unbelievable. Delaney hardly knew him. And he was a social butterfly who got along with anyone and easily talked with anyone. How could she deal with that?

As they reached the lighthouse platform and it looked like he was thinking of going up inside, she asked if he wanted to see the nature trail or if he'd rather move on to other sites. He agreed quickly to the trail, which nearly elated her since she'd always wanted to go out on it and never found anyone who wanted to go with her. She nearly laughed at Eli's suggestion she travel alone when she couldn't even make herself go on the nature trail alone. She'd thought about it. There were so many things she thought about doing. Someday. When she could make herself.

By now, she was starting to think that would never happen, she would never grow out of it the way she'd grown into it. And she had grown into it. She was a carefree happy open friendly child, she'd been told often. So what happened? She hated to be asked, but she often wondered, since nothing *happened.* Things just changed somewhere inside her for no apparent reason. Yes, she had embarrassing moments. Everyone did. Not everyone turned it into a big issue, a constant all-consuming part of who they were. Why did she?

It most frustrated her that she didn't know why and she couldn't change it, no matter how ridiculous she knew it was or how stupid it made her feel. Mostly, it made her feel like she was an awkward ten-year-old instead of a grown woman, a grown woman with a college degree in journalism who couldn't go into her chosen career field because she couldn't make herself go out and interview people. Stupid career choice, but she had things to say that she could say on paper. Delaney did that well, and yet she'd barely passed some of the required classes because they demanded she either talk in class or go interview strangers. She had fudged a bit on those by interviewing her sister or brother-in-law or by taking Trina and letting her talk.

So she had a bachelor's degree and worked as a file clerk, which also made her feel stupid. And uninteresting. And... Why was Eli so pushy about wanting to talk to her?

He did, though. He kept talking as they walked, about plants he saw that they didn't have back in his farmland state, about the varieties of birds, about what kind of fish he would find along the coast that he wouldn't find in Indiana lakes and ponds, and about his travels.

Maybe he was trying to entice her to travel with him. It started to work. He'd fueled her curiosity, which was easy enough to fuel. She could do a travel series...

Delaney stopped. A travel writer. She could write about what she saw. No interviews necessary. Sitting at local restaurants would be enough to get a feel of the people, which Eli talked about a lot, how people were different in different places and that was why he talked to them so often. Maybe she should travel with him and let him do the talking...

"Delaney?"

She realized she'd stopped and shut out whatever he was saying. He stood directly in front of her, close. "Sorry. Got lost in my thoughts."

"I'm talking too much." He reached up to pull a strand of hair from her face as the breeze tossed it.

"No." She studied him as he realized what he'd done, as though they were long-term friends, as though they were far closer and knew each other far better. And she watched him realize she hadn't pulled back.

She liked him. What could she say? He was ... comfortable. Delaney was somewhat shocked by the realization. She didn't last remember when someone felt comfortable. At least as comfortable as possible considering the way he studied her.

When he inched closer, her heart raced. Again. But different. A nice, excited, anticipatory race, not a fearful *I wanna fall into the floor and disappear* race. Because she didn't. She didn't want to be anywhere else in the world, and that was an unusual feeling.

"So how about we go up into the lighthouse? I'd love the full view."

Now it was a mixed race, anticipation and humor at the way he was flirting – she knew the "full view" comment was flirting – and also fear of going up into the very tall lighthouse and looking down. No. She couldn't do that. 172 feet above sea level up on a narrow tower that was top heavy? Not likely. She loved to look at it from the ground...

"Yes?"

She had to answer him. "Um, no. Thank you. If you want to go up, I'll wait down here."

"You don't like heights."

"No." Her stomach turned.

"Ah, you could have said so. I understand that."

"How? You work up there, right?"

"Yeah, heights don't bother me, but some things do."

"Like what?"

He grimaced. "I'll tell you if you keep it to yourself."

"Who would I tell?"

He chuckled. "Okay. Water."

"What?"

"I'm intensely afraid of being in water above my head."

"You can't swim. A lot of people can't."

"I can swim, and I do, in a pool where I can put my feet down on the bottom or at least see that the far side, the deep side, is plenty close enough I can swim to it and grab the edge. I can't go beyond that. I even have to fish from the shore, can't deal with boats. I swim well, actually, and there's no sense in it since I've never had a bad experience with water, haven't nearly drowned or anything, so I don't know why I am, but I am. So I have to say while the ocean is intriguing, it also creeps me out a lot."

A deep relaxation swam through Delaney's soul. Maybe he could understand. To a point. "Okay, so I won't ask you to swim in the Atlantic, and you'll have to understand why I can't go up in the lighthouse."

"I suppose that's fair, although I'll admit to thoughts of getting you up there at dusk, looking out over your ocean and your fish friends, and ... well, maybe stealing a kiss or two." Eli stepped back as he shrugged. "Guess we'll have to figure something else out."

As he headed back, Delaney held still and let his words sink in. Steal a kiss? Why hadn't he just done that? She'd always thought it was a stupid idea to plan a kiss, or to ask permission for a kiss. It was unromantic. Was that a word? If not, it should be.

Of course, a first kiss at the top of the lighthouse would be very romantic, if she wasn't terrified of being up there, but now he'd spoiled it anyway.

Deciding she'd look like an idiot if she just stood there, Delaney purposely ambled slowly so it would look, if he turned around to notice how far behind she was, that he was just walking faster, not that she was bothered. Just because she was bothered, good bothered mostly, by thinking of his lips against hers, her hands against his sturdy chest, eventually his bare sturdy chest if all went well, he didn't have to know she was.

He turned back sooner than she expected, his head tilted, his eyes curious. "Gonna stay away from me now? Did I blow it?"

She took her time, but she caught up and stood in front of him. "I'm not that easily scared, just because I look like I am."

A grin highlighted a sparkle in his eyes. "There's a hell of a lot more to you than you show."

"There is of everyone."

"Is there? I'm not sure about that. Most people show quite a bit, and some show a lot more than I want to know, actually. It leaves no guess work. It's a good thing, I suppose, and I can appreciate those who just *are* what you see, but..." He leaned closer. "I also love a good mystery."

"Do you? Good luck." Delaney walked around him and toward their vehicles. Trina was wrong. She did know how to flirt. She just wasn't so obvious about it.

She let him drive around Long Island as she showed him around, which Eli took as a sign of trust, at least some amount of trust. And, to his admiration, she looked fully comfortable in his truck. A lot of girls didn't. They bitched about the height of it or the maleness of it or looked at the plain interior as though he should do better. Delaney used the top handle to pull herself up and in without pause and buckled the seatbelt without being asked.

Several times during the day while she took him wherever she thought he might want to go, and she guessed well, although she could have taken him to the middle of the parking lot and just talked to him and he would have been fine with that, Eli often told himself to offer to take her back to her car and let her get home. But he was puzzled about whether to try to kiss her when they parted, whether to set his hands on her just-round-enough hips, over the jeans he'd like a little tighter to show more of her curves. And her company was far better than sitting at the motel with the coworker. Or without him. Or wandering by himself.

It was dusk already by the time they left Viking Village where he bought small Scandinavian souvenirs to take to his family. She showed him the fishing boat used in *The Perfect Storm.* He hadn't seen the movie. The water thing. He didn't like to watch movies that showed any threat of people drowning.

The reddish-dusky sky threw a shadow over her face as they stood between her car and his truck. He couldn't believe the day had gone by so fast. "Have I bothered you enough for today?"

She graced him with a light grin. "You saved me from being home in the commotion."

"Nice to know I was helpful in some way. So how about dinner? There's a pasta place near the hotel the guys say is pretty good. Or if there's somewhere else you'd rather go..."

"Do you like Thai food?"

"I couldn't say. Never had it."

"Interested? It's spicy, so if you don't..."

"I love spice." He grinned. "The spicier the better, as far as I'm concerned." At her raised eyebrows, Eli thought he'd taken it a step too far. And it wasn't really true. He liked moderate spice, not extreme. If he couldn't taste the food under the burn, there was no point in the burn.

She gave him the name and address of the place in case they got separated on the road, since it was back on the mainland, but Eli made sure they didn't. And she was easy to follow. She watched to be sure he had room to pull out behind her whenever she changed lanes or roads or came up to stop lights. Courteous. The girl was very courteous.

He took her advice and ordered a coconut chicken soup and mild seafood curry. The silence between them after they ordered and before the food came didn't bother him. Often, it did. Okay, most always it did on a date, but this wasn't exactly a date. He watched her study people at other tables, not rudely, only casually, and noticed her glance at him now and then, covertly. Her face was expressive. Her eyes gave away her interest even if her body language told him to tread carefully.

Eli avoided talk of anything controversial, obeying the no politics or religion rule until they got to know each other better. He couldn't stay with anyone long term if she disagreed too much with his own basic views. And the east coast tended to vastly disagree with his own views, from what he'd heard. People who lived differently did tend to have opposing views and that was fair, but a long term relationship had to have...

Long term? What the hell was he thinking? She couldn't imagine leaving the coast, so she said, and he couldn't, wouldn't, leave his family. Long term was highly unlikely.

He managed to pull himself together and keep talking as though they were only acquaintances and would never be more than that up to the time they stood beside their Fords and fumbled with how to say good night. She didn't jump right in and leave. She hadn't even unlocked her door yet.

So he decided to push. "Should I follow you home to be sure you get there fine?"

"Thank you, no. I'm used to getting myself home."

"Had to ask. Mom would knock me upside the head if she found out I didn't. A bit old-fashioned, but she means well."

"Good for her."

"Yeah?" He tilted his head as he tried to figure how she meant it. "A lot of women get pissed ... sorry, get upset when I try to treat them the way I was raised. Never know how a woman will take it."

"They only get pissed if they think they have something to prove."

He couldn't help but grin, at both the language and the comment. "You don't."

"Of course not. I don't want to be babied and I won't be talked down to, but I see nothing wrong with people being polite to each other, with looking out for each other."

"Exactly." He felt his lungs expand deeply, in relief, he supposed. "Well, guess I'll see you tomorrow at the refuge."

"No, I won't be there. I have an appointment. I'll be there Tuesday."

He felt a pang of disappointment but tried not to let it show. "Okay, Tuesday, then. Have a good rest of the night, Delaney, and a good tomorrow."

"You, too." She turned to unlock and open her door and paused. "Thank you for today. It was nice."

"Oh, no, I should thank you." He stepped closer and thought about giving her a hug, but he felt a withdrawal on her part as he got that close. Instead, he leaned in and set a light kiss on her cheek. "I don't remember when I last had a more enjoyable day."

"Me, either." Her eyes reached out to him.

Eli took a chance and nudged his face closer to hers, waited to see how she would react, and was rewarded when she closed most of the distance and let him meet her lips. He kept it light and quick. A sweet kiss that he felt down to his ... well, farther than he should have for it being so light and sweet. It wasn't the way he'd wanted their first kiss to go. He wanted it somewhere more romantic than in the parking lot of a run-down little restaurant with curry on his breath and gas fumes coming at them in the dark from the road. But spontaneous was nice, too. Her expression as she turned her eyes away and pressed her lips gently together ... was far more than nice. It was beautiful. Expressive.

He'd gotten to her.

And she sure as heck got to him, too. He wanted to make it deeper, to take her in his arms and ... and he wouldn't. Yet. She appreciated gentlemen, and accepted them. He would be that for her as well as possible.

"See you Tuesday."

He could barely respond to her soft, sweet voice as he held her door and closed it behind her.

Eli was frozen in place for some time, wishing he'd followed or ... hell, he didn't even have her phone number. Why hadn't he asked? He would ask on Tuesday. He never forgot to ask for a number. Often, he asked too soon. Often, he'd been given fake numbers. Maybe that was why he hadn't. It was only annoying in general, but with Delaney... He would be crushed if Delaney gave him a fake number.

Crushed? What kind of bullshit was that? He didn't get *crushed.*

Girls got crushed. Young girls. He brushed it off. Plenty of fish in the sea ... plenty of damaged fish in the sea, and the ocean. Not that he was looking for a damaged fish. He wasn't. He was looking for strong and capable, wise, not needy, not clingy, but still soft at times, loving, affectionate. A hard mix to find in the right proportions, which was why he was thirty-eight and single.

When she said she wouldn't be at the refuge the next day, he automatically figured it would be a night off for him, also. Why would he go if she didn't? But he would. As often as he might tell himself not to bother, he would still go. Sap. The girl had turned him into a complete sap. His coworkers would make fun. So would his family.

He had to pull himself together.

~ *Eleven* ~

On Friday night, when they again stopped for yogurt, but not for dinner since she refused his offer, Delaney agreed to go out with him again on Sunday. She'd missed seeing him on Monday, and she declined for Saturday since she needed time at home. And she needed to not look too eager. This time, she made him wait until Sunday afternoon, even if she'd been impressed that he worked Monday when she wasn't there and that he was there every night although he still looked tired from his regular job, and even if he hadn't tried to kiss her again and hadn't asked for her number or address, she wouldn't look too available.

After a couple of hours at the food bank on Saturday, she pulled into her driveway and sat in the car. They were all home. Both cars were there. Delaney sighed and let the CD play, let Enrique Iglesias calm her. Her brother-in-law laughed at her music, so she listened to it only in her room or in her car.

Not that his opinion mattered, but it was hard to handle. Why, she didn't know. She truly didn't care what he thought. Still, she kept her music to herself, and her opinions, too, since he debated everything she said. Always. Because he knew everything.

When the car decided the accessories had been on long enough without the engine running and cut it off, Delaney opened her door. But she didn't get out. She couldn't handle all of those people, even if they were people she loved, other than the one married in. It was too much commotion. Trina rolled her eyes when Delaney dared say as much. What happened when she had her own children, Trina wanted to know. Delaney always said she wouldn't have more than two. Trina said it wouldn't matter: two were as much commotion as five. But Delaney had her doubts. She also wouldn't let them be so loud inside the house. That's what the backyard was for, and yes, they could learn if they were taught. And they would. For her sanity, they would have to learn. If she ever had kids, and that was starting to become debatable.

Closing the door again and restarting the engine, Delaney drove toward ... where? She didn't want to go to the beach. It would remind her of work, her volunteer work. Of Eli. Of his hard-toned muscles, his charming smile, his wavy brown hair. Of his lips. She was anxious for Sunday. Tomorrow. A few more hours.

She soon found herself on the road to his motel and she nearly pulled in, nearly imagined she'd make herself go to his door and knock, and maybe she would if he was alone, but he had a roommate, and maybe his other coworkers were there, too, and they'd snicker about her coming to his door, make comments, look at her like...

No, she couldn't.

So she drove on. Up to Ocean City where for the hundredth time, Delaney considered going into the Art Guild, more to see the inside of the building than to see the art. She loved the colorful 1800's Victorian from the outside. She badly wanted to see the inside, but her sister had no interest. Trina would go, if Delaney pushed, but she would know Trina didn't really want to be there and she'd feel rushed to get in and out and it wouldn't be worth it.

Would Eli be interested? Maybe not. But he did construction, so maybe he would be interested in the construction of the house. Or maybe he just did it because he liked to work with his hands. Because he was energetic and active.

She sighed. He wouldn't want to go see art. He was ... a horribly masculine construction worker who made vulgar jokes with his buddies and liked to talk to everyone and ... and lived in Indiana, where he would return soon.

What was wrong with her to keep falling for men she knew wouldn't stick around? Maybe that's why she did. It was safer. They would leave and never see her again so if she embarrassed herself, she wouldn't have to deal with it for long.

Except she would. Every small embarrassment stayed with her forever. It was ridiculous. She couldn't even get it out of her mind that she'd said something stupid to Eli about supposedly grown men who spent time playing stupid video games. He'd grinned and pointed out the value in it, the coordination it took, and the thought process it demanded, and he didn't seem to take it personally, but she'd been mortified and hardly talked to him the rest of the week as they worked side by side.

How could she dare ask him to go see art? She couldn't. If he said something about it, she'd have too hard a time letting it go. And she wouldn't. And she'd feel like an idiot...

Not that she wasn't used to it. Still, she didn't like it. Some things you just never got used to.

Since she was up there, Delaney decided to make herself go to Ocean County Mall and shop for her nieces and nephews. She parked farther away than necessary in order to avoid the biggest congestion of cars, and she set her mind on her task as she got close to the door. Her body tensed as she went past a group of kids talking loudly and pushing at each other in fun and she kept her gaze away from them as though they weren't there. The mall itself was light and airy with its rounded white ceiling and sky lights and the white and tan shiny floor tiles, but it was more crowded than she expected for the beginning of April. Did that many people still do Easter shopping?

Her breath quickened and she told herself to knock it off, no one was paying attention to her or cared that she was there. Everyone was too busy with their own shopping to bother about hers or with her. She went over the list of current likes and dislikes in her head. They changed every year for every niece and nephew. Two of them were into video games, which she wouldn't do even if Eli did think they were okay. One was into fashion, too much into fashion. The youngest liked anything for about five minutes and nothing longer than that. The other ... Delaney never knew what the oldest was into. She wouldn't wear shirts with any brand logo. She was picky about clothes in general but not about whether they matched. She never wore jewelry. She liked television, too much, but not any one show more than others. An odd kid.

A sign for a store she hadn't seen before caught her eye. A game store. At its doorway, Delaney saw actual board games, puzzles, calendars... perfect. She could get them things to do and think about. But which? She'd barely started to browse when a large woman bumped into her and apologized, and she drew in, trying to make herself even smaller. There were too many people in the store. She couldn't... Her heart raced; her breathing increased enough she started to get dizzy. She had to get out.

Heading toward the entrance with a fast walk, Delaney decided it would look like she was rushing out for a reason, as though she'd taken something or done something she shouldn't have, although she never would, so she forced herself to walk at a normal speed, to look casual, to not panic. Getting into the hallway didn't help much and she wanted to leave, but it would be stupid not to go ahead and finish shopping.

Telling herself she was fine and no one was paying any attention to her, Delaney paced along the mall corridor, away from kiosks where vendors called out to people to get their attention and acted like she didn't hear them so she wouldn't have to answer. Spotting Auntie Anne's, she headed that direction, pulled a few dollar bills and coins from her purse and counted the change, looked at the menu and roughly figured what tax would be and counted her change again before she approached the young smiling girl at the counter and managed to order a pretzel with cheese sauce as she wondered if she should use her debit card instead so she wouldn't have to worry about counting the change right and making a mistake only because she was nervous. Her pounding heart told her she should but it was ridiculous to use the debit card only for a few dollars when she had cash. Instead of counting change, although she had a ton of it, she dropped the coins back in her handbag and handed the girl a ten dollar bill to let her make change. Delaney saw the girl's expression but played like she didn't, mumbled a thank you, and felt her face get warm as she stood by herself and waited on her order.

Luckily, there was a small table in the corner free and she made her way back, pulled a chair out without letting it squeak on the floor, and settled down to sip at her iced tea while her heartbeat slowed.

Was everyone looking at her? Of course they weren't. Why would they? She should have stayed home. At least Eli wasn't with her to see her get so nervous at such a simple thing as walking into a mall alone. She didn't even like it not alone. But alone...

Why had she? A stupid thing to do since she knew it would lead to this. And there was no reason. She was smart, capable, an adult, not a lost ten-year-old. *Why* did she do this?

Fighting the urge to leave the pretzel and drink and just bolt back to her car and go home and shut her door and lock it, Delaney sipped her drink and tore off a small piece of pretzel. She dipped it lightly in the cheese sauce, not enough it would drip because the last thing she needed was to get it on her clothes and have someone notice that she did. Taking a bite, she made herself look around the way a normal person would. Until someone met her gaze and she looked away. She should have brought a book or magazine. Maybe she could go get one, but she couldn't take her pretzel and drink into the bookstore ... was there still a bookstore in the mall? Maybe not. So many had been shut down. Where did they carry magazines? Maybe they didn't. What did people do when not shopping, when resting their feet? Talk. Of course they talked to each other. What about those alone like she was? She supposed they played games on their phones, or texted friends, or talked loudly on their phone so everyone around could hear half a conversation no one wanted to hear.

She looked around again, careful not to catch anyone's eyes, but the only people by themselves were heading somewhere with a mission, or walking the mall for exercise. In the winter she understood, but since it was nice, why wouldn't they do that on the beach instead of adding to the crowded mall? Why wouldn't they want to? She supposed they could like the crowd. She couldn't imagine why, but of course it was possible.

Eli liked crowds. He did well with them.

Delaney was more jealous of that than she could ever tell him. And he would think she was ... what? Crazy? Childish? Self-absorbed? She didn't think she was any of those things. She was only phobic of ... people. A lot of people had phobias, even about such silly things as ... as stepping on cracks. Why should hers be any more crazy? Why was her fear of people worse than her fear of heights? A lot of people were afraid of heights. No one made an issue of it. But be afraid to talk to others...

She supposed it was rare. They didn't understand. How could they? Those who were afraid to talk to people also didn't want to admit it, or couldn't make themselves admit it. Maybe lots more were than she knew and she just didn't know because they kept to themselves and didn't say so. Maybe they were the hermits people made fun of for being crazy when they were no crazier than people who were afraid of germs or spiders or storms. Or water. It was no different.

Except it was, because people took it personally if you were afraid to talk to them.

She had to force herself to stop thinking about it, to think about ... tomorrow. Eli. To wonder about his plans for the day. They'd agreed to meet at his hotel, in the parking lot, where his coworkers wouldn't be standing around watching, but then she'd have to drive because she couldn't leave her car at the hotel when she wasn't staying there. What if they towed it? Maybe she could say she was visiting someone who was staying there, but she didn't want to go in and ask.

She should let him pick her up as he offered. Delaney could call and suggest it. Before they left the refuge on Friday, she wrote her number on the back of her work card and handed it to him. He'd grinned and asked if she still had his. Of course she did. He was glad she did.

Charming Eli. A gentleman. But ... more. The spark in his eyes said there was so much more. An exciting thought since she was more adventurous by nature than she could let herself be in practice, but it was also scary. He was an adventurer through and through. It drew her to him, but it scared her just as much.

Finishing her pretzel while she answered a text from her sister wondering where she was, Delaney took the rest of the tea with her as she ambled back toward the game store. She figured she could take the tea in if she was careful, but someone might say something and she didn't want to deal with that, so she took a couple more swallows and tossed it in a big garbage can in the middle of the aisle next to a seating group that looked cozy for people to rest their feet ... if they wanted to sit facing strangers.

With a sigh, Delaney went in and wandered the games, trying to decide which they might like and which they would say were lame, or whatever the new word for that was. It was hard to keep up. She found a few that looked interesting but she wasn't sure. There was no point in buying something they'd thank her for politely and then shove in the back of their closets. Maybe she'd just get them a mall gift certificate. But they'd buy junk with it like video games or cheap jewelry that would tarnish or fall apart. And it was the easy way out.

Her head spun with the choices and indecision and the people talking so loud around her and pushing through to grab something they showed no indecision about and...

She had to get out of there.

Her racing heart made the blood rush to her face and she wasn't sure she'd keep breathing if she didn't find fresh air. Open air. Open space. It felt like everyone in the mall was staring as she made her way through and out the closest door. But it was a long way from where she parked. She needed to go back in and find the door she went in but she couldn't. She'd look like an idiot if she went right back in the same door, so she walked as though she was in the right place, down around the sidewalk and ... the sidewalk ended. But her car was in that direction. She was at the back end of the mall, a delivery entrance, and she didn't want to walk around there but she also didn't want to go back in, so she kept walking.

Damn. Damn. *Damn.* Why hadn't she just gone back in? Stupid. Who cared what anyone would think, if they would? And they wouldn't. She knew they wouldn't. People thought far too much about themselves to pay that much attention to her and she knew it, yet it made no difference.

Get it together, Delaney. Stopped by indecision and fear, she nearly jumped right out of her skin when her phone rang. Not a text. It rang. She flipped it open and found Eli's name on her screen. She answered with a tentative hello.

"Delaney?"

"Yes, hi Eli. What's up?" She hoped she sounded normal.

"Glad I got the number right. I wasn't sure about a couple of the scribbles you gave me."

"Sorry. Bad handwriting." Only when she was nervous.

"Are you okay? You sound..."

"Yes. Fine." With his voice encouraging her, she headed on around the delivery part of the mall, keeping her eyes out for anyone paying attention to the fact that she was a woman out there alone, but she was on the phone and she heard that discouraged possible attackers...

"Okay." He said it as though he didn't believe it. "Did I call too soon? I was just thinking ... well, I'm bored, actually, so I thought if you were, too, I might pick you up and..."

"I'm not home."

"Ah. I'm interrupting."

"No. I'm..." She decided to tell him, because there was no reason not to. "At the mall. For my nieces and nephews. Shopping for Easter, since it's coming up fast."

"Nice. Find something good for them?"

"No. Maybe. I couldn't decide. I'm bad at that – really bad. Too many choices, you know."

"Not following you there. I like choices, the more the better."

She grinned, despite how much she hated how alone she was in the back of the mall or how hard she was trying to calm her heartbeat so he wouldn't hear the shake in her voice.

"Delaney, is something wrong? You can tell me."

Her eyes watered and she forced it back. No, she couldn't. It was stupid, idiotic. She'd sound weak and childish and she wasn't. She *wasn't*. She was strong. She was. Except...

"I'll let you go. Call back if you want..."

"No, don't hang up. Um, yes. About tonight. If... It'll take me a half hour or so to get back in town, so if that's not too late..."

"Sounds good. Or I can meet you up there. How about I help you finish shopping so I don't pull you away? I'm good at multiple choices and I love picking stuff out. Yeah, I know, a guy who likes to shop. What can I say? And you don't, right? I can help if you want."

"I'd love that, actually. Are you sure? It's..."

"Give me the name again so I can GPS it and I'll be there as soon as I put my shoes on and however long it takes to drive. Where should we meet? Or should I call when I get there and find out where you are?"

Where would she be? For a half hour or more? She thought of asking him to meet her at the library so she didn't have to go back in the mall alone, but it would be silly to drive over for such a short time and she didn't need a book since she was in the middle of the one Eli had laughed about and she couldn't just go in and sit. So she told him to call when he got close, and she went to sit in her car to wait, with her doors locked. As she waited, she studied people who walked past. Just normal people, talking to each other or not, their heads up to see who approached or didn't.

Eli would be there soon. She hoped. And whatever he picked out, she would agree with, for the kids. What did it matter? They would likely shove it in the back of the closet anyway, no matter what she chose. They had too much stuff they didn't even touch.

It didn't matter. Shopping with Eli would be fun. At least she thought it would be. And she nearly cried from the relief of his coming to her shopping rescue. Stupid. She was an adult. People dealt with far worse things every minute of every day and she needed rescue from shopping alone. Truly stupid. She should just let herself become one of those hermits.

Eli saw her before she saw him. Her hair was down for a change; the breeze pushed it into her face, and she kept brushing it back while she looked around at mall-goers wandering outside and at anyone who came out the doors. The girl noticed everything. She watched everything. He constantly wanted to ask what she was thinking as she watched.

He grinned when she brushed hair back again. Maybe here, at the mall where she let him come join her daily life? No, not good enough. He wanted their next kiss, their first deep kiss, to be somewhere private. His body tightened at the thought. He wanted private with her, deeper, closer.

She spotted him and got up, but waited for him to approach. Her jeans were a very light denim, soft-looking, nicely fitted, topped by a simple flowing dark teal blouse with short sleeves that dipped lower in the back than in the front. And she smiled, a beautiful, welcoming smile. "You found it. Have any trouble?"

"Not at all." He leaned in and set a hand on her arm and a light kiss on her cheek. Although he meant to pull right back again, she turned to him, and he met her lips. It startled him, honestly, and it looked like it startled her, too. He had to pull himself together fast. "So? Nieces and nephews."

"Yes. I was thinking a game or two, but I'm not good at this."

"Glad you let me come help. It's good for a guy's ego, you know, even if it is just shopping. Did that sound bad?"

"I'm flattered that I can be good for your ego." She blushed.

"Delaney, you are very good for my ego. And you look great, by the way." He backed away to lighten the mood and offered his arm. She looked at him curiously, and accepted.

Eli didn't understand the big deal in choosing a couple of gifts for a few kids who sounded unappreciative, but she was serious about finding just the right things, so he put his mind on what she said about them, buzzed through the different games and puzzles, and found something for the older three. For the youngest two, he took her out of the puzzle store and down the hall to a toy store he'd seen on the way. More appropriate, he said, for things that would keep younger hands busy.

She tensed when someone closed in on her, so he moved around to block whichever side they were on, casually, as though looking at something over there, with a hand on her back. Trying to remember what he enjoyed as a kid, he suggested Legos for the second youngest, Pirate Legos, since she said the kid was hooked on those movies and loved to swing things around like a sword. For the youngest, he picked up Lincoln Logs. "I used to love these."

"They were better when they were original. Those..." She shrugged. "I've thought of it, but they look fake to me."

He couldn't help but grin. "You played with Lincoln Logs?"

"When I was over at a friend's house. We didn't have toys. We had books and puzzles, some other craft things."

"No toys? Why?"

"Mom didn't believe in them. She pushed us outside to play. I think she just didn't want them all over the floor. She was very touchy about clutter. I think that's why Trina is so opposite with her kids. You can hardly walk through the house most times. Drives me crazy. I keep telling her there can be a balance, but she doesn't listen."

"Yeah, we didn't have a lot, but we did have stuff to keep our hands busy, imaginative stuff like this. Tonka trucks for outside and so on. Of course they tended to rust since we left them out there and Mom always threw a fit about leaving nice stuff outside to rust. Dad would calm her by saying he'd fix them, and he did. Can't tell you how often they were repainted. Still, we left them outside. We figured that's where trucks belonged."

"They didn't get stolen?"

Stolen? "Of course not. We all did it. There was hardly a yard without toys and bikes sitting out front."

"They would've been gone if we'd done that." She accepted the Lincoln Logs container and headed to check out. "So, you are good at this kid shopping thing. Should I ask if you have kids? I mean, I know you said there was no ex, but that doesn't really mean there aren't kids."

Taken aback by the question, Eli had to be amused. "At my age, you mean?" He grinned. "Nope. No wife or ex-wife and no kids, other than the nieces and nephews. Just one of those rare really single guys with a full-time job and his own place who would make a good catch but hasn't been caught yet."

Eli wasn't sure if she thought he was funny as he meant to be or too cocky as most women thought. He saw another woman look over at him with interest and a catch of the eyes that said she'd gladly talk to him if he wanted.

Delaney saw her, too. "A rare bird these days." She edged closer to him as the line moved.

"I suppose. My family thinks I'm far too particular, at least the sibs do. They could be right." He caught her glancing back at the woman when she also pressed closer. Fully amused, Eli leaned in. "So can I buy you dinner since the gift hunting is done?"

"I think I owe you dinner. For coming all this way…"

"All this way?" He laughed. "I drive farther than that just to go see what I can see. Hate being bored. But whichever way you prefer, as long as we can hang out a while longer. What's up here that's good?"

~ Twelve ~

Delaney headed back toward Manahawkin and stopped at Tom's River. Parking at Huddy Park so they could decide where to go from there, she agreed to ride with him to find food. She pointed out Seaside Heights in the distance where the huge Ferris Wheel had been taken out into the ocean, and he parked along Main Street close to a grassy area on one side and several food options on the other. Wandering until they agreed to grab sandwiches to take to the bench along a little walking path, they sat with their drinks between them.

"Can I ask you something?"

She tilted her head at him, wondering why he suddenly felt the need to ask if he could ask her something instead of just doing it.

"You just, uh, like the outdoors so much you'd rather eat out here? Or is there some reason you don't like to eat in a restaurant? Germs? Shared utensil? If so, I get it, I guess, but..."

"Not germs. Crowds."

"Um, Delaney, there are crowds at the beach, too. Pretty much everywhere here."

"Yes, but not at the refuge, and if you walk the beach at the right times, it's not bad."

"Claustrophobic?"

"No." She took a bite of her ham sub with lots of vegetables, hoping the Italian dressing wouldn't run down her face or fingers, and set her focus between the buildings where the Atlantic peeked through the city.

"You sure?"

"I don't mind elevators if they aren't crowded. I can do small spaces. I even hid in the dryer as a child when we played hide and seek."

He shuddered. "Okay, then. I wouldn't even do that."

"I think you'd have a hard time fitting." Unable to resist a smile at his raised eyebrows, Delaney realized she was flirting, and she realized she rather enjoyed flirting with this guy.

In return, he scanned her, being as obvious as possible about it. "Bet you still could, though, if you're limber enough."

"I am."

He choked on the sip of cola he'd just taken. "Damn. That was ... unexpected. Kinda makes me want to ask you to prove it, too."

"I'm not getting in a dryer at my age."

"Nah, didn't mean that." Eli threw a wink and got up to throw his trash away, taking her sandwich wrap, also. Returning, he sat closer. "How about dessert? I'm in the mood for ice cream." With a glance at the little parlor across the road, he waited for her answer.

The place was packed. It was a nice, warm day turning quickly into dusk, and everyone and their brother was out enjoying it.

"Too crowded?"

She nodded.

"Mind waiting here? I'll go get it."

"Are you sure?"

"Yep. What do you want?"

"I'm not picky. You choose."

Eli acted like he was about to make a joke, but thought better of it and gave her a quick nod instead. She watched him dodge cars, raising a hand in thanks when someone stopped for him, saw him talking to an older couple while waiting in line with that ready smile of his, and noticed that he kept checking on her through the big window.

A sweet, protective man. A bit ornery here and there, with some rough edges. Ridiculously talkative. A little too seductive without trying to be. But very sweet. How was he not taken already? He'd mentioned an ex. She figured he had far more than one ex that would have been at least part serious. Did he choose badly, or was there something about him she was missing?

Either could be true. Lots of really good guys made horrible dating choices and got hit hard. It seemed the better they were, the more likely they'd get hit by those kinds of girls. But then, she'd been hit herself often enough. She figured much of that was due to her social phobia, but maybe it wasn't.

He returned with two large ice cream cones, one chocolate, the other vanilla, and sat close enough their arms rubbed. "Should I have gone for strawberry instead of one of these?"

"No. Both are good."

"Which do you want?"

"Either."

"Not fair. Which would you order?"

"Both. I get them swirled."

He grinned. "Nice. How's this?" Eli mashed the cones together as well as he could without spilling them onto the sidewalk.

Delaney smiled and accepted the mostly chocolate cone smeared with vanilla. "One way to do it, I guess." She met his eyes as she licked the top of the swirl, catching it with her top lip and sucking it in.

His body tightened with her obvious flirting, and before he could stop himself, Eli leaned in to kiss her. A sweet kiss. He could taste the ice cream on her lips. A short kiss, only a hint, a tease. A question. She answered by returning it, making it longer, still sweet, gentle. Careful.

"Your ice cream will melt." She nearly whispered it and then licked her cone again.

"Yeah. No kidding." He felt about twelve years old with a school boy crush on a girl out of his league. More so when she grinned. Deciding he better distract himself, Eli got up to walk, offering a hand. When she kept it, walking beside him, on the inside of the sidewalk away from the constant stream of cars, he felt twelve years old mixed with full adult male protective.

The girl was flirting. Full-out flirting. It turns his insides upside-down and every other way. He didn't do this. With other girls, it was more a lust thing. His *silly sex drive* got him in trouble more than once. It was different with Delaney. He could walk around with this girl, teasing, flirting, talking, leaving it at that and still want more, as much as he could get of it.

They walked a distance down the sidewalk and turned back the direction of his truck. It was getting dark by now, but he had no interest in taking her home, or letting her go home, given she had her own car to get back. When he veered onto the little path that looked to go back into a nicely wooded area, Delaney paused.

"We won't be able to see back there for much longer."

"Sure we will. Our eyes will adjust."

She shook her head.

"You don't like the dark."

"No. I like to see what's around me."

Eli bit into the crunchy brown cone and stepped closer. "I'm around you, Delaney."

"Well, that's fine, and no, I'm not worried about you, but..."

"I'm trained, Del. I won't let anyone bother you."

"Trained how?"

"Black belt karate, started when I was a kid. Always loved adventure, activity ... motion in general. And as I said, I'm a volunteer fireman, CPR-trained and such. You're in good hands, so to speak."

"Captain America." A near whisper.

He laughed. "No. Just kinda typical small town Midwest kid who got in trouble if he got bored so my parents made sure I didn't have time to be bored. These small city kid gangsta wannabes have nothing on that. Ridiculous little punks. I've run into them already since I've been here. They found out country boys ain't so dumb after all, or helpless. We take care of ourselves well."

"I can imagine you do. I don't want this anymore."

His heart nearly stopped. He'd turned her off that easily? "Delaney, I'm not bragging. And I would never hurt you. I don't hurt women. I would hurt men who hurt women, as I said, and I'd never apologize for that because I think it's part of a man's job..."

"I meant the ice cream, Eli. I've had enough, and it's running down my fingers."

The ice cream. She didn't want more of the ice cream. His body relaxed as he took the thing from her and went to dump them both in a nearby trash can. She stayed beside him, her right hand out as though wondering what to do with it. He raised it to his mouth and sucked the ice cream from her fingers.

She held his eyes as he did, and she moved into him when he pulled paper napkins from his pocket to wipe it off better. Raising her face toward his, Delaney pulled back again and glanced toward the trees where he'd started to take her.

"You'll be safe with me, Del."

"I highly doubt that." Her voice was soft, but fiery, and she gripped his hand, leading him there herself, not too far in, but away from the sidewalk, into the dark where they had to slow down.

"Is Del okay? I thought I might call you Laney, but..."

"No, not Laney. I hate that."

"Doesn't suit you." He drifted his face closer to hers in the filtered dusk of the shadow of the trees that spread their pine scent through the air and found her lips. With his gut pushing him to pull her body up against his, Eli fought it and listened to his brain that told him to be careful.

"Yes." Her voice was soft, breathy.

"Yes, what?" He let his hands find her waist and fall softly down to her hips.

"The nickname. It's fine."

"Hm." He kissed the side of her head, and in front of her ear, and felt his body react to hers as she came all the way in against him. Finding her mouth again, Eli kissed her deep, long, and hard, and she returned it just as passionately as she slid her hands around his waist and up from his lower back to behind his shoulders. Holding him in.

Delaney tried to catch her breath as she leaned her forehead against his shoulder. She wanted to take him home, and the thought surprised her. She never did things so fast. But she'd never kissed Captain America before, either. Even if he said he wasn't, he felt like he was. He felt strong and safe and ... exciting. And fully interested. She was close enough to know he was. Normally, she would back off, but she didn't. She wanted to feel him. She wanted a hell of a lot more than to feel him this way. "Eli."

"Hm." He kissed her neck.

"I think you are."

"I am what?" He slid a hand around to her backside.

"Captain America. I think maybe you are."

He met her eyes as well as possible through the dark. "Why?"

She allowed herself to slide a hand up from his waist to his stomach, up to his chest, the most incredible chest she'd ever had her hands on, or even close to. "You're not afraid of anything. Know how jealous I am of that? And you can do anything..."

"No, I can't. And I am, actually."

"Really? What?"

"Which *what* do you mean? What am I afraid of or what can't I do?"

"Both."

He chuckled, a beautiful deep rumble she felt on her palm. "What I can't do would take too long to answer. The other I already told you. Deep water. Terrified of it. Makes me feel about four years old at times."

"Yeah."

"Yeah? You mean your fear of heights makes you feel like a child?"

She looked up toward the bat she could hear but not see. "No. But..."

"Something else you're afraid of."

She nodded. "But all the time, or at least far too much of the time. Makes me feel like a real idiot, like something's wrong with me." Her eyes water and she was glad it was dark.

"It's not that big a deal, Delaney. A lot of people are shy."

Her face grew warm and she tried to pull away but he held her in. Her heart pounded. She wanted to tell him, and yet she didn't. She couldn't. It was too hard to say.

Eli slid a hand along the side of her face, down to her neck, resting his thumb just under her jaw. "You're afraid now?"

"No."

"Your heart's beating a mile a minute. Or do I have you turned on that much?" He was teasing. It was in his voice.

"No. I..." She swallowed hard. "Being around people is hard, even not talking, just... I can't even explain it."

"I've kind of seen that already. But you're good outside, right, in fresh air? So it's more people in enclosed places?"

"Um. It's ... worse when I feel like I can't escape. It's not ... the enclosed place. It's..." Dizziness set in. She couldn't do it. She couldn't even tell him.

"The dark's bothering you."

"No. Maybe. It's just ... trying to talk about it. I can't..."

"Okay. Later. We'll talk about it more later, when it's not dark. Okay? Relax. You're fine." He brushed against her lips. "And you're beautiful."

"I'm not."

"Oh Del, yes you are." He stroked a finger along her face.

"If you tell me I am on the inside and that's what matters, I'll punch you. And I don't punch like a girl."

He laughed, a gorgeous laugh. "Thanks for the warning. But that's not what I meant, or was going to say."

"Good." She traced her finger over his chest. "Eli."

"Hm?"

"We should head back to town. It's getting late."

He sighed. Audibly. It nearly made her laugh. "Well, I'd like to argue, but I guess I won't." Instead, he took her hand and walked her to his truck and helped her in. They were silent on the drive to the park to get her car.

~ Thirteen ~

Delaney didn't want to leave him. Standing between his truck and her car in the parking area at Huddy Park, she found herself unwilling to get in her car and drive away from him. "See you tomorrow? Or have you had enough of me for the weekend?"

He grinned and moved against her, with a large hand sliding back through her hair. "My dear Del, I haven't had close to enough of you yet. Take that as you wish."

Unable to resist, she met his lips and wrapped her arms over his shoulders. He tasted of ice cream and smelled of nature and warm male. Noting his hands on her waist move down to her hips and down farther, to her thighs, Delaney realized he didn't want to leave any more than she wanted him to leave.

"Hm." She kept her face close. "We could walk around the park a while. There's a nice little bridge and some benches..."

"I'm game if you are."

It was terribly peaceful walking with Eli in the quiet of the dark, with only a few lights to guide their path. She shivered at a breeze and assured him she was fine, but he wrapped a warm arm around her shoulders, which worked as a nice excuse to close the distance. She took him down the sidewalk along the river and he asked about the standing log structure.

"This area was a fort back during the Revolution. The park is named after a Captain who tried to defend it."

"Tried?"

"They took him prisoner and hung him without a warrant to do so. Guess it cause a huge uproar."

"Right. New Jersey would have been right in the middle of all of it. Didn't think about that, to be honest. So is this a pond or...?"

"Tom's River."

"The town name, right, but..."

"And the river. It leads out to the ocean. They do boat shows here twice a year."

"Boat shows?"

"Showing off boats, some for sale, some for show."

He chuckled. "Coastal version of a car cruise?"

"We have those, too. I prefer the boats."

"Because you love water."

"Right. Want to cross the bridge?"

"Del, I'll follow wherever it is you'd like to take me. Lead on."

"Not in a hurry to get back?"

"Nope. You are my only plans this weekend."

Eli lowered to the steps of one of the gazebos and offered a hand to ask her to sit with him. The river glistened with the breeze and the lights and he wrapped his arm back around her. He thought maybe he could sit right there all night long holding onto Delaney and enjoying the cool, moist ocean air and the sounds of the darkness he always loved. Bats flitted about. He was glad she wasn't bothered by the harmless little creatures. Mostly, he was glad she felt fully relaxed out in the dark, where she said she didn't like to be, within his protection. It signified trust.

Or he was getting ahead of himself. Still, it was her idea. There were few people around, few voices. Car noise interfered, signifying a somewhat major roadway nearby. He didn't smell the exhaust, though. He smelled freshly cut grass and a hint or two of the ocean when the breeze washed over them. And then there was the smell of Delaney. She had a sweet scent to her that wasn't perfume or shampoo.

Nuzzling his nose in against her neck, he tried to figure what it might be. Hard to say. But nice. Feminine. Unfrilly.

Shifting, she met his eyes in a question.

Unable to say anything, Eli lowered his mouth to hers, slow enough she could pull back if she wanted, in case being out there with hardly anyone around would freak her out if he got too close.

Instead of pulling back, she leaned up into him and set a hand on his chest, over his heart where she more than likely felt the heavy thump of his attraction. Her arms were cool, chilled, so he cuddled her in, bringing her up against his body as much as possible while sitting side-by-side. Her kiss was as un-hesitant as any he'd ever had. It was deep and passionate and fully real. Her hand slid up from his chest around his neck, holding the back of his head.

He wanted to take her back to his hotel. Couldn't do that. His roommate would be there. Her place, then. Would she?

Testing the waters, he let his arm soften, releasing her somewhat, and slowly moved the hand to her waist, inching it up.

She broke from the kiss. Gently. Catching his eyes, again with a question.

"You want to take this farther?"

Nearly jumping to her feet, Delaney headed back the way they came. He had to move quick to catch up and in the middle of the bridge, he grasped her hand. "Okay, hold up."

"Eli. I don't... This is so fast."

"Hm. If you say so." He moved in gently and kissed the soft spot in front of her ear. "We can't do it here, anyway. Not that it would be a bad way to get arrested, but my boss might not appreciate it and I'd have to go home. Not real sure I'd want to explain that to the family."

She drew back until she was against the metal railing.

"I'm kidding. He wouldn't fire me. I'd have a hard time living it down, though." Eli tried to make it a joke, but she was tense again and that was the last thing he wanted. "Hey. Not pushing, alright? Just kind of felt like it was going that direction."

"Maybe." Her gaze was out over the water.

"Yeah? Well, you know, we have time. No big rush."

"Not enough." Slowly, she lowered against the railing until she sat on the bridge with her knees up in front of her.

Taking her cue, he sat against the opposite rail, his legs out beside hers, one ankle over the other. "Why's that?"

"You'll leave. When your job's done."

Leave. The thought socked him in the gut. "Well. Guess I wouldn't have to."

She caught his eyes. "You don't want to move here."

"No. But there's no big rush to get back, either. I could stay a while. Find another job when this ends, though I'd have to guess it'll be available for some time to come."

"But you'll want to go back home. To Indiana."

"Yes. Family's there. Otherwise, it wouldn't matter so much. Same with you, I suppose."

"No." Her voice was soft, barely audible across the slight distance. "For me, it's more the place. This is home."

"Place is just place, Del. You don't seem all that comfortable here."

"I'm not comfortable anywhere outside my house, or these days, outside my room."

"Well, then, wouldn't matter much, would it?"

"Eli, I... I'm not right for you. This... We shouldn't..."

Shouldn't? Not really good enough, as far as he was concerned.

Getting up, he moved over beside her, stroked fingers alongside her face, and pressed his mouth against hers. No resistance, only need came through. Want. No way in hell she could deny it with a kiss like that. "Shouldn't we?" He spoke close to her lips. "Don't know, Del. I tend to think we should. But..." He released her and stood. "Doesn't matter if I do if you don't. Still on for tomorrow or should we just call this off now?" He offered a hand.

"Everything okay?" A strange male voice came at them, and then a big flashlight. Someone in uniform. Not a cop. A guard of some sort.

"Yes." Delaney took Eli's fingers and stood up next to him. "Thank you. It's fine."

Eli thanked him, also, for checking and Delaney closed in on him until her head was on his shoulder, her hand on his stomach. Sure as hell felt like she thought it could be a good idea.

Maybe he was right. Maybe they should. At least while he was in New Jersey. Why not? She was thirty-two and hadn't dated in a year or more. She could enjoy him while he was there.

They returned to their cars and Eli followed her home even if she said he didn't need to. He didn't only follow her back to Manahawkin, but all the way to her driveway, pulling in behind her.

She went to him as he stepped out of the truck that he left running.

"Nice little place." He scanned her narrow two-story house with its narrow front porch and a white railing that needed painting. A face appeared in a window, the curtain drawn back just enough for the little girl to look through, gaping.

"Tammy. She's the nosiest of the group." Delaney crossed her arms, partly from the chill in the air and partly because she wasn't sure what to say.

"Well, guess I should let you get in."

With a soft nod, she unwrapped her arms to give him a hug. "Thank you. For shopping with me and ... all the rest."

"No problem. Anytime, Del." He set a quick kiss aside her face and backed away, taking his luscious warmth with him.

"Eli." With a glance back to see the curtain returned to its place, Delaney walked around his open truck door that somewhat blocked the view from the house and gave him a kiss. A nice, lingering kiss. She didn't want him to be too discouraged. "Goodnight. Still on for tomorrow?"

"Absolutely. For breakfast?" He was pushing. They'd agreed to later in the day.

"Okay. Same place or somewhere different?"

"I'll pick you up. Ten? We'll go from there."

"Sounds good. And..." She ran the tips of her fingers down along his face into the stubble that was growing back. "Maybe. Can I leave it there for now?"

Catching her hand, he kissed her fingers. "For as long as you want, or need. Night, Del. I am going to wait until you're inside, so go on in."

With a grin at his super-protective nature, Delaney squeezed his fingers, went up to her door, and turned to watch him get in his truck. He didn't pull out until she was inside with the door closed.

Too revved up to talk or to sleep, she barely answered her sister about who followed her home, made her way up to her room, and turned on her music. Richie Sambora. For the mood Eli had left her in.

She practiced her Flamenco moves for some time, switched to club dance type moves, jumped at her phone's buzz that signaled a new text, and grinned at his message:

"Miss you already. Sleep well."

Sending a quick "You too," Delaney went to take a long warm shower and lay in bed thinking of him until she drifted into slumber.

~ Fourteen ~

Delaney rolled over and looked at the clock. After nine. Damn. He would be there in less than an hour and she had to shower and let her hair dry and decide what to wear and ... and she was being ridiculous. She wasn't sixteen and going on a first date. She'd wear what she usually wore. Jeans. A decent top...

Pattering against the window made her get up and look out. Rain. Hard rain. She sighed. So much for sight-seeing. Would he cancel? Maybe she'd wear her galoshes. They seemed to amuse him the first time they met. He might be amused again, or he'd think she didn't want to bother much for him. So... dress up nicer to show it mattered, to encourage him, or dress casually so it didn't look like she was trying too hard?

Ugh. She *was* sixteen again, or might as well be.

Other than the sex thing. At least at sixteen, she'd only been concerned about whether her date liked her enough for a goodnight kiss and a repeat date. Why had it felt so much more complicated back then when it was actually far less? There was nothing uncomplicated about Eli. On the other hand, he was maybe the most uncomplicated man she knew.

Other than the Indiana thing. Even the sex thing wasn't terribly complicated. She'd known it was headed that direction from the time they sat at the lake park and he fell asleep. It was only a matter of when, and he knew it as well as she did. And *when* only mattered for the way it would affect their relationship. That mattered more than sex. Far more. She had to be careful. She had to be encouraging but not a tease, be a lady for him but not a prude, be accepting but not needy. Finding that line was far more complicated than a goodnight kiss and next date. She *was* sixteen again as far as the nervous anticipation and excitement leading to possible mortification...

Except she wasn't. Delaney was over thirty and she could damn well do what she wanted with him. The chips could fall where they would.

Scuffing to her closet, she pulled a dark blue lacy cleavage enhancing bra off the hook where it had hung far too long, removed the loose T-shirt she wore as pajamas, and eyed herself in the full length mirror inside her closet door. She couldn't have it on the outside of the door so she'd have to look at herself too often. Inside was safer. All the way around.

A glimpse of a quote she'd printed out and stuck to her wall caught her eye:

"Avoiding danger is no safer in the long run than outright exposure. The fearful are caught as often as the bold."
Helen Keller

Helen was right. Worrying changed nothing, except the heart rate, the stress level, and probably the illness level. Delaney needed to stop worrying and just ... just let herself have this, try this. With Eli.

Maybe he would work. Someone would. She had to believe someone would. Why not him?

Skimming through the rest of her closet, she pulled out a clingy knit top, not tight, but not loose, and went to her drawer to get her favorite jeans, the ones that fit just right, the ones she usually only wore around the house. They had some stretch to them and sat low on her hips so she usually wore a long blouse over top that partly covered her backside. Not today. The top went just to her waist. She didn't wear it often. If she leaned over, her back would show, if she didn't have a jacket on, anyway. She'd have to think of somewhere they could go inside where she could take the jacket off and...

And maybe stay with him.

Except it was Sunday and they both had work in the morning. And she'd only known him for three weeks, barely more than that. It felt longer since they worked together most every night for a couple of hours, but still, three weeks.

Did it matter? Maybe not. What did matter was that her sister would know if she didn't come home, and her brother-in-law, and they'd make a big deal out of it, and Delaney wasn't sure she could deal with that. They were already hassling her about her date the night before, and no amount of saying she hadn't planned it made them stop. She'd yet to tell them he was picking her up in ... forty minutes. And she hadn't showered.

Throwing her robe over her shoulders and gripping it in the front, she rushed out of her room to the bathroom door ... and someone was in it. The shower was running. Hell. She was tempted to go out the back door and strip and let the rain wash her off. Of course she wouldn't. She wasn't shy about being naked, especially, but there was a point. And if she was going to be arrested, she'd rather do it with Eli, caught in the act. Delaney grinned at the thought.

One bathroom for the eight of them wasn't enough. She wanted her own bathroom back, her own house back.

Figuring deodorant and a dusting of cologne would have to do, she slipped into her blue bra and matching panties, glanced at herself in the mirror, shrugged an almost satisfied okay, and pulled her clothes on. Her hair... it needed to be washed. She couldn't leave it down, and she felt scroungy not washing it, but unless she used the sink, she had little choice, and it was raining anyway, so she pulled it into a loose braid and told herself she'd go out to meet him so it would just look wet.

She really needed her own space back. For so many reasons. So she could simply invite him in, and let him stay.

The doorbell rang and she jumped. He was early.

Her hands shook as she tried to force her feet to the door. It was hard enough when she was prepared. She wasn't yet. Should she have guessed he would be early? Maybe. He was too together not to be early.

Doing her best to calm her nerves, Delaney headed down the stairs and stopped when she saw him kneeling on the floor talking with Paddy who kept tugging his sleeve and telling him to *look, look!* while Tracie, the ten-year-old, told the child to leave him be. Eli dealt with it well... until Pat butted in. Her brother-in-law asked his daughter why she let some guy in the house and Tracie said he was there for Aunt Laney.

Eli offered a hand and introduced himself.

"You're a friend of Delaney's?" Pat scanned him with an *I'm judging you and I don't approve* look. Of course he didn't. Eli was a good fifty or sixty pounds lighter, fit and trim, a couple of inches taller. Pat didn't trust anyone who wasn't as out of shape as he was and yet he bitched if Trina gained a couple of pounds.

"I am. We're headed to breakfast. You're Pat, I would guess."

Gathering her nerves and shoving them back, Delaney went to rescue Eli. His smile was relief, she supposed. Except he leaned down to kiss the side of her face with a hand softly set on her back. "Hey, Del. Ready? I know I'm early."

"Shows, too." Pat smirked. "What's up with the hair, Laney? No time to wash it?"

She flushed as Trina came over and scolded her husband with an apology that her oldest was hogging the bathroom at the same time she introduced herself and the two kids hanging about, then sent them away.

"I'll wait if I rushed you. It's no problem."

She skimmed a hand over her hair. "That bad? I'm sorry. I don't like to wash it at night because it gets frizzy, and I got up late. It's the gel that makes it look like this in the morning. It's not as unwashed as it looks, but I'll..."

"It's fine." He kissed her head, her unwashed hair. "Up to you, but I think you're beautiful as you are."

Pat snickered. "Yeah, he's trying hard to get some. Good luck, buddy. Rumor has it she's a pretty cold fish. Guess that's why she hangs out with them."

Delaney nearly melted right down into the floor as Trina yelled at her husband. Kind of yelled. More of a *now don't do that again* useless lecture as she did with her kids.

"Gotta say, man, I wouldn't even talk that way about a girl I didn't like, much less to family." Eli rubbed her back. "Let's get out of here."

"Um, maybe today's not..." Her voice shook.

"Hey, don't worry about it. Come here a minute." He took her fingers and led her to the front door, away from them, as she considered dashing up to her room and bolting the door and turning the music on as loud as her stereo could go and stomping as hard as she could with her heal-toes, her shoes on, just to annoy Pat. But Eli pulled her in against his body, held her with a strong soft grip, and again kissed her head. "It's not your fault the guy's an asshole. You're fine. Just don't cancel on me, Del. I've been up since five a.m. looking forward to having the day with you."

"I'm not cold, and I'm sick of hearing it, just because I don't respond to their vulgar comments or jump in bed with anyone who buys me a beer when I didn't want it. I'm *not* cold. I'm careful."

"And you tell me as though I don't know that already?" He gave her a soft kiss and ran a thumb over her cheek, his palm cupping her face. "I know, Del, and I'm not trying to *get some*. Not that I'd object, either. And let me tell you, whether or not your hair was washed this morning's got nothing to do with it either way. I'm not anywhere close to that finicky. Damn, did I seriously just use that word?"

She chuckled, and when he hugged her again, she melted into him instead of into the floor. "I want out of here."

He was quiet for some time. "You mean for today?"

"No. I... I don't know. No, I just want them out of my house. Is that wrong? I know they're stuck. I know. Their insurance company is taking forever and it's not their fault but it's not mine either and I'm..."

"Overwhelmed."

She nodded against his chest.

"I can see why. Come on. Get your galoshes so your feet don't get wet and let's go find somewhere quiet to be. Anywhere you want."

"You don't have to. I won't blame you..."

He raised her face with gentle fingers and met her lips. "I want to tell you something. The day I met you, I was ready to get out of here. The attitude got to me. The misery, the flooded moldy houses. The looks on people's faces. My hands being tied – that, maybe more than anything, was frustrating me..."

"You're leaving." Her heart nearly stopped. Delaney thought she might rather have it race.

"No." He glanced over as Paddy raced through to the other room yelling at almost the top of his lungs. Eli shook his head then returned his attention, his round expressive eyes peering into hers. "Del, I'd rather live here with you in your madhouse than to leave now."

"You're insane."

"Maybe. Maybe not. Depends."

"On what?"

He leaned in close to her ear. "On whether I'd have to sleep on the couch or if I could be at your side."

Her stomach turned, a good warm turn. "Are you sure you're not, Eli?" Grabbing every bit of her guts, she met his eyes. "Trying to get some."

"Well, it's not my main goal, but it could be on my list. It's not about the sex, though, Del, if that happens, and like I said, I'll never push you. It's about far more than that."

"Let's go." Delaney grabbed her jacket and called back that she was leaving. Since Eli didn't seem bothered about getting wet, although it was down-pouring by now, she didn't rush, either. Rain was good for the hair, especially when it needed to be washed anyway. He also didn't seem bothered about his truck getting wet but, as he got in behind the wheel, she asked if she should bring towels.

He wiped the back of his arm across his eyes to clear the moisture. "Nah, it's been wet. I get flak for it not being perfect inside, or very new, but you know, I don't have to have a shit fit about the rain, either, and that matters more to me. The running parts are taken care of. Otherwise, it's a truck, not an exhibition. Here." He reached back through the space between their seats to the full back seat, and handed her a soft worn blanket. "If you want to wipe the rain off your face."

"Thanks. What year is this?"

"2007. Got her brand new, first new vehicle I've owned. I do most of the work on it myself, or with my cousin's help since he knows more about mechanics than I do." He turned the engine, and the heater, on. "Your brother-in-law know you don't like to be called Laney?"

"Yes. That's why he does it."

"Your sister seems nice. Why does she put up with him?"

"She thinks he's funny. I know. I don't get it, either."

"You got the brains of the family, right?"

With her face dried enough, she set the blanket over her legs. "And you can say the rest. I do know it."

"The rest?" He looked up out the front windshield at the dark clouds roiling past.

"I got the brains; she got the looks. I know, and that's really fine with me. As far as I'm concerned, I'm the luckier one."

His head tilted and he touched her chin. "Nah, not true. She has a cuteness about her, and I can guess she had more attention in school..."

"Still does, even with five little banshees and the ring on her finger."

"You know, guys who fall for that are just setting themselves up, in general. No offense to your sister. She does seem nice and she got the short end on this deal, but that's not always true with the cutesy, popular girls. And I can say that 'cause I've done it myself, but I had my eyes opened good and I'm sure as heck glad I did." Eli slid warm fingers from her chin to her cheek and back over her hair. "You're beautiful, Del, and it's more a genuine beauty, not so cutesy. Might not get as much attention, but it's more deserving of it, as far as I'm concerned." He leaned in to give her a light kiss. "Guess I should take you to breakfast as I said I would."

She didn't argue, although she wanted him to explain more. Had he fallen for someone like Trina? Cute. Bouncy. Not so bright but into fun. If so, why had he taken interest in her when she was so opposite? Maybe because she was opposite and he figured that was safer. If he wanted safe, though, he was truly barking up the wrong tree, as he'd said about something else. Delaney wasn't safe. She was full of issues.

The boy didn't understand what he was getting himself into.

He took her to a little café with dark red vinyl booths and white gold-speckled Formica tables along the window opposite the bar-type food counter instead of the crowded place out on Long Beach. Still, she was too quiet. Bothered. But when Eli asked, she said she was fine. "So where do you want to go today?"

"Wherever you want. What do you want to see?"

"No, Del, today is yours. You took me all over hell last weekend to show me the sights. Your turn to do what you want."

"We did that yesterday. It's your turn again."

"Nah, yesterday was keeping me from being stir-crazy. No more. So what would you do today if I wasn't along with you?"

"Stay home."

"You'd rather be home?"

"No, I wouldn't rather, but that's what I'd do."

He forked in another mouthful of pancake smothered in syrup and gave himself time to swallow as he tried to think how to get her to tell him what he wanted to know. With a swallow of coffee to wash it down, he figured he'd just go straight at it. "What would you do if you had someone with you who's interested in the same things you are and happy to spend as much time as you'd want to do them?"

"I'm not sure there is anyone like that."

"Just play along. What would be at the top of your list?"

"I'd probably go to the arts council building to see the inside."

"Where's that at?"

"Back where we were last night. It's a gorgeous old house, from the 1800s, and I've wondered about the inside, if it's just as pretty..."

"So let's go."

She set her cup down and looked up, wide-eyed. "No, you don't want to do that."

"Why wouldn't I?"

"It's basically an art gallery."

"Okay. I'm not some culture deficient backwoods plowboy who doesn't appreciate art, Del, if that's what you're thinking."

Her face reddened and she looked away. "No, but no one wants to. Not even Trina will go with me, or her daughter who says she's into art stuff and paints ... well, some really weird things, but no one except me and ... older people, I suppose, want to go...."

"Hell, I'm older people. That count well enough?"

"You're not. You have to be my age, right at."

"You're ... what? Don't make me guess. I'm bad at it."

"I'm thirty-two, and you have to be about the same. Maybe younger? You can admit it if you are. It doesn't matter."

He grinned. "Thank you kindly, ma'am. I'm thirty-eight."

"No, you're not." Her surprise was too genuine to miss.

"Honest to God." He crossed his heart and looked up to ... the ceiling since they were inside instead of out.

"I'm impressed."

"Hm." He leaned closer. "How about you remember that line for a better occasion?" With a wink, Eli was glad she grinned.

"You're a horrible flirt."

"Yes, ma'am, I am, and I've been on my best behavior so far so I wouldn't scare you off. If I get carried away, say so."

"I don't mind."

His heart skipped a beat or two or three. "Well, let's go up and see that art building. Then we'll decide what next. I plan to keep you out all day if it's alright."

"So far it is."

So far. Cute answer.

Asking for the check since she was obviously done and he'd had plenty enough, Eli stood and held her chair and then held her jacket. He saw a woman look over and could tell it wasn't exactly because of him but more because of his actions, he figured. The idiot she was with had been playing on his phone the whole time they were there, even through her trying to talk to him. The ring on her finger said she was probably married to the inconsiderate ass.

To tell the guy he was, Eli walked a little too close to the table and bumped his arm.

"Watch what the hell you're doing." The guy grabbed at the phone he'd nearly dropped and glared.

"Me? Seems it should be you. A girl like that who gets neglected the way you're doing is a girl who deserves better and should find it." With a tip of the head to the girl, he gave Delaney his arm and led her away.

"You can't do that here." Her voice shook as they stepped outside.

"Can't do what?"

"Talk to people like that. They don't... We mind our own business. People get irate when you don't."

"What's he going to do?"

"Follow you out." She glanced back.

"Let him."

"Eli..."

"He won't, Del. Relax. That one is too fully self-absorbed to give a rat's ass what I think or to even bother to defend her if he did think I was hitting on her. Still needed to be told. I hate seeing that. What happened to talking to each other face to face?"

"I know. I agree. But..."

He kissed her quick and easy. "You really gotta learn how to relax." Before she could protest, he kissed her again. A deep kiss, only for a second, only long enough to taste the pecans and maple syrup on her tongue.

"You're just determined to get us in trouble today, aren't you?"

"For telling him to pay attention to his wife?"

"Well, and for kissing me that way in public. I'm not sure how it works in Indiana, but people here don't like that, either."

"Thought you said they minded their own business."

"Until you do something that bothers them personally."

"Maybe the wrong things bother them if my attention to you is wrong and that guy is right. Come on. Rain's going to start again. Let's get you in the truck before it does."

Getting the engine and heater running, Eli decided that tease of a kiss wasn't enough and he leaned over, pulled her face to his, and made it better. His fingers brushed over her wet braid and he trailed to the end of it, pulled out the elastic, and started to separate the hair, setting it free as she needed to do for herself. She was too tightly wound and he didn't think it was natural. She needed to be more free.

Her hand exploring his chest, his shoulder, his nape with cold fingers that made him shiver said he was right. And she was just as much a flirt, though more subtle. It was in her eyes and the way she touched him, the way she accepted his affection, his kisses, his wandering hands, and leaned in asking for more without saying so.

He wanted to take her home to Indiana, to meet his family.

It was too soon. It was far too soon. But she was... She'd fit right in with their openness, their friendliness, their acceptance. He'd have to call ahead, warn them she was quiet and not to say she was, not to mention being shy, or to notice it at all, or at least not to act like they noticed, and maybe she would be comfortable enough to loosen up and just be part of them. Part of him.

Damn. It was far too soon for that thought. Not that it mattered that it was too soon, since the thought was there.

Eli separated gently from her lips. "On to the art."

Delaney lowered onto the sand overlooking the bay and gripped Eli's hand when he sat next to her. The art society visit had gone better than she expected. He not only didn't push her to hurry, but he talked with her about it, about her thoughts and his own, about the architectural detail and what kind of time it would have taken to get that kind of craftsmanship. Eli mourned the loss of craftsmanship, not only in architecture, but in everything. It was all fast and cheap now, whatever *it* happened to be. Assembly line molds. Ten hands on one product doing ten different parts of something instead of one skilled and passionate artist creating the whole product. He said it showed.

He was in process of making furniture for his house, which he'd built with help from friends and family. A small house, he said. Delaney truly wanted to see it. Maybe she'd go with him for the Fourth as he hinted, to visit, to see his house, to meet his family. Except they were talkative. Friendly. All she needed was to have a panic attack in their midst.

Thinking about it bothered her, so she thought back about their day instead. When he found that Asbury Park was only about 45 minutes from home, from her home, and they were a third of the way there already, he insisted he had to see it. Just because it was Asbury Park. She suggested they wait a couple of months since it wasn't officially open again yet, but he wanted to grab the opportunity while he knew it was there.

Of course what he meant was he might not be around for a couple of months yet. But she took him up and they wandered as she pointed out some of the damage. Luckily, most businesses got through pretty well, but others had their entire oceanfront windows

with frames blown into the buildings. Some were still closed. Many
were reopened. There was normal flooding cleanup with tons of sand
dumped up over streets and sidewalks, broken wood and glass and
such scattered everywhere. A lot of the boards on the boardwalk had
been ripped up by waves and wind although the area had just gone
through a big renovation within the past couple of years and much of
it was new.

Eli had stood for some time in front of a ripped-up section of the
boardwalk with a piece of yellow caution tape fluttering in the breeze
from the metal barrier it was anchored to, right next to the Paramount
theater. He commented on how strange it was to see one spot so
devastated and the one just down from it, its ornate yellow and green
decorations and tons of glass untouched. Like a hurricane, he said,
that demolished two houses in a row and jumped up over the next to
land on the one on the other side. He'd seen it first-hand. Not
something he'd ever forget, anymore than he'd ever forget what he'd
seen so far along the Jersey coast.

She took him into the Stone Pony to get away from the
devastation, and so he could say he'd been there. A landmark since
the early seventies, the music venue was far enough off the ocean that
its boarded windows and sandbags protected it well. They had almost
no damage, and even locals who didn't go there were glad to hear it.
She'd heard music lovers who had never been in the area were just as
glad, since to some music enthusiasts, it was as much a shrine as
Graceland. Since they were up and running quickly, they'd been
holding benefits for others not so lucky.

Cleanup was progressing quickly on the boardwalk. It had to, she
told him, since it was a big money maker. He glanced at her but didn't
comment. He already knew how she felt about so many people still
displaced from their homes. But the tourist trap was being well taken
care of. She supposed it was beneficial to the community and tried to
see it that way.

He listened intently to everything she told him about the area and
bought a few knick-knacks to take back to a few of his family with the
Asbury Park or Jersey Shore logos. After a time of walking around,
they were both ready to go somewhere without destruction, so

Delaney took him to Jersey Mike's in Manasquan for subs. He was far too excited about finding a Philly cheese steak in New Jersey and had so much trouble deciding, he ordered two full subs for himself. She had her usual buffalo chicken wrap and he tried that, also.

The man was in "hog heaven," he said.

Delaney hadn't been ready to call it a day when they got close to Manahawkin, so she detoured him to the little public beach on Bayshore. Once the weather warmed, it would get crowded, at least on weekends, but for the moment, they nearly had it to themselves.

"Another beautiful place. It would be hard to leave this." Eli let his gaze travel to Old Barney as its light flashed over at them, breaking through the dusky blue and still cloudy sky.

His soft deep voice next to her ear, on the blanket he'd brought from the truck and lay over the sand, pulled her from her thoughts and back to different thoughts she didn't necessarily want. "I'm sure there are beautiful places in most areas, aren't there?"

"Absolutely. Just depends what you call beautiful."

With a sigh, she took her shoes off, got up, and ambled down to the edge of the water, focusing on the soft sand between her toes and cool water lapping up over her feet. The bluish-brownish-green ocean rippled from the wind and the pull of the moon, stirring and mixing its colors, and with the coming darkness, the line between water and sky was hard to see.

She hadn't been to the little beach front in some time. She'd have to make more use of it as the weather continued to improve, bring a book and sit out here away from noise, from her family, from the crowded house...

"What are you thinking, Del?" He set a warm hand on her forearm.

"I'm hoping you're still here in a couple of months."

His chest rose and fell deeply enough she could see it without looking directly at him. "Yeah. So am I."

"Are you?" She couldn't resist studying his face as she asked. "Thought you were homesick."

"Not so much anymore." He kissed her forehead. "I don't suppose there's any way you'd think of leaving the coast?"

Leaving. He wanted it to continue? Or was it only a general question? Wanting to believe the first thought, Delaney shrugged. "I have thought of moving, actually."

"Have you? Away?"

"Up to Lakewood. Not much of a move, but I'd be out of the house and they could have it. I wouldn't give it to them, of course, but I could sell it."

"What's in Lakewood?"

"The Strand Theater. Music in the park every summer. A shopping district that's easier for me to take than the mall. It's a pretty, quaint little area. They even have a minor league baseball team."

He ran his hand up her arm, to her shoulder, and brushed fingers through her hair. "Yeah? Which team does it support?"

"Phillies. Which I don't follow, but…"

"You're a baseball fan." He looked amused.

"Yes. I follow the Marlins."

"Florida? Why? Because of the beach?"

"I like a couple of their players, and their name. Especially since they're the Miami Marlins now. Sounds better."

He chuckled and traced the other hand over her hip and down to her thigh. "We have a minor league team, too. Indians. Indianapolis, of course. I'd be glad to take you."

Definitely a hint that she could move to Indiana. "Is it close to where you live?"

"Couple hours. We'd probably want to stay over."

Stay over. A nice thought. Delaney claimed his hand and started walking again, silent, until he asked how serious she was about selling her house. She was serious enough she'd checked into its value and knew she would make a good profit, if the market was good enough for it to sell, and she supposed it would be once cleanup was finished. He looked shocked at her wanting $200,000 for it, but that was fair considering neighborhood values and other Mercer Avenue selling prices.

"House like yours in Kentland would only be around $70,000."

"Really? Why?"

He chuckled again. "Maybe because it's in the middle of farmland in the middle of nowhere. Now if you have land, that can be pricey. Houses by themselves aren't, in general."

"The middle of nowhere doesn't sound all that bad to me." She was talking to herself, but he stopped walking.

"Be careful, Del. You're starting to make me think I have a chance of moving you out there."

Maybe he did. "Where's the nearest beach?"

"That would be up at Lake Michigan. Just over an hour. I work up there at times, and down in Lafayette."

"Why?"

"Kentland has exactly zero high rise buildings and not much construction need other than homes and small offices and such. Better money in high rise. More fun, too." He winked.

"If you say so." She stroked a finger down his shoulder to his chest. "An hour to the beach. That's not bad."

He kissed her. Suddenly. Without warning. Luckily it was getting dark and the beach was nearly empty, because his hands roamed, not as far as she wished but enough to want to take him somewhere private. She heated with his touch and moved against him, her stomach next to his, her breasts flattened against his chest.

"You're going to get me arrested yet." He mumbled in her ear, a soft deep sexy sensual sound.

"I don't think I'm doing it."

A light smirk graced his face. "Oh Del, you are, for sure, doing it. And I don't think you mean not to."

"Is that so?" She slipped out of his arms, stepping backward through the sand.

"Del..."

Something entwined her foot and she hurled toward the ground and landed on her rump.

"You okay?" Eli pushed a large branch away and offered a hand.

"Except I feel like an idiot." She didn't take his hand. She stayed right there and tried to pull some semblance of dignity back.

"Yeah, well, you're a beautiful idiot." Eli lowered beside her, met her lips, and pressed her backward with a strong arm supporting her head, until they lay together in the sand. "Except you aren't. An idiot." He supported himself with one arm, his body leaned over hers, and smoothed hair from her face. "I'm highly tempted to take off work tomorrow and ask you to do the same and..." He stopped.

"And what?"

"And keep you in my arms all night long."

"It'll get cold out here soon."

"Well now, I didn't mean to keep you out here in view of others." With a grin, he got up, brushed sand off, and helped her to her feet. "Guess I better get you home before I let myself think about that any longer."

~ Fifteen ~

"How about we leave early tonight?" Eli sidled up to Delaney's side as she crouched to pull something rusty from the muddy sand. "We deserve the time off, right?"

She caught his eyes and started over to the large scraps pile to dispose of what looked like a small connecting beam of some kind. "What did you have in mind?" She ambled, in no rush.

"That sub place. Don't laugh."

"Jersey Mike's? Again?"

"Couldn't try them all in one meal. Might take a few trips."

She grinned, dropped the metal piece with the rest, and cocked her hands on her hips. "I bet you'd be fun to cook for."

"You like to cook?"

"Love it, when I don't have to worry about a bunch of kids being finicky about everything I make. I cook healthy and I experiment. They don't like anything beyond the basics. I shouldn't say they don't like it; they won't try it. Drives me nuts. When, or if, I have kids, I won't coddle them like Trina does. They'll try whatever I make."

"You'd force something they don't like on them?"

"No, but they need to know whether or not they like it before they say they don't."

Eli was taken aback at this side of her. He agreed, at least to an extent, but it would be interesting to see her around the kids more since that mattered to him, how she dealt with children. "Actually, I am fun to cook for. I'll try anything. At least once." He pulled a little twig from her hair. "We can do that instead. Up to cooking for me tonight?"

"In your room?"

"No, most I have is a coffee pot and tiny microwave. I meant at your place."

"My family's there."

"Figured. You're not allowed to bring guests to your own home?"

"Yes, I'm..." Her mood shifted. Fast. Like a wave in a storm. "It's my house. I can. But ... you've seen it. It's noisy and Pat says things..."

Eli closed in against her. "Delaney, I don't care what he says and you shouldn't." He gave her a soft kiss, heard a whistle nearby, turned to give the guy an amused grin, and pulled her closer. "I don't care what they know, either. About time we stop hiding it, right? They've all been rooting for me to get you to accept a date. I'd say you've done that."

Her face reddened. Her body stiffened. She tried to move away.

"Hey." He wrapped a hand behind her head, fingers entwining with her ponytail, and met her eyes. "It's not like they can't see it, and it's not like they don't know why I'm here. They knew the first day I came and saw me watching you. So what? You're an adult. Who cares what they know? Unless you know, you're married or something and this could get you in trouble."

"I would never do that to you." She relaxed, only a touch. "Or to myself. Eli..."

He met her lips. Not long enough. "Let's go. They'll understand."

Her fingers ran along his sides, the hard nails tracing a line as she pulled back. She took his hand with a light nod.

He noticed how she kept her face averted from her volunteer colleagues. Embarrassed. He didn't think he'd ever seen a woman embarrass so easily or so often, at least not since junior high when girls naturally embarrassed easily. These days, it was rare. Girls said whatever they damned well wanted, and as bad as his language was, many of them were far worse. They also tended to do whatever they wanted. A good thing, to an extent.

He gave Gloria a quick "see ya tomorrow" and chuckled at her request to "behave, at least as well as I would." It made Delaney's face even more red, her grip on his hand tighter, her body more strained.

Deciding not to make it worse, Eli kept a slight distance as she unlocked and opened her door. "So, I'm going to head to the hotel and shower. I'll come over in a bit and you can decide whether you'd rather stay in or go out." She didn't answer. "Okay?" Damn, the girl looked like she was in front of a firing squad. "Del, what?"

"Sorry if I embarrassed you." She fidgeted with her keys and her chest rose and fell. "But coming to the house... I don't know."

"Hey, I've been there already. I still like you, anyway." She didn't laugh. "That was a joke. I'm not that touchy, and I don't give a flying f... I don't care what your brother-in-law says. Won't change how I feel about you."

"You don't really know me." Her voice was shaky. She kept her gaze on the ground between their feet. "This... This is hard and I can't make you understand. I'm not the same with them as I am with just you. I mean... I can't make you understand."

"Try." He raised her face to his. "Del, I listen. Honestly. Some of us men do."

She swallowed hard and grabbed a deep fast breath, her eyes still away from his. Unwilling to let her be so nervous with him, Eli closed in and touched her lips gently. When she tried to back away, he moved with her, kissed her harder, set a hand on her back to hold her against him, to calm her, but it did the opposite. Her breath became jagged, her body tense. Too many people still around, he supposed.

He gave up. For the moment. "Okay. I'll wait on the cooking thing. That's not a big deal. I just hoped you'd let me in a bit more. That's all. But whatever. I'll give you time."

Her chest rose and fell hard and fast, her arms crossed in front.

"So, subs? The one across from the park?"

She nodded but didn't look at him.

"Delaney, are you alright to drive?" Her hand, as he claimed it, said she wasn't while her lips said she was. "Let me have your keys."

"Why?" She finally raised her eyes to his.

"I'm going to lock this back up and you're coming with me."

"I can't leave my car."

"You can for a bit. We'll come right back." He noticed her eyes dart to a couple of kids walking past. "How about some ice cream as an appetizer? Then we can come back for your car and think about dinner. I'll get it swirled this time." When she didn't answer, as though she couldn't, he pried her keys gently from her hand, hit the lock button, and led her to his truck. She didn't object, but she was distant.

Eli had seen her nervous plenty, but never like this. And he didn't get why. It wasn't like he'd humped her right there in front of everyone. It was only a playful kiss. Not a big deal. If she was that afraid of public affection, he was going to have a damned hard time with that.

Delaney kicked herself mentally over and over. Stupid. It was so *stupid* to act like that. She'd kept telling herself to knock it off, it didn't matter that they saw the kiss, even if she did work with them every day and they might say something she wouldn't know how to answer especially since she didn't know what exactly would come of her relationship with Eli, if anything more came of it than it was, or that they wouldn't say anything but would smirk behind her back, or maybe tell her sister she'd been making out in public, although she wasn't, it was nothing really, just a quick casual kiss and it shouldn't bother her, but he wanted to have dinner at her house, with her brother-in-law's big mouth and her sister's tendency to ramble and tell stories of Delaney whenever she dated anyone, which usually stopped the dates right then and there since Trina made her sound silly and jealous and snobby...

And no matter what Eli said about not caring what they'd say, he didn't know he wouldn't. Or he didn't know he would. And he would. Or her stupid inability to even speak to him just because she was nervous for no reason would get to him, and he'd go home.

To Indiana. Without her.

She'd never see him again.

But then she wouldn't have to worry about what Pat would say anymore or what Trina would tell him or if anyone who saw them together would make an issue of her and "another" temporary worker, this time one "taking advantage" of the storm. He wasn't. He truly wanted to help. Why else would he volunteer with her after work?

To *get some*, Pat would say. Maybe. It sure as hell was getting close to that. He hinted often enough. Eli didn't bother to deny it.

And then he would go home.

Stupid. She was *so stupid*. Even if she wasn't. She *wasn't*. She was smart. Capable. And...

And half crazy.

She wasn't, though. She wasn't crazy. She was only nervous. Nervous didn't equal crazy. She still functioned, still held down a paying job and did two volunteer jobs that were around people, more or less, more less than more to be honest, but still, it was a step and she'd been trying to keep taking steps, to force it to stop.

At least she didn't just hide in her house and apply for disability like Pat said she should if she was really that bothered by people. She couldn't say it hadn't crossed her mind, and it would be fair considering her disability was as hard for her to manage as many were. Definitely harder on her than the guy she knew who had a "bad back" and "couldn't work" but had no issue surfing and carrying mostly naked girls around on the beach. If it was okay for him, why shouldn't she?

Because she wanted to defeat it, not give in to it.

It was why she'd said yes to Eli, had agreed to breakfast when he first asked. Another step. Just breakfast and sight-seeing. Casual. She could have been fine if it stayed that way. This ... this was too fast. Far too fast. She couldn't deal with it all so fast. She had to have time to think, to take smaller steps.

But it was April. He planned to be home by July at the latest, maybe sooner. There wasn't much time for her to decide what she would do.

Her breaths came faster as he pulled up in front of a café that advertised ice cream. It was busy, as usual in the evening. She only went during the day when she was off.

"This okay?"

She heard his voice but her ears buzzed and her head swirled with the noise of the radio and his voice and the thoughts of people in the café and on the street, or so she felt. She didn't actually hear their thoughts but she felt their presence and it was overwhelming in her current state. She had to calm down. Answer him. Delaney, *answer* him.

"Hey." Eli touched her face and she pulled back. "What in the hell's wrong? You don't want to be out with me tonight?"

"No. Yes. Eli, yes, I... I can't..." She glanced over at a group of people going into the café. They were laughing, smacking each other in play, so easy. It was so easy for them to just hang out and laugh and talk without caring what other people thought...

He started the truck and she again yelled at herself for being an idiot. He'd take her back to her car and tell her to get lost and she wouldn't try again. She couldn't take this step again if it would lead to this, to coming so close and ... and...

He pulled around the block into a parking area away from the main street where there was no one around, and turned off the truck. "Better?"

"I'm sorry." She barely got it out between her racing heartbeat and the pain seeping into her head.

"It's worse than you've said." Eli unbuckled his seatbelt and then hers and shifted closer as well as he could. "Want to talk?"

Her head shook while her brain screamed yes. She did. But she didn't. She couldn't. It was too stupid...

"Okay. It's fine..."

"It's not. I'm sorry. You can take me back to my car. I'll understand." Her words were staccato through her hard breaths. Her face was hot. Her palms were sweating and she just wanted to crawl down onto his floorboards and sink into it like ... like an oil stain.

His strong hands aside her face kept her from doing it. Eli pulled her closer, trying to catch her eyes. She knew he was but she couldn't. Her head still swirled, still echoed as though every thought she ever had was bursting through all at once like a canyon, or like she'd heard a canyon did, she'd never been in one, or to one...

His lips pressed against hers. Her body tried to object but her fingers gripped him, his shoulder, his ... thigh. He made the kiss deeper, held her tighter.

Delaney shuddered against his body, that part of it she could reach with the console between. Her head lowered to his shoulder. His gentle words told her it was fine and he wasn't taking her anywhere. She was staying right there with him as long as she needed, until she was up to going in and getting ice cream.

The thought tensed her again and he caressed her skin, spoke to her. She didn't even know what he said since her ears were plugged with the swirl of her echoed thoughts all jumbled together and the fog from blood rushing through her brain, or at least that's what she thought it was that made everything sound enveloped in ... in a thick fog that distanced her from everyone, everything. It didn't matter what he said. His voice was soft, gentle. Soothing. She kissed his warm neck. The growing-back beard scraped her cheek. His hair tickled her nose. He smelled of ... of the ocean and ... and mildew. He'd been working in an old house, he said. The stench on his shirt was bad.

Delaney had to wonder if it was Trina's house. Not likely, she supposed. It was still waiting the okay from the insurance company and they would be in Delaney's house blocking her from any real peace and quiet for who knew how long. But the smell was nice on him, somehow. Reassuring. He was there to help.

She'd desperately needed someone to be there to help who wouldn't look at her like she was nuts, who wouldn't walk away...

Or who would take her with him when he walked away. Back home.

Could she?

Delaney found herself calming at the thought of being in the middle of nowhere with him. Maybe not a bad place to be. Not crowded. Open. Quiet. Nature. Not ocean, but still nature.

He tried to find her lips again and she let him as she wrapped her arms around his shoulders. She'd been so afraid of doing this in front of him, but so far, he was still there.

When her body relaxed and her kiss became more about passion than escape, or fear, Eli slid his hand under her shirt to her bare skin. She'd said he could take her back. He knew what she meant. She expected him to walk away because ... because she was far more than simply shy, more than simply nervous. He had to wonder how often it hit her like this.

With a deep breath, she lay her head on his shoulder and held tight.

"Delaney. When you're ready, you can talk to me. I'm not going anywhere." He kissed her ear. Nudged her face up to his. Kissed her mouth, teased her lips.

She ran a hand down his chest, her breathing back to normal, her gaze focused, the flush easing out of her cheeks.

"Better now?"

She nodded. "I'm sorry..."

"Don't apologize. You're right. I don't understand. But I'd like to understand. Later. For now, just relax. I'll go get us a couple of cones. You're okay here? Lock the doors behind me..."

"I'll go."

He studied her face. "Are you sure?"

"Yes. If you won't be bothered when I close in on you. I might."

"Be my guest." He brushed her lips. "Anytime, Del. Truly. I mean it. Whatever I can do."

"I try to fight it. I do. I'm not ... looking for attention. I hate attention. I mean I hate attention with a passion. So I'm not..."

"Hey. We'll talk later. I want you calm enough you can drive."

"I'm used to it. I do okay. I just put my music on and it relaxes me enough to drive as long as I'm careful."

His gut ached at the thought. "I'd rather you didn't. And if I have to, I'll take you home and take a cab back to get your car."

"No, it's fine. Really. We can go in."

Eli saw her rub her fingers together hard, as she often did when she started to look nervous, and he kissed her again. A long gentle reassuring kiss. An *I want to be with you for an awfully damned long time to come* kiss. He hoped she would take it that way.

"Thank you." She spoke against his lips in between prolonging the long kiss with smaller *I don't want to back away from you yet* kisses.

He chuckled. "Please tell me that was for the kiss."

"Oh. It could be. But I meant ... for trying to understand."

"You know what, Del? It's kind of nice to have someone who won't laugh at me for my water thing since you ... and I mean, I'm not glad you have to deal with this and I hope we can help you get over it, at least to some extent, but I mean..."

"Yeah. That's nothing compared to this, right? You can just avoid deep water." She stroked a finger over his lips. "The food is good here, too, if you want to grab a sandwich. I'll cook for you another night. Let me prepare for that first. I do better with new situations if I have plenty of warning. Is that going to be too hard to deal with?"

He slid his hand around the side of her head. "I'll remember that. No last minute surprises."

"Well, it depends. Just not with..."

"Social situations. Got it. A sandwich is fine. Then ice cream. I'm in the mood for it. Swirled, of course." He threw a wink and went around to open her door.

After she was sure the kids were in bed and it was late enough Trina and Pat wouldn't knock on her door, Delaney locked it, changed into bicycle shorts, a skinny tee, and her long flowing skirt, and turned her stereo on. Spanish guitar. Trina had teased her years ago about listening to Spanish guitar CDs instead of Billy Idol or whoever her sister's current interest had been – Trina flitted between bands too fast to keep up – so she kept it to herself.

For practice.

Or release, really. She wasn't practicing for anything. She wouldn't show anyone. It was only for her. Flamenco. With Spanish guitar. It was graceful and aggressive both. Her mother had told her she'd been an aggressive, headstrong child, but she didn't remember it. She did feel it. She loved the foot stomp that felt like saying *don't screw with me* as she wished she could actually say now and then. She loved the fifth position hands, straight over her head, as though readying for battle, curving them down slowly, hands first, elbows up still in ready position, fingers and wrists doing their own dance that said *look here, be wary*.

At least that was how she saw it. Flamenco was her release. And maybe it was crazy for a Jersey girl with uncertain roots but certainly not Spanish or at least not enough to tell if she had any Spanish heritage to be so tuned into Spanish guitar and Flamenco as though it was a part of who she was.

It was her other side, the one no one saw. Aggressive. Prepared. Sensual. Seductive. Dangerous.

Part of her was. It just didn't show. Until she danced. Alone.

Her long days with Eli had her tired fast, and the very small space of her bedroom became annoying fast, so she switched the music to something more calm. Bryan Adams. *If You Really Love a Woman.* She loved the song with a passion and let it flow through her fingers, her wrists, her arms and head and shoulders and hips. Delaney thought of Eli as she danced, as she absorbed herself in the words, the music, the passion, the grace ... and the aggression.

He would like this side of her. Delaney was sure he would. If she could ever show him.

Inside the café, she'd clung to him and let him order for her. After paying, he'd wrapped an arm around her shoulder and kissed the side of her head, sheltering her the best he could from the crowd. When the order was ready, they took it outside, across the road where they sat in the grass to eat, on the blanket he again pulled from the truck. He went back in for ice cream, which he got in cardboard bowls so they could take it back to Delaney's car at the refuge. Everyone had gone by then, and he opened the bed of his truck and helped her up on the tailgate where they sat side-by-side eating their ice cream while they looked out over the water.

They'd stayed for some time and pushed their passion farther than they yet had, but not too awfully far before he said he'd better let her get home.

He followed her home, walked her to the door, possibly hoping for an invitation to come in, which she couldn't give him, and gave her a sweet kiss that very nearly changed her mind. She wanted to invite him in. She wanted to tell the people invading her house to get out, so she could invite him in.

With her thoughts too distracting, Delaney gave up on her workout and put in Enrique's *Hero.* Her favorite of his. Something she'd wanted for the longest time. And maybe she found him. Eli. Her hero who kissed away her pain.

Slumping onto the floor at the foot of her bed, she shoved her hands over her eyes and tried to make herself believe she could defeat this thing, at least enough it wouldn't chase away her Eli.

~ Sixteen ~

Delaney prepared for her date by putting her music on, an Andrew Lloyd Webber compilation, and moving along with it, this time with more contemporary moves she saw on dance videos and imitated, plus her own freestyle.

She had few actual CDs. Mainly she bought them in downloads and backed them up on her external hard drive. A few, though, she wanted to be able to hold in her hands. This one, she bought in hard copy.

At a knock on her door, she sighed and opened it to Trina.

"Sorry, but could you turn that down a touch? We can hear it through the floor."

"Is it actually bothering you? Everyone's awake by now, or they should be."

"No, not me. You know I like music loud. But..."

"Then tell your husband that I can always hear his, too, and he can deal with it."

"Laney..."

"Don't call me that. You know I don't like it."

"I don't know why not. It's cute. You can loosen up a bit, you know." Trina tossed her highlighted hair.

"So can he. I'm leaving in a couple of hours. He can put earplugs in for that long if he needs."

"Delaney, he's just in that mood right now..."

"So what's new? Really, Trina, you have to stop letting him boss you around like this."

"He doesn't..."

"Yes, he does." When her sister started to get emotional, Delaney backed off. "Fine, I'll turn it down. And I'll be gone most of the day, so don't worry if I'm late."

"Going out with Eli again? You should bring him for dinner tomorrow. Let us get to know him."

"I don't think it's time for that. Trin, I need to get ready." With a polite nudge, she got her sister out the door. Bring him for dinner in the madhouse? She didn't think so, even if he said it would be fine, he could deal with it. She couldn't.

Over the past week, things had settled down between her and Eli. They still worked close together at the refuge but he kept a respectable distance. Some nights, they'd eaten together, others they went on back to their own places. He gave her a small kiss before they separated, behind cover of his open truck door. It both reassured her and frightened her. She was anxious to see what he had planned for the day, since he asked if he could make the plans. Delaney agreed with some hesitation. She didn't like surprises. She liked to plan ahead. But she didn't want him to think she couldn't be at all spontaneous, or didn't trust him. Although she supposed both were true to some extent.

Trying to put it out of her mind, she turned the stereo down and lost her thoughts in the music, the dance, the release. The only real release she'd had in years. Her dance.

Showered and dressed, in layers since she didn't know where they were going, a pretty yellow tank top, loose and flowing, topped by a short-sleeved brown shirt over denim capris since it was supposed to be warm, Delaney studied herself. He'd never seen her in anything but jeans. She supposed she should look like a girl for him at least once. The capris were more fitted than she liked. They looked fine, not too tight, but the tank top was the new high low style that dipped nearly to her thighs in back while swooping up almost to the top of her jeans in front. It showed her shape well, or it would if she had to take the button-front shirt off. Why shouldn't she show her shape? She worked hard to make it what it was and keep it there, despite all of her recent splurging.

But it started to make her nervous and she didn't need that on top of not knowing their plans, so Delaney changed her mind and slipped into her loose jeans. And her boots. They felt protective.

Take another step, Delaney. Just one more small step.

The voice in her head made her pulse race, but she took a long deep breath with her eyes closed and thought of Eli's face, of his hard shoulders, his chest, of how she'd love to see them uncovered.

Another step, Delaney. You can do it. You can.

With one more deep breath, faster this time, she changed back into the yellow tank and brown shirt over blue jean capris. While her guts were functioning okay, she put her boots back and opted for the yellow and brown dance-style shoes she loved and had never worn. Grabbing socks and tennis shoes to take with her in case he had something active in mind, Delaney hurried down the stairs, yelled a goodbye, and went out to the porch to wait for him. The last thing she needed was a comment about her outfit. Then she'd have to go right back up and change.

She didn't have to wait long. By the time he got out of the truck and headed toward her, she was nearly in his arms.

"Hey Del, I would have come to the door." He kissed her cheek.

"I'm saving you from that. Pat's in a mood."

"Sorry." He ran his eyes over her. "You look great, and what do you know, you have legs and toes."

Her heart pounded. "Are you being facetious?"

"Not at all. Well, maybe about the toes, since I have seen them on the beach a couple of times." He hugged her with another kiss, aside her head this time. "Relax. You do look great. And I'll be happy to keep you out away from your brother-in-law all day."

"I'd like that. Not just to be away from him, but..."

His grin nearly melted her knees right down to the pavement. "Good. I have tickets to the Blue Claws. Okay with you?"

The Lakewood minor league team. "Sounds great, actually."

"You know..." He stroked fingers down her arm. "A girl who likes baseball and is willing to let me make plans without asking twenty questions is a girl hard to let go of. Fair warning, Delaney."

The girl *knew* baseball. Eli found himself turned on by the fact. A lot of his family did, girls included, but with so many of them playing in school leagues, it wasn't surprising. Delaney sipped on her beer, regular, not light, to her credit as far as he was concerned, and fussed quietly about bad calls and bad plays.

Eli set an arm around her shoulders. "You're supposed to yell at the umps when you're mad, not mutter so they can't hear you."

"I don't yell."

"No? Never?"

"Yes, at times, but not in public."

"At rock concerts even?"

"No. I haven't been to many, anyway."

She looked embarrassed so he let his fingers play with the hair over her shoulder. He was glad she had it down, natural. "Why not?"

"They're crowded, and unless you buy the expensive seats up front, you have to climb way up into the bleachers and..." She shuddered.

"The heights."

"Yeah. Stupid, huh?"

He leaned in to give her a kiss, a quick one, so it hopefully wouldn't embarrass her. "Stop calling yourself that. You're not." At her questioning gaze, he took her beer, put it in the holder, and set both hands on her face. "Delaney, you've said it I don't know how many times since we've met. But you're not, and you need to stop saying you are. It's hard on your soul to talk about yourself negatively."

She flushed and turned her eyes away.

Eli kissed her again, gently, and made it longer than he intended, but it was nice, accepting, and she set a hand on his shoulder, ran it down to his chest...

"Hey, this is a family place."

Releasing her, he looked back at the guy behind him. With his kids there, and his wife, Eli supposed. "Sorry. But we've just started dating recently and I like her a heck of a lot. Thought she should know I do."

The man's look softened into a head shake. "Great. Show her elsewhere, not in front of my kids. And good luck, but be careful or you'll end up like this instead." He shrugged his head toward his family and his wife gave him a glare.

With a grin, Eli caught Delaney's even redder face and lowered his arm to take her fingers. He leaned close to her ear. "Kinda thinking that might be okay with me. What do you think?"

She hesitated, only a moment. "I think it's too soon to think that far ahead."

"Meaning you're gonna play hard to get?"

"No. Meaning I am hard to get. Especially all that far." With a slight raise of the corners of her mouth, she grabbed her beer and crossed her legs with a light lift of her chin.

He chuckled to himself. A good challenge was fine with him. It had been far too long since he'd had one. Too many became immediate leeches when he so much as paid them attention. He couldn't stand a leech. Not these days. When he was younger and showing off and ... well, far too easy to *get* himself, yeah, a leech was fine for a while. Didn't take him long to get bored, though. And he couldn't stand to be bored.

Delaney forced herself to stand up with him during the seventh inning stretch. And she did need to stretch. She wasn't used to sitting so long. When *Take Me Out to the Ballgame* started, she grinned at Eli as he sang along. He had a nice voice, baritone, rich, in tune, unlike some around them.

"You gotta sing it. It's part of the ritual." He tilted his head.

She shook hers. She didn't sing in public. Ever.

"Come on, Del. You know the words."

"I'm enjoying listening to you."

With a grin, he sang louder. A goofball. He really was. And she felt like an idiot being the only one who wouldn't sing and she thought it might be less obvious if she would, or act like she was. She held a tune well enough even if her voice wasn't near as nice as his, but she couldn't do it. The thought of it burned a pit in her stomach. Luckily, the song didn't last long.

"Want another beer?" His fingers teased her leg.

She nearly accepted, just to ease her nerves. "Thank you, but I had enough. I don't hold it well."

The sparkle in his eyes was just too darned charming. "Coke, then?"

"Water maybe. It's warm. Finally." Her damp tank top stuck to her back where it had been pressed against the seat.

"Whatever you like. Staying here or coming with?"

She absolutely did not want to stay there alone.

Eli held her hand tight as they weaved through the small crowd and she stayed close to him, close enough her breast rubbed up against his arm at times. Not intentionally, but his glance said he took it that way.

People pushed to get to the front of the counter and Delaney withdrew from it as well as she could, mentally, focusing on Eli, on his fingers, his strong arm, his boyish excitement and ease. She drew into him when someone very large crowded behind her.

"Hey bud, want to back off an inch?" Eli shrugged his free hand at the guy.

"Mind your own fucking business. I got a right to stand where I want."

"Not right on top of my girlfriend, you don't. *Back* off."

Delaney started to panic. The guy was big. Obnoxious. But he backed off. Just enough.

Eli moved her to his other side and set an arm around her. Protectively. *My girlfriend.* It was cute. Sweet as hell, if she let herself acknowledge it. Most of her dates had been ... modern, detached, figured she could fend for herself. She could, at least to an extent, but still, men were built to be able to deal with each other physically far better than women were built to be able to deal with them if they got aggressive. It was natural instinct for males to protect females, especially those they cared about, the same as it was in the animal world. It was nature, instinct. She was afraid men had lost too much of that instinct, which was a shame. Apparently not all of them had.

Relieved when they got their drinks and moved out of the crowd, Delaney stopped him and slipped an arm over his shoulder. "Thank you."

"It's just water. I'll do better later if you want..."

"I mean with that rude guy. Thank you."

He stared at her for some time. "Have you ever in your life had a man treat you like a lady?"

She couldn't answer. Had she? Her father, she supposed, although he went a little too far and wouldn't even hug her because it *wasn't appropriate.* He hugged Trina, though, because Trina insisted. She had

no brothers, no male cousins who lived anywhere near. Her dates...
No, not even close.

He took her silence as a negative. "That's fucking ridiculous.
Excuse the language." His face lowered to hers. "It's about time
someone did."

She felt herself draw in. "No, it's fine. I take care of myself. I was
taught to do that. Always have. It's safer..."

"Del, yeah, you're right. And you should. I can already see you
take care of your sister and her family, and sounds like you took care
of your parents a lot, too. And the wildlife. The food bank. That's
great. It is. But now and then, don't you want someone else to take
care of things a while so you don't have to?"

She couldn't think of it. She couldn't let herself think someone
would. He was there temporarily...

His lips met hers and his arm slid around her waist. A short kiss.
Too short. "Game's starting."

She nodded. But she didn't move away.

"We can blow off the rest if you want. Outcome is pretty well set
by now. Not much to watch. How about an early dinner? Hot dogs
aren't doing it for me."

"I know a good diner nearby, but it's my treat this time since it's
far past my turn."

He chuckled. "There are diners everywhere I look. Never seen
anything like it."

"Yeah, kind of a Jersey thing, so I hear. You don't have them?"

"We do. Not nearly so many. Mainly full restaurants or fast food.
This in between is kind of nice. I could get used to it."

Delaney didn't dare hope he meant longer than while he was in
the area working.

Delaney noticed him get quieter as they ate. It wasn't an
uncomfortable quiet, only a ... a thoughtful quiet. The man was deep
in thought and she wasn't sure she wanted him to be. She liked his
upbeat, open, fun side. It helped energize her, which was hard to do.
She had plenty of determination, drive, even stamina. Energy was not
her strong point. She loved his. This quiet side was new. But it was

nice in a way.

As they left the diner, which he seemed in a hurry to do although he claimed to like the food, Enrique's *I Like It* came on and she stopped a second.

He looked at her curiously. "You like this?"

"Yes. One of my guilty pleasures." She shrugged at his raised eyebrows. "It's fun. I know the words are kind of..."

"Yeah, kind of."

She felt herself blush. Right there on the sidewalk in front of the diner, in front of the kids hanging out, he wrapped an arm around her, his hand firm on her lower back ... and started dancing. Damned near grinding, as the kids called it.

"Eli..."

"Dance with me, Del. The words are kind of..." He spoke next to her ear. "Turning me on, to be honest. Although I detest cheating. I seriously detest cheating, even barely."

"Me too." She slid her arms around him but she wouldn't give in to dance. Not there, with eyes on them. "But not here."

"I'm not trying to *get some* here, just dancing." He backed up, just a touch, swiveling his hips to the beat. Very sexy. The man danced as well as he sang. The kids nearby laughed, a fun laugh, not mean. They were enjoying the fact the guy they probably thought of as old would stand on the sidewalk and dance to Enrique Iglesias. Very, very sexy. She flushed again, this time not from embarrassment, well maybe that, but because she couldn't pull her gaze from his hips, from his...

"Come on." He tried again to get her to join him. Her feet felt like steel, bolted into the cement, as she shook her head, as a couple of nearby girls said they would if she wouldn't. Jail bait girls or near enough. He paid no attention to them.

"You can do this. Just move, back and forth." He set his hands on her hips. Her face burned. Her heart raced and her head rushed, swirled, until she was almost unsure where she was and could hardly see him. Her head shook and she backed away. She wanted to sink into the sidewalk, melt like butter in summer, into a stain no one would notice.

"You can't dance? Thought you said you did."

With a heavy breath, she crossed her arms in front of her. She danced. Well. Just not in front of anyone.

Delaney heard voices in the background. Laughing. At her now. She should have just danced with him. She'd look less idiotic. Except she wouldn't. She'd be stiff and look ridiculous. And she'd think about it for weeks, about how ridiculous she'd looked when she knew she could dance far better than most of those kids who were laughing. If she could let herself.

Eli gave up, slid an arm around her back, kissed her head, and walked her to the truck. When he got in, he didn't start it. "Where to next? That's all I had planned."

She couldn't look at him. "Doesn't matter."

"Maybe we should've stayed at the game."

Tears threatened, except she couldn't do that, either. It was too humiliating. She was going to lose him, just because she couldn't dance in public, couldn't sing in public, couldn't... She couldn't push herself as fast as he was trying. Maybe he was trying to help. Maybe he thought she just had to keep going out there, keep pushing, but he didn't understand that every time she got so flustered, it only made it harder...

"Okay." He didn't talk all the way back to Manahawkin ... and he didn't take her home as she expected. He crossed onto 72 and drove out to Long Beach Island.

She hoped it was a good thing, but she couldn't be sure since his face was firm, almost cold, and he said nothing. Delaney couldn't make herself ask. He drove the entire length of the island and parked in the lighthouse parking lot.

Her head was spinning, fuzzy with nerves, fear, frustration. Silence.

His radio stayed on when he switched off the engine. Country. She was starting to like it more the more she heard it. Except this song. A stupid song. Some of them really were.

He clicked it off. "Stupid song. Gives country a bad name."

She glanced at him and wondered if she'd said what she thought out loud. As fuzzy as her head was, she could have.

"So why the sudden *get the hell away from me* act after as close as you got at the game?"

What? That's why he said they should have stayed there? Her head shook. "I didn't mean it that way."

"No?"

"I don't dance in public. I don't. I can dance. I can't in public."

"Why? I wasn't asking you to talk and no one else was close or crowding in on you."

Her head started to thump and she looked out the window, her side window, away from him.

"You know, I know people who are kinda nervous in public, but still, they dance and talk and all. Maybe they just learned how to control their nerves and you could..."

"You think I don't?" She looked back.

"Not so well, apparently. And hey, it's not a criticism. I hate deep water, too, and I avoid it when I can, but when I can't, I at least act like it's cool until I can get away..."

"So do I."

"Yeah? Not today, you didn't. Or the other day."

She felt a highly combustible mix of anger and frustration welling, too fast. She *did*. He had no idea *how much* she did. How much she controlled it so people only thought she was a snob instead of realizing she was terrified of having to talk to them even to give directions which she'd likely mess up because she'd be too nervous to think. She controlled herself very well, considering the pounding heart, the spinning head, which no one knew about because she controlled it and she didn't talk about it. All they saw was silence. Stiffness. Nothing more. She hid it damned well. He was an idiot.

She jumped when he touched her arm and flashed a *leave me the hell alone* look. Defensive. She needed to just go home and start trying to recover. Again. From her defenses being so far penetrated. It would take forever to rebuild them, to feel secure enough to try again.

"Fine. But I want to show you something before I take you home." He reached into his glove compartment and plugged an iPod into his stereo.

Music started. Enrique. *I Like It*. He had it on his iPod?

Eli answered her question before she could force herself to ask. "I have a huge amount of music, all kinds. I like pretty much all of it. So no need to worry about guilty pleasure music with me, or what I'll think about it." He switched the song. Backstreet Boys. And again. A female voice she didn't know. "Phoebe Snow. From the Sixties. Forget who introduced me, but I take a lot of flak for that when it comes on. Couldn't care less."

"She's from here. From Jersey."

"You know of her?"

"Her name. I don't know her music."

With a nod, he switched it again. She recognized the song but couldn't place it. "Spice Girls. Go ahead and laugh."

She did have to grin.

He switched it again, back to Enrique. *Hero.* "I love this one, actually. Kept thinking someday I'd play it for a girl, the right girl."

Delaney bit her lip, holding herself in. It was her song. He couldn't have it. He couldn't *love* it. That was intruding too far.

"So? Going to stop worrying about what I think any time soon?"

She shook her head. "Probably not."

He stared a minute, then laughed. "Damn, Del. I love a good challenge, but give me something here. Anything."

"This is one of my favorites, too."

"Is it? Sexy song, really."

"Sensual. Sensual's better than sexy." She embarrassed herself by correcting him, but it wasn't sexy. It was sensual. She liked that about it.

"Yeah."

Delaney caught his eyes. She knew hers were moist and tried to blink it away, but he touched her face. She found herself moving toward him, wanting to be closer. She wanted...

He kissed her, gently, questioning.

She wanted ... far too much. "Eli."

"Hm." He kissed her neck as he cupped her head in his large, strong, gentle working hand.

"You should know ... I do control it."

He pulled back just enough to see her face. "Del, I didn't mean... I'm sorry, it was a stupid thing to say. I just never..."

"No, you probably haven't." His expression told her he was confused. "I ... have severe social anxiety. To the point it's a disorder. A lot of people have anxiety in public. I know. But not like this. Not to the point it interferes with their daily life and everything they do. This isn't just... I have panic attacks, not as many anymore because I've learned to control them for the most part, and I try not to let it stop me, but there are things I just can't... I *can't*. And can't isn't a word I use lightly. I hate it, actually, but..."

"Panic attacks. From...?"

"Trying to talk to people. Just talk. Especially if there's even a hint of conflict in it. That turns me into a red, stammering mess and I'm never sure I'm not having an actual heart attack. A real one. Or dance. That I really can't do and it frustrates me more than you can imagine, because I can. I'm a damned good dancer. I do Flamenco, actually, which I have never in my life told anyone, but I can't even do simple club dance around ... anyone. Ever. I panic if I try."

"Flamenco." He looked confused again.

"It's Spanish."

"Yeah, I know what it is, but... Del, have you seen a therapist or something? Something to help..."

"I *can't*. Eli, you *don't* get it. I don't tell anyone. I'm trying very hard not to have a heart attack right now just from telling you and I ... I can hardly ... breathe. Because it's... It's stupid and I know it is and it's embarrassing to even admit it but you have to know I can't just ... decide to get over it and ... and dance with you in public, no matter how much I wish I could and I do wish I could. I would. Eli if I could without..."

He took her in his arms as well as possible around the console and kissed her head. "Relax. Just breathe, Delaney."

She fought hard not to let herself cry out of frustration, out of his kindness, the way she was finally able to tell someone. "I only know what it is, only recently, because of the internet, the research I've done, trying to find some answer, anything to help, because no, I can't go to a therapist. I can't even make the phone call. Other people talking about it online, kind of, with memes mostly because it's so damned hard to actually talk about, is the only way I know I'm not the only one fighting this."

The first time she'd read someone else's symptoms, Delaney cried. They were hers. And this person understood. Really understood. The way no one else could. Just knowing it was real, that she wasn't crazy, and a lot of people were affected by it made it easier. To some extent. Not enough. "Most of us who have this horrible fear of being around others, of even speaking to another person, hide inside and stay away from people. It's easier, they say. Maybe it would be, but ... you're right. I do want to be around people, and I can't. I keep trying to fight it and some days I think I'm actually getting somewhere and then the next, it's right back and I'm afraid someone will think I'm having a heart attack since it feels like it and ... and maybe someday it will be a real one..." Her heart raced so much her chest hurt and she could hardly see him through the haze in her head.

"Okay, baby. Breathe. Just breathe. It's okay." His kisses trailed along her face back to her lips. "I'm sorry. I didn't get it. I do, kind of. It's like if I had to go out in the middle of an ocean in a rowboat, I'm assuming, except a lot more unavoidable. Yeah?"

"More if you had to be in the ocean where you couldn't see land, in only a life preserver." She felt his shudder. "It's not always that bad. Some days it's the rowboat instead."

"Damn, Del. I can't even..." He kissed her head, stroking her hair. "So you'd dance with me on the sidewalk if you could?"

"Yes. In a heartbeat." She relaxed as his thumb brushed over her cheek. "I can't tell you how much I wish I could. Not even on the sidewalk, but, at a club where everyone is dancing and I look more an oddball because I won't. Or even, just ... talking in a group of people without getting red and having them look at me because I'm red and flustered. I can't tell you how much I wish I could. And I've tried. I keep trying, but then... Even talking to people I work with and see every day makes me nervous and I can't stop it. Sometimes I'll go to the refuge thinking I'll join the group, talk to them, and I freeze. I can't. I know you don't understand it because I don't even understand it. But every time I try and have to fight off an attack, it's harder to try again."

"How do you live that way?"

She swallowed hard. "By myself, mostly. When I have to shop, I put my head on anything else, try not to see anyone, and pretend they aren't there. I walk past people I know all the time and they think I'm..."

"Snubbing them."

"Yeah, and you know that's fine because then they leave me alone, which is what I want."

"No you don't." He turned her face back to his. "No, you don't."

A large fast breath engulfed her. Like a huge wave. Nearly drowning her. "No." She sputtered out an answer. "I don't. But it's ... the only way I can function."

"What are you so afraid of? I mean, with water, there's the drowning thing, and sharks, jellyfish... So..."

Her head shook. "Nothing. Everything. I don't know why. There's no reason. I read ... it's a chemical imbalance that hits in young teen years and that must be right because I didn't used to be. And there's no reason. I had a normal childhood. I was always a little touchy about being yelled at or scorned, but..."

"Maybe there's something you can take?"

She pulled back.

"Del, I'm only... I just can't imagine how you deal with it."

"What would you do?"

"If..?"

"If you got stuck in a rowboat in the Atlantic with no paddles and the only way back was to jump in and swim. Would you?"

He shuddered again. "Yeah, I ... would probably panic and drown if I got out too far. My guess is I'd think I could and I'd get in the water just to have to pull myself right back up in the boat."

"That's what I do. Over and over. It just doesn't get me anywhere. I do try. Sometimes I get farther out than before and I think it's getting better and something happens and ... I just climb right back up in that boat and think maybe I'd just rather stay there and die of starvation or dehydration."

He was silent a while. "So what calms you? What do you do to relax?"

She danced. Alone. But she'd talked too much about that already.

"The water. Walking along the beach. Swimming, except I hate to do it around others. Hard to avoid that here."

He rolled his eyes. "Swimming. Great. I can't help you do that, not outside a small pool."

"You can walk along the beach."

"Yeah. Makes me nervous but I can."

"Does it?"

"By the ocean, it does. Lakes are fine. I fish on lakes, only on shore, not in a boat. Didn't realize the ocean made me nervous?"

"No. We've been... I keep dragging you out there. You should have said so."

"Well, you know. I keep trying, too. And I know you love it, so there is that."

"As much as you love being around people."

He dipped his head in acknowledgement, then he opened his door and came around to hers. "Okay, so come on."

"Where?"

"To help you relax since I made you so upset."

"You don't have to."

He leaned in and looked up at her with a light grin. "I know I don't have to. I want to. Are you coming?"

As though she could refuse. They walked silently, holding hands like teenagers, and he led them down to the beach where she slipped out of her shoes. If he was nervous, Delaney couldn't tell and there was some comfort in that, like maybe people really couldn't tell she was, either. At least until it went too far.

The beach was mostly deserted and dusk was falling in around them. Eli headed toward the big flat boulders on the edge of the water, beside the walking path. He leaned way over the metal railing until it hurt Delaney's stomach and peered down farther from the lighthouse, where the wall between the boulders and path was higher, then he slipped under the railing onto the wet rocks.

"Eli..."

"Come on, Del. This is not comfortable for me so..."

"Then come back up here."

"Come down here. I want you to do something."

The possibilities of what he might ask her to do swirled in her mind and became increasingly sexual-natured until she had them both undressed. *Get your head out of the gutter, Delaney.* Talking to herself, she gave in to him.

They made their way over the mostly flat boulders and she enjoyed the cold strength of the stones beneath her feet mixed with the softness of the water-sanded surface. Eli held her arm, protective. She was sure if she slipped, he would either hold her up or land underneath her to soften the blow. She knew he would. The thought of landing on top of his body engrossed her thoughts far too much...

He stopped and cast a glance from where they'd come and then above the wall beside them.

"Nervous?" By now, he looked it.

"Beyond belief."

"Eli, we can..."

"Show me."

She paused. He was close. Very close. "Show you what?"

"A couple of Flamenco moves. I want to see it."

Her heart pounded. "No..."

Quickly, he moved in and claimed her mouth. A hand behind her head threaded through her hair, the other beneath the back of her shirt, beneath her tank top. "Del." He whispered beside her ear. "You're safe with me. I don't care if you're nervous. I don't care if you stumble. Just show me. A couple of moves. Nothing more."

"Oh Eli, you don't understand..."

He took her hand and set it against his chest. His heart was pounding as bad as her own, or so it felt. "I think I do, at least right now, at this moment. We stay down here too long and I may have the heart attack. So we're on equal footing, right? At the moment?"

"Maybe."

"Maybe? What else do I have to do? Actually go out into the ocean?"

With her ears ringing, Delaney shook her head. She'd already talked to him, told him something she'd never been able to say, already had the heart attack feeling, nearly to the point of passing out. It was too much...

"Fine." He took his shoes and socks off, set them aside, then pulled his shirt over his head, dropping it onto the rail.

"What are you doing?" She could barely ask while staring far too much at his bare skin...

"Getting in the water."

"Eli. Not here. The tide..."

"I want to be on equal footing, so to speak. Should I lose the jeans, too, or will that make things worse?" He started to unbuckle his belt.

"Don't." She took his hands to stop him before she realized exactly where his hands were and how close to his nearly naked skin she was.

"So, keep the jeans on? Gonna make it harder to swim that way. I can do it..."

"You're not going out there." Releasing his hands, Delaney couldn't keep her eyes from roaming. As she took in Eli's glorious strong sexy tanned chest in the shadows of Old Barney's light, she nearly changed her mind about not letting him take the jeans off. She'd always been told to picture people in their underwear, that it stopped nerves. It always made it worse for her. But Eli... "Damn, you're sexy." She heard herself say it and flushed more.

"Sensual." His voice teased as he repeated part of their earlier conversation. "I work hard." He kissed her neck. "And I play hard. And long. In case you're wondering."

A groan escaped her lips but she was far too flushed already to let it bother her. "Sensual. Yes. And sexy. Both." She allowed her fingers to wander along his stomach, his tight abs, to his back...

"You're stalling."

"Yes."

He chuckled. "So how about getting this out of the way?" Eli slid his fingers from her collar down to the middle where it was buttoned and undid them, slowly.

Delaney thought she might pass out. She hadn't actually done it before, although she'd been dizzy enough often enough from the panic attacks. But this... getting part undressed with him part undressed, outside, and trying to dance, on the rocks...

She clenched her eyes and made herself breathe slower to calm the dizziness. Waves splashed beside them against the boulders. Seagulls called overhead. She focused on the smell of the ocean ... and on his fingers, sliding her shirt down her arms.

"You okay?"

With a nod, she opened her eyes and met his. The deep dark blue eyes so concerned about her. She touched his face, and his lips, sliding her arms over his shoulders.

"Mm. Nice, but no more stalling. Show me." He backed up to give her space and draped her shirt over his. "By the way, that's a wonderful color for you. You should wear it more often. And you should wear less more often. Talk about sensual. Damn, Del. You have to stop covering it all up."

"You're making me more nervous."

"No excuses. Dance." He lowered onto a boulder, sitting, like an actual audience.

"I don't have music."

"Want me to sing?"

"Yes." He wouldn't do it...

But with a sparkle in his eyes and his lips turning up just a touch at the edges, he started to sing. An Enrique song. Delaney had to wonder if he was showing off or being facetious. Except he knew the words.

He stopped when she didn't start. "Not good enough?"

"You sing well."

He grinned and leaned back on his hands so he was nearly half-reclined and looked fully comfortable. "If I'm going to do something, I sure as hell mean to do it well. Dance, Delaney. Quit stalling."

She grabbed all the strength she had inside and positioned herself to be ready for the chorus of *Stay Here Tonight*. Pointed? She let the thought consume her, to add passion to her movements, and focused on his expression.

It took time to relax enough to do it right, but she did. And she was right. He loved this side of her, too. It was all over his face.

As his voice faded out into a stare full of emotion, Delaney moved over to him. Eli reached up to grip the hem of her tank top in a suggestion to come closer, and she leaned down to meet his lips. But she wasn't close enough yet, so she sank to his side, holding the kiss as the damp cold of the stone penetrated her capris and cooled the top of her feet. Slowly, carefully, she straddled him and wrapped an arm around his head.

"Delaney." It was a furtive whisper, a question.

"Yes." She caught his eyes. "Eli, yes."

"Where? I don't want a cheap last-minute hotel. Not for this. I want ... more for you, for..." He played with the bare skin of her lower back and kissed her bare shoulder. "Ideas?"

"Still have that blanket in the truck?"

"Sure do."

"Come on." Forcing herself up off his warm, hard, inviting body, she waited while he retrieved their shirts and led him back up to the beach, back to the truck. He slid his shirt over his shoulders but left it unbuttoned. Delaney carried hers with her shoes. All the way to the truck. The soles of her feet were toughened from all the time she spent barefoot outside, which seemed to impress Eli.

He put a hand on her rear as he held the door. And when he got in and started the engine, she leaned back in against him, over the console she wished wasn't in her way, claimed his mouth, and slid a hand under his shirt to his bare chest.

Surprised at herself for her aggression, she nearly backed away, as she normally did. Nearly pulled back into her hard-to-build private shelter that she didn't want to lose. But her Eli... She'd been wrong twice. Very wrong. Not this time. Her Eli was different.

Or so she hoped.

"Plan to do this right here?"

"Hm. Maybe."

"Del..." He forced a bit of space with a hand against her cheek, his gaze strongly on her eyes. "You know I plan to go back home. To Indiana."

"Yes." She forced herself to not get emotional about the thought.

"Okay. Just wanted us to be straight on that, before..."

"I don't care." She slid her hand up over his shoulder. "Maybe I should, but ... I don't. I'll hate when you leave. I *will* hate when you leave, but I know you will, and I don't care. I want this. And don't think I'm ... desperate or anything. I'm not. To be fully honest, I've never cared much about ... if I did or didn't. I've never even cared much about it after I did. But Eli..."

"Damn, you've been with the wrong men."

"Yeah. Big time. Just twice, only two... I'm not..." She gave him a soft kiss and slid her hand down the front of his shoulder, under his arm, and up, holding him in. "I do care ... about having more. With you. I need more of you." She kissed his neck, trailed her lips down his chest. "Elijah..."

The sound of her saying his full name turned him on in ways he wouldn't have expected. "Not private enough here, Del. Come on, baby. Let's find somewhere more alone. Point the way."

She kept her hand on his thigh as she gave him directions, back off the island, into the refuge, down a long narrow road, onto a dirt road where she warned him to take it slow because of pot holes. Sprinkles spattered his windshield and he grimaced.

"It's okay. It'll stop. Here, just a few feet more, turn left there."

He peered through the growing dark and the tangle of tall trees and weedy shrubs surrounding them with assistance from his headlights down what looked more like a bike trail than a road. "You sure about this?"

"Yes. No one will be here."

"I can imagine why."

"Don't worry, Captain America. I'm here with you and I won't get you lost."

"Cute." He pulled into a circular dirt-rock area with a metal fence in front of what looked like an overview, and turned to back the bed of the truck close up against the tree line, away from the path. As soon as the engine was off, he felt like an idiot. "Hell."

"What's wrong?" She tightened her grip on his thigh.

"This is." Eli ducked his head to look around the place through the windshield. Desolate. Well, tree-filled desolate. Dying, broken branches mixed with those trying to come back.

She moved her hand away. "Sorry. I thought it might be... You said private. I come here a lot just to think, to get away. No one else does, not that I've seen."

"No, Del, what I mean is..." He shifted to face her and reclaimed her hand. "This feels too much like ... a one-night-stand secret rendezvous kind of thing instead of..."

"Is it?"

He tilted his head to wait for what she meant.

"A one-night-stand. Is that what you have in mind?"

"Absolutely not. And I don't want it to feel like that. There's gotta be ... a nice place, hotel or something that... This isn't the way I wanted this to go. Thought I'd have time to..."

Delaney leaned in, pulled his face to hers, and met his lips. A sweet kiss. Short. And she kept her mouth close to his. "Elijah, are you always so set on how things *should* go?"

"Uh, yeah, I am kind of a planner. Guess it's my line of work. If you don't plan well, you don't tend to have what you need when you need it and things don't go right."

"I think we do." She teased his lips. "Have what we need." Her fingers ran down his chest between his open shirt and she unbuckled his seatbelt. "Was our first kiss not as nice because it wasn't what you'd planned?"

"Oh Del, our first kiss, and every damned kiss since then, was and is spectacular." As proof, if she needed it, he undid her belt, her seatbelt, while he caressed her lips, found her tongue, and slid a hand up under her loose flowing pretty yellow tank top to her bra. A lacy bra. He would be almost disappointed if it was black because that wasn't her and he didn't want her not to be herself with him. Of course he figured if it was black it would show through the yellow, and it didn't. She was a lady. Not even her bra straps showed under her tank.

It didn't take long to realize why they didn't. No straps. A strapless. So it wouldn't show. Delaney was absolutely a lady. His mom would like her; Eli was sure of it. Was he honestly thinking of his family now? Idiot. Too soon for that. Maybe.

Her hands under his shirt, pushing it off his shoulders again, told him maybe it wasn't.

Delaney kissed his shoulder, trailed a finger down to his waist, to the hem of his jeans, and slipped her fingers inside, barely.

"Yeah, we're gonna have to be able to get closer. Didn't think about doing this when I picked this truck, I have to tell you."

She chuckled. "I'm glad."

"Hold on a minute." Slipping the rest of the way out of his shirt, he tossed it into the back seat, set the interior lights to stay on so it wasn't pitch black, got out to lower the tailgate, rolled back the tarp, jumped up into the bed, and pulled his thick sleeping bag and foam cushion from the big plastic box he kept camping gear in. With the thing unrolled, he jumped back down and went to open her door. "Your chariot, or best I can do." He slipped an arm under her knees.

"I can walk."

"This stuff is hard enough to walk on in boots. Not going to have you bruise up your pretty feet."

"Eli…"

"Come here, Delaney. Just let me be happy with the excuse." He took her in his arms, despite her ridiculous protest that she was too heavy, which of course she wasn't, and carried her to the bed. She sat on the open tailgate and raised her eyebrows at his accommodations.

"I sleep in the truck now and then. Comes in handy when I get out where there aren't motels." Hands on her thighs as he stood between her legs, he reached up to kiss her neck. "This okay or you want me to go find us a room? Or you wanna change your mind by now?"

She set her hands alongside his head and kissed him long and warm. When she released him, he gripped her top and she allowed him to pull it over her head. Beige. A lacy beige bra that nearly blended with the color of her pale skin.

Forcing himself to take it slow, he stayed there in front of her, enjoying her caresses, enjoying caressing her bare skin, and watched her reaction to his more intimate caresses, a beautiful, passionate expression, eyes closed, head dropped back. She would damned well care about this afterward. At thirty-two years old, it was about time she did.

Cold raindrops began to pelt his back. Hell, not now. He wanted this. He wanted her now, here, in his truck out in the middle of nature. Eli looked up at the sky with a grimace.

"It's okay. It's not cold." She gripped his arm. "Come up here with me."

"We'll get soaked." He teased her skin.

"We'll dry. I don't care, Eli. Come up here."

They would dry easily enough, but their clothes wouldn't, and no way in hell could he resist. Climbing up into the bed, he pushed her clothes through the back window, then took his camping lantern out and stuck it on the roof of the truck for better light. With any luck, the bugs would buzz around up there and leave them be as dark fell harder. She joked that he'd turned his truck into a lighthouse.

"Come here, Captain America."

"Wow, Del, way to give a guy performance anxiety."

She grinned and pulled him down against her.

Performance anxiety. The guy was far too modest. With the rain falling softly and Eli hiding her from it with his body until he got the sleeping bag pulled up around them, Delaney ran fingers through his wet hair and pulled him down close against her.

"Not exactly the way I'd planned things, but..."

"Not planning is good at times, too. Eli..." She kissed his face beside his ear. "This is a huge first for me, and it was perfect."

"A first?"

"It matters. This will never *not* matter."

"Oh Delaney, you don't realize what you're doing to me." He kissed her forehead and held her, still and silent.

The rain filtered into sprinkles and finally stopped, and it didn't matter. Except the cold of the night began to seep through and mosquitoes started to buzz their heads.

"You're getting cold." He swatted one away from her face.

"Hm." After the shiver, she couldn't argue. Still, she didn't want to move away from his bare skin, his luscious masculine smell, his strong arms. Ever. She realized she would never want him to go home. She stroked a hand down his chest. "What if I decide to visit? When you're home, in Indiana. Would it be okay?"

He set a soft kiss on her wet hair. "What makes you think I plan to leave you?"

She had to think about how to answer. He'd just said he wasn't staying. He'd made it clear. "You said you would."

"I said I'm going home. Doesn't mean I plan to leave you." He shifted to kiss her neck, her shoulder. The wet and heavy cold sleeping bag stuck to her skin and contrasted with Eli's warmth and hardness.

For the hundredth time, Delaney wondered if she could actually pick up and move just to be with him. She had family, too. But he seemed to truly enjoy his. Delaney silently scorned herself for the thought. She enjoyed her family, some of them. And it was all she knew. This place that he liked but he wasn't in love with. She wasn't sure she was, either, except she loved the water, the ocean. How could she live in the middle of ... what, exactly? She had to know before she could make a choice, such a big choice. "Tell me more about Indiana."

He kissed her head again and described his parents' house where he grew up: the big open field behind it where they had campfires and slept in tents just because; going to school with only thirty other kids in his entire class, which she found unbelievable; and then he broadened the description to neighboring towns and the closest cities. Cornfields. Beans. Dirt. Dirt roads. Basements where he and his sister used to roller skate. Bailing hay for spending money as a teen. Farm markets where families and small farmers bought what they didn't raise themselves and took extra of what they had to sell.

She shivered again as she waved away the pesky bugs.

"Better get dried off." He gave her a quick kiss, pulled out from the wet bag, and slipped into his boots.

She chuckled as he made his way down off the tailgate, carefully. "You're missing a few things." Delaney scanned his naked body. "So you're a farm boy who's afraid to walk on rocks?"

"We farm boys wear good boots for protection. We're tough, not stupid." He threw a wink. "Figured you might want to dress in the back seat so you don't get your clothes wet. Quit laughing, Del, and come here." He wriggled his fingers at her until she went to him, and he carried her to the back door.

He dressed beside the truck and then carried her again from back seat to front, her legs straddling his waist. As Eli stalled with his arms under her rear before he released her onto the seat, Delaney started to think she could maybe fall very deeply in love with this man. She shouldn't let herself think it so soon, but she'd always thought you should know when someone really right came to you and you just needed to wait long enough. It would happen when it happened.

Maybe she'd been right.

She let him walk her to her door but hesitated when he said he'd see her in. Eli decided not to push. They'd stopped for burgers since he'd worked up a good hunger again and sat in there for the longest time, with his shirt over her tank since it was long and fell down over her capris that were damp from the rain. She'd chuckled when he pulled an extra T-shirt out of his big plastic box, one of three he kept there just in case.

When they decided they'd taken up a table long enough, he drove her home and they sat outside and talked, in her driveway. The curtain fluttered back enough to show Trina's face for a brief second, which meant she and Pat were still up. Delaney didn't want to deal with comments, or for Eli to have to hear them, so she stopped outside the door of her house that wasn't so much her own anymore and gave him a long hug.

He breathed in her scent, her outdoor oceany earthy scent. "Can I see you tomorrow?" He wanted to take her with him. Overnight. Somewhere private. And try again, better this time. Then wake up beside her.

"Yes."

"What time can I come?"

"How soon are you willing?"

"Five a.m.?"

"Okay."

He pulled back. "You're not serious."

"Are you?" She held his eyes and stroked a finger down his shoulder, down his arm. "I am if you are."

"Let's make it six, then. Five is a tad too early for a Sunday morning, even for me. Dress warm, in layers."

"Okay. Guess I should give your shirt back."

"Hold it for me. I know where you live."

She trailed her fingers down to his hand and caressed his fingers. "You know I'm tempted to..."

"To what?" When she stayed quiet, he kissed her face above her ear. "Tempted to what, Delaney?"

"To not let you go. Tonight, I mean. Yet. Okay, that didn't come out quite right. I mean I wish, tonight even more than I have for a long time, that I had the house to myself."

"Would you ask me to stay?"

"Yes. Would you?"

Eli kissed her nose. "Absolutely."

Delaney threw her arms back over his shoulders, nuzzled her face into his neck, and held tight, her hands wrapping around his head, her chest pressing into his with her heavy breaths.

"Come here, Del." He took her hand and led her over to an old porch swing that could use a coat of fresh paint. The white glowed yellow under the porch light. "This thing still stable?"

"Yes. I read here at times."

Eli could picture her there with her thick hardcover Dracula book ignoring the activity from the houses and street around her, with a pillow at her back and her bare feet pulled up. Offering an arm, he cuddled her in, gently, carefully, aware others could see, including whoever might spy out her window.

"Hm, I could almost sleep right here if I had a blanket."

Stay right here ... forever. The music ran through his head. "Tempting. Until we find better arrangements. I can grab the one out of the truck."

She raised her face to his. "Oh, no. I wouldn't... Too public."

"I'm right here, Del."

"Yes, but you need to sleep, too."

"Okay, so would you sometime consider camping with me? Away from everything so we could sleep out under the stars?"

"Absolutely."

Eli gave her a light, short kiss and cuddled her as close to his body as he could get her. At least with snooping eyes on them. Next time they were alone... Next time it would be right.

Though he had to admit it felt pretty damned right as it was.

Could she *visit Indiana?* Visit, hell. He was damned sure going to do what he could to get her to move to Indiana. With any luck, he would have another month or so to convince her she could, and to give her a promise to make it worth her while.

<h1 style="text-align:center">~ Seventeen ~</h1>

Eli pulled in to her drive just before six and chuckled when she came right out. He went to meet her and again said he would have come to the door, but before he got the words all the way out, her hands were under his denim jacket, around his back, and she gave him a light kiss.

"Good morning to you, too." He squeezed her gently. "You're wide awake for it being so early."

"I'm good with early. Not so much with late. Sorry I drooped so fast last night."

"Don't be. Early works well for farm boys, even though I'm not one, technically."

She slid her hands up to his chest. "You look good."

He laughed. "You're easy to impress." Eli was in old jeans, an old tank top, a flannel shirt, and his denim jacket. Nothing impressive.

"I'm not, actually. I'm very hard to impress."

"But this impresses you?"

"Yes. Much more than suits and ties." She met his lips again.

"Don't tell George that."

"Who?"

"My oldest cousin. The black sheep of the family. Stockbroker or something like that. Has to do with big money, anyway." He rolled his eyes with a grin. "The one who always got all the girls. 'Course, now he has a wife and six little ones, all girls, which I find hilarious since he's already worrying about those girls with the kind of boy he was…"

"Six? Even worse than Trina."

"Yeah, he always did tend to go overboard. Kind of all out there, you know? What you see of him is just what he is. Good guy. I give him a hard time but I respect the hell out of him these days."

"Aren't you? Just what people see."

He shrugged. "I do keep some things to myself. I'm the quiet one of the family."

"Wow."

He laughed and set a hand on her hip. "Was that an insult?"

"Not at all. I just can't imagine..."

"You'll be alright." He caught himself at her curious look but decided to push a bit more. "When you meet them. It'll be fine, Del. I'll be right there and you can hang on to me or tell me to take you away for a few minutes whenever you need."

The look on her face... He couldn't tell what it was. Fear of all those loud people, maybe. Or because it sounded as though he assumed she would go back with him. He supposed he did. She hinted often enough. And he sure as hell didn't want to leave her.

Whatever it was, she'd brushed it off by the time they stopped at the little fishing store to grab licenses and bait and a couple of poles and got to the pond. Daylight was just breaking and he'd hardly set everything on the ground before she gripped his hand and pointed in the distance, across the lake where birds of some kind rose as a group and flew up into a pink-hued dusky blue sky.

"Piping Plovers. They're shore birds that nest in the sand. They're on the endangered list, and we have nearly a third of New Jersey's population of them on the refuge. About 78 percent of the refuge is actually salt marsh, you know. It's the most productive land on earth. Seriously. I know you have some rich farm land back west, but the marsh is super important as feeding grounds and a fish nursery and..." She shrugged. "Not that you wanted to know all of that."

"Why wouldn't I?"

"Trina says I'm showing off when I point out things I know as though I think I'm smarter or something. She hates it." Her voice lowered. "And she says it's why I don't date much, or for long. If it bothers you, you can say so. I'll stop."

"Don't you dare." Eli pulled her face up to his. "I enjoy seeing your enthusiasm for what you love. You don't show it often, and when you do, it's like you're giving me one more little piece of yourself. Don't stop, Delaney. Share anything you want with me, anything you're willing."

She held his gaze with so many thoughts brewing he wished he could pull them out of her head. Finally, he had to ask. "What is it? What are thinking? Or trying not to say?"

"I um..." Her chest rose and fell hard but her gaze remained on him, searching, studying.

He stepped closer. "Tell me what you're thinking."

"Too much to possibly... I don't have near enough words, or the right words, to possibly explain... Eli, I..." She touched his face. And she tried to speak but faltered.

"Yeah. Me too."

Her expression changed to add curiosity.

"Del, I have never in my life even half thought I'd remotely consider leaving home, for good, that I could leave my family. Never. For anyone. And I still..."

"You don't plan to."

"No, but... I don't know. Maybe I would. Would you?"

"Maybe. If it ever came to that. It would have to be worth it, though. Moving... I have trouble just packing for weekend trips. It would be hard..."

"On your nerves."

She nodded, searching his eyes for his reaction.

Eli brushed his nose against hers, lingered, taking her in, letting her decide... And she closed the distance, teasing his lips for what felt like the longest time with a soft hand on his chest, again under his jacket, under his flannel shirt. After a long soft kiss, he moved his lips to her ear. *I would sure as hell try to make it worth it for you.* He didn't say it aloud. Too soon. "So, do you know how to cast?"

"Of course. And I think whoever catches the biggest fish should make the other one clean them all."

"You know how to gut and clean fish? Thought you were only in the rescuing business."

"Rescue can mean a lot of things, Forrester." She gave him a grin and strutted over to claim one of the poles. "All the things I know how to do might surprise you. One benefit of not wanting to ask others for help. You just learn to do it yourself. I'm good at a lot of things."

"Why do I not doubt that at all?" She'd darn sure make a good farm wife type. Not that he had a farm or wanted one. But if small stuff happened at the house, maybe she'd fix it instead of calling him at work like that... He wouldn't go back there. He'd learned that lesson fast. And permanently.

By the time her stomach started to growl, they had stripped to their tank tops in the unseasonable warmth that felt actually hot after the cold March weather and Eli planted kisses on her bare skin now and then. Delaney admired his strong tanned shoulders but made herself behave. They caught plenty of fish of all kinds but none big enough to keep. Eli suggested getting even with the stubborn big fish by finding a couple someone else had already caught and cleaned and let them cook it. He dumped water from a bottle into a bowl, added some soap, let her wash her hands first, did his own, and poured clean water over both.

"You're a regular Boy Scout, aren't you? Well prepared."

"All the way to Eagle, thank you very much, with a community service gold award."

She asked him to explain and stroked a finger down his chest as he talked about how few scouts made it all the way to Eagle and while most community projects consisted of cleaning up a park or building a bench, Eli had organized a fundraiser to rebuild a local amusement park that had burned while sitting vacant due to lack of funds to keep it maintained. He managed to get several local bands to play for free, had an artist friend design a logo and had T-shirts made for $3 each that he sold for $20 each, and got support from every town around plus many businesses, small and big. He'd raised enough with the community's help to restart the park, and in the meantime, drew attention to it from farther away. He'd been seventeen at the time. The park was still thriving.

"I'm impressed again."

"Still not the right time, Del. But so am I. You cast like a pro."

"Well, I had to show off. I do that." She teased with a grin as her stomach growled louder.

"Time to eat." Throwing everything in the mesh holder along the side of the bed, he helped her in with a hand on her rear and took her suggestion for a good fish sandwich.

Eli loved the looks he got when she touched him, casually, but with meaning, on the arm, the face, the stomach when they were in line and someone crowded her, and how she completely shut everyone else out and focused solely on him. He figured Enrique himself could walk past her and she wouldn't even notice.

Maybe that was too far.

They talked about going back to try for bigger fish, but clouds were moving in. Rain clouds, she said. Stratocumulus. It would rain before the day was over. So they opted for a movie and she leaned against him in the dark, in the back row, reacted to his fingers caressing her leg, then her thigh, her inner thigh as he grew more bold and she didn't show any sign of wanting him to pull back. During the love scene, she brushed the backs of her fingers over his chest and he leaned over to kiss her. Her hand ran up around his neck to the back of his head, pulling him in, and she caught his eyes when he inched farther up her thigh.

By the time they left the theater, they were both quiet, both wanting privacy. He didn't have to ask if she felt the same. He could sense it.

Inside the truck, he hesitated. But he had to ask. "If I get a separate room, will you stay with me tonight?"

"Oh, Eli, I wish I could say yes."

"You can say yes. You're of age. It's only your business. We can stop and get your things..."

"No, I can't... If it was just my sister I would, but..."

"Okay. So just home?"

"Don't be angry."

"I'm not angry, Del. I'm nearly forty years old seeing an absolutely beautiful and wonderful woman I'm very much interested in spending more time with and somehow I feel like I'm sneaking around like a kid who should go home and do homework. I'm a little frustrated, but I'm not angry. I can get my own room full time so you can come and go as you please..."

"I can't let you do that. It would be too expensive."

"Hell, I don't care right now. Last night... Damn, it was nice but it was too rushed and ... I want to do better than that."

"It was beautiful, Eli." She stroked his face. "Wasn't it?"

"I just said it was."

"You are angry."

"I'm not." He sucked in a fast deep breath. "I'm not angry, Delaney. And if it wasn't going to rain again, I'd take you right back there. Of course the sleeping bag's still wet..."

She leaned over, far over the console, up on one knee, and gripped his face to pull him in for a kiss. A long, deep, passionate kiss. Damn his lack of control – he couldn't keep his hands off her...

"Mm, hell. Okay." He turned the engine on and told her to get buckled while he could still drive.

She gave him different directions this time. Closer, down a sandy, rocky road. With a barrier blocking it. When he stopped, she got out to move the barrier aside and motioned for him to go through. Then she replaced it and got back in.

"Still trying to get me arrested?"

"I work here. I'm allowed. But no one will know. Go that way."

When he parked where she told him and turned off the engine, Delaney got out again and into the back seat. "There's a lot of room back here for a truck."

"Yeah, I have to haul others..."

"Come here, Forrester. Let's get you unfrustrated."

~ Eighteen ~

Grabbing her handbag, Delaney took a deep breath as she stepped outside to get a break from the closed-in area of her daily work space. The worst part of her job was the windowless room. The more time she spent in it, the more she thought about the possibility of travel writing.

On Sunday, she'd brought up the thought to Eli, admitting to her journalism degree and how she'd thought it was ridiculous to get such a thing when she couldn't make herself use it, but maybe she could. Her credentials would be at least something to put on an article query.

Eli jumped all over the idea. He swore she would be perfect for the job and he asked to see her work. Trouble was, she didn't have any, other than what she'd done for school years ago. By Wednesday, he'd convinced her to let him see that, then, if it was all she had. She still wasn't sure she should have agreed.

Pulling out her phone to turn on while she ate lunch at the staff outdoor area on the other side of the building from East Bay Street, Delaney also pulled out her notebook. She had thoughts of starting with her own area, for practice. And it would give her something to do other than bury her head in her book for the half hour.

The thought of someone possibly asking what she was doing, since almost no one wrote anything with pencil and paper anymore, made her nervous. But it was fine. She was prepared to say she was only putting stuff down she wanted to remember, which was largely true. If she did move with Eli at some point, Delaney at least wanted to have her written details of the small things she noticed, things she loved and things she didn't. They wouldn't ask, though. She'd made it too obvious she was not there to socialize.

Her phone buzzed and she opened it to find Eli's message. All week, he'd been leaving her a message to find during her lunch hour, just *hope you're having a good day* type of messages. She answered with the same.

This one was different: *Wish you had a full hour for lunch today ;-)*

The man had actually typed a winking face. While she tried to figure out what he meant and how to answer, Delaney heard her name and looked over to see another employee telling Eli it was a restricted area.

"He's with me."

"Yeah well, he's not an employee." The guy she recognized but never talked to although he'd tried to flirt a couple of times scanned him.

Hurrying over, Delaney set a hand on Eli's stomach and accepted a kiss on the side of her face. "What are you doing here? You'll never get back to work in time."

He shrugged. "Things are slow. Might take the rest of the day off. Where can we go nearby to eat?" He raised a plastic bag with a luscious smell of fried chicken emanating from it.

"Back of your truck? I don't have time to go far."

With that charming grin and a light nod of the head, Eli offered his arm and escorted her over to where he'd parked around the corner. As soon as they were out of sight of the employee area, he leaned down for a quick kiss. "Damn, I've missed you."

"It's only been ten hours, if that."

"A long ten hours." He winked. "You like fried chicken?"

"Who doesn't?"

"Oh, trust me, Del. I've been yelled at for offering it. You woulda thought I was forcing it down her throat." Yanking the tailgate down, he rolled the tarp back a few notches and helped her up to sit at the edge.

"Sounds like you haven't been treated as well as you should be, either, Forrester. I might have to fix that for you."

Eli pushed himself up onto the tailgate and gave her an ornery smile. "Think you've been doing that already, but I'll take more."

"Gladly." Leaning over the food sitting between them, Delaney gave him a better kiss. "And I missed you, too."

While they ate, he talked some about his job, how it frustrated him that they weren't doing much anymore with so much left to do and it kept getting worse. The thought hurt her stomach. His crew wouldn't be able to stick around if they weren't working enough. It was too expensive. He'd have to leave.

"Hey." He wiped his fingers and reached over to touch her chin. "We have no word of leaving yet, okay? Not even rumors. So all's good for now."

She nodded. For now. But that would change. It was likely to change way too soon.

"And uh, when you have more work I can read, bring it on." Hopping down, he went around to the back door driver's side and returned with a folder. Her folder. Her old school work. "This, Del? This is some really good writing."

"Yeah? You're not just being nice because you kind of like me and all, right?"

He chuckled. "Kind of like you? Okay, then. No, I'm not just being nice. I wanted more of it. Honest to God." He crossed his chest again with a look to the sky.

"Thank you."

Clearing the food stuff away, Eli moved over beside her and kissed her fingers. "That's what you need to be doing, Delaney."

"Yeah, well, I could do it for places around here just fine, but that only goes so far."

"You'll have to travel to be a travel writer."

She nodded. "And it makes my stomach hurt to think about doing that. You have to actually ... get embedded enough to see more than the big tourist trap things."

"Right. Well, you know with my love of talking to people in different places and your way with words, we could make a good team."

"You have a job."

"We can work around that. Long weekends, holidays, and such." He smoothed fingers along her face and into her hair. "Maybe do that kind of thing in colder regions during the warm months and then take a month or so during the winter to run around where it's warm since I don't work much in the winter. We could go wherever you want to write about."

Delaney studied him, his face, his soft voice, the question in his eyes. A good team. They could be. Depending. On a whole lot of things.

"Could you travel with me okay enough?"

She gave him a grin and a soft kiss. "Easily. That would be the easy part."

"Mm, and I hate to say it, but I think I've kept you past your half hour lunch allowance."

"I don't care."

"No?"

"No."

"Good. Then come here a minute." Eli helped her off the tailgate, led her to the side of the truck, and opened the door, blocking the already limited view of the public area of the building. Sitting at the edge of the floorboard, a foot propped on the side rail, he pulled her between his legs.

Delaney rested her arms on his shoulders and leaned in for a kiss. He was cautious, his eyes questioning her, so in answer, she moved in as close as she could get and claimed his mouth. His hands slipped under her blouse to her waist.

"Mm, Del. Don't suppose you can take the rest of the day off, too?"

"Wish I could." She kissed his neck. "But I do have to get back."

"Not gonna get fired for being late, right?"

"No. I'm never late, so I'm sure they'll look past it this once. Just don't think I'll make a habit of it." She stroked the side of his head, his beautiful soft wavy sun-streaked hair.

"Yeah, well, I'm hoping we'll pick up and get too busy again." He lowered his hands to her hips and skimmed her outfit, the dark brown separated skirt that felt more like pants with a dark coral hi-lo blouse, somewhat loose but not too big. "This is a nice look for you. You look good out of your jeans."

"Thank you. Should I pick you up after work this time since you've been doing it the past three days?"

"Well, let me think about that and I'll text you." With a nudge to indicate he was standing up, Eli closed the door behind them and walked her back over to the employee entrance.

"Thanks for lunch. It was better than the sandwich I packed."

Unable to resist, she wrapped her arms up over his shoulders.

He kissed her forehead. "Glad you enjoyed it. Nice to have a non-particular girl."

"And I think I'll make you explain that one later." With a grin, she ran a hand down his chest and backed away. "See you soon." Delaney couldn't make herself say goodbye. She could never make herself say goodbye to him.

Eli stood and watched her until she was inside. In front of her coworkers, she'd hugged him, flirted, ran a hand down his chest. Without getting flustered. They didn't necessarily work with her. It was a big enough place Delaney maybe didn't know them at all. Still, it was nice. A sign of comfort with him? Or with herself? Or just one of her better days?

She'd been far different the past few days, smiling, teasing. They even went to Rhode's Den, where he'd first approached her at the bar, for drinks the night before and she'd looked perfectly okay. Of course, they sat on the patio rather than inside, and that seemed to make a difference. But if she'd been nervous, she'd hid it well.

Maybe they could take another step. Heading back to his truck, Eli pulled out his phone and did some searching. Then he drove over to her house.

Finally, four o'clock came and Delaney grabbed her handbag, so much more than ready to get out the door. She turned her phone on as she paced down the hall, nearly ran into someone and apologized, then realized she'd just apologized like a normal person, without worrying about it.

She felt good the past few days, but beneath it lingered the knowledge that it wouldn't last. Delaney often had a few good days triggered by a good event or a rare good outing. Anyway, at least she was giving Eli that much for now.

At the buzz of her phone to say it was on and ready, she checked for his message. Nothing. She frowned. He was supposed to let her know if she should pick him up or meet him or just go home so he could pick her up. Did something happen? Did he decide to go back to work and... No. He said he was taking the day off. Maybe he got bored, though. He might have... They'd already lost a couple of rescue people during cleanup due to accidents. He couldn't...

Stop. Just stop. He's fine.

Her heart had started to race again and she forced it to calm. He was fine.

Telling herself he was did little to actually calm her sudden nerve flare-up, until she got to her car. Delaney stood staring. Rose petals were scattered along her dash and a single long stem red rose was propped against her steering wheel. Inside her car. How did he get inside her car? The doors were locked. She tested it to be sure. Locked. Who was he? Houdini?

Delaney fumbled with her keys, got it unlocked, and picked up the rose to inhale its sweet scent. Her eyes moistened. Yes, maybe she would have to move with him when he went home.

Inside, she found a sticky note: Go on home, Baby. I'll meet you there.

Home. Home ... was wherever Eli was.

With another slow inhale of the rose, Delaney gathered herself enough to be able to drive, glad it wasn't far, and that he'd be there before long.

Her breath caught when she pulled onto her street. He was there already. Pulling in, she checked his truck. Not there. Not on the porch. He wouldn't have... Forcing herself to stay calm, Delaney grabbed her rose along with her handbag and made her way inside. "Trin?"

"Well, there she is." Trina nearly hopped into the front hall. "Aw. How pretty, Laney." She tilted the rose to smell it.

"Where's Eli?"

"Living room. Entertaining Tammy and Paulie. Wow, Laney, he's a real sweetheart. Why didn't you say so?"

Her gut twisted. "What have you said to him?"

Trina shrugged. "Nothing, really. Why?"

"Did he just get here?"

"No, he's been here, oh, half hour or so. Maybe more. Definitely more."

Delaney shoved a hand through her hair and veered around her sister to the living room. He was sitting on the floor with the six- and seven-year-olds on either side of him building something with Paulie's erector set.

"Hey." She crept in farther, wondering how worried she should be, how much *nothing, really* Trina had said.

He looked up and smiled, a sweet smile. "Hey, yourself."

"Why are you here so early?"

"Had nowhere else to be. And your sister invited me, after I begged her for your spare key. She wasn't so sure about that one."

Her spare key.

"I also invited him for Easter dinner this Sunday since you hadn't yet, and he already agreed." Trina plopped into the chair beside Eli as though they were old friends.

Excusing himself from the kids, Eli got up. No jeans and tee. He was in gray khakis and a dark green collar shirt, the sleeves rolled.

"Look at you. What's the occasion?"

He grinned. "I'm hoping you'll agree to a nice sit down dinner for a change?"

Sit down. In a restaurant, not take-out or buffet-style, but an actual restaurant. She cringed, but only a light cringe.

Taking her side, he set a light kiss on her head. "Hope it's okay that I'm here."

She shrugged, since, what else could she do or say? "Thank you." Delaney nodded toward the rose. "That was sweet."

"You're welcome. So. Dinner? I'll wait if you want to change, but you look great already."

Debating between wanting a few minutes to freshen up and not wanting to leave him in the madhouse alone any longer, she told him she'd be back in a minute, told Tammy to stop badgering him to come back and play, and touched his arm a second before she went to the kitchen to put her rose in water and then up to her room, first to breathe in the silence and then to change her top to something nicer that hadn't already been worn all day. She also switched out of her work flats and into a pair of her heels, ones that matched the pale green blouse she'd put on that was made of ridiculously soft, flowing fabric. With a quick bathroom stop, she brushed her hair out, then added a small barrette to hold part of it back at her nape since she'd had it back all day and it showed that she did.

Breathe, Delaney. Just breathe.

With her eyes closed, she took a couple of deep breaths, and went down to him.

Eli wondered if it was a mistake going to her house, talking with her sister, and accepting the dinner invitation without Delaney being there. He'd only meant to show her it was fine, he could deal with her family's chaos, since he wanted her to deal with his. Her reaction said she didn't appreciate it, though. Too soon, maybe. Too impetuous, Bill always told him. *Slow it down, kid. Stop acting like your pants are on fire.*

Could be Bill was right. It did tend to get him in trouble. On the other hand, it was nice to get to know Trina somewhat, and the little ones. He had a whole different feeling about them from what Delaney said than he had now. They were a tad undisciplined, granted. But they were sweet-natured, as was their mother, even if she was a bit too emotional. And Trina did adore her little sister. It was impossible to miss and hard for Eli not to let that influence his opinion of her.

When Delaney came back, he stood again to meet her. She'd fixed herself up more, although it wasn't needed, and he gave her a smile. A beautiful girl, even if she didn't think so.

"I hope they weren't getting on your nerves." Her shoes clicked lightly as she came to him.

"Nope. Not at all." He set a hand on her back and kissed her head. "Ready?" She gave Trina a quick goodbye and almost yanked him out the door away from them.

"Whoa, Del. What's the rush?"

She looked wary. "Are you sure they weren't annoying you?"

"That's nothing. Just kids being kids. I'm well used to it."

"Really? Because they're..."

"Kids." He shrugged. "Weren't you and Trina wild and messy when you were young?"

"No. Mom would've locked us in our room. We wouldn't dare have acted like that. You said your mom doesn't take that, either, right?"

"Uh, I said she doesn't take flak from anyone. We got away with a hell of a lot, though, just kid stuff, nothing major. Kids have to be kids while they are. Once we grew, we knew better and we wouldn't disrespect her for anything." He tilted his head at her. "You really think they're abnormally rotten?"

"Compared to us? Yes."

"That's kind of sad." Eli had to wonder if that was part of her issue, that she'd been forced too much into herself. Of course, Trina was not nearly the same. That girl was more outgoing than he was himself. So it couldn't be only that. "It's okay, though. Hang around me long enough and I'll help bring the wild, rotten kid out of you."

"Don't count on that. That kind of behavior gets too much attention. I told you before, you know, that I'm not the girl for you."

"Yeah, well, I kinda think you're wrong on that count, Delaney. And I intend to prove it to you." He gave her a quick, soft kiss, then led her to his truck and helped her in.

Normal kid stuff. She was too stodgy, is what he meant. Too reserved or prudish. But she had to be. Childish behavior got too much attention, attention she could not deal with. Maybe what she'd meant was she wouldn't be able to deal with him if he got too outlandish, too attention-seeking. Like dancing in front of a diner to music too young for them. How did she ask him not to do it without taking too much wind from his sails? And she liked the wind in his sails, loved his outgoing, friendly nature. She did. But how was she supposed to deal with it?

"So I found a place out by the lighthouse I'm dying to try and I'm dragging you with me. Sound okay?"

"What is it?"

"Daymark. Supposed to be a nautical term of some kind. Looks light and open inside."

"You found it?"

"Yep. Phone search."

"Trina's favorite place. You just happened to pick that?"

"I'll admit I did ask her about it. I was looking at a couple of them and she steered me that direction."

"You know it's on the more expensive side?"

"Don't care, Del. Like I said, I want to enjoy the place while I'm here, and the way I figure, I'm giving back some of what I'm making."

"Still going to be able to pay your bills back home?" She felt herself flush at his grin. "Sorry. Not my business. I just... We've been going out a lot."

"Yeah, I'm good. Don't worry. About tonight, either."

Eli loved the place. It was casual, but nice, light-colored and open like the beach during the day. Delaney said it was nice and she said her food was wonderful, but she was quiet. Even when they went out to the lighthouse to amble along the shore – and the sight of her dressed so nice with her skirt-pants swaying in the light breeze, her heels carried by their straps in one hand, had him thinking far too impetuous thoughts – she was quiet.

He was waiting for her to ask more about the *unparticular girl* comment, as she said she would, but she either forgot or decided not to ask. Since he was far too curious himself not to ask, Eli took her hand and led her down to the wood rail wall holding the sand back where they could rest their feet on the stones below, just out of the water, and spread the blanket over just enough area to keep it off her clothes and soften the narrow rail.

By now, the soft swish of waves rolling up onto the sand and receding was familiar enough he wasn't too bothered. If he had to, he could deal with the place long term. And if she wouldn't move, he was thinking more and more that he might.

"So, I have to ask." Eli stroked hair from her face. "What's the story with you and the temp worker?"

Her eyes shot to his. "Trina."

"Yeah, I wasn't prying..."

"What did she say?"

"Only that she was surprised you even talked to me, considering your last adventure, as she called it."

Delaney got up and walked away.

Hell. Grabbing the blanket, he followed. "Del, wait up." He

grasped her hand.

"And you wonder why I didn't want you there. She never knows when to keep her mouth shut."

"Okay, but, hey, I'm not..."

She walked away again.

Eli followed for some time and then caught up and walked beside her for some time, until she slowed down. With a fast rise and fall of her chest, she lowered onto the sand, her knees pulled up in front, her arms wrapped around them. He took her side, facing her, and waited.

"He worked at the same place I did, not where I am now, but a trucking center. I was in admin and he was in logistics." Her voice was soft, her eyes out on the Atlantic. "He'd been there a few weeks and always smiled as we passed in a hallway or something, and always came over to talk to me if he caught me in the break room, until I finally went out with him. He said he'd just moved to the area and always talked like he meant to stay. Usually, we just went to Lefty's to hang out, no big deal. I still had the house to myself then and he started asking if we could hang out there because his place wasn't company ready yet. I thought that was kind of odd, but bachelor's, you know, or what I've heard about bachelor pads made me think he possibly didn't care about having it company ready."

She grabbed another deep breath and waited while a couple walked past. "Okay, so I was stupid and I walked right into it. He was there for a temp job and he wouldn't go out and about anywhere with me, including out here, because now and then his wife and kids would come visit and hang out on the beach. Of course he hadn't bothered to tell me he had a wife and kids."

"Ouch."

"Yeah. I should've known, right? We went out for about three months. I finally found out because I turned the corner at the office and heard him laughing with his buddies about his quiet little beach girl who hadn't figured out yet that he wasn't staying, not that I'd say anything to anyone, anyway, since I didn't talk much, which he liked just fine. The really stupid thing is that he wasn't the first one. The other wasn't married, just didn't bother to say he was only there for the summer. Guys looking for summer flings. They're everywhere

here. They don't give a shit how much they have to lie, either." Her voice was shaky and she got up to walk again.

Eli walked by her side without saying anything to give her time to unwind first. When she stopped, looking up at the lighthouse with its large light turning in circles above their heads, he risked touching her face.

"So. It's not like I'm not used to it." She shrugged. "I still mean what I said, though." Delaney looked him in the eye with determination atop her past pain she tried to hide. "It will always matter, Eli. This. Us. Even if you... He was never that big a deal. I just feel stupid that I couldn't see it. But this..."

"You're not stupid." He cupped the hand behind her head and moved close in front of her. "Delaney, you're not stupid. He's just a huge jackass. I've had my share of those, too, but no, I don't blame myself for someone else's stupidity or selfishness and you shouldn't, either."

"I only blame myself for not seeing it."

"You shouldn't, though. And..." His shook in resignation. "I guess now I get what my family's been trying to tell me."

"About the particular girl?"

"Yeah. Trust me, I was far more naive with her. Even moved her in with me. Nearly two years. She had the wool pulled all the way over my eyes, despite the warnings from family and friends who I just figured couldn't see her the way I did. They were right. Lesson learned the hard way."

"What did she do?"

"She spread shit about me. Fully untrue stuff. When we were together, she was all sweet and loving. No sign she was anything but happy. But if she got pissed at me, about any little thing, she'd go run her mouth anywhere she was. Some of the stuff she said, completely made up, but..." He shoved a hand through his hair. "I still run across it at times and have to set the record straight. Not everyone believes me, of course. She was a hell of a good liar. I mean, top professional kind of liar."

"Wow. I don't even... Why would anyone do that?"

"Got me. She's some kind of psycho."

"I'm sorry." She ran fingers along his stomach, the backs of her fingers. "And then you have to deal with me and my... Not really fair to you, is it?"

He grinned and lowered his face close to hers. "You know, Del, I'd much rather see what it is I'm up against straight out than to think everything is what it isn't. You're fine."

"But, you realize those things you like to do, like dance in front of diners to music you're too old for, and be in the middle of crowds, and talk to everyone you meet..."

"Yeah, I get it." He brushed his lips against hers. "We'll work around it, Del. Just, maybe, if you get ticked at me about anything, tell *me* and not everyone else in the world, yeah?"

"Because I would be able to do that?"

He chuckled. "Well, I guess there is that. Wait. What do you mean music I'm too old for?" He backed up with a teasing scornful look. "There's no music on earth I'm too old for."

"Really? Those kids outside the diner would argue."

"What do they know? They're still kids." When she smiled, a relaxed, genuine smile, Eli took her hand and led her back to the wood rail wall, stepped over the edge onto the rocks, spread the blanket out, and lowered to sit against the wall, beckoning her to sit with him.

She grasped his hand. "You're okay here?"

"Yep. With you, I am." He kissed her head and wrapped an arm around her.

Delaney brought her knees up, turned his direction to rest on top of his thigh, and lay her head on his shoulder. "I want you to know I never thought I'd be able to tell you about..."

"Thinking I'm too old for teenie music?"

She chuckled. "Well, maybe that, too, but I mean about my ex, with as embarrassing as it is. I... It's getting so much easier to talk to you than ... even to Trina, really. I'm not sure how, but it is."

Eli's stomach tightened, a nice joyful exquisite tightening, and he pulled her face gently up to his. "I'm glad, Del. You don't need to be worried about embarrassment around me. It's all good. We all do stupid things and we all have those moments. Doesn't matter."

With a soft kiss, she set her head back against his shoulder and her body heaved in a deep sigh. Of contentment, he hoped.

Nineteen

She woke to a knock on her door. Not *her* door. The front door. Then the doorbell. A glance to her side told her it was five a.m. On a Monday.

Delaney jumped up and slipped her old robe on. Heading down the stairs, she heard a gruff voice. Pat. Telling someone to leave.

"Just get her for me or I'll go up there." Eli.

"Like *hell* you will. Just because you spent the day in my house yesterday doesn't mean you can..."

"*My* house, Pat. Not yours." Delaney rushed to interfere and opened the door farther. "Hey. What's wrong?"

His face, shadowed with overnight hair growth, softened as he turned to her. He was dressed for work. "Morning, Del. Can I come in?"

"Of course..."

"Do you know what *time* it is?" Pat half blocked them.

She straightened and met his stare. "Do you know that besides the fact this is still *my* house, I'm *not* sixteen and you're *not* my father?"

"Wouldn't want to be."

"Something we agree on. I have the door. You can go back to bed." She saw the shock on his face, but Delaney stood her ground, dismissed him, and took Eli's hand. "Sorry about that. Do you want coffee? I'll make some..."

"No, I don't have long. I tried to call you last night, but there was no answer."

"My phone is off at night. What's wrong? Your family? Did something happen?"

"Nothing like that." He slid a hand through her hair. "My crew is being sent down south for a few weeks. Big job there, South Carolina. High rise work."

A huge *NO* welled up inside, but Delaney managed to hold it down. "You have to go?"

"Or quit, which I did consider, but it's my crew and I can't leave them hanging with no warning."

"No, of course." A few *weeks.* "You're leaving soon?"

"About now. Delaney..." He moved in and ran a hand down her arm, over her old robe. "I'm sorry. I bitched about the short notice but they'd tried to reach me all day yesterday. Didn't feel like answering when I was with you and your family, on Easter. I um... They're going back to Indiana after this job. Too much they won't let us do here and we're spending too much time spinning our wheels..."

"You're not coming back." Her eyes moistened, but she managed to hold herself together. It had to come. The morning after he spent the day with her family, with Trina talking too much and Pat being so rude and Delaney refusing to let him stay over, because of the kids, and because she didn't want the comments. Hard to believe it was a coincidence. "Okay." She heard herself say it. Calm. Controlled. Unemotional. Just okay. And it was. It was fine. Easier to just end it there...

"Come in July for the reunion. Will you? I'll be home by then."

"Why?"

He tilted his head. "What do you mean, why?"

"Eli, it's okay. I did expect it." She leaned in to kiss his cheek. Not his lips. He smelled incredible, like he'd showered and...

"You're taking this as a break up."

"Isn't it?"

"No. Del, no. I can't abandon my crew, and I can't afford to quit without a backup. I have plans, things I want to do..."

"I get it. It's fine. You didn't mean to be here long. I knew that..."

"Stop brushing me off and tell me you'll come to Indiana. Or come to South Carolina on a long weekend or even for a week or so. You have vacation days, right?"

"Not enough for both, and..."

"Fine, then I'll get up here when I can while we're still along the coast and you can save your time for Indiana. Will you come?"

"I don't travel alone."

"I'll come get you, then."

"From Indiana, just after you get home? Don't be ridiculous. It's ... how far?"

"About thirteen hours, but I mean I'll come back here when they head home. I'll take a short leave of absence and we can go together. Just to meet my family for now. I won't ask for more than that until you see the place and meet everyone. See if you think you can be comfortable there. I know it matters. Tell me you'll at least come check things out."

Delaney hesitated. He could say now that he'd come back for her, when it was still new, when they'd been together so often, before he had time to think...

He gripped her hard around the waist and claimed her mouth. His tongue caressed hers, teasing, as he untied her barely-tied belt and slid his free hand inside her robe. The strong long beautiful fingers made their way up from her stomach to her rib cage.

She dug her nails into his arms to keep hold and he released her lips. "Del." His voice was hoarse, light, firm. "This is not a breakup. I am not like that other guy. I plan to call you every chance I get, no matter the time. Keep your phone on. Answer it. At work, too. Just tell them your boyfriend is crazy possessive and missing you and needs to be able to stay in touch." He moved his mouth to her neck. "Say you will, Delaney. And tell me you'll come home with me."

"Yes. I'll leave it on. And I'll answer no matter the time."

"And you'll come home with me?"

"Mm, well. How about you ask again in a couple of weeks?" That would give him time to think. She'd give him that before she'd let herself think this could be more than temporary. "If you haven't changed your mind by then, ask again and I'll agree to at least visit. As long as you don't find another girl in South Carolina and decide to take her home, of course. I wouldn't want to..."

"Not gonna happen. Two weeks. I will ask you again in two weeks, so be ready for that." Eli moved both hands to her back, under her robe, over her shirt, and gave her a deep kiss. "Just don't be surprised if my family and my buddies do what they can to help me convince you to stay."

"And you really think this quiet little beach girl would do okay in the middle of cornfields surrounded by your big family?"

"Well, first of all, we'd have our own place. You're not the only one who owns a house, and mine isn't crowded. So, you'd only be surrounded during event-type things and not otherwise. Second, I think you'll do fine with them and I know they'll just love you. Third ... well, if it doesn't work out for you, don't think I won't be willing to take you somewhere that will. Okay?"

Her eyes moistened as she held his gaze. "You're getting pretty serious here, Forrester. Be careful with that. Because I may have agreed to be your New Jersey fling, but I'm not moving without damned good reason. Just so you know."

"I wouldn't expect otherwise, and you're not a fling, Del, not close." He gave her another semi-deep kiss and started to back away. "I have to go. Damn, I don't want to."

"I'll be here."

"Hm, you better be, and it might sound bad, but I'm really just as glad right now you're not the social butterfly type so I have to worry less about guys hitting on you while I'm not here to deal with it."

Delaney ran fingers through his beautiful hair. "Don't worry. I'll likely go back to my baggy clothes because I'll be too busy pouting to care how I look."

He kissed her nose. "You're still beautiful that way."

"And you're stalling."

"Yes, ma'am, I am." With another kiss, he slid his hands away from her body to capture her fingers and stepped backward. "I've gotta go, baby. I'll call when I get there."

"You better." She felt her whole system cringe when he released her. "Be careful when you're up there with the birds."

He grinned. "Always. And you ... don't let anyone screw with you or get to you. Think of me right there at your side and call when you need, or when you want. If I'm up with the birds, I won't be able to answer, so don't worry, but I'll call back. Just know I will call back and hang in there till I do. Okay?"

"Yes. It's fine. I'm fine, really."

He set his palm against her cheek. "You're beautiful, and maybe the strongest damned person I've ever known in my life. Remember that, too." Eli kissed her forehead and opened the door. "Oh, nearly forgot. I want to trade you iPods until I come back."

"Why?"

"Because your music is part of you. What you love says something about you." He closed in again and wrapped her in his arms. "Let me that far in, Delaney. I know it's hard for you, but take that step with me."

Her iPod? She had odd things on it, at least what he would think is odd. Spanish guitar. Ricky Martin, which he'd laugh about. Old stuff like Captain & Tennille. A lot of Richie Sambora. And ... classical. Fauré and Sorozábal ... to even the Lone Ranger soundtrack. And Mary Poppins. He'd think she was a real fruitcake.

"Delaney." He brushed a hand through her hair, her hair that was probably messy, along with the fact she was wearing no makeup and dressed in her old robe, and...

And he didn't care. He still looked at her the same as when she was dressed well. And at least she didn't have the Spice Girls. She didn't think he was crazy for that, no matter his age. She thought it was adorable. Fully, utterly, charmingly adorable. How could she refuse him her quirks? "It's in my room away from where a kid will grab it. You can come up."

"Should I take my boots off?"

"Not if you can't stay." She took his hand and led him up the old worn-in-the-middle wood stairs.

Delaney was nervous about letting him inside her room, but if she was going to agree to share her whole music list, him seeing her room was nothing. It was ... bland, really. Nothing to see. And maybe that would turn him off, but she was who she was and he'd have to deal with that.

Or not.

Eli didn't look at her room at all that she could tell. He closed the door, scooped her up, and lay her on the bed. With a glint in his eyes, he eased her robe away from her body.

"You said you couldn't stay." Delaney caressed fingers through his hair.

He grinned at her T-shirt. "Bon Jovi?"

"Um, yeah, it's ... old. I bought it second-hand years ago."

"They're from here, right?" He pushed the shirt up over her

stomach.

"Yes. Close... You said..."

"Why didn't you get one from a concert?" His thumbs swept lightly over her.

"Haven't been to one. Eli, you said you can't..."

"I can't stay." He leaned down and kissed her again, lifting her up with him, and stripped her of her robe, and the shirt. "But I'm damned well going to, since we actually have a bed for a change. And because I'm pissed about having to leave you."

"You'll get fired."

"Doubt it." He kissed her neck. "They should have given us more warning, and they know we're all pissed they didn't, so they'll give us some leeway." He stood and pulled his shirt off, pushed his jeans down to the floor, and kicked out of his boots. "Besides, along with being the crew boss, I'm their any height man. No limits." He came back to her. "They kinda need me."

"So do I. Lock the door." Delaney whispered. As he did, she slipped out of her underwear and lay back against her pillow, enjoying his grin as he came to her.

Eli reluctantly redressed as he watched her get back into her robe. Damn he didn't want to leave. But he wasn't ready to quit, either. Of course he could find a job locally, but then he'd have to have a place to stay and pay it himself and ... it was too soon for that, and he didn't want to stay in New Jersey. He wanted to take Delaney to Indiana, to open spaces, to where there were fewer people everywhere she went, and see if it would help her.

She stroked a finger down his chest. "I'll walk you down."

"Del, the music. It's what I came up here for, remember?"

"Is it?"

"You thought it was an excuse?"

"Possibly. I don't mind."

"You're beautiful." He brushed her lips. "It wasn't. And I didn't intend to stay. Just couldn't help myself when I saw you and the bed in the same room. It was nice here, too."

"Hm." She slid her arms around him. "More than nice." With a soft kiss, she backed up again and went to her dresser, returning with a tiny square iPod. "This is all I have. Not really a fair exchange since you're giving me a big one."

He chuckled. "Are we still talking music equipment?"

She blushed slightly as she caught his meaning.

"Let's just say I'm glad for you to have it, whichever you want to take that to mean. But I have to go." He grasped her fingers and walked with her down the stairs and out to the porch. "Take care of yourself, Del. Damn, I'm going to miss you."

"Me too. And by the way, I am impressed. Right time yet?"

"Absolutely right."

She gave him a light, teasing kiss and backed away, calm, in control. Making it too easy. He was glad not to have a scene, but she could have looked just a tad bit more like it bothered her.

Delaney stood at the door until the taillights of his truck faded out of sight. With a sigh, she closed and locked it and considered taking the day off work and trudging out to the store for an expensive bottle of wine and a pint of super chocolately ice cream with a jar of maraschino cherries to top it off. She supposed she wouldn't. If she was going to go to his reunion, she'd need to save her days.

"What in the hell are you doing?"

She jumped at the booming voice behind her.

Pat descended. "My *children* are in this house. You can't bring your *lovers* in here, in the broad daylight..."

"They're asleep, unless you just woke them. Keep your voice down." She tried to move around him as her face got hot.

He grabbed her arm. "That's totally inappropriate..."

"Why? You don't sleep with your wife in the house with your children here?" She wanted to punch him right in the mouth.

"My *wife*. See the difference? And at night, not..."

"Not your business, Pat." She yanked her arm away. "I didn't do anything in front of them and they are still asleep." Delaney headed up the stairs.

"You know he's using you for how easy you are."

She swung back. "Easy? First I'm cold and now I'm easy?"

"Sleeping with him already. *Easy.* And he's not coming back. That was the oldest excuse in the book. *Have to leave for work.* Right now. And you fell for it. It was a *lie.*"

"That's not true."

"No? Cade down at the store heard them talking at that bar they hang out in. Looking for easy pickups while they were in town. Your boy there was with them, planning it just like the rest. You were temporary amusement to him. Again. How 'bout the next lost puppy you pick up, you don't bring home? Do it somewhere else."

"Don't talk to me that way." She heard her voice shake and saw him gloat at her nervousness, which pissed her off. *"Don't* talk to me that way. And if you don't like it, you can get out of *my* house. Because it is *my* house, not *yours*, and I'll bring in whoever I want *whenever* I want. Don't like it, *get out.* Just *go.*"

"Delaney?" Trina's confused voice filtered down the stairs. "You want us out?"

A huge pit twisted her stomach as she turned to her older sister who was always much more like a little sister, the emotional, sensitive little girl who always wanted everything to be right and everyone happy. And it showed all over her. But it also made her trust this jerk when she shouldn't have.

Trina crept close, her voice low. "Laney, tell me. You want us out?"

"Trin..." She couldn't tell her. Staring into those watery green eyes, Delaney couldn't do it. "It was just an argument. Forget it. Eli just left, going out of state, and I'm..."

"Out of state?"

She explained briefly.

"Oh honey, I'm so sorry. He was such a cutie. Wish he'd stayed around longer, but you did know it was temporary. You said as much. Don't take it out on Pat, okay? It's alright, honey. We understand. Don't we, sweetie?" She wrapped a hand around his arm. "Come. I'll make us all breakfast. It's early, isn't it?"

"Too early to be up." Delaney gave her sister a light hug. "You know you can stay as long as you need. I'm... I'm going back to bed." Holding her tongue so hard it nearly gagged her, she hurried up the stairs, closed the door, and flopped back down on the bed where Eli had just been. Not coming back. Knew it was only temporary. No. It didn't feel temporary. He wanted her to go with him to Indiana, to see his family. He had a house. They'd have a place of their own.

They'd talked about it? Which meant they were talking about her. Being used. Again. How many of them? Cade had a loud mouth.

Delaney clenched her eyes and rolled into a ball. Oh Eli, no. Please.

Please.

How could she go back into town? To the hardware store she'd helped support while buying stuff for the cleanup, the extra gloves, the big garbage bags, the tough ones to hold heavy stuff, the hoes and shovels she shared and sometimes lost to have to get more... How could she go back? Or anywhere they might be, whoever *they* were who knew, as though it wasn't already hard enough to be out. She'd have to go to the huge warehouse-like store instead, but she hated them. They made her cave in on herself. Still, it would be better than having to face the looks, the comments. Would they comment? Cade might.

Maybe when Eli called, she'd say yes and lock him into taking her to Indiana just to prove them wrong. *If* he called. Just in case, she turned her phone on. It buzzed. Twice. Once to say it was on. Next... a message she'd missed. Flipping it open, Delaney cringed. He'd called already.

"Hey Del, just wanted to apologize for running out so fast. Okay, not true. I wanted to hear your voice. Hope you went back to sleep. I'll call later." A pause. "And I uh ... damn, I can't do it through a message, so ... I'll call later. Have a good day, okay?" Another light pause and the phone clicked.

He couldn't do what through a message? Was Pat right? Was he going to tell her he wasn't coming back? It didn't sound like that. It sounded friendly. Or ... laughing. Was he laughing at how he'd fooled her? Why would he want to hear her voice? To enjoy it more than if he did it by message?

"*Stop* it, Delaney. Just *stop*." Putting the phone down, she turned to the other side and tried to go back to sleep. She could still get an hour in before her alarm would wake her for work. Couldn't do what over the phone? Maybe she should call him back. But he'd said he would call. He was driving maybe or talking with his coworkers. Explaining why he was late. Would he? He wouldn't tell them… He could just say he'd stopped to tell her and leave it at that. He wouldn't say more.

Or he would. Particularly if Pat was right. He'd brag about it.

What did it matter? They were all going away, down south and then home to Indiana. No one here would know anything actually happened between them. They could guess but they wouldn't know. If Eli didn't talk too loud or in front of the wrong people.

He wouldn't. Damn. Would he? Of course he wouldn't, after the way he talked about that girl who said stupid stuff about him. Of course, a lot of people accused others of doing what they did themselves. It happened. She'd seen it often enough. Did he have her fooled just like the last one?

Pulling the pillow over her head, she tucked herself back into a ball. He had her iPod. He had to return it. He would be back. Unless he wanted it for extra ammunition to make fun of her. But he'd left his. Maybe. Maybe it was an old one that didn't work and…

She got up again and turned the thing on. It seemed to work, at least. Fumbling for her headphones, she plugged them in and hooked them in her ears. It worked. She scrolled through his list. A ton of music.

Half falling back on her bed, she made herself get up enough to get under the covers and lay listening to his music on shuffle. She had to sleep. Focusing on the lyrics, on Eli's smile, his hugs … she felt herself drifting off.

He would be back. It felt far too real for him to not come back. She had to believe in him. He deserved that much.

~ Twenty ~

Eli shifted his truck into gear and cursed himself for starting to say too much. Not for starting to say it, but for waiting, for not saying it before he left as he nearly had. He'd always thought men who claimed it was hard to say were just pansies. Personally, he'd never felt it, not like this. He never expected to feel it and be afraid ... not afraid. Cautious. It was too soon.

Or he was more pansy than he wanted to admit.

After all, he could have fought harder to stay. Other companies were hiring. He could have taken one of them up on it so he could stay with her. Then what? Go home where people would know he'd ditched his company? One owned by a local family guy who had worked his way up from nothing and now employed just as many others as he could, including boys to mow the grass and run errands. Even with profits down, he'd kept his staff working. Eli couldn't ditch him.

At times, he thought about moving to a big city where he had more chance to work on skyscrapers and walk across the beams like tightropes. The only problem was, while he loved the temporary excitement of big cities, he did not want to move to one. He was more a hit it hard short term and then back off to recharge kind of a guy.

And he didn't want to be away from his family and have to miss the get-togethers. It wasn't something he'd give up easily.

Neither was Delaney.

Of course, the big family meals could be a drawback for her.

He needed to call her again. Checking his watch, he decided she would be on her way to work and he didn't want to call while she was driving. He'd wait until she was at work and leave a voicemail. Play a game of phone tag. For fun. Just to tease. Maybe he'd give hints about what he wanted to say, or what he didn't want to say, with each message. How? That could be a puzzle, but he liked puzzles.

He supposed that could be why he was so pulled to Delaney. The girl was definitely a puzzle. An earthy-airy, hidden-open, sexy-subtle grounded but set off from others puzzle. How could he not love that?

Delaney chuckled at his newest message. *All's well that doesn't end. Will call back soon.* He was a goofball. Seriously a goofball. But he made her laugh and that hadn't happened in ... since sometime before she'd lost her parents. No one she'd dated made her laugh. His first message only left her puzzled, the second raised her eyebrows. *To climb or not to risk the fall is always the real question. Will call back soon.* Definitely a goofball. And Pat was definitely wrong.

He kept calling during her "closet" hours, as he called them, when she was in the back filing everything she'd organized earlier. Delaney had told him her method, the routine she didn't break. One hour organizing, fifty minutes filing, five minutes briefing her manager, and the other five minutes for herself. He could easily call during her five minutes, or even during her organizing time since she could sneak in a call as she worked. So he was playing a game.

She didn't mind games, as long as they were fun, interesting, intellectual, not just childish. Or mean. Delaney didn't think Eli had a mean bone anywhere in him. And she missed him already, which was ridiculous since she never got to see him during weekdays anyway.

If he wanted to play games, she would play along.

During her next five minutes, she called him back, hoping to get his voicemail. He answered, but she was prepared. "Hey, can't talk. But you're not as cute as you think you are. Call later." With a grin, she forced herself to hang up, although she wanted to hold him on the phone since she had him.

Thinking back over her message as she worked, Delaney got that panicky feel in the pit of her stomach. It was a stupid message. Insulting. She'd thought it was cute when she came up with it; now ... he'd think she was an idiot, or trying to play a game she wasn't equipped to win, or to even give him a run for his money. He was too naturally charming and funny. She wasn't. She tried, but it always came out as trying too hard.

When five o'clock neared, the panic increased. He hadn't called again. Hadn't left another message. She could turn her phone off.

Pretend the battery died. Say she had to work late. She wouldn't. Any of it. Maybe her comment wasn't funny. Maybe it was kind of moronic. But it wasn't mean and he would at least know she meant to be funny. It was in her voice. She heard it herself. He would have had to hear it.

Her phone rang as she walked out the door and despite her nerves, she jumped to answer. "Hey." Delaney realized she'd already picked up his habit of saying hey, which she never did. "Did you run out of sayings to butcher?"

"What?"

She cringed at Trina's voice. The only time her sister called the minute Delaney left work was when she wanted something. "Thought you were Eli. What do you need?"

"Eli? Didn't he leave?"

"He's been calling today."

"More than once?"

"All day." A slight exaggeration but close enough.

"Why?"

Delaney rolled her eyes as she reached for her keys against a strong gust of wet wind. "Because he misses me. What do you need?"

The silence told her Trina was trying to figure out whether to believe her, or why he would miss her already. "Um, would you pick up 7-Up and juice on your way home? Tracie is throwing up all over the place and I can't leave her."

Wonderful. Delaney hoped she hadn't been close enough to the girl to get it. "Why doesn't Pat stop for it?"

"He's already home."

"So? He can't go back out?"

"He's had a long day and..."

"Really, Trina? Are you serious? She's his kid."

"Fine. I'll wash the puke off and leave the poor kid and go myself..."

"Forget it. I'll stop. But remember, I'll be at the refuge for a couple of hours first."

An audible sigh passed through the line. "You can't forget that for one night?"

"So Pat doesn't have to go back out? No. I'll grab it on my way home. Best offer. Give her water until then. That's better for her, anyway. Bye, Trina." *What a useless, pathetic father,* Delaney mumbled to herself as she got into her car and tossed her phone on the passenger seat. She'd stay single forever before she did that to herself. Would Eli go back out to get whatever his child needed? She thought he would. She thought he might do darned near anything for those he loved.

Except stay.

Of course that wasn't fair to ask. And he never said he did.

A beep on her phone made her want to throw it out her window. Trina again? Begging? No, it would have come through. A message. Delaney started the car to let it warm and checked. Eli. He had called as soon as she got off.

"Uh oh, I wasn't prepared for a message. Thought you'd answer. You're off now, right? So um... Sorry, kinda tired from the early morning and travel, so nothing not cute. Call when you get a chance. I'm off the rest of the night and already bored as hell and wishing you were here. Going to the refuge? Talk later."

Nothing not cute. Was that a slam? He didn't sound happy.

Delaney started to call him back but the car was running and she didn't talk on her cell while driving so she decided to get to the refuge first and talk to him while she worked, for as long as he wanted.

By the time she parked and called back, he didn't answer. She supposed he could be in the shower ... and the thought of him in the shower made her want to be there with him. He had another roommate, she expected, maybe the same roommate always there playing loud games on his laptop, or a different one who liked to be out and they could have the place alone...

A message. Should she leave one? "Um, well, I guess I expected you to pick up, too. I'm here working but call back and work with me. If you want." She nearly said "Love you" but luckily caught herself. And she was flustered as she hung up without being sure how she did end the call.

Listening to the message, Eli wished he'd taken his phone with him. But last time he'd done that, he'd dropped the thing in the toilet and had to get a new one. Besides, that was too intimate for where they were. Or too disturbing. He knew men who talked and peed at the same time. Hell, he even knew women who did, but he'd been totally turned off by it when one did it to him.

At her voice, he grinned. "Is this live or is it Memorex?"

"What?"

"You know, that commercial."

"Oh. I don't ... guess I don't remember it. Nice to hear your actual voice, though. How was the drive?"

"Long. The guy who rode with me didn't stop talking. Once. Not for two minutes. Wow, that's exhausting. Do I do that to you? I had to wonder if you felt the same. And you can say so. I know I talk a lot and I am now." He forced himself to shut up for a second to let her answer.

"No, I enjoy hearing you talk. And you do stop for two minutes now and then."

"Ah, a way to politely say it could be for more than two minutes now and then?"

"No." There was effort in her voice. "Not at all, Eli. You don't bother me."

His heart flipped. And he rolled his eyes at the corny thought. But it did. He was too old for that. She was... She was delightful. He loved how delightful she was, how different. How she said his name that made him like it better. How... how much he missed her already. He loved that he missed her. He was insane.

"Still there?" She called out, with less effort.

"Yeah. So tell me what you're doing right now." He settled back against the outer wall of the little motel and enjoyed the warm moist air of South Carolina as she described the little cove where they were working that had not only storm debris, but also new debris, packaged food wrappers stuck under twigs and shoved into the sand. Kids, she said. She didn't understand why parents didn't teach their kids to be more respectful, not only of nature, but of other people who didn't want to walk along the shore and have to look at their garbage.

He could hear other frustration in her voice and pushed her to tell him about one of the kids being sick, about her sister's request and the idiot's laziness. She didn't call it that. She was trying to be nice. Eli was infuriated but tried to be nice about it, also, since it was her family.

"Del, tell them you're not going to be home and then get yourself a nice room away from them so you don't catch it."

"No, I don't want to spend money that way. And I don't…"

"You don't like to stay alone."

"No. And you know if I didn't even do that with you, while you were here, I'm not going to do it now."

He had to think about that a second, and lowered his voice as a group of people wandered not far away with what looked like a couple of six packs in paper bags. A night or two in a hotel with her, unhurried, unbothered, would have been good. Would have been very good. Of course so was making love in the bed of his truck. Outside. In the rain. And in all honestly, he'd love a repeat performance of that.

She asked about his roommate and he said he'd changed out to the guy who rode with him and along with being on his phone, he insisted on the television being on and talking over it while leaving it loud enough he could hear it as he talked. It's why he was sitting outside the room against the building. "Like I said, dealing with these guys, or anyone, during the day is fine, but it's different at night."

"Maybe you're the one who should get his own room."

"Yeah. Like you said, not much point without you to share it." Eli took a chance and pushed a bit. "It's beautiful here from what I've seen so far. If you ever feel like coming down for a couple of days, you could probably catch a train. I'll look into it for you. Just get on, take your book and ignore everyone, and I'd be there to meet you the minute you step off. Promise."

"I'll think about it."

Silence came between them but it was a nice silence. Comfortable. "So maybe call me back before you go to bed? And Delaney, you should stay away from there. Or at least keep your mouth covered as you go through and up to your room. Open your window to air it out…"

"I think it won't matter."

"It does. That's airborne and…"

"And I'm starting to think I might have it already. I'm … going to go home."

"Oh, honey." He caught it as it came out but not fast enough, and he didn't care. "Wish I was there to take care of you."

"So you'd get it, too? I'm already hoping you didn't get it from being here yesterday, or this morning."

"I don't usually, but I'd risk it even if I did." Eli wished he could hold her and take care of her, since he didn't have much confidence her sister would do it while busy with her kids. Heck of a time to get pulled away from her.

And yet, she said she would maybe come visit him.

Twenty-one

Three days of lying in bed barely moving followed by four days of trying to get her strength back and not going anywhere but work, and Delaney wasn't sure she wanted to go back to the wildlife refuge. Not without Eli. She was still overwrought about feeling so crappy and hearing his loving voice over the phone try to comfort her.

He'd begged for the house phone number in case ... just in case. She didn't use it any longer. Too much of it, nearly all of it by now, wasn't for her. They'd taken over, like the flu bug that crept into her insides and knocked her for a loop, despite her best intentions, her family had taken over her whole life. All of her energy.

Had she said that while sick? She vaguely remembered someone bringing her soup now and then. And water. But ... she'd said something about invaders. No privacy. Had told someone to get out.

With a groan, Delaney forced herself out of bed. She couldn't not go to the food pantry last minute just because she didn't want to be around anyone, not even long enough to get from the car to the front door, or from her bedroom door to her car. It was late spring but still cold. A new flock of tourists had invaded to look at the beach. Why weren't they somewhere warmer? Like South Carolina. Eli liked people. He wouldn't mind them crowding in.

Why didn't she just go to South Carolina? How far was that? It took Eli much of the day to get there. She didn't want to drive that far... And why not? She could. Her sister's gift to her every year was an auto club membership, at Pat's suggestion, since she didn't have a husband to take care of car things for her and she didn't do it well enough herself, he said. A dig in the form of looking like he gave a shit, which he didn't.

Delaney sat back down on her bed. She could go alone. She had to start just doing it, to show Eli she could so he wouldn't be so wary of her always needing him at her side when she went out. It wasn't fair to him. Trina said often enough it wasn't fair to her. And she was right.

Delaney had to learn to do more on her own, more than work and volunteering, to stop letting it hold her back.

A rush of panic flooded in as she thought of all the things that could go wrong if she drove that far alone. Even if she had call-in roadside assistance, she'd have to stand alongside the road and wait for the tow truck by herself if she had a flat tire or whatever else. She knew how to fix a flat. Her father had taught her the process, but it did no good when she wasn't strong enough to pry the lug nuts off. If a hefty muscular guy stopped to help, she could tell him how to do it, but she figured most guys knew that much, too, and she didn't want some strange man to stop and help her. Even the guy they sent out would be a stranger and ... and she was being ridiculous. They would know who was dispatched and have it on record. He wouldn't dare knock her out and steal her car or anything with his name on record. But then, how would she know whoever stopped wouldn't be only acting like he was called and...

Darn her imagination. Or her paranoia. Whatever it was that always made her see the worst that could happen was not at all helpful.

She had to defeat it. She needed to just do it and find out it wouldn't be as bad as she thought. It wouldn't. It never was. Almost never. She always terrified herself for no good reason. Ludicrous. Idiotic.

She could drive to South Carolina alone. Surprise him. Book a room ahead of time and just call and tell him to come. But what if he didn't? What if he wouldn't appreciate the surprise?

Stop it, Delaney. Just stop. She took deep breaths and closed her eyes to calm her nerves, to slow her heart rate. It didn't matter. She'd just missed three days of work. She couldn't leave again. Unless she said she had a resurgence of the virus and ... and she wouldn't.

She wasn't going to work today. To volunteer. It had been a hard week, beginning with Eli's sudden departure, and she needed down time. To go do something alone. Where people were. She could. Maybe she'd start at the library and ease into it. She could walk down there since it was close, let nature — what there was of it not covered by buildings and sidewalks and fake-trimmed shrubs that looked ...

fake — ease her into strength and calm and go browse books. What would she look for? Nothing in particular. She could just browse. She loved to do so but she didn't often because she kept wondering if someone would ask if she needed help and have to say she didn't and act like she was comfortable being there so they didn't think she was … looking for … sex books? Heaven forbid since she was thirty-two and single, well, kind of single. Or that she was waiting for someone or just killing time and using the library that way instead of just using it or maybe she was looking up … how to build a bomb or something since everyone was so jumpy about that lately. She didn't look dangerous. Except her nervousness made her look guilty and she knew it did so it made her more nervous about someone noticing and wondering what she was doing...

She didn't want to go to the library. She was still in the middle of the book Eli laughed about since her free time, her non-working time, had been taken by keeping him company.

Maybe Delaney would take it to the park where she and Eli had gone together. And then she could go grab a sub from Jersey Mike's and think of how Eli loved them. She could take her book in and sit by herself as she ate, except it was Saturday and the place would be packed. She could grab a handful of sunflower seeds leftover from when she still had a feeder, take the book and the sub both to the park and eat there on a bench as she fed the birds or ducks. She didn't mind birds crowding. They were nice companions. Quiet. Well, not always so quiet, but at least they didn't talk to her or ask her anything.

Great. She would look like the old bird woman from Mary Poppins. Except she wouldn't sing. Not in public. She would dance in public before she would sing in public and there was no way in hell she would dance in public.

"You're insane, Delaney. You know you're insane. Just go out. Anywhere. Just *go*."

Shoving herself onto her feet, she determinedly plucked a bulky sweater from her closet and grabbed old baggy jeans, then put them both back and pulled out clothes that actually fit her shape and dressed without letting herself think about how well they fit her shape since her shape was fit enough. It wasn't spandex or anything. How girls could wear that stuff outside their house, she couldn't imagine. She wouldn't even wear it inside her house, not without something loose over top.

And on the other hand, she was kind of jealous that they could let themselves and not be bothered by it. Delaney often studied people who could. Not only in spandex but in anything that drew attention. Or even laughing aloud, acting silly. Talking in a big group. She studied people who did and wondered how they did, how it would be to be able to do so without having a heart attack and dropping onto the floor and then being even more embarrassed at the attention that would get. How would that be? Delaney wished she could find out.

She had a friend once who had year-round constant allergies and no matter what she did, she was always stuffy. Sometimes she was less stuffy than others, depending on the season, but she always was. Delaney remembered her telling about the one time she cleared all the way up so there was no congestion at all to try to breathe through and how elated she was ... and it only lasted a couple of minutes. She said she nearly wished she didn't know because she'd never forget and it was wonderful and she couldn't get back to that.

So maybe Delaney didn't want to know unless it would stay away for good, her fear. It would be too heartbreaking to think she'd conquered it and to have it come right back at her.

With a sigh, she figured she might as well trudge along trying to find something that would help, as her old friend had. A shame the girl had moved away. Delaney had been fairly comfortable with her.

Dressed and ready to go, she hesitated. Was she going to volunteer, or go out on her own?

A glance at her silent phone told her the answer. She needed to prove to him she could go out on her own just fine and be okay with it. More than that, she had to prove it to herself, to tell herself she wouldn't hold him back too much if he wanted to stay with her. Delaney needed to know she wouldn't.

With still no word from Eli and fatigued from her day on her own out shopping and wandering and eating lunch in the park while wondering the whole time if people paid attention to the fact that she was alone, if they felt sorry for her — a dreadful thought, Delaney closed her bedroom door, turned on her music and turned it off again, and plugged Eli's iPod into her dock. She didn't care if she disturbed everyone in the house. She turned it loud. It was the only thing that truly calmed her soul, her dance, alone, when no one knew. If asked about the noise, the thumps from her feet they could hear on the kitchen ceiling, she would say she was working out. It was true. Dance was an incredible workout. *How* she worked out wasn't their business.

There was something about dancing wildly alone that you couldn't get any other way in the world. Someday she would have more room again, could unrestrain herself more.

Hopefully, someday, that would extend to more than her dancing. For now, it calmed her soul and used the energy she had been using with Elijah Forrester.

Before she lost herself in her impromptu routine, Delaney sent him another text: *Hey, Forrester, getting tired of the game? You don't have to be cute, you know. :D*

Delaney hoped he would answer soon. It was far too late at night to still be up there with the birds.

Twenty-two

Two days since she'd talked to him. He wouldn't answer. She'd left texts and voice messages, asked if she said something wrong, tried joking the way he had although it took her far longer to be creative than she figured it had taken him, and since she called to message him the night she'd gone out by herself all day and had an okay time wandering shops, small shops with intriguing little things she just wanted to look at and not buy and thought of him whenever she started to get too tense ... ever since that message, she hadn't heard from him.

Was she being clingy? In case she was, Delaney decided not to call again. He could call when he wanted. If he wanted. If he didn't, at least she would know to stop bothering; she'd realize he couldn't deal with it. Someone would. Or so she supposed. Someone who also didn't like to go out and mingle. Someone who preferred to stay home and ... and how would she find that?

It didn't matter. She didn't want someone like that. She wanted Eli. She would give him space and he would call again when he was ready. When he did, she would ... what? Sound annoyed that it had been so long, that he wouldn't even answer her and tell her he needed space? He could say so.

Of course there was always the thought that something happened while he was up there working with the birds, but Delaney absolutely refused to believe it. He was smart, well-trained, careful. He'd be careful. The crew boss. You didn't get to be crew boss unless you were well-trained, she expected. She also realized no one he worked with would have her number to let her know, and neither did his family. How would she find out? She didn't have their number, either.

It didn't matter. She wouldn't allow that thought. He only needed space.

And she needed to be out, not around people, but out of the house. Trina's house. Trina had made a mission to find things that were as much like what she had as before. They were all over

Delaney's house, things that made no sense, that only added clutter and stuff to dust and weren't even pretty. At least they weren't to Delaney. They were modern. Slick shiny black and silver and red. Bright red. It felt intrusive. And cold. Trina said they were energetic. Delaney couldn't imagine. Having that stuff throughout her house drained her energy. Her own softer things, furniture of wood rather than metal, accessories in blues and greens, were stashed in her room or pushed to the side, some of it was in boxes in her closet until she had space for them again. To share space for that cold aggressive unfriendly ... stuff.

Eli liked red, also. Would his house be red and modern?

With a shiver just thinking about it, Delaney pulled out her old jeans, a baby doll tee and a matching thick flannel shirt in blue and brown plaid, pulled on her matching blue socks, and slipped into her low brown boots that were kind of shoes but boot-like. Not a feminine look, but what did it matter? She'd been wearing the same outfit when she first met Eli and he didn't appear to care that it wasn't feminine. He'd been attracted to her anyway. He was a working man. She supposed he appreciated that she looked like she knew how to work. Of course just because that attracted him short term, maybe it wouldn't long term. Maybe he'd found some girl down in South Carolina who wore those beautiful long flowing casual dresses wherever they went and he met her walking along the beach and was so struck by the image he couldn't help saying hello.

And she probably didn't yell at him about kicking a starfish. Although he wouldn't do that again. Delaney at least accomplished that much. He understood sea stars now and she'd even seen him pick one up and move it back into the water. She hadn't had the heart to tell him it was too late for that one and he should have left it alone. It was too sweet that he did it, that it now mattered to him.

Not sure where she wanted to go, she found herself driving out to the beach where she'd met him, where there was no work to do and she could wander along and enjoy it. Delaney wanted to pull her boots and socks off and tread through the water, but it was chilly and she was still getting over the flu remnants.

Maybe Eli had caught it? But he'd been gone for over a week

now, so she would know. He hadn't sounded at all sick last time they talked. He sounded energized. He was heading out with a friend to go see a lighthouse down the beach a ways, a friend who agreed to go up into the thing with him. Maybe a girl.

Delaney stopped suddenly. It was a girl, in a long flowing feminine skirt, one who would go up into the lighthouse and give him that kiss above the ocean he'd wanted with her.

Was Pat right? She'd often thought men understood each other far better than women ever could, and vice versa. It was possible the jackass, as Eli called him, was right.

She bit her lip, traced back away from the water into the dry sand, and plopped down, her knees pulled up in front, her arms wrapped around them. Why else would he stop calling and refuse to answer? He felt guilty. He'd kissed the pretty feminine flowing girl up in the lighthouse and couldn't admit it.

Her stupid fears. She was the idiot. She should have gritted her teeth and just gone up.

Maybe she would. Maybe she would go prove to herself that she could and then tell him and he would forget the pretty frilly girl and come back and she could actually wear the light blue dress that looked like the color of the sky on a nice day, not gray and cloudy like now; the dress she'd bought long ago because she loved it but had never dared to wear it and ... and he would stay.

She could go change now. Put it on. Go up into that damned lighthouse and take a cell photo and send it to him and maybe he would return *that* call.

Of course she wouldn't. Not today. She needed time to convince herself she could.

Instead, Delaney stared out over the grayish-greenish beach, over the water rolling in large waves against the wet shore, sliding back out to slam against water coming in, the force pushing some of it up into foamy waves that settled again just to repeat the process. A natural process. In and out. Like oxygen. Breathing. In and out. A simple thing. Like talking to someone in conversation. They speak. You speak. Sometimes it came together and one would back down and wait and then the first would crest and wane and make way. Simple.

Natural. In and out. Back and forth. Give and take. Such an easy process. Speech. Laughter. A look. A smile. Second nature. Something you do without thinking. Just talk. Answer. Listen. Repeat. Simple.

If everyone else could do it, so could she.

She did with Eli. Simple. Just listen and respond, consider, debate. Admit when you don't know because sometimes you just don't and it's okay. *I don't know.* How hard was that? Her brain worked just fine when it wasn't fighting rushing blood and heat. She knew it did.

What was so hard about it?

Scooping a handful of light brown sand into her fist, she let it fall out in a funnel of her fingers. She'd seen a highly magnified photo recently of what sand truly looked like. Amazing. Each piece was so much more than it seemed when held in a fist. You only had to look close enough. People were just like that. Unique, more than anyone really saw, since they didn't look in such close detail. She knew she was. There was so much inside ... and it just stayed locked inside, avoiding magnification.

She sniffed back the sudden emotion and wiped her eyes on her sleeve. Too much inside. And too much fear to let it out.

"Eli. Call me." She'd spoken aloud and saw a couple turn their heads and ask what she'd said. "Nothing." Shoving herself to her feet, she allowed a long scan of her blue-green-gray ocean, her brown-tan beach, and the blue-yellow horizon, at her existence wrapped up in this place, then brushed the sand from her palms and went home to make dinner, something different, unique. Something the kids would complain about but she would enjoy creating.

Twenty-three

Thursday night, Delaney went back to the refuge. It was hard since she hadn't been there in over a week and they asked about her, about Eli. Surprisingly, she was okay with them asking, and she managed to answer pretty well. Without her voice shaking. And it was okay. She even worked beside an older couple she'd talked to briefly here and there. An interesting couple. Married for 36 years. Delaney would have to be ... 68 before she was married 36 years and that was if she got married now, in a few months. To hit a fifty year anniversary, she'd have to live to be 82, which she hoped she would. A 75 year anniversary was out of the question. Other than by some miracle.

With a sigh, she checked her phone again to be sure it was still working and went back to picking up garbage. The same thing on each stretch of beach. Debris. Splintered wood. Bits of rusty metal. Garbage that was just garbage – papers, wrappers, plastic. Old and new. She often wondered, as she picked up wrappers that obviously hadn't been there long, why she bothered. Kids, and maybe sloppy selfish adults, would still throw their garbage down instead of taking it to a trash area. Why clean up after those people? They didn't learn. If they could catch them and make them do clean up duty, maybe they would. But they wouldn't catch them. It was pointless.

And yet she hated her beach being so littered.

Not *her* beach. She hardly used it. Other than to work on it. For others. Why did she do this? Because it needed to be done. Because she had no reason to be home other than to shower and sleep. Because ... because she wanted the beach and water clean.

Putting her headphones on with Eli's iPod, she moved farther away from others as she worked. It kept her occupied enough Delaney didn't realize it was time to go until everyone else headed that direction.

Barely saying anything to Trina in response to ... whatever she said about dinner and there wasn't much left but there was some of whatever it was, Delaney trotted up to her room, grabbed her old sweats and went to take a long shower. But someone was in there. She waited a couple of minutes and decided she might as well eat first, whatever was left.

Which was almost nothing. And it had cilantro, a ton of cilantro, the way Pat liked it. That's what Trina had been saying. Probably payback for her making something the other night she knew the kids wouldn't eat. Delaney left it in the pan and made a peanut butter and jelly sandwich and took it upstairs.

Closing her door to eat in privacy, she stared out the window and wondered what he was doing. He could at least let her know. Just a text if he didn't want to talk. Something. A pit began to form in her gut. Something happened. He would never be so rude on purpose. He'd at least have the nerve to say so if he didn't want to talk to her. How did she find out?

The bathroom door was still closed when she was done with her sandwich, and she knocked hard. "Are you really *needing* to be in there or can you do whatever you're doing in your room?"

Tiffany's cocky arrogant voice came back that she was almost done with her nails. Thirteen-year-olds. She rolled her eyes.

"Do them in your *room*, like I've asked you. I need to shower."

"I don't want the smell in my room."

"And I don't want you *tying up* the bathroom."

"Is there a problem?"

Delaney turned to Pat. "I've told her to do her girl stuff in her room. *This* room needs to be shared."

"She's not your daughter. Leave her discipline to me."

"What discipline? She does whatever she wants. In *my* house. *My* bathroom. The *only* shower I have. I have to have *some* say in my own damned house. And don't dare talk about my language or raising my voice. This is my house and I have *no* say and *no* privacy and *no* respect. It's not fair and it's not right..."

"Fine. I'll put my kids in a little hotel room and make them live on top of each other and sleep on the floor..."

"I'm not asking you to leave. I'm asking for cooperation. Respect."

"You gotta earn respect to have it. Haven't learned that yet?" He threw a sly grin.

"Have *you*? You haven't earned it. Not from me. And say what you want. I don't care. Teach your kids to cooperate with me or *I* will teach them. I *mean* it, Pat." She went back to her room and slammed her door and paced. He needed to be told. She knew he did. But Trina would have a fit. It would be a huge fight between the two and all her fault and ... and she should have just kept her mouth shut because it would do no good. She'd yelled before. She'd pleaded with Trina. It made no damned difference at all other than a two week pouting episode.

Delaney wasn't up to that. She just wasn't. Their insurance was paying temporary living. They should use it instead of giving her a very small amount of rent from their allowance and pocketing, or spending, the rest. She knew he blew it. She knew he did. And he used that little bit of rent to act like it put him in charge. The jackass.

When she heard the bathroom door open and voices, she stormed right back out and through them, shut the door with a bang, locked it and turned on the water hot. She was cold. She shouldn't have worked outside so long while getting over a virus. Eli would fuss at her. If he ever called her. Maybe he lost his phone. But he'd get another one. They'd give him the same number. With as often as she'd called, he couldn't claim not to have hers even if he didn't remember it.

He'd at least want his iPod back. He had a lot of great music on it, some she'd never heard but was starting to enjoy. A surprise that she would. Not always her style. But a lot of different styles. Everything, really. At least he wouldn't laugh about hers.

And she wouldn't even care if he did if he would just call and tell her why he was mad at her. She'd back off if he wanted. Hell, at this point, she'd even move to Indiana if he wanted. Maybe he was only waiting out the two weeks she told him to wait...

The thought struck her hard and she stopped scrubbing the shampoo into her hair. She would move. Out of state. To Nowhere, Indiana, as he called it. If nothing else, it would get Delaney away from Pat and the undisciplined kids who had taken over her house.

Their grandparents' house, as one of them reminded her at times.

Maybe they should keep it if they wanted it that bad. If Eli never called her again, she could still sell it to them and find her own place, a smaller place. Maybe just an apartment where she wouldn't have to worry about maintenance and lawn care.

A sting in her right eye told her she'd let shampoo run down her face. Cursing, she washed it out the best she could, washed the rest of her quickly, and scrubbed herself dry. She'd start looking for places. Online. It was time. When Eli came back, they would have privacy. He would come back. She had his music.

Throwing her clothes on and going back to her room, Delaney heard her sister say they needed to talk, but she didn't answer. While her laptop was turning on, she picked up her phone. Should she try again? It had been two days since she tried. Okay, a day and a couple of hours. Either way.... Why not? Didn't he owe her at least the courtesy to tell her why he was mad or if he'd found someone else?

While her anger was still fueling her determination, Delaney flipped her phone open. But it rang and startled her all to hell. Eli.

Finally. Should she answer sounding mad or relieved? She was both. She might as well accept both would show. "Hey, so did you finally think of another way to destroy a good quote? Took you long enough." Silence came through. "Hello? Don't fuck with me, Eli. It's been a bad week and I really need you to just *tell* me why I haven't heard from you. If you're sick of me, say so. I can take it. I'm strong, remember? So just *say* it."

"This isn't Elijah."

A female voice. Delaney's stomach turned worse than when she had the flu. "Uh, who is this? It's Eli's number. Or it was..."

"Yes, it is. I'm his mother."

She was going to be sick. His mother called from his phone? Her eyes clenched. "What happened? Is he okay?" More silence from the other end. "Please. I'm ... a friend of his..."

"I know who you are." The tone was rather unfriendly.

Delaney eased out a long breath through tight lips. "Is he okay? I'll stop calling if he is, and if he wants me to stop. I just... Tell me he's okay. Please."

"Elijah is..." She stopped.

Delaney sank onto her bed, her hands shaking. "No. Please..."

"He's here. Don't get the wrong idea."

There? He was there? She heard a muffled voice in the background. Light. Strained. Eli. "What's wrong? Can I talk to him?"

"Only for a minute. He asked me to find your number and hand him the phone, but he's supposed to be resting, so before I do, I want to be sure you understand not to strain him..." The muffled voice came again. It sounded like *Don't scare her, Mom.*

"Is he sick? Should I ask him or..."

"There was an accident. Some young boy driving far too fast swerved to miss an animal and pushed Elijah right off the road."

Delaney clenched her eyes. "How bad?"

"He will recover, although we weren't sure for a while. It'll take time. I'm not supposed to tell you more, or even that much. He's already frowning at me and I don't want to upset him, but I do not want him to talk long."

They weren't sure... She swallowed hard. "Only a few seconds. Take it back if it bothers him. Just let me have a few seconds with him."

After some mumbling in the background, Delaney heard his voice. Kind of his voice, the *hey* she loved by now. It brought tears to her eyes, but she pushed them away. "Hey back. I guess I don't have to ask how you are. Can I do anything?"

"Yeah. Tell me you'll give me a five minute tonsil search when I get back there to see you. I could use one."

"Oh." She had to swallow hard to stay in control. "Of course. How long are you... Are you home?"

"Nah, kind of stuck here at the moment."

"In South Carolina?"

"Yep. Mom came out as soon as they called her. Sorry it took me so long to get back to you. Wanted to be able to talk first. I hear I missed about a gazillion of your calls."

"Not quite that many. Oh Eli, can I come? I'll help with whatever you need. Can I?"

Silence invaded.

She gripped her comforter hard in her hand. "Elijah?"

"What about your job, Del?"

"I don't care. About any of it. Not even the house. They can have it if they want it. Put your mom back on and I'll arrange with her, okay? You rest. And hey..."

"Tired of talking to me already?" His voice was too strained. She could hear his mom ask for the phone.

"No, baby. Never. I want you to rest. Listen to your mom. And I ... I hope she'll still let me near you after what I just said when I thought it was you. I'm sorry..."

He chuckled. A hoarse harsh chuckle. "Yeah? I gotta hear that. What'd you say?"

"Never mind. I'll work it out with her. Just give her the phone..."

"Not till you tell me. I could use a laugh." He sounded in pain.

"Eli, please, just...."

"Not gonna happen. Tell me. You suggest another trip out to the woods? I'm okay with that. We'll have to get another truck and you'd have to drive. I can manage the rest in a few days."

Delaney blushed. "Isn't your mom right there?"

"Yeah, and she's rolling her eyes. Don't worry, Del. Whatever you said, she's used to me."

Quickly, so he'd stop asking, she repeated what she said and how she thought he was tired of her or...

"No, baby, never. Don't ever think it. You don't know how bad I've wanted you here. They wouldn't let me on the phone till now. Come if you can. Just be prepared. I look kind of a mess, so they say. It's okay. I'll heal. Don't let it scare you if you come. If it will, wait a while."

Tears rolled down her face. A mess. Her poor baby. "I'll be there just as soon as I can get there. You rest now, Eli. That's an order. You know I..." It wasn't the right time to say it, not over the phone. It should be in person.

"You what?" As well as in pain, he now sounded tired, far too tired. His mom asked for the phone. "Del, you what?"

"I love you, Eli. I hate being away from you. Rest now. Follow orders, and I'll be there. Okay?" Silence. Maybe she shouldn't have.

"Still there?"

"I love you too, Delaney. Should've told you before. Can't wait to see you, but drive safe, baby. Take your time."

She heard his mom say she'd taken the phone from him and her voice was different. Softer. Curious. It took Delaney a minute to answer and then ask where he was so she could go find him.

The thought of him banged up enough it would scare her, so he said, nearly broke her down but she wouldn't. Instead, she called work and left a message to explain and said she didn't know how long she would be gone, and they could replace her. And she called her contact for the food pantry to let them know someone would have to fill in. And Gloria at the refuge, who almost made her cry with her concern for Eli and her request for Delaney let her know how he was and to keep her informed.

Next, she threw a few essential things together, added the blue dress just because, printed out a map with directions – even though she had a GPS, she still liked printed maps – turned her laptop off again to take with her, and went down to tell Trina she was going to visit Eli.

She didn't tell her sister about the accident. Pat was right there and she didn't want to hear his comments. Trina urged for more information, but Delaney wasn't giving in. She needed to go, to get to him.

Her poor baby. Almost taken out by a stupid kid who swerved for an animal. *Stupid* kid. As much as she loved animals and respected them and would never hurt them voluntarily, she would never do something so stupid. If the road had been clear, fine. But... *Oh Eli.*

Suddenly, she remembered he'd had a friend with him. They'd been going out to the lighthouse. She should have asked if he was okay. Damn, she hoped he was okay. Eli would feel horrible if someone riding with him...

Delaney couldn't think of it.

Eleven hour drive. And it was after eight o'clock at night. She could drive for about three hours or so and stop to sleep a bit and get there by the next evening or late afternoon. Of course it meant she would have to get a hotel room alone, late at night, but she could.

And she would.

With Eli's iPod plugged into her stereo to help calm her nerves, she tried not to think about how he looked or about the long drive. Before she realized it, Delaney was leaving New Jersey. Alone. A suffocating weight she hadn't noticed before evaporated into the dark night of a new state. She'd done it. She untied her ropes, her frazzled oily grimy ropes that held her down into the littered marshlands of a life too long lived in fear and dread of the unknown, and took a big step out of bounds.

Delaney nearly cried with relief. She wouldn't. She had to drive. She had to get to Eli safe and sound and take care of him and assure his mom she could take care of him, that she could be good for him. He was close to his family. She had to fit in, at least well enough, or at least convince them she would be good for him.

First she had to convince herself.

At quarter after twelve, her phone rang. She was still driving, but there was almost no traffic so she slowed down as she answered.

"Tell me I didn't wake you." His voice was hoarse.

"Eli, how are you? Shouldn't you be asleep?"

"Been asleep most of the time. Woke up and Mom's finally asleep. She's been watching me like the proverbial crow..."

"Hawk."

"I get watched far more by crows around my place so it seems more appropriate."

She grinned. "Okay. Did she go get some rest?"

"Yes and no. Asleep in the chair. Can't get her to leave." He groaned, a painful groan.

"Are you okay?"

"Answer me first. Did I wake you?"

"No, I'm ... driving."

"What? Now? Del, you should've waited till morning."

"Couldn't. I want to be there with you."

Silence came from his end and she saw light alongside the road ahead that had to be at least a large truck stop.

"Damn I love you, but stop somewhere and get some sleep. I can't have you..."

"I just saw a sign. I'm about to pull over."

"Good. I'll let you go, but call me back just as soon as you're safe in your room so I know you are. Don't argue. I hurt like hell and I'm annoyed even more, so I get to win this one."

"Okay, baby. I'll call you back in just a bit. But sleep if you need. I'll leave a message and leave my phone on. Okay?"

"Not so sure I like being called *baby* by a girl."

"Hm, well. You can drop the macho stuff and just deal with it. I'm hanging up now. I'll call back."

"Careful. Get a good place and an upstairs indoor room. I'll pay it back for you if I need..."

"You don't need, and I can manage. Talk to you in bit, baby." She was coming to the exit and wanted to be off the phone, so she hung up and grinned at his expression as she assumed it. He didn't like being called baby? That was just tough. Granted, he was strong and mostly fearless. He worked high up on thin beams with only a few straps around his hips and thighs and waist as protection. He was the one willing to go highest. Nothing but water scared him.

Yeah, he was plenty macho. But he was also sweet and gentle and loving and ... and in need of strong arms to help him recover. She would darn well baby him as much as she decided, and he could deal with it.

~ Twenty-four ~

"So cuz, your girl should get here soon. Think she's gonna be able to handle us?"

Eli sipped the nasty soup of whatever kind it was and eyed his cousin. "Take it easy, Ranger. I don't want her chased off. It'll be hard enough for her to deal with everything."

"Think you'll get her to move?" His brother helped to steady the bowl and Eli let him take the thing. He could hardly sit up enough to eat, or drink. It was damned annoying. He hated it. He'd never been weak in his life. Even as a baby he'd held his head up alone on his first day for some inordinate amount of time that surprised the nurses. His mom bragged about it often enough. Even as baby of the family, he was the strongest. This wasn't close to acceptable.

"Are you okay? Need anything?"

"Stop hovering like a mother hen, if you don't mind. Mom's doing it enough. And yeah, I don't know. To be honest, I'm surprised she's coming down here."

"A girl who wouldn't come when you're lying here like this is a girl you don't want."

"You don't get it, Bill. She's kinda skittish. I need you both to tone it down, just until she gets used to you. Will you do that?"

"Skittish?" Ranger shrugged his hands. "You gotta be kidding. You? And a *skittish* girl?"

"Just take it easy. This is gonna be hard enough. I look like hell, right? Mom won't give me a damned mirror though I know she carries one, so I know it's gotta be bad."

"Kinda bad, yeah. I'd say it's kinda bad."

Bill shoved their cousin and Eli had to know. Before Delaney got there, he had to know what she was walking in on. He pushed until his brother gave in to him, as he always did, and helped Eli get up to hop to the bathroom, with his cousin on his other side since his foot was fucked up and wrapped up.

The sight in the mirror turned his stomach. A red puffy line covered in bright blue stitches ran along his nose and up his forehead. Other parts of his face were scuffed. An eye was black and blue. "Fuck."

"It'll heal." Bill tapped his shoulder. "Come on. Back to bed."

"Gotta piss while I'm here. Shut the door."

"Can you do it by yourself?"

"I bet I'm gonna. Go." He waited just until he heard the click. Not like he hadn't done it in front of them before, outside camping or working, but it was different in the hospital.

And he wasn't strong enough to stand. He got dizzy, so he sat to piss. Like a girl. She might as well call him baby since he felt like one. She couldn't see him like this. He should have told her not to come. To wait. Until he could at least stand up to piss again. At least that long. And maybe until he didn't look like Dr. Frankenstein's monster.

Frankenstein. It echoed in his head. She'd said it. When?

A knock and his brother's voice asking if he was okay made him push to stand again. At least he didn't have jeans to deal with. The horrible green hospital gown fell back down to his thighs as he held tight to the metal bar with his one good hand, trying to stay steady on his one good foot.

Bill came in and gripped him under the arm, told Ranger to help, and breathing hard while leaning far too much on them, his good hand gripping his brother's shirt, he got back to the side of bed that by now looked like nothing but relief...

"Eli."

Delaney. And he was hobbling, his backside mostly uncovered, his head spinning from the effort.

Bill looked over his shoulder. "You must be the Jersey girl my kid brother's been talking about." He tugged the back of Eli's gown together.

"Yes. Should I..." Her voice showed her worry.

"Bill Forrester. I'd offer a hand but they're kind of busy holding the kid up and protecting his decency. If you give us a minute, we'll get him back in bed..."

"Don't call me a kid in front of my girl like this isn't embarrassing enough. And she already knows plenty about my *decency*. She can stay."

Eli turned toward her, with Bill's help, and Ranger's snicker in his ear.

"Oh, Eli." She glanced down at his wrapped foot and found his eyes. "You didn't have to do this to get me to come. You could have just asked."

"I did ask. Didn't work, so had to get more extreme. Do I get my tonsil search? You did promise..."

"Elijah. Get back in that bed."

Delaney turned with a start toward the woman, a sturdy woman, but fit, in shape. She was a bit taller than Delaney, about sixtyish by guess, with mostly gray hair, the rest the same light brown as Eli's, and the same strong oval face. She was in jeans and a plain tee, with a thin sweatshirt over top and unzipped. Nothing at all fancy about her, which was nice and completely unexpected. "You have to be Eli's mom." She flushed at the woman's tilted head and raised eyebrows.

"Why? Do I look old enough to have been through two boys and a girl who might as well have been a boy?"

She flushed more. "No, I... You look like him."

"Well, thank you. Bill, get him back in that bed this instant. I don't care who's here. Elijah, you can just follow orders and use that bed pan like the nurse said, like it or not."

"Mom..."

His mother stopped him in his tracks and got him tucked back in. Then she rubbed a hand over his head and came to Delaney, one hand on her hip, studying her, the other vaguely offered. "Ellen Forrester. And you're Delaney, if I had to guess."

"Yes. Delaney Griffin. It's nice to meet you." She looked back over at Eli and wanted to go to him but she wouldn't dare insult his mother. A strong woman. Afraid of nothing, Delaney supposed, but with kind eyes.

Bill said something about her just getting there and that she hadn't had time to even give Eli a kiss yet...

"Come here, Del."

She met Eli's gaze and went to him. Unable to help herself, she stroked his beautiful hair. His strong face was broken up and battered, but his eyes were still warm and soft...

"Remember how you said you feel like Frankenstein's monster when you dance in public?" He gathered her hand in his, the one not bandaged. "Well, now I look like him, so I guess we make a good pair, huh?"

"No, you don't. How bad is it? I mean..." She looked at where his brother had put his foot back in a hanging blue sling.

"Kinda bad. They're not sure at this point if I'll be able to walk on it normally again." He squeezed her fingers and pulled them to his lips for a quick kiss. "You can run now if you want. I won't blame you."

She felt her eyes widen and her mouth open to answer him, and couldn't. Run? Her head shook. She had to sit. Whether or not she should, she sat on his bed, leaned in carefully, and touched her lips to his. "I can't run, actually." She met his eyes. "You'd have too much trouble keeping up and then I'd feel bad."

He grinned and the guy she hadn't met laughed. "I like her so far. Sure she's from the east? Thought they didn't have no sense of humor."

Ellen Forrester gave the man a look. "Didn't have *any*. And don't be rude, Ranger."

"My cousin. Takes some getting used to. Don't let him bother you." Eli stroked her hand with his thumb. "Thought this might freak you out. Freaked me out just now when I looked at it."

"Elijah, is that what you were doing up?" His mom stood on the other side of his bed.

"You wouldn't give me your mirror. Can see why you didn't. But it's okay enough since she didn't run. Del..."

"What can I do for you?" She stroked fingers along the uninjured side of his face.

"Don't go anywhere." His eyes fluttered as though he was forcing them to stay open.

"I won't. I'm going to stay at your side and take care of you until you're healed."

"I may not..." He swallowed hard and took a breath that looked like it hurt. "I may have just screwed up my future, what I'd planned. I don't know now ... what's going to happen or..."

"You are going to heal just fine, Elijah Forrester. You have to.

Know why?" She played with his hair and forced her voice to calm as his mom wandered farther away. "Because I want you to hold my hand tight when you take me up into that lighthouse and kiss me there. I thought about going up alone just to tell you I could, but I can't quite, so I need you to go with me. It's a lot of stairs, Eli, so you have to heal. And you will. I'll help make sure of it."

"Del, they say it could take a good bit of time. You'll have to go back to your job, your family..."

"No, I don't have to. So if you don't want me here, you'd best say so right now. Otherwise..."

"I want you here more than about anything in the world." He looked far too emotional. Tired. In pain.

She kissed him. Lightly, since his family was in the room. "Good. Because that's a hell of a drive. Wouldn't want to have wasted my time."

He grinned. Slightly.

"You're tired. Sleep, baby. Do whatever you need and tell me if you need me to do anything. I don't care what it is." She leaned close beside his ear. "As you said, your decency doesn't matter with me. That was a cute view of your cute behind, by the way. How many nurses have you showed it off to?"

A light chuckle rumbled her hand on his chest. "First time out of bed. You had good timing." He squeezed her hand as she sat up again. "Hoping my brother will see fit to at least bring me some shorts since they cut the others up and tossed them."

"What? Why?"

"Will do." Bill set a hand on her shoulder. "Had to cut everything off and toss it. Blood was everywhere and they had to check him. The kid's lucky. The truck doesn't look like one anymore."

Her stomach turned.

"Don't scare her worse. I mean what I said. Both of you." He glanced at the two men. "Del, I gotta sleep. Tell me if they don't behave. You'll be here when I wake up?"

"I'll be here." She stroked his hair. "I love you, Elijah. I'm not going anywhere. No matter what happens." She kept her face down close, stroking his hair until he relaxed. Asleep.

Her body gave in to a deep shaky breath and she bit her lip as she studied him. Her beautiful Eli, all broken and battered. In pain enough he nearly...

"Come with me, dear." His mom took her side. "The boys will stay with him. You and I are going to get coffee."

"I don't want to leave..."

"You're exhausted. If you plan to take care of my boy well enough, you need to take care of yourself, too. Come."

Delaney couldn't argue. Before she left the room, his brother came to her and gave her a large hug. She felt herself draw back. She didn't do hugs. She didn't. Only with Eli. She didn't even hug her sister. But this man, Eli's brother, felt secure, welcoming. Too secure. It broke through her defenses too far. Her body quaked with tears she couldn't hold back. Her Eli. In so much pain. She could have lost him.

"Hey, he'll be alright." Bill spoke softly as he kept hold. "The kid used to get himself into all kinds of scrapes. He heals fast."

She nodded, trying to convince herself, to let him convince her, and pulled back to wipe her eyes. "I'm sorry. I don't do this. Really, I don't. I..." She looked back at Eli and started again.

"We've all been there already. Don't you worry about it." Bill patted her arm. "Go on with Mom and I'll look after him. Ranger, walk with them and bring coffee back if you would."

Again she couldn't argue although she wanted to stay right beside Eli and just hold onto him. Delaney supposed he wouldn't sleep well enough that way, though, so she let his mom lead her down the hallway, with Ranger – was that his real name? – on her other side. She felt them watching her. She had to pull it together. But she was tired, too. And emotionally spent.

In the cafeteria, they found a back corner away from everyone and Ranger went to get coffee after he held both of their chairs.

"So you drove all the way here by yourself?"

She nodded at his mother and rubbed fingers across her eyes. The woman handed her another tissue. "Thank you. Yes. A long drive."

"You like to drive."

"No."

"No? Why didn't you fly?"

"What?" At the idea, Delaney stared. "I didn't... I never have. I just wanted to get here so I came."

"Just like that. After I called you."

"Yes."

Ellen studied her a moment. "You love Elijah. Honestly?"

"Yes." She felt herself well up again.

"He's used to having his family around. It's who he is. He might very well give that up for you, but I'm afraid... Don't get me wrong. I'm not trying to discourage this, or you. I'm just afraid, especially now, that for him to be away long term..."

She nodded and thanked Ranger for the coffee.

"Especially if he doesn't heal all the way. If he needs extra help..."

Extra help. The thought made her shudder. It would nearly kill him to be held back. He wasn't used to it the way she was. It was harder than he understood, and she didn't want him to have to understand.

"It's going to be hard on him, even if he does heal well. It'll still be a long road."

Delaney sipped the strong coffee and nodded. "I know. He's not used to being held back. He's..." She nearly said *Captain America* but decided against saying that much.

"He's used to being able to do about anything he puts his mind on doing. Always could. This will be a whole new ball game. Can you deal with him when he gets frustrated? Have you seen it yet? You haven't known each other long."

"No, I... Yes, I've seen it to an extent. Not much."

Ranger snickered. "He can be a bear. Just a warning. Tends to surprise people since he's so friendly mostly. Don't let it get to ya, though. Just tell him to simmer his ass down. Usually works. If it doesn't, call me or Bill and we'll settle'im down."

"Randy, don't make it sound worse than it is." Ellen set a hand on hers. "He is part right. Eli can be somewhat bear-like when he's upset, but he would never hurt you. He's all bluster and no bite. Still, it can be hard to take if you're not expecting it."

A bear. Yes, she imagined so, just from the bit of frustration she'd seen. But she couldn't deal with this discussion right now. "I know he wouldn't. I'm not... This is all ... a bit much. It was a long drive and I don't like to drive and..."

"You're right. I shouldn't have started the conversation that way. Randy, go on up and take that to Bill. If Eli wakes, come on back and get us."

He nodded at the order and turned to Delaney. "Didn't mean that to sound bad. He wouldn't ever hurt a girl. He's a good guy. Just gets moody at times is all, and you seem kind of ... well, he told us to take it easy. I wasn't sure why he'd take up with a girl we had to be careful with, when he told us to, but I can see it now. He finally picked up some sense, it seems."

"Randy." Ellen gave him a look.

"Yeah, I'm talking too much. Sorry if I said something wrong. And so you know, Aunt Ellen's the only one still insists on calling me my given name. It's Ranger. I hate to be called Randy. Even my own mama doesn't call me anything but Ranger." He stuck out a hand. "Good to meet you. Glad you're not what I expected." With a quick handshake, he left.

Delaney wondered what he expected based on whatever Eli had said.

"Never mind him. A rogue, that boy. We keep trying to make him into a civilized man. That girl he's been chasing for years might just say yes if he'd try an iota or two."

"He seems nice."

"Yes. Nice. But... Anyway, tell me about yourself. Eli hasn't said much. Something about a sister and kids."

Delaney told her only the basics about her living arrangements and family history.

"You lost your folks at the same time?"

"Yes." Her hand shook and she set her cup back down. "A few years ago. An accident. Drunk driver. We were told they wouldn't have felt anything, but I saw them, and I find it hard to believe." The image of their bodies still haunted her. "Trina refused to go ID them and there was no one else to do it, so I did." She shuddered.

"Oh, honey." Ellen squeezed her hand. "And all of this... You must be a mess about now. You hold it together well."

"I had to. I took care of everything. Trina was a real mess. Always Daddy's girl and she just..." She grabbed a deep breath. "Anyway, I know Eli wants to be home. He made that clear from the start. His family is important, I know."

After a moment of silence, Ellen rubbed her chin. "You're planning long term with my Elijah."

"I hope so." She heard herself say it and was amazed she could be so open with this woman. But she was fairly comfortable with Eli's mother. There was such a strong similarity, and Ellen Forrester was very down to earth. Delaney was actually more comfortable with Eli's mother than she had ever been with her own mother who never made sense to her, and vice versa. Or she was so tired from the long night, the early morning, and the long tense drive that she didn't have the energy to be too nervous. "Right now it's... Like you said, it hasn't been long."

"His injuries frighten you."

"No. Other than I know they'll frustrate him, but I can deal with that. I'm not afraid to take care of him. I've done it. I worked at a nursing home for some time. And I can work to support us. I'm used to that, too. It's... He's sociable, super outgoing, and I... I don't know if he can deal with me. Long term. Even if he says he can, it's early yet."

"You're not sociable?"

"It's complicated. Yes and no."

Ellen studied her more and then eased back in her chair with a deep breath. "Well, maybe I shouldn't tell you, but when you talked to him yesterday over the phone..."

Heat surged up through Delaney's face. "I'm sorry. For the language. I thought he... I don't talk that way, really."

"Don't worry about it. I've long known my youngest would have to have someone strong-willed, and I'm not that uptight. As I said, I've raised boys and Eli was never one to hide things from me. Not much I haven't heard." With a light grin, she took a sip of her coffee and leaned forward. "Delaney, the boy was so anxious to talk to you we hardly heard him say anything else since he woke up. Made us all plenty curious. He never talked about his dates, about girls specifically, other than to Bill. In general, yes. He made no attempt to hide his thoughts about them in general. Bill had to tone him down at times."

Delaney wasn't sure whether to laugh or cry. Instead she took a large swallow of the coffee and kept her focus on the table. "He's a terrible flirt. I told him he was."

"He is that. But he's only been serious about a girl once."

"I know."

"He told you about her?"

"Yes. Would it sound bad to say I'd love to strangle her for him? I know he wouldn't do it, but I'm not sure I wouldn't."

Ellen chuckled. "You and me both and a few others of us, also. Whatever you might hear, if you come out to visit, just know some of it is from that ... girl, and it's not true."

"I know Eli. I know better."

"Good." Tapping her thumb against the paper cup, her voice softened. "You told him over the phone you love him." It was half question.

Her eyes watered with her nod.

"First time?"

She nodded again and held her breath to keep control.

"He cried."

Delaney looked up then to find moisture in his mom's eyes.

"That boy has been through some hard times, partly of his own making, and he's been in pain more than he'll admit, including now. Still, I haven't seen him cry since he was maybe ten years old. He did, though. He tried to hide it from you, not from us. I knew then..." Ellen took both of Delaney's hands in hers. "My boy is truly in love with you. You mean the world to him."

Unable to stop it, tears flowed down her cheeks.

Ellen moved closer to hug her. "I'd say you have a good chance at long term if that's what you want."

She felt herself nod again, but she couldn't speak. He'd cried when she said she loved him. Oh Eli. *Her* Eli. He was.

When it was dark and Eli was asleep, Ellen asked her to go back to the hotel, to share the room they had and rest since she looked exhausted. The boys would stay. Delaney tried hard to insist she was staying. She didn't want to go share a room with his mother who she hardly knew. She was stressed enough already. But the nurse said she needed to leave since it was past visiting hours and she wasn't family.

It wrenched her heart to walk away from him. With a kiss to his head, she let her gaze linger on his face and she suddenly hurt so bad inside she wanted to scream. Her Eli. He'd joked about it, said it was ironic that after he'd spent so much time with her helping out critters that it would be a critter that nearly did him in. It wasn't, of course. It was a stupid boy who should have his license yanked for being so stupid. The kid was just fine. He got his car under control and ran back to help Eli, said he felt just terrible earlier in the day when he came to check on the man he'd nearly killed. Delaney couldn't even look at him, even with Eli joking with the boy that he'd got his girl to come down to visit. Luckily the friend with Eli only had a few scratches. The truck had come to rest on the driver's side in the ditch. His airbag hadn't worked. Eli also joked that he'd have to have that fixed.

"Come, Delaney." Ellen put an arm around her and she felt herself withdraw, but she gave in since she didn't have much choice. More than half numb, she knew Ranger was driving them. She felt herself obey orders and get out of the car when they got to the hotel. But when they had the room door open and told her to go on in, she froze. "No. I'll..." She stepped back. "I'll get my own room."

"Sheets are clean. Room got redone after we left it this morning." Ranger was staring, curious.

How could she explain she couldn't share a room with a stranger? Not even Eli's mom. They both stared like she was crazy, or...

"The boys won't be here till we relieve them at the hospital in the morning. You're fine here with me." Ellen insisted.

Delaney's heart pounded. She wanted to go back to Eli. She could sit in the hospital waiting room. She couldn't sleep there like some did, but...

"Randy, call down and have them send up a bottle of house wine if you will. This girl needs something to help calm her. You drink wine?"

She found herself nodding. Not often, but tonight she would. How else would she deal with staying overnight in a hotel room in a strange city with Eli's mother after everything else without crumbling? She wouldn't crumble, though. She'd learned long ago not to. And Eli needed her.

You're about the strongest person I know. Remember that.

Delaney couldn't imagine how he thought so, but she would try hard for him.

~ Twenty-five ~

Eli cringed at the pain, but he made it into the wheelchair with his brother's help and assured Delaney he was alright. Alright, but frustrated. Six days in the hospital and still so damned weak. At least they were letting him get up to use the toilet, not that he gave them much choice. They gave him crutches that hooked to his forearm since he couldn't put pressure on his left wrist at all, but with some lingering dizziness from the concussion when he stood, so far he was still stuck in the chair and he couldn't even push himself because of the wrist. He could do almost nothing.

At least he was out of the hospital and sharing a room with Delaney in a hotel, a nice one. Finally. It only took smashing his truck into a ditch and against a couple of trees.

"Hey." She touched his face. "It's going to be okay."

"I feel damned useless."

"You're not."

He pulled back. This wasn't what he'd planned, not how he wanted her to get to know his family. Bill told her to never mind; he was too busy pouting to be nice enough, but he'd get over it. *Pouting.* He wasn't pouting. He was pissed. It could have at least waited until he got her home, until she met the family, got comfortable with them. If she would. Now she'd feel obligated. He sure as hell didn't want that.

Eli also did not want her helping with his daily needs. That was something old married couples did, not new couples still getting to know each other, not even engaged yet. Too personal. It was bad enough having to let his brother and cousin do it.

Getting wheeled into the hotel room, obviously a handicapped room, Eli rolled his eyes when Ranger commented on the "cool" extra stuff in the bathroom, like a shower with no floor ledge so the chair could be wheeled right into it and then the poor sap could move from the chair to the fold-out seat. Wasn't going to happen. He'd hop with one foot first and hang on with his one good hand.

"So, we're right next door." Bill nodded to the connecting door. "If you need anything, just knock." His brother was talking more to Delaney than to Eli, which also pissed him off.

"We're good. What's the plan from here, since everything's been arranged around me without my input?"

"Alright, Elijah Samuel. Enough now." His mom moved in front of him with a hand on her hip. "Fussing at those trying to help you won't help you. If you disagree with the plans we've made, you can say so."

"Doesn't matter." He looked over at Delaney, who had been keeping her distance the past couple of days. "Is your vacation time gone by now? Headed back to your fish while they take the invalid home to heal and be a general pain in the ass to everyone?"

"I um..."

"It's fine. You might as well."

"Okay, Eli." Bill stepped between. "You want to lie down? Probably a good time to rest since you've been pushing yourself enough today. Let me help you..."

"I'll get there if I want to."

Ranger snickered. "I want to see that. Go on, cuz. Get yourself there."

"Shut the hell up, would you?"

Laughing at the rebuff, Ranger put an arm around Delaney's waist. "Told you he can be a bear. Want to leave Bill here with him and share my room instead? Bill ain't scared of him at all."

"Just get out. We're good." Eli pushed one wheel, then reached over to the other side to push the other one so it wouldn't go in a circle. Gritting his teeth, he kept trying to get the thing where he wanted it to go.

Bill shook his head and turned to her. "Do you need anything?"

"No. Thank you."

"Okay, then. I'll leave him to you. About time. I'm getting tired of dragging his sorry ass around. Good luck. Yell if you need us. And don't let his tantrums get to you."

"Stop treating me like I'm three, would you?"

"Come on, kid. You know I'm teasing." Bill pushed the chair over beside the bed. "I'm here for you as much as you need, like you would be for me and have been for plenty of others. Nothing but arrogance and stupid pride keeps you from accepting help after you've been so willing to give it, and you know better than that. Don't be too proud to accept help as you need it. Understand?"

He couldn't answer. He was too frustrated, working too hard to stay in control.

"Okay, so." Bill set a hand on his shoulder. "We'll do something about dinner in a couple of hours." Moving to Delaney across the room, he set a hand on her back, told her again to be sure to knock if needed, and ushered Ranger and his mom out of the room.

"Can I help you lie down?" She finally came to him and ran fingers through his hair.

He pulled away. "No."

"Okay, do you want the television on?"

"Hell, no." The thing had been running near constant in his room to keep Ranger entertained.

She sat at the edge of the bed. "What do you want to do? Feel like taking a walk? It's beautiful today. This warmth is wonderful."

"A walk? Are you serious?"

"Well, I meant..." She sighed. "Eli, are you not sure you want me to go home with you? You can say so if you don't."

"I told you I do."

"Yes. But you don't act like you do."

"What in the hell am I doing?"

She walked back across the room. "You know this isn't easy for me, and I don't know what else..."

"For you? It's not easy for *you*? Would you *look* at me? You stand there looking so incredible, with every man turning his head and feeling *sorry* for you being stuck to *this* – I can see they are, so don't argue – and this isn't easy for *you*? Damn, Del, did you start dressing like that *now* just to rub it in?"

She looked down at her blue jean capris and the perfectly-fitted navy top that was buttoned low enough to tantalize but high enough not to show anything, as though she didn't know she was driving him crazy.

"Telling me you haven't noticed them? Especially that one in the lobby eyeing you like... Good looking, wasn't he? And on two good feet. Maybe you should have said hello."

"I don't know who you mean."

"You're serious."

She met his gaze. "I haven't seen anyone look at me. At all. I try *not* to see anyone, remember?"

"Yeah well, you're missing out."

"I'm not interested in anyone else. Eli..."

"Maybe you should be. Someone who'll stay by the coast with you, someone who can still go on walks with you..."

"You will, when you heal."

He rolled his eyes. "Hobbling like ... like Frankenstein's monster with a line all the way down my face? Yeah, that'll be great. You better find someone else to climb the lighthouse with."

"Is that what you want?" Her voice was soft, shaky.

Hell. Of course it wasn't. But she should. The way he looked, he was bound to get her all kinds of attention she didn't want.

Delaney went to the connecting door and knocked. Bill was right there. Again. He'd been right there for her the whole week Eli had been stuck in that damned hospital bed.

"What's up?" He glanced in at Eli. "Change your mind about lying down?"

She grabbed her phone off the table and walked out.

"Hell. *Delaney.*" Eli tried to get his stupid chair to move with one hand, which didn't work at all. "Bill, get me out there."

"What did you say to her?"

"Never mind, just get me out there."

"You know, if she walked out on you, I bet she had reason. Damn, Eli, that girl is bending over backward trying to make you comfortable and you're being nothing but a jackass to her."

"Lecture me later. I don't want her out there alone."

Bill stared a moment, went back to the other room, and returned. "Mom's going after her. Maybe she can get the girl not to leave your sorry ass, although I'm not sure she shouldn't."

Delaney walked through the hotel lobby without looking at anyone, her phone clenched in her hand. What had she done wrong? She'd only tried to help, and she tried not to be pushy about helping. Still, he'd barely spoken to her for the past four days, and when he did, it felt like he was irritated with her.

Walking past the outdoor pool, she went down the steps that led to the beach and kept going up to the edge of the sand on a hilly area where she could look out at the Atlantic, her Atlantic, just a few hours south. South Carolina.

With a sigh, she sat in the grass, her arms wrapped around her knees, and took a deep breath of warm, moist air. Now that she'd had time to think about it, she enjoyed the strange view of palm trees and the warm humidity and the soft southern accents. A beautiful place. If he didn't want her to go home with him, maybe she'd move down to this area. At least it was warm.

"Delaney?"

She jumped at the voice coming from behind her. His mother.

"Mind if I sit with you?"

Of course she couldn't say she did, even if she did. She'd wanted quiet, and space to think, since she'd had none of that from the time she arrived at the hospital. Her phone rang and she looked at the ID. Eli. She stared at it, trying to decide whether to answer, until Ellen Forrester took it from her hand, answered to say she was there with her and he could cool his heals for now.

"Hope you don't mind." Ellen set the phone on the grass between them. "Sometimes that boy just needs a firm hand. He was always that way. Sweet as could be and he'd do anything for anyone, but heaven forbid anything block him from what he wanted to do."

Delaney set her gaze on a sailboat in the distance bobbing in the waves. Anchored, not sailing.

"Are you thinking of going on back home?"

Gritting her teeth, she tried to figure out how to answer. Yes, part of her had been thinking about it, and especially now since he hadn't even bothered to say he didn't want her to go.

"We would understand if you need to go give your job notice and have time to ... get things together, to let Elijah get adjusted at home.

I know once he adjusts, he'll be back to himself. I do hope you'll consider not throwing the whole thing out just because of the way he's acting right now, not that we would blame you, of course, but in the long run, it might be worth at least staying in touch."

Staying in touch? Was his mother telling her she should go home? Had he told her..?

"Honey, I'm not trying to discourage you. I think you could be very good for Eli, but you seem to be having a hard time with this and there's no use helping someone else if you hurt yourself that way. None of us would want you to do that."

Her head shook of its own accord. "No, it's not... I just don't know how to help him, what to do. And..."

"You have a hard time being away from home? He said you wouldn't come. Those first two days when he rambled about you, he said you didn't travel alone, so you wouldn't come."

A deep breath overtook her and Delaney shook her head again, trying to pull her thoughts together enough through her racing heart and fuzzy head to answer with some kind of sense. "I'm..." Okay, she had to just say it. *Just say it, Delaney. It's Eli's mother and she needs to know.* "I ... have social anxiety disorder. Since I was a young teen. I don't talk about it. But this... being around people is hard and it's harder with his family because I know I come off as ... snobby or unfriendly, and I'm not, but... He's the first one I was able to talk to about it. Ever." Heat flushed up from her chest to her neck to her face. "I already quit. The day after I got here, I called and told them I wasn't coming back. He asked me to stay with him and I expected that meant he wanted me to go back home, to help him, or just be with him, but I'm not so sure anymore. And I'm not sure I can be what he needs, with my... He'll have a hard enough time with this. I can't make it worse. I don't want him worrying about me while he's trying to deal with his injuries and his frustration." Unable to sit still, she grabbed her phone and stood.

Ellen stood beside her and took her hand. "Thank you. I know it was hard for you to talk to me, but honey, don't think we're looking down on you in any way. We're not. We're all rather embarrassed by the way Eli's acting. This isn't him. Bill is likely giving him a good lecture about now..."

"No, I don't..." Delaney felt her eyes widen. "I don't want to cause trouble. He's having a hard enough time right now and I hate seeing him struggle this much."

"Trust me, this is what they do. Elijah gets all full of himself at times and Bill brings him back down to earth. Randy, well, he's Randy and always finding something to laugh about, which Eli finds ... well, he puts up with him better than anyone else I know. The boys are just fine and very well used to each other. No need to worry." She grinned with a slight head tilt.

It reminded Delaney of Eli so strongly, tears came to her eyes.

"Oh, Delaney, my Elijah is a wonderful man. I'm awfully proud of the way he turned out, like all of my kids, but Eli, especially, has something about him..." Ellen shrugged. "However, he's not perfect, as none of us are. He can be headstrong, impetuous, and too surly when he's annoyed. It's just part of who he is. But that's the thing, honey. We all have our strengths and we all have our weaknesses. The trick is to find the right person, or people, to balance that all out."

With a light squeeze of the hand, Ellen released her. "If you'd like to stay with us on the ranch, rather than with Elijah, until you're more settled as to want you want, or until he remembers the manners he's been taught, you're very welcome. And that said, I'm going to go check on my surly son and see if he's calmed down by now. Coming?"

"I'm going to take a walk before it's dark. Will you let him know?"

"Of course. You won't go far?"

With a simple head shake, Delaney took her shoes off and wandered down to the water. She needed to be by the water.

"By herself?" Eli started to push out of the chair and then cursed at the pain in his left hand.

"Alright, cuz. That's not gonna help anything." Ranger took his shoulders and pulled him back. "Want me to go?"

"Randy, you stay right here and leave the girl alone. Eli, she needs some time to herself. Let her be."

He nearly argued, but he knew better than to argue with his mom. "What did she say? She's not leaving?"

"Do you not want her to leave?"

"Of course I don't..."

"Then maybe you should tell her that. Anyway, she said she wouldn't be long. She's out by the water. I could still see her from the porch area when I came back."

By the water. Of course she was by the water. "Take me out to the porch." He looked back at his cousin, who was giving him that *don't order me around* look again. "I'm sorry. You don't get it, though. Just please, help me get out to where I can see her."

Eli noticed the stares as Ranger pushed his chair out onto the deck spread with tables overlooking the Atlantic. His cousin had to walk around and move a couple of them out of the way in order to get the chair over to the railing. He didn't see her. Where'd she go?

"Over there." He pointed at a ramp leading from the porch down to a sidewalk. "Please."

His cousin chuckled, apparently enjoying being in charge just a little too much, and wheeled him over to the ramp down onto the sidewalk, down as close as he could go without having to ask Ranger to push him into the grass.

"That her?" Ranger pointed down the beach in the distance.

Breathing a sigh of relief, Eli nodded. Her shoes were in her hand as she walked ankle deep through the waves.

"Gotta say, cuz, if you blow this with her, you're a freaking moron. That girl's..."

"Be careful."

He chuckled again. "I was gonna say beautiful. Or maybe cool. She's pretty cool for a girl."

Eli nodded with another sigh. "How can I take her away from this, from her ocean? It's a part of her, Ranger. I guess that's part of my trouble. Other than knowing she shouldn't have to play nursemaid to a broken up construction worker. How can I tell her she should give this up for me? Look at this place." Palm trees swayed, or at least their feathery branches did. Tufts of white highlighted the ocean as the wind pushed at the water. The sand here was white rather than tan. Hard on the eyes when the sun bounced off it, but kind of stunning to look out at. "And Jersey is ... well, to me it's better than this. Less humid. Less hot. How do I tell her to leave it for me, especially like this?" He motioned toward his mostly useless body.

"You can't." Ranger shrugged, locked the wheels, and sat in the grass facing him. "You can't tell her she should. Not your place. And yeah, she looks pretty connected to all of this. Hard to blame her. Hell, I'm tempted to move down here where it's this warm in the spring and where I could take the boat out on that ocean and just go like hell. It'd be hard to leave. Especially for some guy being such a jerk to her, never mind how you look. Can't imagine what she sees in you, really. You're right. You can't ask a girl like that to go live in the middle of the dirt and play nursemaid for your pathetic bitchy ass."

"That wasn't my intention."

"Well, if I were you and had that pretty little thing drop everything for me just 'cause I ran into a tree, I think I'd stop being an ass and start acting grateful."

"I get it. You're right. I get it." Something caught her eye up farther on the shore and she went to investigate, bending down to the sand, watching. She picked something up, but he couldn't tell what it was. She was too far away. By herself.

Eli picked up his phone, then thought better of it, and put it back down. Delaney went back into the water, a bit deeper to where it occasionally splashed up onto her capris, headed back his direction. Her gaze was at her feet, or just in front of her feet. Again, Eli wished he could pull thoughts from her head.

Nearly back in front of the hotel property, her shoulders rose and fell, and she left the water on a path toward the hotel. When she finally raised her head, she saw him and stopped walking. With another rise and fall of her shoulders, her eyes now on him, she headed his direction, taking her time, not bothering to put her shoes back on when she reached the grass. He couldn't quite read her expression. Calm. Thoughtful. Unsure, maybe. She stopped a few feet in front of him.

"Del, I'm sorry. I'm just... This is bullshit. I hate this, being so damned helpless, and I don't... I don't mean to take it out on you. I just don't know what to do with myself..."

"I know."

"No, you don't."

Her shoulders straightened; her chin raised. "Don't I?"

"Why? Have you *done* this? Got *stuck* in..."

"Eli. Come on, man." Ranger stood and touched his shoulder. "Chill the hell out already. She's on your side."

"It's fine. Can we have a minute?" Delaney glanced at Ranger, who gave her a nod and left, then returned her attention, which was now plenty easy to read. "You know what, Forrester? I dropped everything for you. I took only enough time to call into work and pack a few things and then I drove down here, by myself through the middle of the night, stopped to get a hotel room when I got too tired to drive, mostly because I was so tense from being so afraid for you on top of driving alone out of state where I've never been before and lying at the hotel to say there were two of us so I wouldn't look like I was alone and then I couldn't even do the breakfast buffet on my own so I grabbed something greasy from my car instead, which upset my stomach since it was already gnawing at me. I found my way to the hospital, asking directions and meeting your family by myself, really, since you were pretty out of it, and stayed in a room with your mother and sat at the hospital with your brother and cousin the past six days, knowing they've been judging whether or not I'll be good enough for you. Don't argue. Of course they are, as I'd expect, but I'm not exactly at my best right now and I can tell what they're thinking. My nerves have been at the top edge of overboard for the past week. I've thought about going home I don't know how often. But I didn't. Instead, I called up and quit my job and told the food bank to find someone else. Because after all of that, I was still willing to go home with you, to be by your side and help you deal with this. And you think I don't understand?

"Don't I, really? You think what I have to deal with is less debilitating than this? It's not. I promise you it's not. You know how much I would love to be a travel writer? I would love it, if I could, but the thought of being out in places I don't know and having to talk to people enough to have a good story makes me sick. Literally. Not to mention that I'm a dancer, Eli. Inside, that's what I am. But I can't do it outside my own room. I dance like Frankenstein in public because I'm so damned afraid of people watching me, looking at me, that I can't just ... be what I *am* inside. If I could, I would be so much more than I am, but you don't get it. You *really* don't.

"You think your *temporary* injury is debilitating? Try *this*. Every day of your life. Knowing you can't step outside without being nervous, that you can't go to a club and just ... just be there and talk and laugh without wondering if you'll go into panic mode and have someone think you're having a heart attack and call 911 just to make it all worse and having a doctor stare at you like you just wanted attention when the *last* damned thing you want is attention. Try having to take a stupid monotonous boring back room job when you're trained for bigger things because you *can't* face doing what you're *trained* to do. Try it, Eli. Then you tell me I don't understand that you're frustrated right now because for a few weeks, you can't do what you normally would. Tell me *I* don't understand.

"I've been sick to my stomach the whole week, trying to hide it, trying to look like someone you can count on, and you act like you don't even want me here. So yes, I know you're frustrated, but..."

"Come here, Del." He reached out a hand, but she was just out of his grasp. "Please."

Raising her hand, she set something in his instead of taking it. A star fish, missing a leg and a half. "It was out of the water too long to save it."

Eli studied the thing with rust-colored streaks down the center of each beige leg. It was different than the one he kicked. And it reminded him of his own body at the moment. *Out of the water too long.* He swallowed back emotions trying to escape and met her eyes. "You don't want to move to Indiana."

"I was thinking about staying here a while."

His heart pounded. He'd blown it, like Ranger said. "Del, what? Alone?"

She shrugged. "I'm always alone. I'm used to alone. Even when I'm in a crowd I am because I have to be, I have to shut everyone else out in order to function. The only times I haven't been shut off..."

Her head shook and she looked back toward the water.

"Is when you're on the beach with your fish friends." He was half teasing, and half just trying to stay in control of himself. She wasn't coming with him.

"Home for the sea stars is the ocean. They have to stay near the water or they shrivel up, like that one."

"And you think you'll shrivel up without being beside the ocean, Delaney?"

Her head shook. "Home for me is ... where you are."

A straggled breath crept through his body, nearly stifling him. Where he was? "Del..."

She met his eyes. Hers were wet, barely controlled from spilling over. It made his do the same, and she looked away.

"Elijah, the only times in my life I have felt not alone, not shut off, didn't feel the need to hide myself ... is when I've been with you. I feel ... like you opened this huge heavy door that's been weighing me down to let who I am start to come out. Or, at least I did feel that way. But if you're going to be different around your family, if what I had of you was only ... a travel adventure, and this is who you really are, I can't..." She wiped the corners of her eyes.

"You know why I love sea stars? They rejuvenate. If they have the right support, they can heal themselves and start again. But they have to be where they can do that."

The right support. Maybe he wasn't entirely useless if... "Come here, baby." Damn his foot, he needed to be closer to her. "Delaney, you're right. I've been a huge ass and I'm sorry. I felt for sure you'd walk away after this and I guess..."

Her eyes touched his. They were still moist, hurt.

"Hell. I'm sorry. You want me to stay here with you? Say the word, Del. I'll stay."

"I can't help you well enough right now."

"I'm not asking for your help. I'm asking for your company." He reached out a hand. "Please." Still, she held her ground, so Eli put the Starfish in the little bag hanging from the arm of his chair, lowered the leg covered from toes to calf with a heavy cast to the sidewalk, and balancing his left forearm on the chair's arm, he started to push himself up with the right.

"What are you doing?"

"Coming to you since you won't come to me."

"Don't..." She moved in and held him back by his shoulders.

Eli grasped her around the waist and pulled her on top of his leg. "That worked better than planned." He grinned and brushed her hair back with his good hand. "I'm sorry, Del. The thing is, I don't want to go back home this way, with blue thread all along my face and hardly able to do anything myself. I had a hell of a time convincing that nurse I could wash my boys by myself with my good hand, had to get pissy with her before she gave in. Hell. I've been doing that myself since I was a toddler. Not gonna stop now. Every time I have to piss, Bill or Ranger stand outside the door like..." He sighed. "But I'm sorry. It's not your fault. I just didn't want to take you home like this. It's going to be hard enough, with them converging on you, and if I look like ... like I was run over by my truck, you know..."

"If I offer to help you wash, are you going to get pissy with me?"

He started to answer and then caught what she meant. Eli couldn't help a grin. "Well, now, that just might be worth all of this. But I can still do that much. Gotta sit down to do it, but I can do it."

"Good to know, Forrester."

"TMI?"

She kissed him with her arms sliding up around his neck, then rested her forehead against his. "I am so sorry you have to deal with this. I am. I'm trying to figure out how to help, and you keep shutting me out. Maybe I deserve that after all the times I kept you shut out because it was too hard, but I want to be here for you like you have been for me and..."

"I know, baby." He set a kiss on her forehead. "Okay. I'm an idiot. I'm the one who didn't understand, although I've been trying. I'm sorry. I do want you here, Del. More than anything." He ran fingers through her hair and cuddled her in as well as he could. "You really had someone call 911 for a panic attack?"

She nodded. "I tried to tell them to just go away, to leave me alone."

"Where were you?"

"Not now. Okay?"

Of course not now. They were too much in public, and people had to be noticing. Who wouldn't stare? Eli realized she was sitting on his lap, and had kissed him, there where people could see. She felt like he was opening a heavy door? And he'd nearly blown it.

"So, how about you stay here with me a while?" Eli ran a finger alongside her beautiful face. "Since you quit and all, anyway. We can get a by-the-week room, and I can keep seeing the same doctor. At least until I get these stitches out and start healing, and once I can manage better on the crutches so I don't feel so..."

"Vulnerable."

"Yeah." He caught her eyes. "Hell. Is that it? That's how you feel every time you go out in public?"

She nodded.

"It's a really shitty feeling."

"It is." She rested a hand on his chest. "Okay."

"Okay? You'll stay here with me?"

"Of course. I'll do whatever I can to make this easier for you."

"Damn, I love you."

"So, you're back again? You're the Eli I fell in love with?"

"Yeah. I'm so sorry, Delaney..."

"Stop apologizing. You're fine." She brushed her lips against his, briefly, teasing. "Just don't refuse to let me help you."

He chuckled. "Oh, Del, trust me. I'm kinda looking forward to seeing if you meant the kind of help you offered."

"If I wasn't starving, I'd take you back to our room and prove how much I meant it right now."

A loud groan caught the attention of a couple walking nearby. "Sorry, but this girl's going to be the death of me yet." When Delaney ducked her head against his neck, he apologized to her, even if it maybe didn't sound too awful apologetic.

Grabbing his phone, he dialed his cousin. "Hey, Ranger. You guys hungry yet? 'Cause my girl's starving and we gotta take care of that."

"Yep, I am, but you could have just waved me down." He raised a hand from up on the hotel deck. "On my way. Don't let her try to push your heavy ass around. And don't try to get out of that chair by yourself again. You about gave me a heart attack."

"What? You've been up there watching us?"

"Damn right. Thought I might have to come steal her away from your rude ass."

Eli shook his head as he hung up. "I think my cousin has a thing for you."

"No. He just doesn't object to me being with you, and it's the first time he hasn't objected to a girl you've dated, so he said."

"Just how much have you been talking to him while I was knocked out?"

"Well, he's known you forever and he talks even more than you do."

Eli groaned. "Yeah, great. And you're still thinking about going home with me?"

She grinned and kissed him.

Delaney felt Eli's anxiety while he made his way through the little restaurant with windows overlooking the ocean. He was using his crutches instead of the chair since he didn't want to be wheeled in, but he was struggling to get the hang of them and people looked over like they were waiting for him to fall, not that Bill would allow that, with the way he stood guard on Eli's other side.

She held his chair as Bill helped him finagle his way into it, a chair facing the windows instead of the rest of the diners. And she took his hand as she sat next to him.

He grunted, breathing hard. "Wouldn't be so bad if I could use regular ones."

"Not until that wrist heals." His mom took his other side. "Be glad it's not nearly as bad as your ankle and leave it that way."

With the smell of something rich and cheesy, Delaney's stomach growled and Ranger joked about liking a girl with a good appetite as he pushed Bill out of the way to sit next to her. She expected Eli might answer it, but he only glanced at his cousin.

"Are you okay?" She asked quietly.

"Trying to figure out what I'm gonna be able to eat with one hand."

"Pasta worked for me when I had to."

He tilted his head. "When did you have to?"

"I fell on ice and broke my right hand way back when. Made writing hard, too. I couldn't stand to ask anyone to cut anything for me, so I ate pasta that didn't need a knife."

"Guess that would work."

"Or you could suck it up and let someone cut the steak I know you want." Bill eyed him over his water.

"Not in public, I'm not. Pasta it is."

Delaney set a hand on his leg for a moment. She never would have believed he could understand public embarrassment with as outgoing as he was, but obviously he did. It was far harder to watch it bother him than to deal with it herself.

During dinner, Eli broke the news that they planned to stay in South Carolina for a couple of weeks or so, and then head up to New Jersey to get Delaney's things together.

Bill raised his eyebrows. "How do you plan to get there?"

Eli shrugged. "Del's car. She'd have to drive, of course, but at least I'd be there with her."

"Okay, but you're too heavy for her to handle, and you're not very steady yet, no offense." Doubt covered his brother's face. "I can't stay. I've got to get back to work. You need to come on home for now so we can help you."

"I don't want to go home like this. Looking like this. Barely able to function." His voice was soft, far more than normal.

"Elijah, we're you're family. We'll keep anyone else away, if you want."

He nodded toward his mom but didn't meet her gaze. "Call me vain or whatever. I don't... Either way, Delaney needs time to get her things together and there's no sense going all the way to Indiana and having to turn around and head back east. It makes more sense to do it all at once. After a couple of weeks down here, I'll be plenty steady enough."

"And how do you plan to get her things from New Jersey to Indiana?" Bill took over again. "I assume that's what you're doing."

"We'll hire a moving company, since I can't do it right now.

Otherwise, I'd just rent a truck and drive it there myself."

"I can do that." Ranger dropped his fork and stared at them. "Hell, I'm laid off anyway. No wife to be worried if I'm there or not. I'll stay if you want. While you two are doing your own thing, I'll go beach bum the hell out of the place and then help her move whatever she wants loaded and drive the truck behind you. Still leaves her driving the car since we can't put three of us in a moving truck, but hell, she drove down here alone, so..." He shrugged. "I'd be glad to stay here a while. It's damned near paradise, as far as I can see."

"Until a hurricane comes." Delaney heard herself say it, barely. Then she wished she hadn't because they got quiet and Eli explained about her sister losing her house during Sandy, and of course they all said they were sorry...

"So what's it like dealing with a hurricane coming your way?" Bill glanced at Eli, as though wondering if he should ask. "I mean, we have tornadoes now and then and a heck of a lot of tornado warnings, but most of us have sturdy basements to hide in, and if not, a friend or relative we can go shelter with does. And parts of some places get flooded, around the river, but then there's the higher parts of ground to get up out of it. Where do you hide from gale force wind and that amount of water at the same time?"

"Inland. You don't hide. You run." Delaney focused on Eli's fingers caressing her arm.

"And your sister's family sheltered with you. How far inland do you live?"

"Not far enough. Manahawkin. We flooded some, too, and some buildings were damaged. We had to pump out the cellar of the house. I lost a few things, but nothing major. The worst part was the kids and seeing how scared they were. It's hard to tell them not to be when you are."

"Were you down in the cellar?"

"No, we were more worried about the flooding than the wind, where we were. Trina kept the kids in the bathroom with the door closed during the worst part of it."

Eli tilted his head. "And you?"

"I kept watch out the window. For flooding. In case they needed to move upstairs."

"What about your brother-in-law? Why didn't he do that so you could be in there with your sister?"

"He was out blockading roads and such. He works for the local transportation department. That's why she wouldn't go farther west to get away from it. He couldn't leave, so she wouldn't. I think she also expected it was more talk than anything, just headline stories. It's hard to tell, since everything sounds like it's going to be catastrophic anymore."

"Right." Bill shook his head. "Sorry you lost some stuff, and I'm really sorry about your sister's house, but I'm glad you all came through okay."

"Thank you. Stuff is just stuff. Trina doesn't think so, but it is."

"Agreed. Although a house can be a part of who you are almost. So I understand why she'd have a hard time with it."

"I'm not sure she ever liked the house itself too much. She likes ... mine better, because it's the family home. It's only right that she should have it now."

Eli took her hand. "You've decided to sell it to her?"

Delaney touched his eyes a moment. She knew what he was really asking. "Yes. I can rent a place. It would be easier and less expensive, and then she wouldn't have to relocate again. The kids want to be there..."

"Or you can just move your things into my place and not bother with renting."

Delaney felt the stares, but she couldn't answer in front of everyone. "We'll see."

"What else did you plan to do with it when we pick it up and move it to Indiana?"

"I thought I might just put the big stuff into storage for now, in Manahawkin, and take only what I need for a few weeks. That way, I can just drive and we don't have to worry about a truck right now. That can wait."

"Hm." Eli released her hand to take a swallow of his cola. "Well, I'm thinking we should take Ranger up on his offer and keep him around to help out."

"That's fine, but..."

"Good. We'll start with that and go from there. I'm about ready to go lie down a bit." He tried to hide a grin when Ranger snickered and mumbled something about lying down until Ellen hushed him.

~ Twenty-six ~

Ellen and Bill decided to do some sight-seeing while they had the chance. His mom especially wanted to run by St. John's Island to see the Angel Oak Tree that was said to be 500 years old or so. In a couple of days, they were flying back to Indiana. First, they wanted to get Eli settled. That would be the next day's adventure. He wasn't up to much more for one day. Regardless of how he tried to hide it, he was weak yet, shaky. It exhausted him to get from the car back to the hotel room.

Ranger came in long enough to be sure Eli was set. When he told Delaney to knock if she needed help of any kind, with a wink, Eli kicked him out.

Sitting at the edge of the bed, he gripped the front of her shirt and tugged her gently until she stood between his legs. "Come here, Del."

"How much more *here* do you want me to get?" She wrapped her arms over his shoulders and kissed him, glad they were finally alone, for the first time since before he left New Jersey.

"Hm." He kissed her nose. "I mean sit with me." When she curled a leg up to sit close, facing him, he brushed fingers over her face. "Tell me about that day."

"What day?" She ran fingers through his soft hair, thinking about his offer from earlier, or rather her offer he said he'd take her up on. Talking was not exactly on her mind.

"The 911 call."

"Eli..."

"Del, you're safe with me."

"I know."

"But?"

She sighed. Really, she was just tired of it being between them, having to talk about it, having to explain.

"Delaney, I just went to a nice restaurant with blue stitches all over my face, my left fingers sticking out under this cast nearly as blue since they're still bruised, and my right leg wrapped up three times bigger than my left while fumbling with crutches made to be as obvious as possible. You saw the stares. And you said it didn't matter. You made me believe it didn't. Mostly." He stroked her face again. "Don't be embarrassed with me."

"I'm not embarrassed, Eli. I'm ... worn out. And I'm glad to finally be only with you for a change. Can't we just..?" She kissed him, a light questioning kiss.

"Mm. Yep. I had that in mind, too." Suddenly, he swiveled around, taking her down to the bed, his body half on top of her supported by his good hand, the other up over her head. And he kissed her deeply.

"Are you up to this?" She stroked a finger down his chest.

A sly grin took over his face. "Oh, yeah. I'm definitely up to this, baby. First, though..." He kissed her neck and her jaw. "Tell me. Get it out, Del. And then I'll help you relax again."

A deep breath and his peering gorgeous loving eyes made her give in. The terror of the day came back as she described how her sister dragged her to a club the day Trina turned twenty-one and wanted to party and insisted Delaney go with her. Trina pulled her out to dance. She felt herself stiffen at the memory, at the whispers and stares while Trina danced cute and playful and flirting at her side and kept tapping Delaney's arm and saying, loudly, "Come on. Dance. I know you can. I've seen you do it in the bathroom when you thought no one was around." The laughter. The looks. Trina egging it on until Delaney went to sit, by herself, sipping her cola. She was designated driver. It was her job to watch over her sister, to be sure she got home safe. Delaney would have given most anything right then to be able to down a whiskey and cola or two or three or four, to talk some guy into buying them for her since she'd been only nineteen. She couldn't. So she sat alone... until a couple of guys came over to talk. Cute. Dressed well. One of them leaned in close and asked her to dance and she refused. The other tried and she refused him, too. Someone had bet they couldn't get her on the dance floor.

It was humiliating. She could dance. She danced well. She wanted to prove she could. And people pressed around her, urging, so she gave in to one of them and he put his hands on her hips to help her move when she was too stiff, and her armpits got wet, and the small of her back, and she worried if they could see her sweat, if she smelled through her deodorant, and the palpitations got strong enough to scare her, and they laughed more and she couldn't breathe...

"Okay. Delaney, okay, relax." Eli. She was back with him then, her heart racing as though they were still there, the cute strangers, laughing, making fun... "I'd like to go find those little assholes and pound them into the ground with my one good hand. But hey, you don't have to worry. I won't do that to you. Okay? I won't ask you to dance in public."

"Well, maybe slow dances. With you, I can do that, as long as you don't mind if I hang all over you."

The sly grin returned. "You hang all over me on a dance floor and I'll be strutting out the door like the proudest peacock you ever saw."

"That's one bird I haven't seen, actually."

"Yeah? Well, we'll fix that. Just a warning, though: they're not friendly birds and they're loud."

"Hm, guess I won't ask for one as a pet, then."

With a smile, Eli held her eyes as he stroked her hair. "I love you, Delaney. If I start getting pissy again, just punch me in the nose and I'll stop."

"That's not funny." She traced a finger alongside the blue stitches. "Anyone tries to get near your face and they'll have to deal with me."

"Is that right?"

"Absolutely. And don't think I won't. I can yell at times."

"Good." He set soft kisses along her face, her nose, her forehead. "Damn, you're beautiful. I can't wait to show you off."

She pulled his head down to claim his mouth and absorbed herself in him, his tongue, his fingers, his neck and chest and shoulder, his sensual scent she couldn't place but loved just the same. She started to unbutton his shirt to find more skin...

He grasped her hand, slowed her down with a soft kiss, and then just held her close for some time.

"Are you sure you're up to this?" She whispered beside his ear.

"Oh yeah. That part of me's working fine. I'm just enjoying the thought of having you here beside me all night long for a change, in a bed, even. Kind of thought I might take my time, since I've got the time to take."

"Take as long as you want, Elijah Samuel."

He groaned. "Yeah, great. Guess I should have known not to irritate my mother around you."

"It's a beautiful name."

"Family names. Elijah was the first American in our line to be born here and Samuel was a great uncle to some degree lost in the First Great War."

"That's nice. Who is Bill named after?"

"Our grandfathers, William and Henry. Rosemary is named after our grandmothers. You really want to go into family history now?"

"Well, I thought maybe you were trying to stall."

"Not stall, take my time. Two very different things. But since we're at it, who are you named after? It's not a real common name."

"No idea. Something she picked up out of the blue, as far as I know. For both of us."

"Really? People do that?"

"Mom did. Dad said he couldn't care less what we were named, just so long as he could pronounce them."

"And what's your middle name? Because if you can pull mine out, I should be able to do the same."

"You can't. I don't have one."

"Try again."

"I'm serious. She didn't bother, for either of us."

"Interesting."

"Hm. Quit stalling, Eli."

"I'm not stalling."

"No?"

"Maybe a tad."

"Okay. Why?"

"Well... I'm kinda ... marked up across my chest, too. So don't be alarmed or anything."

Across his chest. "The seatbelt."

"Right. At least it was there, though, and kept me from flying through the window, so there is that."

With a deep breath, she set her head against his shoulder, her eyes clenched.

"Hey, it's fine, Del. I'm still alive and kicking and ... the hell with taking my time. We'll do that later." Eli kissed her neck and traced his lips down to the V of her blouse. He was fairly adept with unbuttoning it using only one hand.

Delaney sat up and took it off for him, then pulled the sheets back and urged him to move farther up on the bed, which he did using one arm and one leg, rather well. When he started undoing his own buttons, she took over. "Let me." The sight of the bruising over his chest and down his side hurt her heart, and she lay him back slowly to set easy kisses along the blue and purple and reddish marks.

"It's alright, Del. Come here."

She moved back up to see his face and he sifted fingers through her hair. "I nearly lost you." Her eyes watered, the thought of it slamming back in with the reminder.

"Yeah, I nearly lost you, too, just because I was stupid."

Her head shook. "I'm not going to be that easy to get rid of."

"Good thing. I'm not always easy to live with."

"I'm not used to easy." She claimed his mouth, surrounding him with her arms and her body.

"Mm, I've missed you." He wriggled around to kiss her neck as she kissed his shoulder, as she stroked his bare skin down to the sweats. He couldn't get jeans over his cast, and his sweats were far easier to get off, out of her way. They could take it slow later. She needed him. Needed to feel his need of her, his acceptance.

He was right. In bed was nice. Not being in a hurry, in the rain, fighting off bugs, or with a time limit of any kind was nice. A couple of times he got annoyed by what he wanted to do and couldn't, having to keep the weight off his hand, but Delaney soothed him back into calm surrender and took over as she knew she would need to do for a while.

Always before, Delaney had kept her eyes diverted from his when they made love. A defensive move. Not this time. She met his eyes, challenged him, accepted his challenge, took charge as needed, surrendered when the time called for it.

With her hands alongside his head, she kissed his soft, beautiful, sweet lips and peered down into his eyes. "I love you, Elijah. And I mean I love you so much more than I have words to tell you."

"I love you, too, Delaney. And I can deal with anything as long as you're by my side. I don't even care how corny that sounds. That's how far gone I am."

"So." She settled against his side and stroked a finger over his chest. "Tell me more about your family. I like to be as prepared as possible for new things, you know."

A chuckle emanated from deep in his chest. "Now, that's gonna take some long amount of time."

"That's okay."

"Are you stalling, Delaney? Because that's not really what I had in mind for the rest of the night."

"Thought I should let you recharge in between."

"I damn sure hope you only think I need recharge time due to my current condition."

"Hm, I don't know. You are getting kind of old, you know."

"Old?" He laughed and turned her onto her back. "I'll show you old."

Twenty-seven

Eli beat his good thumb against his chair as he waited for Delaney. His doctor had given him clearance to do a small amount of walking on regular crutches as long as he kept the brace on his wrist. The thing was awkward as hell, but he was managing for short periods of time. It would be a long four weeks ahead, which was how long he'd have to protect the fracture on top of the two weeks he'd already been healing, longer if he wasn't careful enough with it. The ankle was still an unknown. Tricky area, they told him, with its multiple fractures. But Delaney was sure it would heal well, so he made himself believe her and told himself it would.

At least the stitches were out of his face and he wasn't so scary-looking.

Eli was more grateful than he'd be able to express to his family and friends and neighbors back in Indiana. The fundraiser they did to help with his expenses while he healed, only a couple of days after hearing of his accident, still overwhelmed him with gratitude. He'd told Bill they hadn't needed to, they'd be okay. Eli had money put back, but his brother told him to accept graciously, the way Eli always gave help.

Before his mom and Bill left, they'd found a by-the-week hotel with a handicap-equipped ground floor kitchenette unit with two rooms where Delaney cooked for him every night and he promised to return the favor when he could. Now and then, Ranger stayed for dinner. Often, he ate out instead while borrowing Delaney's car to *go out and beach bum*, as he called it. Bill offered to renew the rental for him, but Delaney insisted there was no reason Ranger couldn't use her car instead.

Eli looked back toward their room. Del had told him to stay out until she was ready. Why, he didn't know. Not like he hadn't seen her get dressed plenty often. Or undressed. The thought made him grin. She'd become far less nervous about the whole thing and he'd been crazy wrong about how sex with her would be. The girl fully made him forget his annoyance when she tried. "Hey, are you ready?"

"Keep your pants on, Forrester." She called out through the slightly cracked door.

"Guess I'll have to since I need your help to get them off. Unless that's a hint I should come on back there?"

"Is Ranger back yet?"

"Yeah, he's rolling his eyes at me, but I can send him away."

The door opened and Eli lost his grin as he stared.

"Damn, she looks like a girl."

He whacked his cousin on the stomach and put his attention back on her. She was in a light blue dress with thin straps and a deeply curved neckline to match the curve it showed of her waist before it flowed out softly, swaying as she moved, down nearly to her beautiful feet covered only in flat brown sandals. "Wow. Del, you're ... stunning. This is nice. Nice... no, not the right word..."

Ranger laughed. "You've got him tongue-tied. Never seen that before. Put your tongue back in your mouth, Eli, before you bite it off."

Delaney leaned down, her hands on the arms of his chair, her face close to his. "Thought I'd wear the blue since yours is gone." She gave him a light kiss and backed up. "Ready to go?"

"Yeah. Anywhere. Just stay at my side."

"You got it."

Eli scanned the Charleston lighthouse and wished he could take her up to the top. But it wasn't her lighthouse, and it wasn't as romantic as Old Barney, being square and black and white, all modern-looking, which Ranger thought was cool but Delaney shrugged about. She much preferred the old round red and white one on Morris Island to the much newer one on Sullivan's Island. This one, though, at least had an elevator most of the way up. Still, she wasn't interested. It wasn't her lighthouse, she said.

It was their last day in South Carolina, after nearly a month that included his hospital stay. In the morning, they would drive up to New Jersey and stay for a week or so until everything was taken care of. She'd told Trina she was headed to Indiana for a while. For how long, she hadn't said. Eli didn't even know. She only agreed to visit and see how it went. She hadn't mentioned selling the house to her sister. She wanted to do that in person.

The whole thing was far easier with Ranger along. Delaney often let him drive since he liked to drive and he offered to do at least most of it up to New Jersey, also. If there was one thing Ranger was good at more than others, it was vehicles: driving, fixing, hauling, whatever they needed. Eli was far more comfortable having his cousin along for the journey than he would be if it was only the two of them, between her nerves and his current condition.

Ranger had taken it on himself to make jokes or flirt with Del when she got tense, and for some reason, she liked him anyway. He was also taking on the guardian role well, too well maybe, but it seemed good for him. She talked easily to him and Ranger admitted it was kinda a boon to his ego that she would, that she trusted him already. Trust wasn't something his cousin was used to getting, considering his wild childhood. Eli always had, though. He'd always been right there pulling Ranger back out of trouble and including him in whatever was going on when no one else would. He never thought he'd have to take Ranger up on his constant insistence he'd return the favor someday, but he was sure as hell glad to have him around about now.

Eli was actually nervous about taking her home, maybe as much as she was about going. The attention he got because of how he looked, because of the chair or the crutches, was hard for her. He could see it was. The stares. The purposeful avoidance. Not to mention his crew flocking around so often just to check in with him, since they were still working in the area. That came in handy, too, since one or two would stay with him while Ranger went grocery shopping with Delaney. Still, she was constantly tense.

Except in his arms, naked against his skin. It was the only time Eli felt her fully relaxed.

He supposed, in the middle of the raucous family reunion, he could pull her off aside somewhere and relax her before they went on with the day. Of course he couldn't take her off in the woods in the truck, since the thing was sitting somewhere in an auto graveyard. He hated losing that truck. He'd been through a lot with it, and he'd been with her the first time in it, and the second. He'd wanted to have the thing for years to come, and to find some repeat performances, rain or no rain. But he'd get another. Things were just things, as she always said. They could make new memories, as soon as he was able to drive again.

Considering the walk from parking area to beach front looked longer than he could deal with yet, Eli let Ranger pull out his chair and stabilize him while he hopped over to it. Delaney held his good hand as Ranger pushed the thing down over the boardwalk. With luck, it took them fairly close to the water. From there, his cousin helped him out of the chair and over onto a ledge of grass-covered sand. Comfortable enough to sit and enjoy the view of the calm ocean and white-sand beach, the tall beach grass...

Delaney sat next to him.

"Go ahead, Del. Walk around. Ranger'll go with you."

"I'm not leaving you here alone." She brushed fingers through the hair on the back of his head.

With a shrug of his good hand, he scanned the area. Several people wandered around the beach. Some tourists, some locals, so he guessed. Nothing threatening. "I think I'll be fine. Go on."

"Are you sure?"

He pulled her in for a quick kiss and told her again to go.

When Ranger got her to agree, noting they both had their phones on hand, Eli grabbed a deep breath and watched her walk, still unaffected but more confident, her head up, her gait easy other than the sand shifting under her bare feet. She'd left her sandals with him.

He wanted to be at her side. Damned useless foot. The longer he watched her in the near distance, pulling her skirt up just enough it wouldn't get water splashed as she treaded through the edge of the tide, the more annoyed he got. She needed him. She was finally getting somewhere with her anxiety, starting to look like she could come out of it at least enough to do small everyday things without it being so hard on her. Eli needed to be on his feet at her side. He cursed and threw a small rock as far as he could get it toward the water.

"Are you okay?" A woman came around from somewhere behind him. A gorgeous woman with reddish brown hair, maybe not quite her natural color, a trim but sturdy figure, and dancer's calves that barely showed below a thin beach cover-up dress thing. Delaney had finally told him she hated how square her calves were from her dancing, but he found them sexy.

The woman glanced over at his chair sitting along the edge of the wood planks and down at his cast. "I understand the frustration. Want to talk?"

"You're a dancer."

She hesitated and a man came up to her side. Eli about jumped out of his skin. A large thick man with a dark discoloring running along his face. A hell of a lot more noticeable than Eli's stitches had been, even in blue.

"Don't worry. He's not as scary as he looks." The woman ran fingers over the guy's back. "I guess you've seen me dance."

"No."

"But you know who I am?"

"No. Should I?" He couldn't help glancing at the man and considered calling Ranger's cell to tell him to high-tail it right back.

"You're not from around here, judging by your accent. How did you know I was a dancer?"

"Your legs." He felt his face get hot as the man eyed him. "Sorry, I mean ... I'm not staring or anything." Although it was hard not to since her cover-up hardly covered a two-piece bathing suit and she'd walked up to him while he was sitting on the ground. "You have dancer's calves, like my girlfriend. She's... walking on the beach. With my cousin. Since I can't right now." Suddenly, Eli understood Delaney's nervousness about talking to people. A truly horrid feeling.

The woman smiled, a gorgeous smile, and offered her hand. "I'm Caroline. This is my husband, Dio. And you're right; I used to be a ballerina, professionally. These days I teach dance in between raising our little hellions, the ones making a bunch of noise behind your back. Okay, guys, come this way."

Eli turned enough to see three small children about the same size but with very different looks all come running his direction. He thought he might have to shelter his foot, but the large man grabbed two of them at the same time, one in each arm, and the other flung herself at Caroline.

"Triplets?"

She laughed. "They are. That's what happens when you marry an ultra viral farmer, I guess." Introducing them by name, she sent the four-year-olds out to the sand to play, warning them not to go past the line they knew they couldn't cross.

"Is that going to work?" Eli watched them run off toward the water.

"It better." Dio stayed on his feet, edged more toward the kids, watching until they stopped abruptly, looked at their parents, and sat down to play.

"We're here all the time. They know their limits." Caroline sat next to him. "So, what happened to you?"

Delaney could have walked along the Atlantic with the waves washing up over her feet far longer as she listened to soft southern accents and kids splashing in the shallows. But she didn't want to leave Eli too awfully long. Ranger said he'd be just fine; he was still plenty capable even broken a bit. It wasn't as enjoyable without him, though.

When she got close enough to see him, she quickened her pace. Some guy was sitting next to him, a big guy. Ranger noticed, too, and tensed as he overtook her pace. But Eli smiled when he saw her, and Ranger unwound and put his attention on a woman in a two-piece suit playing at the edge of the water with three kids.

"Hey, baby. I expected you to be longer."

She glanced at the large man with a scar across his face and her stomach knotted, but she walked up in front of Eli and took the hand he offered. "I missed you."

"Yeah?" He threw her a charming smile and looked at Ranger, then over at where his cousin was staring as the man beside him stood. "Delaney Griffin, Dio Troy. He lives right around here. And, Ranger, *that* is his wife, and his kids. Just so you know. My cousin, Randy Forrester. He goes by Ranger."

Ranger pulled his eyes from the woman and shrugged. "Nice to meet you. You're not going to take my head off, right?"

"Not for looking. I'm very well used to it." Dio offered Delaney his hand. "Nice to meet you. I've been keeping him company, but I should go rescue the wife by now. Good talking with you, Eli. If you come back this way, give us a call."

Delaney sat next to him as the guy left. "Why does it not surprise me that you made a new friend out here?"

"Hey, I was sitting here minding my own business. His wife saw the chair and came over. Guess she had a lot of foot trouble of her own and a couple of surgeries, but she's back to dancing. Told me not to give up on it."

"Yeah, that guy looks worse than you do." Ranger was still standing, staring as Dio headed toward his family. "What's with that?"

"Childhood burn accident. I guess he avoided people as much as you do, Del, until she helped him deal with it."

Delaney wrapped her arms around him and lay her head on his shoulder. "We all have our traumas, right?"

"And with any luck, someone on our side to keep us going through to the other side." He raised her face to his and kissed her.

"Yeah, okay. I'm gonna swim if you two are starting that."

Eli told Ranger to go ahead. "Hope he doesn't push it too far with Caroline."

"Who?"

"Dio's wife. I think you'd like her."

"Are those kids all the same age?"

He chuckled. "Yeah. She joked about her farmer and fertility or something like that."

"Farmer?"

"Well, animals mostly. She's kind of an animal freak, but land animals more than sea animals. Like I said, if we were to stay here, I think we'd have a hang-out couple already."

Delaney pulled back. "You're not thinking about staying?"

"No. Just..."

"Hey." She pulled his face to his. "You can't hide from your hometown forever, and you look fine, you know." She traced a finger over the reddish line. "You're still incredibly sexy..."

"Right. One-handed and one-footed with this mark down my face?"

"Yes, even like that. For an old man, anyway."

"Again with the old man thing? I haven't proven otherwise yet?" He rolled half over top of her, lying her against the grassy sand, stroked fingers along her face, and kissed her. "So, what would you say to spending the evening around a campfire instead of at some restaurant?"

Delaney ran fingers through his hair. "Sounds nice, actually, depending. Where?"

"Dio's. He invited us. Wasn't sure you'd be interested since you don't know them, but..."

"With Ranger, too?"

"Of course."

A twinge of nerves hit her stomach, but still, it sounded better than a public place.

"Just them and their kids and us. No one else, Del."

"Okay."

"Yeah?"

"I can't hide forever, either. Someday, it would be nice to have hang-out friends again. So it'll be a good test, right?"

With a smile, Eli sat up and pulled her in close against him. They watched the kids play in the water and sand, with Ranger playing along like he was one of the kids, and Delaney found herself very much wanting to be a family, with kids. Eli's children would be beautiful. They would.

Of course, they were still missing a step before she could let herself go very far with that thought.

~ Twenty-eight ~

The first night back in New Jersey, all she and Eli wanted to do was eat and crash. Ranger did all of the driving, so Delaney wasn't sure why she was so tired. Emotions, maybe, knowing after the next week or so, it could be some time before she would be beside the ocean, and her sister. Part of it was also the tightness she felt in her stomach when they crossed the New Jersey state line. It was home, but it was also where so many hard memories were set.

Ranger had gone to scout out the beach. He had his phone and wouldn't be far, he'd said. It didn't matter. Delaney and Eli used what strength they still had to change and climb into bed and cuddle together. She didn't remember one minute past that.

After breakfast at Mustache Bill's, since Eli had told his cousin about it at some point during the drive, they went out to the lighthouse. He'd used his crutches to get into and out of the diner, but now he let Ranger help him into his chair, which either meant his ankle was hurting or his left armpit was, since he leaned mainly on his armpit to keep the pressure off his wrist.

By the time they got to the benches overlooking the Atlantic, to the side of Old Barney, Ranger was wiping sweat from his forehead. "Wow, another beautiful place." He stood on the other side of his cousin, looking out. "Sure you don't wanna settle here with her? 'Cause you know, I might be convinced to join you."

"What about your girl? Giving up on her?"

"Nah, she'd come. She hates Indiana. Part of the reason she's iffy about staying with me, since I plan to stay there. Could change my mind, though, if you stay here."

Eli threw him a grin. "I'd be flattered, but I know it's more due to Delaney than to me."

"Well, she's definitely the prettier one of the two of you. But you need me more." He winked at Delaney.

"Guess I can't argue that. Can you help me hop over to the bench?"

"Yep." Ranger gave him an arm to help him up and Delaney sat next to him. "Mind if I go wander a bit? Got my phone." He didn't wait for an answer before taking off toward Old Barney.

Eli set an arm around her. "Nice to be home?"

Home. Where she'd always lived. Unsure how to answer, Delaney wrapped an arm around Eli's and leaned in to set a hand on his stomach, closing her eyes to enjoy the gentle breeze, the ocean smell, the cry of gulls ... all of which she was leaving. For her Eli. Possibly for good, depending. And it was okay. This would be locked in her memory always. It would always be part of who she was, both bad and good. All of it.

He stroked hair out of her face and brushed it behind her ear. "Still okay with walking away from this?"

"Yes."

"Sure?"

"Absolutely. *You* are home, Eli, as I said. This is just a place."

"Delaney." He started to speak, then stopped, stared several seconds, and let a deep breath raise his chest. "I love you, Del."

"Yeah, you better. This is a hell of a step for me."

He stroked her face and his eyes moistened. "I know. And I know it scares you. But we're going to make it. I'll help make it work for you."

"Me, too. I'll keep trying, you know. I might go back and forth a bit, but I won't give up if you don't."

"Never." It was nearly a whisper and he took his arm from around her to fumble in the pocket of the loose khakis he'd started wearing since he could get them over his cast. Finally, he pulled out a small box and opened it.

Tears came to her eyes as she stared at the gorgeous solitaire with a starfish design etched on each side.

"I don't want you to put your stuff in storage, Del. I want you to bring it to Indiana."

"Eli. Are you sure? You don't want your family to meet me first or..?"

He caught her mouth in a sweet kiss and leaned his forehead against hers. "Baby, I would move here for you if you wanted, or about anywhere. Whatever I need to do to make it work for you. I'm not an ounce concerned about what anyone else thinks. I want you to be my wife. Marry me, Delaney. Please."

She chuckled and kissed him. "Yes. Eli, there's nothing in the world I could ever want more."

To celebrate how crazy she was to agree, so Ranger said, with a hug for them both, Eli took her to the Sandcastle for dinner and surprised her by taking her to a room with a balcony overlooking the ocean.

"So." Lying up against his warm, naked skin beneath the luxurious bedding, Delaney held up her ring to admire it. "How did you manage to do this when I haven't been away from your side for the past month?"

"Ranger and some phone calls. Nearly gave it to you the last day we were in South Carolina, but I wanted to get you up here first and give you another chance to be sure you could leave it."

She kissed his chest. "Good thing I said yes, huh? You could have been stuck with a starfish ring."

"Nah, I'd just wander the shore kicking the things until some other crazy fish girl yelled at me about it."

She chuckled and shifted to prop herself half on top of him. "Is that right? Any crazy fish girl would do?"

"Delaney, absolutely no girl in the world but you would ever do for me. Come here."

"How much more *here* do you want me to get?"

"All the way, baby. Just as close as you possibly can."

Twenty-nine

Trina cried when she saw Eli on his crutches and she touched the side of his face before she gave him a long hug. "I'm so glad you're okay. I can't believe she just took off and didn't tell me. She had to *call* me. I was so worried. I probably irritated the heck out of her texting for updates. How do you feel?"

"A hell of a lot better by now. And thank you."

"Trin, okay, he needs to sit. We've already been out taking care of some things. How about letting us in my house?" Delaney caught Eli's amused glance.

"Of course. Can I help?"

"Got it covered." Ranger offered a hand and introduced himself, then took Eli's side to catch him if needed. He made it up the stairs to the porch by propping his left arm on the railing and using the crutch under his right arm. He was tired, no matter what he said, and Delaney gave the little ones hugs when they ran up to greet her, but moved them out of the way so he could get through.

Pat was actually polite for a change, asking if Eli wanted the recliner so he could prop the foot up, and the kids looked at him funny, but the younger two talked with him as he settled into a chair, a regular chair. Delaney finally asked them to stop asking questions about his *owies*, as they called them. When it didn't work, Ranger sat on the floor beside the big toy box and asked what they had to play with.

Delaney told Trina a little bit about South Carolina and then broached the subject of Indiana. And the house maintenance, which made Pat start to stiffen. "What would you think about buying it from me?"

Trina's mouth dropped.

"If you don't want it, that's fine. I'll sell it instead..."

"Wait. Sell it? You would *sell* our house? We grew up in this house. And where would you live when you get back? You mean you'd rent the room out or..?" She glanced at Eli and her eyes widened. "Wait. Are you..?"

Delaney raised her hand to show her ring. "I'm moving to Indiana. Eli has a house already, and..."

"You're engaged!" She jumped up and gave Delaney a big hug, and then Eli, and then calmed fast. "Moving? You mean for good moving?"

"Yes."

"You can't... Laney, you can't leave me."

"Trina, it's fine. We'll visit, and you can visit."

"Anytime you want." Eli rubbed Delaney's hand. "And I've gotten kind of used to this whole ocean thing, so we can drop by now and then."

"You're leaving?" She wiped at her eyes as Pat rolled his and told her to calm down, her sister wasn't falling off the end of the earth, to which Tammy said there wasn't an end, it was a circle like a ball and Pat said it was only an expression.

"So. Are you interested?" Delaney wanted the conversation back on track. "In buying the house?"

"Of course. Whatever the market value is now, we'll pay it."

Pat cleared his throat. "Trina. We've discussed this."

Delaney looked from one to the other. "You've discussed buying my house without me mentioning I wanted to sell?"

"Figured you'd be moving out soon." He glanced at Eli. "There are a couple of things we need to discuss first." Pat sent all of the kids to their rooms. He wanted to offer much lower than market value, due to the roof needing attention and the HVAC needing replaced and considering the rent they'd already paid her to live there for six months. Delaney expected it, but the amount he suggested was far too unreasonable.

Eli squeezed her hand. "What's wrong with the roof?"

"Shingles are warping. Has to be replaced."

"The whole thing?"

"You can't do just part of a roof."

"Yeah, you can." Eli held Pat's gaze. "Maybe I should go up and look at it..."

"Are you kidding me?" Delaney nearly throttled him.

"I'm not letting you get shafted, Del. Doesn't look that bad from the ground."

"I'll go look." Ranger stood. "Got a ladder?"

"You can't just go up on my roof without..."

"My roof." Delaney stopped her brother-in-law. "It's still mine. Yes, he can." She turned her attention to Ranger. "You know about roofs?"

He snickered. "Oh yeah, one of my dozens of jobs. I did Eli's for him, all of it, with some help from him and a couple of nephews. I'll look at the HVAC, too. If it's gotta be replaced, I can do it free labor. Might just need maintenance."

"Wow, you're handy to have around."

Ranger grinned. "Glad you think so. Of course, your fiancé could do any of it, too, if he wasn't lame."

With Pat unable to argue and Trina pushing at her husband to agree it was fair, Delaney hugged her sister and walked out with Ranger to find a ladder. It hurt her stomach to see him up there, but Eli had come out as far as the porch and assured her he was fine.

It needed only some patching, Ranger said, and he could do it in a couple of hours or so. The HVAC, as he suggested, only needed a good cleaning and some minor repair stuff he also knew how to do.

Delaney hugged him. And he bragged to his cousin about getting such a nice hug.

When it was time for the cleanup crew to meet out at the refuge, they ran by to see Gloria and the others and to share their news. Gloria also fussed over Eli and Delaney wasn't at all sure her fiancé wasn't starting to enjoy having women fuss over him. Of course, the big test would be when he got home.

Figuring it was the least she could do, Delaney treated the boys to a local seafood dinner from Off The Hook at Viking Village and they took it out to the beachfront to enjoy as the sun faded over the ocean.

~ Thirty ~

A huge relieved breath filled Eli's lungs as they pulled into Kentland's town limits.

Delaney looked over at him. "Does that mean we're close?"

"It means we're here. Pull into Casey's. Right there." As she stopped, he waved at his cousin in the truck behind him to come to the car window. "If you want to go on to the house, I'll give Del a quick tour of the town first."

"Tour of the town? You're kidding me, right?" Ranger peeked in at Delaney. "Sweetheart, this *is* the town."

"Okay, go on." Eli pushed him back out the window. "We'll be there in a few."

"Yeah, like a few seconds behind if you give her the whole *tour*." Ranger muttered as he shrugged and went back to the U-Haul.

"Is he exaggerating?"

"Only slightly." Eli took her hand. "You okay?"

"How big is it? I mean, how many people?"

"Oh about ... seventeen-hundred. On a good day."

She stared as though trying to decide if he was kidding. Before he could clarify, Jeff from up the street came over to his still-open window. "Eli, well what do you know? Heard about your accident. Doing okay? Home to stay now? Was that Ranger I saw in the truck?" He ducked to look in across the car at Delaney.

"Yes. To all of the above." He introduced her to Jeff, and to Bob who came over, and Sheila. "Hey, we'll be around later. Long drive from Jersey. We're going to go get settled and call in to let my folks know we got here."

"My guess is they'll know before you're home." Sheila laughed and poked at Bob. "Nice to meet you, Delia. See you around."

Eli didn't bother to correct her. He gave Delaney the sign to pull away and threw a wave. He was sure to point out the library which seemed to impress her, the large park, the main shopping area, the three different pizza places, and the liquor store with a teasing question about whether they should stop and grab something. She was quiet, though, other than a comment or two about a beautiful house, and he led her ... not to his place, but to his parents'. A sudden attack of the nerves, he supposed. Eli was starting to wonder if dragging her way out to the middle of nowhere had been a mistake. Stopping to tell his family they were back would be a convenient excuse to put off dealing with her reaction to his house, and to being in his house when he couldn't yet manage to be there on his own.

She didn't say anything about it. She just followed the directions he gave with a slight nod and he called Ranger from his cell to tell him where they were and they wouldn't be long.

Delaney pulled onto the large concrete parking area as she looked over at the rust-colored brick two-story ranch with darker rust shutters fronted by a thin open porch and a mulched flower bed boasting its spring colors. By the time she got out to bring his crutches to his door and he was up on the things, his mom and dad and Bill and Shirley were heading at them.

Trying to keep an eye on Delaney through hugs and introductions and questions about the trip, Eli wondered again if he'd messed up, if they should have gone on home. She was tense, more than she had been in some time.

"You look a lot better than when we left." Bill set a hand on his back for a second and walked beside him to the door.

"Feel better, too."

"Did you leave Ranger behind?"

"Almost had to. He fell in love with the place." Eli lowered to the couch and reached a hand to Delaney, keeping hold as she sat on the edge of the couch at his side.

His dad talked about the driving time and how it was tough to have to do it all rather than switching, how tiring it was, even if they had made it a two day trip rather than one, mainly because of Eli's ankle since it got to hurting too bad if he didn't elevate it now and then.

"Where are the little monsters?"

Shirley play-nagged him for calling her babies that. "They're over at Gia's. Bill figured you might stop by here and didn't want to inundate Delaney too much all at once.”

"You could've brought them. I've been missing my hugs. And Del's used to kids. Her sister has five of them. Wouldn't be any kind of shock to her.”

"We nearly had to bring them, once they knew we were coming over to see you." Shirley shook her head and focused on Delaney. "I swear most of the time they'd rather be with Uncle Eli than with me and their dad. They'd move in with him if I allowed it, and on days...”

Eli laughed. "That's 'cause I get to be the uncle and not the parent.”

"Meaning he spoils them rotten." Bill rolled his eyes. "And sends them back to us.”

"Yeah, well, Mom's not the spoiling rotten type, so someone's gotta do it for them. Let me guess. You were afraid I still looked like hell and might scare them.”

"There was some of that." Bill glanced at Delaney's clenched fist, the one he wasn't holding. "And I wasn't sure what you would be up to. Really nice to see you doing so well, kid." He grinned at Delaney. "I told you he healed well, and you've obviously managed to keep him out of trouble since we left.”

She looked at Eli and her fingers tightened against his.

"How about we go and grab some drinks?" His mom asked Delaney, suggesting she go with her.

"We're not staying." Eli rubbed her hand with his thumb. "We only stopped for a minute to say we were back.”

"Take them with you, if you'd like. Come, dear, I'll show you around the house while you stretch your legs. I'm sure you need it after that long drive.”

Delaney was half glad for the excuse and half annoyed that they didn't just go home. She was tired. And... her ring. She curled her left hand so Ellen wouldn't see it accidentally. Pointing out the kitchen, his mother also pointed her toward the bathroom in case she needed to freshen up from the road, and said Delaney could join her in the kitchen.

She grabbed a deep breath as soon as the door was closed. A large bathroom for a hallway bath. It smelled of something floral but not overwhelming. Delaney wasn't sure where the smell came from. There were no countertop freshener things, no bowls of potpourri. The walls were a pale green, the minimal decorations a vine pattern in cream and dark green. The house was bigger than she expected. It was casual, elegant, very together, as she'd expect from Ellen Forrester, but bigger.

Taking more time than she really needed, Delaney grabbed another deep breath before she opened the door, and nearly ran straight into Eli.

"You okay?" He tilted his head at her.

"I'm fine."

"We can go when you want."

"Eli, it's fine. Really." She touched his face and he caught her hand, his thumb rubbing over her ring.

"Can we go ahead and tell them?"

"That's up to you."

"I figure someone'll see it soon, anyway."

She moved in to plant a quick kiss on his lips. "Whatever you want. I'm fine."

"Okay, then. Wait here for me." He headed into the bathroom and she closed the door for him and leaned back against the wall, telling herself she was as fine as she told him she was.

"Is everything alright, dear?" His mom, with a tray of sodas and glasses with what looked like tea, stopped on her way from the kitchen.

"Waiting for Eli." At the raised eyebrows, she searched quickly for a reason. "He's more tired than he wants anyone to know, and he's been up on his crutches a lot today already. I just..."

"Yes, I see it, as though he can hide it from his mother. Alright. Give us a shout if he needs us. In the meantime, you might want to check the wall farther down."

Delaney followed Ellen's nod to a wall full of photos, some in compilation frames, others in single frames. He played baseball. She grinned at the succession of yearly photos of him in his team uniform, bat held on his shoulder, the happy proud look all over his face in every picture. There were some of him and Bill in their Boy Scout uniforms and some of who she expected was Rosemary in a Girl Scout uniform. Random photos of them all playing. And full family photos, not yearly, but regular full family photos.

When the door opened, she called his name to let him know she was there and he took her side. "Mom sent you here, didn't she?"

"Yes. You didn't tell me you played baseball."

"I did tell you was active. Just one of the things they let me do to keep me out of trouble."

"These are beautiful." She gazed at the family photos again.

"I bet yours are, too. Bring any with you?"

"No. We didn't... I have some random pictures, but nothing like this. We didn't do this."

He tilted his head with a frown. "I can't even guess what it would be like growing up without family being a priority."

Delaney shrugged. "Trina always had a ton of friends. I'm good at keeping myself occupied. It worked."

"Hm. This is going to be some kind of different for you, Del. Come on, let's do the obligatory time before we can escape."

Everyone looked up at them as they returned to the living room, to include four new faces. The woman rushed over to give Eli a hug around his crutches, with the other three, a male adult and two kids right behind her. Rosemary, his sister, her husband Max, and their nearly grown kids who also gave him big hugs.

Rosemary hugged Delaney, too tight, but luckily the others only offered their hands. "We had to come. I know you're not staying and we maybe should have waited, but oh, Eli." Rosemary touched his face. "You scared us all so bad. We all wanted to rush down there to see you. Bill told us to stay put, but I nearly ignored him. If the kids didn't have so much going on, I would have, you know. You look okay, though, well, other than all of this." She waved a hand along his frame. "How are you feeling?"

"Bill was right. No need for a big hospital audience. And I'm doing well enough for now. I've been well taken care of."

At that, she turned to Delaney. "We've heard so much about you from Bill and Mom. It's so nice you came along with him. I hope you're staying a while? I know Mom offered you a room here, but we'd welcome you, too, and we're not far from Eli."

"She's staying with me, but thank you." Eli set a hand on Delaney's back.

"Are you sure? I mean, Ranger's staying with you until you're better, right? So you'll have help already..."

"Rosie, thank you. She's not here to help me out."

Delaney wanted to escape. Too many people. Too many presumptions.

"Okay, how about letting him sit as he needs to by now." Bill took her other side, reading her thoughts, maybe, but it worked and Eli threw his brother a grateful nod.

As he headed toward the couch, Eli stumbled. Delaney shoved a hand against his chest and grabbed his arm. Once she realized he was steadied again, she felt his heart pounding beneath her hand.

"That could've been bad." He looked at the coffee table just in front of him.

"Are you okay? Did you hurt your wrist?"

"No, hope I didn't hurt yours. Good catch."

Delaney realized her heart was pounding every bit as hard as his and that his family was swarming him again. "You just insist on being the center of attention, don't you?"

He laughed. "Yeah, and I'm going to drive you crazy, probably."

"Um." Bill had moved around to Eli's other side and grasped her hand, the one on Eli's chest. "Something we should know about?" He looked at the ring.

Eli shrugged. "Other than that she agreed to let me drive her crazy the rest of our lives?"

Commotion broke out with a houseful of congratulations mixed with good reflexes/good catch appreciation mixed in, until Bill took her hand again. "Welcome to the family, Delaney. You'll be a nice addition. Now, take him on home and make him put that foot up before he falls on his face and needs more stitches."

"Sure you're okay?" Delaney had the car started, but she took his hand.

"That was uh ... a little traumatizing. I could see my face planting right on the edge of that table." Eli felt shaky just saying it. "Not exactly the way I planned to announce our engagement."

"That doesn't matter. You didn't hurt yourself more, did you?"

"Stepped on the ankle. Doesn't feel great. But you know what? I'm starving. How about we stop to grab pizza to take home?"

"You have drive through pizza?"

He chuckled. "Nah, but we have a Monical's."

"A what?"

Eli shook his head and told her it was where he'd hung out as a kid, had taken dates, had met with friends after football games or movies. It was casual. Giving her directions, he called Ranger to let him know where they were and that they were bringing food.

He had not counted on running into an old friend who stopped to talk and called another old friend over while they sat at a table to wait on their order. Delaney did okay with it, but she kept looking at him to answer when they asked her questions. He should have just taken her home and sent Ranger out for it.

Finally back in the car, with his old buddy walking him out and a promise to give him a call soon, Eli apologized.

"It's fine. Anywhere else you need to go?"

He heard an edge to her voice. "Changing your mind already?"

"No. Are you? You're the one stalling from taking me home. Why?"

"Del." He brushed hair from her face. "I know you say stuff is just stuff and a house is just a house, but ... I put my heart and soul into my house, planning for the right one to share it with in time. I designed it myself, built much of it myself, well with plenty of help from Ranger and a few others. So if you don't like it or don't feel like it fits you..."

"You built your own house?"

"Well, construction is what I do. I brought in an electrician to double check what we'd done to be sure it's safe, but the rest... I guess I'm being too vain again. Still..."

"Eli, I've yet to find anywhere, other than the refuge and your arms, that fits me or that I fit. You can't worry about that. I fit you.

That's what matters. Or maybe I don't and that's what's worrying you. Your family isn't sure about me, other than Bill and Ranger, anyway. I see it..."

"They're just not used to non-talkers. As soon as they know you as well as Bill and Ranger do, they'll like you every bit as much. Nope, that's not worrying me at all. My house is ... well, the only part of me you haven't seen."

"Then it's time I do, right?"

"Okay, baby. Then let's go home. Want me to drive?"

She leaned over to kiss him. "No, but I'll be glad for you to take over with that when you can." With a touch of his face, she pulled out.

He took her back out of town, past his parents' house, past where he pointed out Bill's house and Ranger's trailer, to a long gravel drive where they came to a wood panel and stone two story ranch. Or one and a half; only part of it had a second story. There were large windows and a covered porch that extended the whole front of the house. As she got closer, Delaney could see an open patio on one side with short stone walls that matched the house. The large parking area, also gravel, was on the other side and she pulled into the spot closest to the porch. The U-Haul was at the far side, the door open. It was nearly empty.

"You built this?"

"Yep. Let me take you in to really see it before you..."

"It looks like you."

"That a good thing?"

"Would I have said yes to coming here if it wasn't?"

"Well, how about withholding judgment till you see the rest?"

"Okay, but I was right about you ... before I saw the rest."

He chuckled, gave her a soft kiss, and opened his door. Ranger was there, grabbing the crutches from behind Eli's seat and helping him out before Delaney had even closed her door. He was telling her, or Eli, what he'd done already, said the pizza smelled good and he'd eat before he finished what he could do himself, that he had help coming over in the morning to get the big things.

Delaney only half heard him while she studied the place. Eli's home. On the way in, he told her about things he still meant to do but hadn't had time yet and wasn't sure now how long they'd take to get to. She let Ranger take his side up the steps since he was strong enough to catch him if he stumbled again, and then they stepped inside and she lost her breath.

"Is that good or bad?" Ranger half-whispered.

"Not sure yet. Del? What do you think?"

She would have chosen it herself. Part casual, country style and part elegant, classical, it was open, airy, light. The walls were a very soft blue bordering on white, the furniture medium oak highlighted with fabric in blues and greens of different shades and different patterns, all simple, small patterns. The doors and window frames matched the wood of the furniture, and the floor, a real wood floor of narrow strips. The ceiling was vaulted, also oak, with two skylights and two rows of dropped lights running along the lowest beams.

"Del?"

She nearly couldn't answer him. It was like ... like walking into a place made for her. Like some kind of fairy tale meant for a casual Jersey girl rather than a princess. "This." She set a hand on his chest. "This is gorgeous. You designed it?"

"I did, with some help picking out the fabrics and such. Rosemary is good with that and knows me enough to know what I'd pick if I'd wanted to do it."

"Did... um..." Unsure she should ask, Delaney continued when he gently raised her face to his with a question. "Your sister is ... the only woman to help..?"

"The ex didn't live here, Del. She's never set foot in it and not one thing here belonged to her. Okay? I was in an apartment at the time, still getting this done enough. Like I said, I've been saving it for the right girl, the one it fits. So, let me show you the rest of the place."

He walked her through the living room to the connected dining area, to a big fresh and open kitchen in the same colors and same wood. The countertop and large island with a separate sink were pine green, textured, not glossy. A large sliding glass door with pulled back Venetian blinds the same color as the walls led out to the patio.

Eli took her out through the door. Above the low stone wall was a tall planter that wrapped all the way around the patio, in the same wood as the top of the house. Openings on each side of the wall against the house allowed passage to either the front or back yard. A black metal patio set and a nice big grill filled in the open space.

"I may put gates in eventually. Still thinking about that. The plan is to put small vegetables and herbs and such in the planters, which I'll need to get done soon if we're going to have it this year at all."

"Doesn't that usually go in a garden?"

"Rabbits get to it in a garden. Hoping this will work better."

"You have rabbits?"

He laughed. "We all have rabbits, not invited."

"Yeah, bad for gardens, but they make good eating."

She looked back at Ranger to see if he was kidding. Apparently he wasn't. And she had to admit she'd never tried it. She also admitted she wasn't sure she wanted to try it.

"Come on back this way." Eli hobbled the way they'd come, pointing out a mud room/laundry area around the back side of the kitchen, plus a half bath, so he could go in and out right there in between working on the yard without messing the rest of the house. And then to the other end of the house where there was a full bath and two bedrooms, one unused so far where Ranger was stacking her boxes, and one Ranger was using to house sit, plus an office with a large window facing the front yard where he said he planned to put a daybed for extra space if needed.

"How much company do you plan to have?"

He grinned. "Well now, company isn't my biggest plan for these rooms." He pulled her in against him as well as he could without dropping the crutches. "They're for the kids."

"What kids?"

"Ours." He searched her eyes, waiting for a response.

"Is that so? Aren't you jumping on that trigger a little too fast, Tonto?"

"I tend to do that. Haven't noticed?"

"Hm. And where's your room?"

"*Our* room is up there." He nodded at the stairs that went up to the open area overlooking the living room that she'd tried hard not to look at.

"Um." She glanced at his crutches. "Going to be hard with those, isn't it? Should we stay down here until you're healed?"

"As long as I've been away from my own bed sleeping in hotels? Not a chance. Even if I have to sit on my ass and push myself up and down with my one good foot and my one good hand, I'm sleeping in my bed. Come on. I want you to see it."

Her stomach hurt going up the open stairway to the open loft, both with railings, but too open railings, close enough together a small child couldn't possibly get through. Her gaze did, though. But his room was wonderful. Even if there was a big window with window seat on one wall that he said she could use as a reading nook. How she'd do that when the thought of getting close to that window that looked down...

Forcing herself to wander closer, she saw that it looked not only down but out over a very large pond surrounded by trees.

"My fishing hole for when I don't want to go out and about. It's actually a lot more shallow than it looks, but the back part of it's deep enough..."

"Yours?"

"Yep. Thinking I might put some sand and a mini lighthouse out there around it to help you feel more at home."

Delaney's eyes moistened as she wrapped her arms gently over his shoulders. "So tell me, how often should I expect your family and friends to just drop by?"

"No, they won't. Already made that clear. This is my oasis, Del. And yeah, I do need one at times, too. They'll call first and they won't hover. I guarantee it. Of course Ranger will be staying here a while, at least until this wrist heals so I can move about easier, but he'll respect your privacy."

Overwhelmed again, but in a much nicer way than when they drove into his town, Delaney gave him a soft kiss. "This is... you're right, more than just a house. It's you. I love it."

He squeezed her with one arm. "One more room to see." Eli took her back down the stairs, hopping again, which scared the heck out of her and made Ranger hurry over to be sure he didn't tumble down. After resting a bit with a few chosen curse words, he accepted his cousin's offer to get his chair and led her to the back of the house, to ... a room with all windows and a hardwood floor, open, the only furniture stuck up against the one solid wall. It also overlooked the pond, and a large back patio.

"It'll make a usable dance space, right?"

She looked back at him from the center of the room.

"I had a playroom-slash-entertaining room in mind for it, but it'll be the best place for you to..."

"My shoes would mess up the floor."

"Doubt it. If they do, it's wood. I'll sand it down and refinish it. I don't want you worrying about that, Del. What do you think? Will the windows bother you?"

Probably. At first. But she could get used to it once she was sure people wouldn't just stop by. It faced the back of the house rather than the front. There were no neighbors anywhere close enough to just look in, and trees outlined the yard beyond the pond.

Delaney shook her head and went to sit on his legs. "A man this concerned about a girl's needs is a man hard to let go of, Forrester. Fair warning."

"Well now, it doesn't come cheap. There's a price to pay, you realize."

"And what is that?"

"You have to put up with me and my irritable moods. Not to mention the family. Maybe cook for me now and again. I'm kind of getting used to your odd meals, even if they are healthy."

"I think I can manage that." She slid a hand down his chest. "If you'll do some of your famous barbecue for me now and again."

"Ah, and who have you been talking to?"

She grinned and kissed him.

Ranger asked if they'd be okay for a while so he could go check his trailer and stop to see a couple of people, and Eli told him to go on. When the front door banged, he gave Delaney directions to find a large old blanket, let her help him wheel out to the back patio, to the far edge, and had her spread it over the grass.

He got himself down onto it with some gentle help, and grasped her hand. "Come here, baby."

"I don't know. That glint in your eyes says I probably shouldn't."

"Does it now? Come here."

With a grin, she settled beside him and looked out over the yard.

"So what do you think? And be honest."

"I'm always honest with you." She scanned the property, the house, and then she scanned him. "It's you. Inside and out."

"We can make it yours, too. Decorating isn't my thing. You can do that. Make it yours, Del. Ours. I don't want it to be just mine. I built it for a family, not just for me."

"Oh Eli, you have a ways to go yet in understanding me. What I mean is ... I love it, just as it is. Like you. Inside and out. I think I can be really, very comfortable here."

A large grin covered his face and he pulled her up closer against him.

"One thing." Delaney ran fingers through his hair. "Mind if I use part of the money from my house to put in a pool? I love to swim, but not in public, so I don't much..."

"Well, let me see." Eli looked over at a spot he'd already picked out for that, when he could get to it, back along the tree line, which meant he'd have to also put up a leaf netting to keep them out, along with a fence big enough to keep the kids from getting into it on their own. "That spot right there." He nodded toward it. "Pretty secluded. It'd make a nice skinny dipping opportunity."

"Don't count on that."

He laughed and pulled his shirt off, or tried to get it off.

"Getting hot?" She ignored his struggle and teased his stomach with soft fingers.

"More frustrated than hot at the moment. Want to help me out?"

"How long will Ranger be gone?"

"A couple of hours at least."

"Sure about that?"

"Absolutely. He'll be off to find his girl. May not be back till late tonight, or even morning."

"Well then, you get that shirt off and I'll help you with your frustration."

He stopped pulling at the thing and looked at her. "I think you're not understanding me well yet, either."

She grinned and ran a finger down around the hem of his jeans. "Oh, I understand you. But I'm enjoying watching Captain America have trouble with his own shirt. I bet you can do it."

"This is payback, right?"

"Absolutely not."

Her grin said otherwise, and he nearly tore the thing off but he got it off. She moved around behind him and caressed him with both hands, giving his shoulders a gentle massage to help ease the strain in the nearly constant-aching muscles from the crutches. Every night she'd massaged them, even over the past week when she hadn't felt well herself and couldn't do more than enjoy lying close as he did whatever he could to help her feel better.

The way she kissed his shoulder and slid her hands down around to his stomach told him she was very much willing and ready to relieve his frustration. Although it was no longer frustration. It was only plain enjoyment, sexy and sensual. Both.

"Come here, Del."

"How much more here do you want?"

"All the way, baby. I want this all the way."

Thirty-one

They'd been in Kentland for barely over a month and Delaney was already able to walk around town without feeling terribly like a fish out of water. Eli's cousin Gia mentioned needing help at the animal shelter and Delaney volunteered. Since then, Gia, who was twenty-four and bouncy enough to remind her of Trina with less attitude, had been attached to her hip, whenever she could pull her from Eli's side. Delaney even got away with adopting one of the puppies, an eight-month-old mixed breed that always came right to her and nudged her ankle. He was black and brown and shaggy with a sweet face, and he was always pushed aside by the other dogs, so she couldn't leave him there. Eli teased that he'd have to buy more land if she worked there long, with as big as her heart was. She had to wonder just how much land he thought dogs needed.

"Move out from under my feet, bud. You're going to get stepped on." She shook her head. The little mutt followed her everywhere she went and whined when Eli made him stay downstairs for the night. Ranger was already at work building him a house off the patio and Eli was doing well with training him to stay where he was told to stay, except out from under Delaney's feet. Nothing they said stopped that.

"Hey, baby." Eli rolled his chair into the spare bedroom where she kept her makeup and hair supplies so she could be downstairs with him in case Ranger wasn't around. She was supposed to be dressed and ready to go. To the reunion. "You're not ready."

Delaney ambled over and brushed fingers through his hair. "Sorry. Trina called. And you shouldn't be pushing yourself with that wrist yet. Call for me next time."

"It's good. I'm being careful. All okay there?"

"Yes. She went on and on about a benefit concert for storm victims at the Strand this fall and said I should go and she'd go with me if I was there. Still trying to make me guilty for leaving her, I suppose. It's not something she'd normally want to do."

"Is it working? Do you feel guilty?"

"No." She leaned down to brush his lips. "I'm too happy right here with you."

"Mm, good." He gripped her thighs. "Since you're not ready anyway…" Releasing her, he rolled over and closed the door.

"Hold it right there, Forrester. I need my beauty time if I'm going to go out there and get swamped by even more of you overly friendly types." Pulling her old T-shirt over her head, Delaney laughed when he grabbed her with his good hand and pulled her up close. "I have to get ready, Eli."

"Yeah, you do, but I want a couple of kisses first. And Chance, you can just relax. I'm not hurting her." He shook his head at the mutt trying to jump up around the chair. "Just thought I'd relax you a bit."

Delaney wrapped her arms over his shoulders, lowered onto his legs, and kissed him as he teased. "Keep that up and we'll be late."

"That a promise?"

She grinned and pushed out of his grasp. In front of him, she changed out of her sweats and into her new jean capris, the ones he helped her pick out that fit just right, and topped it with the fitted soft, flowing ombré coral shirt, lighter on top and darker at the bottom, that he'd said looked like a Jersey sunrise.

Wearing actual colors was quickly becoming an addiction, especially since he enjoyed it so much when she made the effort to "look like a girl" for him. There were still days she stuck with her baggy blues and grays, and days she just could not make herself leave the house other than to the kennel, but he told her she should let herself have those days and not worry about it. If they had to have milk or bread and she stalled until he realized she wasn't about to do it, he called Ranger.

Mostly back at his own place by now, Ranger and his girl were still checking on him constantly, asking if they needed anything, and they had no trouble running into the store and bringing it out.

Delaney liked Crissy a lot. She was sometimes a bit hard to take, being ridiculously open about everything, but she was fun and loved to joke and nothing bothered her. She kept Ranger in line without being needy or overbearing. The manager at Monical's, she often brought Eli leftover pizza or wings, joking that he had to keep his strength up and the "rabbit food" Delaney fed him wasn't going to cut it for a "strong, vigorous man" trying to get back on his feet. She flirted with him like crazy and he gave it right back. Now and then, Delaney and Ranger would let them have at it and go walk around the pond, mostly as an excuse for Ranger to ask how Eli was, really, and how things were going without being overheard.

At first, she'd been hesitant about talking that much to Eli's cousin, but it was nice to have an understanding ear and Ranger so obviously wanted things to work well for both her and Eli that she let herself talk to him. Bill dropped in often, also, always with a call first, but Ranger almost felt like her own big brother rather than Eli's brother, or cousin. Eli teased her about it, but more seriously told her she was very welcome to talk to Ranger as much as she needed. He wasn't at all worried.

Eli couldn't have been prouder of Delaney if he tried. He could see how nervous she was as everyone and their uncle had to come over and talk to her, circling her like buzzards over injured prey. They did it to him, too, but he'd expected it and brushed it off alright. At least his wrist was out of its cast and he was using the hand to a decent extent. Delaney held her own, also, stayed in control, and caught his eyes at times when she needed a quick rescue. He put it on himself, said he wanted her alone a few minutes, and led her away from the pack.

He heard all kinds of shaded compliments about picking better this time and not losing her and so on. His dad still lectured now and then for moving her in without the right ring on her finger. *If a girl's good enough to live with, she's good enough to marry, son. Don't mess this one up because of that earlier mess.* Eli assured him the engagement ring wasn't only for show, that he wanted to give her time to acclimate before pushing her for a date. He'd also wanted to watch her around the kids. Luckily, his concerns after seeing her with her sister's kids were unfounded. She was good with them, not down on the floor playing good with them, but she listened and talked with them and wasn't bothered that Renee, Eli's *pet niece*, as his family called Bill's hyperactive, sweet little five-year-old who followed him nearly as bad as Chance followed Delaney, gave Delaney hugs almost as often as Eli got them.

The family also joked that he wouldn't have to break off the engagement since Renee okayed Delaney. She'd always refused to even speak to his ex. He figured he should have paid attention to that.

By now, dusk was falling and sections of the sky matched the color of Delaney's shirt. She now had it covered by a lemon yellow sweater that made her own coloring stand out.

Bonfires had been started around his parents' yard. Kids were settling in with quieter games or drowsing against their parents' sides. It was time. He gave Bill the sign and had Ranger help him up out of the wheelchair to his crutches.

Delaney set a hand on his stomach when he lost a bit of balance. "You've been on these enough already today, don't you think?"

"One more time and I'll quit for the day. Promise." He took her hand and kissed it. "Come here, Del. Want to show you something." His family cleared a path for Bill to drive the truck into the yard and park it sideways.

She walked with him as he hobbled over. "It's the same."

Eli grinned. "Pretty much. Bill did some searching for me. A year newer, but close to the same. And he's had the airbags checked. Think you can drive this till I can?"

"Of course."

"Ever drive anything bigger than your car?"

"I'm not some pampered city girl who can barely drive, if that's what you think, Mr. Forrester. My papa had a truck. When they yanked his license, I drove him around. Trina wouldn't. She was afraid of him."

"Papa?"

"Mom's father. A sweet man. A bit on the odd side, which is why they had to pull his license. He started braking for ... well, apparitions, letting them cross safely." She shrugged. "Still, he lived to be ninety-three, and I was his favorite companion. So yes, I can drive this fine."

"You never fail to surprise me, Del. I learn something new about you every day."

"Get used to that. You have a ways to go."

"Looking forward to it. And that said..." He nodded his head to the side and went around to the back of the truck. With his good hand, he lowered the tailgate.

She grinned at the sight of the big plastic box in the back, a near replica of the other one. Her eyes said she was possibly wondering if he had a sleeping bag in there yet. He didn't. Yet. But that would come.

"Hop up here." Eli patted the tailgate and she pulled herself up like a pro as Ranger brought a box from the back seat to set beside her.

"Open it."

"Nothing's going to jump at me, right?"

"Other than your little mutt who's yipping because he can't reach you? No."

Ranger picked the dog up to make it hush and Delaney unfolded the bent in flaps. When she looked sure nothing would jump out, she peeked inside and pulled out a few of the magazines.

"It's full of all the travel magazines I could have the gang find for me over the past month. And..." He reached in to pull out the market listings book, for travel writing. "We're going to redo that front office and make it yours. Now that the hand is starting to work, I'll make you whatever kind of shelves you want and anything else you need. You need this, too." He pulled a travel guide out listing all of the major beaches around the country.

Setting the magazines back in the box, Delaney wrapped her arms over his shoulders and kissed him. Intensely. Never mind the family standing around. The comments. The laughs. They were friendly laughs and she understood they were. She was part of them. He could feel she was already fully a part of him.

"The doc says this ankle is healing better than he would have expected."

She leaned back to find his eyes.

"Another month and we should be able to start roaming the country now and then."

Settled on a damp log around one of the bonfires, Eli kissed her head when she rested it on his shoulder. Much of the extended family had gone on home or to their hotels or a guest room for the night. His close family was all still there, to include Ranger's girl. Even with her being fiery and mouthy, Delaney seemed to like her a lot so far.

Chance was snuggled against her feet, despite Eli telling him he could back off. Expecting it might work better if the mutt had a buddy to play with, he told Delaney she should pick out another one to bring home. She said she named him Chance since that was how they'd met, she and Eli, by chance. He wasn't so sure it was, but it didn't much matter to him how or why they'd met. It only mattered that she'd stayed.

And he didn't want to wait long to make it more official. With another kiss to the side of her head, he cuddled her in close. "So you have a date in mind yet?"

She turned with a question in her gaze. "A date?"

"When do you want to get married, Del?"

"*Eli.*" His sister scolded from a couple of logs down. "You don't ask a girl that in front of your family, even if you are thinking about it right now. Never mind him, Delaney. He's always been that way. Waits forever and a day before he decides to do something and then wants it done right now, this instant. Drove me crazy."

He shrugged. "Hell, she's already said yes and I can't imagine she'll want anything too big so..."

"How do you know she doesn't? You better give her the wedding she wants, since she left her home for your pathetic ass and came out here to a bunch of flat dirt. I can't imagine leaving the beach if it was me. It has to be beautiful." Rosemary shook her head. "Really, Delaney, you tell him what you want."

Del rubbed a hand over his leg. "He's right, simple and not too big would be perfect."

Eli gloated at his sister. "Told you. Think I don't know my bride-to-be? I'm thinking September, except I'm not sure I'll be able to handle Ireland by then." He heard Rosemarie's groan...

"Ireland?"

"You aren't supposed to *tell* her your honeymoon plans. Wow,

Eli, we should have talked first."

He brushed off his sister, as he was used to doing. "Where I want to take you, and I'd be pushing for earlier, but I don't want my foot slowing me down when we go. By fall, it should be good."

"Oh. Eli..." She slid a thumb along his neck and met his eyes. "You don't like to fly. Do you plan to take a boat to Ireland?"

He shuddered. "Hell, no. At least the plane's only a few hours and I won't have to see the fact that we're over all that water. You get the window seat, as a forewarning."

She smiled and gave him a soft kiss. "How about October?"

"Particular reason?"

"Yes. October is when that storm came. It's why I met you. I can give myself a one year mourning period for my home, for the devastation. And then I'll start again. Well, I have already, but..."

"October it is. Want to do it here or in Jersey?"

"It would be hard for your family to get there, wouldn't it?"

"Nah, they can manage; at least most of them can. End of October isn't busy season here, and it's fair enough to have it at your home since we'll be living here. It'll give Rosie an excuse to get to the ocean."

Ranger's girl smacked a hand against his chest. "If you're going to the ocean again, you better take me with you this time."

"Guess I will, then." He threw a grin at Delaney. "Told you she'd move there with me."

Crissy rolled her eyes. "Don't get too full of yourself, Ranger. I said I'd visit with you, not move with you, least not without a ring I won't."

"Figured that much. You're saying you want a ring and you'd actually wear it?"

"You know darn well I've been waiting for you to get the guts to ask me, so don't even..." She stopped when he put a ring in front of her face.

"Okay, so, you'd move with me?"

Crissy took the ring and shoved it on her finger like she was afraid Ranger would take it back, then stood and turned around to sit on his legs facing him with a hard kiss. "You know I'd go anywhere with you. Hell, I'll even stay here with you. About darn time you asked me, too. I was this close to dumping you for someone who would."

Ranger laughed and looked back at Delaney. "Sure you don't want to force Eli back to Jersey? We'll come with you."

"No. I'm good here." She stroked Eli's hair. "But it would be nice to do a beach wedding."

"You got it, baby."

"In October when it's cold." Rosemary groaned again. "You can't wait till next summer?"

"No, I think I can't. What about you, Del?"

Delaney grinned. "I think I can't, either. And this is one time I don't mind saying it."

Delaney couldn't help but grin when Eli pulled into Casey's, as they had the first time she'd come to his town. It was now her town, as well. She looked down at her wedding ring as he turned off the engine; it sparkled in the sun that warmed the cab of the truck, even in early November.

"Need anything while I'm in there?"

She shook her head. "Want me to go instead?"

"Absolutely not. It's cold and you're not dressed for it. Probably get snow in a day or two." He leaned over to give her a quick kiss. "Stay in here where it's warm, Del. Turn it back on if you need, when I'm done getting gas. Going to grab milk and bread to hold us till tomorrow."

She smiled at her husband and watched him walk around the front of the truck to her side, and then watched him in her side mirror as he pumped gas and chatted with someone at another pump.

Snow would be appropriate, she thought. A wiping the slate clean kind of thing as they started their new lives. And it would keep Eli home and inside more often, she supposed.

His foot was doing well, but it still threw pains at him now and then. Between that and the cold, they decided to push off their honeymoon until summer, which was fine with Delaney. Their home already felt like a constant honeymoon. At least for now it did, even if Eli was back at work. So far, he was staying on the ground until he could trust both wrist and foot well enough. At times he came home annoyed, but she knew how to deal with it, and she wasn't always sure he wasn't acting more annoyed than he was just so she'd deal with it. She didn't at all mind. On days she wasn't in the mood, she took Ranger's advice and told him to chill his ass out.

It had taken them forever to walk over two hundred steps to the top of Old Barney since they stopped often, but she hadn't minded that, either. It gave her an excuse to rest without having to tell him why she needed to rest so often.

He'd started to notice, though. And she'd nearly told him there, at the top of the lighthouse, with her heart racing from the sheer height of the thing and from the beauty of the scene before them. Maybe also from the thought of being Delaney Forrester. A new identity. A new start. She'd been surprised how much easier she'd found it to talk to her coworkers at the refuge and any stranger Eli chatted with during their wedding reception and their mini honeymoon in New Jersey. The nerves were there still, but with no sign of panic. It was near impossible to feel panicked with her protective husband at her side.

Now to extend that to when he wasn't at her side. By now, Delaney believed she could, if she took it slowly enough.

Their week at the Sand Castle had been exquisite. Her favorite part was looking out their window at the lighthouse as twilight fell and she snuggled in his arms. Eli's favorite part was the Jacuzzi in their room. The owner of the amusement park he'd helped to save years ago booked the room for them and paid for the week as a wedding gift. Such a contrast to their simple wedding at the refuge where she'd worn her galoshes under her white wedding gown to make him laugh, and then danced with him barefoot in the sand. They did only slow dances, but he was happy with that.

Eli surprised her with tickets to the Strand for the benefit concert and she'd wiped tears at the beauty of the Garden State Philharmonic, at the reason for the benefit, the reminders of those terrible storm days and immediate aftermath, and maybe a few for leaving her home and her sister. They took Trina and her oldest daughter, since Pat wouldn't go, and Trina promised to come visit, to see Delaney's new home.

They'd spent several more days driving back to Indiana, meandering into little towns, driving only about four hours a day or so. As far as she was concerned, those days were every bit as exquisite as the luxury bed and breakfast on Long Beach. She'd taken notes along the way since it was becoming habit to think about the little details of places she could possibly use.

Delaney nearly jumped when Eli opened the back door on his side of the truck and let a swirl of cold air in. He set a couple of plastic bags on the floor and handed her a small pot of deep red mums as he got in beside her. "Girl Scouts were selling them. Couldn't say no."

"Glad you didn't. They're beautiful. I've never had mums. Mom used to go up to the big chrysanthemum show in Morris Township. I'm ashamed to say I was never willing to go with her. Wish I had now. It was the only flower she ever planted."

"Maybe I should've picked up more?"

"No, it's okay." She ran her fingers over the delicate-hardy petals. "This is nice. Thank you for not being able to say no." Delaney leaned over and gave him a quick kiss.

He looked at her a moment, then started the truck, pulled forward, and backed into a parking space. "Be right back." He left it running with the heater on. In a few minutes, through her side mirror, she saw four girls in uniforms carrying flowers ... to the bed of the truck. Delaney got out to investigate.

"Got you a few more." He threw a wink.

"Eli..."

One of the girls bounced, excited that they could go on home now. He'd bought the rest of what they had, in all different colors.

"Now remember, the deal is you have to come help plant them on Saturday. Bring a parent or two and I'll have hot dogs and burgers as a job well done treat. Have them give me a call." Eli brushed a hand over one of the girls' heads and she grinned.

Their leader thanked him and congratulated Delaney on their marriage. "You should know, if you don't yet, he's a pretty popular guy around here. We're all anxious to get to know you."

Eli slid a hand around Delaney's waist. "Therefore, the cookout. Couldn't say no to that, either. Still glad I couldn't?"

"Yes, it'll be nice." Delaney supposed it was time. So far, she'd stayed mainly within the boundaries of his family and the animal shelter, and her new job. But she was Mrs. Elijah Forrester now. What she did would reflect on him. It was time to let him help pull her further out of her self-imposed shelter. Eli, in turn, promised to take her up to Lake Michigan or just over to Lake Erie now and again, where they could walk along the shifting sand. He even said he'd consider swimming with her at the beach once it warmed enough. Delaney didn't care if they didn't swim. Walking along the water, grasping her husband's strong bare arm, would be enough.

Eli scratched Chutzie's ears when the shaggy mutt looked up at him as though wondering if he was forgiven. Delaney had named him well. She said he had far too much chutzpah for his own good, and she was right. It had taken the dog about thirty seconds to have all ten mums knocked over with dirt spilled all over the porch.

Chance was, as always, at Del's feet, behaving well.

They sat out on the patio overlooking the pond as a gorgeous sunset half hidden by their mostly bare trees threw a reflection in the water. He could feel snow moving in from the crispness and smell of the breeze. Delaney had taken to wearing his big old coat that she'd found shoved in the back of a closet. He told her they could darn well get a new one for her if hers wasn't warm enough for the Indiana winter, and they had. Still, when she was outside with him, she wore the old one. Some things didn't change, he supposed, and to be honest, he found it sexy. *Sensual.* Sensual was better than sexy. She'd been right about that, too.

He had his iPod on shuffle, plugged into the outdoor speakers he'd splurged on, and he watched her bounce a foot to the music at times. Now, she closed her eyes and leaned her head back to Richie Sambora's *Weathering the Storm.* "Okay, Chutzie, off my feet." Eli nudged the dog out of the way and went to his wife, offering a hand. "Dance with me."

She grinned and accepted. No hesitation. He held her close as she moved easily with him. Over the past months when he kept insisting, when they were alone, he felt her relax more and more. Some days she'd agree to faster dances, but most often, it was still the slow music she was comfortable with. He'd yet to try outside the house, around others. It would come in time.

Now and then he watched her practice the Bolero, or other Spanish dances. Most often when she danced, though, he gave her the space she needed to just be herself without him in the way.

Delaney raised a hand behind his head to stroke the hair over his nape as she moved with him. She loved dancing with her Eli, her husband, and she loved that he was never bothered if she was stiff. Some days were still better than others. She still didn't know why, but it was okay because at the end of a bad day when she went to bed exhausted mentally from the strain of her job as assistant editor for the local paper or from grocery shopping or whatever else needed done, he was there with a hug and a kiss and often a neck massage. Often more than that. The man was darned near insatiable. She hoped the months to come wouldn't be too hard on him.

"Eli." She spoke gently beside his ear.

"Too tired for this?" His hands drifted down to her thighs.

"No." She gave him a soft kiss. "I love you."

His eyes sparkled. "I love you too, baby. And damn am I glad you're my wife."

"So am I. But we might have to put off our Ireland trip longer than we expected."

"Why's that?"

"I might have a hard time walking around a lot by then." She took his hand and set it against her stomach.

He leaned back slightly and studied her. "Yeah? I was starting to wonder, and to be honest, I was hoping... Am I getting ahead of myself?"

She chuckled. "Son or daughter? What do you think?"

"Oh, a son, for sure. The first of a whole bucket-load of them."

"Whoa, cowboy. Better buckle that thing right back up. I'm not having that many."

He laughed and scooped her up into his arms. "We'll see."

~~ ~~ ~~

EllaMKaye.com

Acknowledgements

I need to start by thanking all of those brave souls fighting social phobia, or social anxiety disorder, as it's called now, for sharing their struggles through social media. Even that much is not easy to do, but it's so important to realize so many of us are fighting this thing. The first time I saw a meme depicting the way I felt when I went out in public, I stared at it for the longest time. What do you know? It's "a thing." It's real. It's not just me. I'm not crazy.

Yes, this book is very close to my heart because it's personal. Over the years, I did my best to hide it, but seeing other brave souls come forward makes it easier for others to do the same. Writing this story was part of my determined recovery process, along with a way to help others understand.

Yes, recovery *is* possible for social anxiety disorder. It can be done. We do not have to let it win and keep us hiding in the dark.

If you're one of those fighting it, I'm thinking of you and hoping you can find the strength to win the war, if not every battle.

If you're supporting someone fighting it, bless you. I know that's not easy, either. A little understanding and a lot of patience go a long way in helping your soldier win those battles.

Caveat: Every mental disorder affects every individual differently, and this book is not meant to be a catch-all of symptoms, or of help/advice. It is fiction, and the characters are inspired by a mix of personal stories and research, but they are not representative of anyone in particular.

Also, my thanks to my wonderful beta readers and editors, without whom this book would not have shaped up to its potential:

Andra Marquardt, an expert on picking up even the smallest detail.

Liz Ferguson, always my strongest supporter and always there when I need a reader to pick up silly things I overlook.

Annette McRoberts: A little thing like small bits of encouragement is a huge thing to struggling authors.

And of course, to my husband, Rulon, without whom I would be unable to spend so much time on this crazy writing journey.

Music Mentioned in this Story

(I do not own any rights to any song/album/artist listed. All are used fairly under
US copyright law. Permission for use of artist and titles is not required nor implied.)

Ricky Martin: *I Like It*
Richie Sambora: *Stranger in this Town* CD
Sugarland: *Stay*
David Bowie: *China Girl*
Spanish guitar
Bryan Adams: *Have You Ever Really Loved A Woman*
Enrique Iglesias: *Hero, I Like It, Stay Here Tonight*
Back Street Boys, Phoebe Snow, Spice Girls,
Captain & Tenille, Gabriel Faurè, Sorazábal,
Lone Ranger soundtrack, *Mary Poppins* soundtrack

About The Author

Ella M. Kaye uses her art and psychology background to create contemporary love stories with mental health issues set around the creative arts. Each of her books fall under one of three series: Dancers & Lighthouses, Artists & Cottages, and Songwriters & Cities. Kaye has been writing romantically inclined literary fiction that branches into straight mainstream in both novel and short story form under the name LK Hunsaker for more than two decades. After many moves as a military spouse, she is settled in western Pennsylvania where she enjoys the abundant foliage and recreational lakes along with the hilly vistas.

Shadowed Lights is the second book in the Dancers & Lighthouses series which can be read in any order.

www.ellamkaye.com
www.lkhunsaker.com

Other books by Ella M. Kaye

(For previews of each book, see EllaMKaye.com)

Pier Lights (2013)
Dancers & Lighthouses Series

Caroline was a relevé away from becoming prima ballerina when, partly due to her own actions, she was injured enough to end her ballet career. With a strong determination, along with some help and hindrance from her antisocial tendencies, Caroline returns to her beloved Folly Beach, finds a grittier dancing job, and makes up her mind to land on top.

Due to a disfiguring facial scar, Dio hides away on his South Carolina farm during the day, where keeping watch over his aging and mentally failing mother strains his time and energy. Venturing into Charleston only for his night job in a strip club allows him to keep needed contact with others while maintaining distance.

When the two collide amid the glow of the lights from the pier, their personal scars push them away, and pull them in, like the ebb and flow of the Atlantic.

~~

Pieces of Light (2014)
Dancers & Lighthouse Series

A Cape Cod grade school teacher. An Irish ballroom teacher visiting for the summer. A little girl who needs a lot of guidance and understanding.

On the shores of Provincetown, Massachusetts, three independent spirits are brought together by unpredictable tides of rapid change. Emma has survived an unsupportive marriage while supporting her family. Fillan is trying to balance his passion for dance with the realities of obligation. Eleven-year-old Patty has been tossed around by her mother's inability to deal with her own life, much less her daughter's autism. When fate brings them together, they must determine whether joining their lifeboats will provide an even keel or throw them further off-balance.

~ ~

Shadows of Greens & Memories (2015)
Artists & Cottages Series

Francis Barrett returns to her hometown of Storm Lake, Iowa to take care of the family holdings, such as they are, after her father passes. While turning his garden shed into a small but livable cottage, she runs into an old flame she admired from afar but never dared speak with during their high school days. Using her secret passion of oil painting to unwind from long days of clearing out the mess, Francis finds her father also had a secret passion and left behind a tale of a man she didn't truly know.

George Frederick McKenry never left the Midwest town where he was born other than brief travels with his four children, who he now has custody of since his ex moved into a condo with her new boyfriend. Running into the one girl from school who rebuffed him when he asked her out, G.F. can't help checking on her and making sure she's getting along alright. False assumptions and past resentments fade as Fran and G.F. let down their guards in order to create new memories.

~ ~

Shadows of Blues & Echoes (2016)
Artists & Cottages Series

Gillian Hart has big ambitions while working as a reporter for a small circulation paper in Denver, Colorado. When her editor and friend assigns a story about some rich businessman who chucks it all to live in the woods alone outside Durango, she does her best to fight it. With no choice but to give in, Gillian determines to use it as a stepping stone.

Hank Dennison wants nothing but solitude while he recovers from a life-changing devastation he has managed to hide from the public. The last thing he wants is another nosy journalist badgering him, especially one who knows nothing about survival in the wilderness and taxes his waning strength. Noticing the darkness of depression that weighs her down, despite her attempt to hide it, Hank determines to keep her off the path that led him to his own illness.

~~

Shadows of Rust & Reels (2017)
Artists & Cottages Series

By day, Holli Jacoby is a jewelry artist in her hometown of Williamstown, West Virginia. Abandoned by her family, Holli mainly stays to herself, preferring her potter's wheel to the risk of letting others see, and take advantage of, the uncontrollable effects of her bipolar disorder.

Isaac Bradshaw is a welder who spends much of his off time assisting his parents due to his father's declining health. While playing pool, he notices a fiery brunette eye him as though she knows him. He soon learns "fiery" is an understatement, and his buddy warns him against the girl, but something keeps him drawn to her.

Despite their earlier crossed paths and a shared love of adventure, Holli's roller coaster life might be more than Isaac is willing to handle. When the bottom falls out beneath her, their relationship hits a critical test.

~~

A Melody in the Dark (2017)
Singers & Songwriters series (a prequel novella)
published by Fire Star Press as part of the *Music of the Heart* anthology

Meladee Lerner is a single mom and struggling songwriter who moved to Pittsburgh to escape a marriage she didn't want. It's 1979, just after the big snow storm that paralyzed the city, when they run into Niall Dillon, a hard-working young Pittsburgher with strong Irish roots. Niall is making plans to travel the US on his own, but one eventful night gives him second thoughts.

~~ ~~ ~~

Watch for more books from both series, as well as from the new Singers & Songwriters series, coming 2019.

www.ingramcontent.com/pod-product-compliance
Lightning Source LLC
Chambersburg PA
CBHW071230190726

48292CB00007B/2212